PRAISE FOR *THE SHORT DROP*

"FitzSimmons has come up with a doozy of a sociopath."

—*Washington Post*

"This live-wire debut begins with a promising lead in the long-ago disappearance of the vice president's daughter, then doubles down with tangled conspiracies, duplicitous politicians, and a disgraced hacker hankering for redemption . . . Hang on and enjoy the ride."

—*People*

"Writing with swift efficiency, FitzSimmons shows why the stakes are high, the heroes suitably tarnished, and the bad guys a pleasure to foil."

—*Kirkus Reviews*

"With a complex plot, layered on top of unexpected emotional depth, *The Short Drop* is a wonderful surprise on every level . . . This is much more than a solid debut, it's proof that FitzSimmons has what it takes."

—Amazon.com, An Amazon Best Book of December 2015

"Beyond exceptional. Matthew FitzSimmons is the real deal."

—Andrew Peterson, author of the bestselling
Nathan McBride series

"*The Short Drop* is an adrenaline-fueled thriller that has it all—political intrigue, murder, and suspense. Matthew FitzSimmons weaves a clever plot and deftly leads the reader on a rapid ride to an explosive end."

—Robert Dugoni, bestselling author of *My Sister's Grave*

POISON
FEATHER

ALSO BY
MATTHEW FITZSIMMONS

The Short Drop

POISON FEATHER

FEATHER

THE GIBSON VAUGHN SERIES

MATTHEW FITZSIMMONS

THOMAS & MERCER

Text copyright © 2016 Matthew FitzSimmons
All rights reserved.

Published by Thomas & Mercer, Seattle

www.apub.com

Amazon, the Amazon logo, and Thomas & Mercer are trademarks of Amazon.com, Inc., or its affiliates.

ISBN-13: 9781503934276 (paperback)
ISBN-10: 1503934276 (paperback)
ISBN-13: 9781503939295 (hardcover)
ISBN-10: 1503939294 (hardcover)

Cover design by Rex Bonomelli

For my friend Mike Tyner,
without whom there'd be no Gibson Vaughn.

THE HUBRIS

But this is what you pay, Prometheus, for that tongue of yours which talked so high and haughty: you are not yet humble; still you do not yield to your misfortunes, and you wish, indeed, to add some more to them.

—Aeschylus, *Prometheus Bound*

CHAPTER ONE

The lights thudded to life in cavernous sweeps of fluorescence. All around him, Merrick heard the sound of men waking against their will. The groans of ancient bedsprings. Conversations, halted the night before at lights-out, picked up where they'd left off as though mere seconds had passed. Easy enough to resume because they were the same banal conversations as the morning before and the morning before that, stretching back the eight years Merrick had been waking to them.

A finite number of topics existed in prison—life before, life during, and the promise of a better life after. Enemies and friends, women, visitors, commissary, and the sorry state of the food. It didn't take long to hear them all, and from that point forward it was only variations on a theme. Inmates came and went, but the conversations would go on forever. Handed down, mouth to ear, for generations of convicts yet to come. As if the conversations were the only true residents of a prison, the inmates merely transient voices mouthing words first spoken long before. Or so Charles Merrick would be happy to imagine in 142 days, when he put Niobe Federal Prison behind him forever.

Merrick swung his feet out of bed and directly into his flip-flops so that his feet never touched the floor of this detestable place. He made his bunk in four economical, practiced movements. The coarse wool blanket wasn't fit for a dog. Certainly not Morgan—his King Charles spaniel, who had passed while he was inside. He missed that animal: the only loyal creature that he had ever known.

The guards moved through the dormitory, taking the seven a.m. count. They also took count at three and five a.m. It was the hardest part of prison for him—having his sleep interrupted by these feebleminded drones with their little hand clickers because the idea of keeping count in their heads was risible. High-school graduates unqualified even to work in the mail room at Merrick Capital.

"Ready for your big day, Cinderella?"

The guards had been hectoring him for weeks. Ever since the warden had approved the interview, Merrick had thought of little else. He hadn't had a visitor other than his lawyer in years, so forgive him for being excited about it. Guards and inmates alike had mocked him endlessly like jealous children, but he was in far too good a mood to let it bother him today.

The moment the guards sounded the all clear, Merrick hurried for the showers. He would have run if allowed. Ordinarily, he never rushed to get anywhere; around every corner lay more prison, so what was the point? But today he wanted to be first in line, unwilling to risk the hot water running out again. After his shower, Merrick shaved carefully and combed his thick blond hair into its proper shape. It showed more gray than when he'd arrived at Niobe Federal Prison, but he still had it, and that's what counted. If anything, he looked better today. The grueling pace at Merrick Capital had taken a toll on his health and on his midsection. It had taken prison for him to discover a love of exercise. Pumping iron, just like a real convict.

The cheap razor nicked him below the ear, and he dabbed at it with a shred of toilet paper. How he missed his old marble countertop of expensive toiletries. Securing even a sample vial of his preferred cologne had taken serious wheeling and dealing. He'd sacrificed a month's commissary to have it smuggled in for today. He unscrewed the cap and knew immediately that it had been worth it. A generous dab on his clavicle and three, no, four, dabs on the inside of his left wrist—it would take a little extra to mask the stench of this place. He rubbed his wrists together and admired himself in the mirror.

A passing guard caught a whiff and pulled up short. "What the hell is that smell, inmate?"

"Chanel's Pour Monsieur," Merrick said.

"Pour Monsieur?" the guard said, mimicking him in a bad French accent. "Well, you smell like a library's abortion. Now hurry up, Cinderella, before you miss the ball."

Merrick pulled on his unflattering prison-issue jumpsuit and tried to tailor it in the mirror, to little effect. He'd requested his trial suit to wear for the interview and had been laughed out of the warden's office. Probably wouldn't have fit him anyway, because he was far trimmer than when he'd arrived. He would need new ones—fifteen or twenty to start—and hoped his man on Savile Row hadn't retired. One didn't go changing tailors willy-nilly.

At breakfast, Merrick sat alone and picked over what passed for scrambled eggs inside. He didn't like the idea of going into an interview unprepared, but the magazine had rebuffed his request for the questions in advance. As the managing partner of Merrick Capital, he'd given two or three interviews a week. Journalists had lined up for an audience, and his public relations team had prescreened the questions, scripting the meeting to show the Charles Merrick brand in the best possible light.

It would be a new experience walking into an interview unprepared, but *Finance* was a fine, professional magazine with a first-class pedigree. They would surely send someone competent. He didn't know this Lydia Malkin woman, but she would get her money's worth. He was feeling expansive, and the idea of talking appealed to him. Real talk. It had been so long since anyone had asked him a question that required anything of him.

When the hour of his interview arrived, a guard led Merrick into one of the cramped legal counseling rooms. It was bare bones, empty but for a long table and uncomfortable metal chairs. He'd been in it, or one like it, innumerable times. At the table sat a woman about the age of his daughter—maybe twenty-five? She was scribbling notes on a legal pad. Not all that attractive, even if he were being charitable. Probably an intern sent along to get some experience in the field. Fine, fine. Two women were always better than one.

She put down her pen and stood to greet him. "It's good to meet you, Mr. Merrick."

"Will she be long?"

"Excuse me?"

"Lydia Malkin. Will she be long? I don't know how long the guards will give us. They can be . . . unhelpful," he said as though describing the service at a hotel.

"I am Lydia Malkin."

She held out her hand. He looked at it and felt his blood pressure rising at the thought that someone had sent this child to interview him.

"*You're* a reporter with *Finance*?"

"I am, yes."

"What are you? Twenty? Have you even finished college?"

"I'm twenty-six. I have a master's in journalism from Northwestern."

"Do you even know who I am?"

"You're Charles Merrick."

"Good for you. But I know full well that *Finance* does not hand twenty-six-year-olds cover interviews."

She looked at him with surprise. "I'm sorry if there's been some miscommunication. This isn't for the cover."

"I beg your pardon?"

"This is a little profile piece. 'Where is he now?' That sort of thing. Since you're getting out soon."

"A profile piece? Is Peter still the editor?"

"Peter Moynihan is the editor," she said in a weary tone that irritated Merrick.

"And he thought it would be a good idea to do a . . . how did you put it? A 'little profile piece' on me?"

"Actually Peter wasn't all that big on the idea. Initially."

"Initially."

"I convinced him."

"Well, thank you so very much," Merrick said. "For being my champion."

"Perhaps I should go."

He watched her gather up the materials that she'd laid out on the table. In the old days, he would have laughed a reporter out of his office for trying such a transparent tactic. He wanted badly to let her leave Niobe Prison disappointed and empty-handed, but he stopped her because it would have hurt him far worse.

"Why weren't they interested?"

She paused and looked him over, held his gaze steadily, assessing him confidently. He didn't care for it but forced a smile. Much as he disliked to admit it, he needed Lydia Malkin more than she needed him.

"Honestly? No one cares," she said. "Many resent the plea deal you cut with the Justice Department. Eight years for the devastation Merrick Capital caused its investors strikes some as ludicrous. And the net value of the assets seized didn't come close to compensating your victims. Lives were ruined."

Merrick dismissed the notion that his deal had been overly generous. If little Miss Lydia Malkin only knew the half of it. The gift that he'd granted this great country in exchange for so-called leniency. The CIA should have thrown him a parade instead of locking him away in here.

"Not to mention the fact that you were sent to a place like this rather than a real prison."

"A real prison? Oh, instead of this 'country club'?"

"Yes."

"Do you know we don't actually have a tennis court? We did, but they bulldozed it. Know why? Because of the idea that this was a 'country club.' That's discrimination."

"Discrimination?"

"Absolutely. I'm denied a valid form of exercise, because why? Because it's a sport people such as myself enjoy. That's discrimination. They let *them* play basketball. A game they enjoy so much. How is that just?"

"Them?" she asked, attempting to bait him.

He wouldn't play her game.

"So . . . if no one cares, why are you here?"

"To find out if prison changed the man known as Madoff Junior."

"Madoff Junior?"

"That's what they call you. You haven't heard that?"

"Of course I've heard it. I just can't believe it stuck."

"Why not?"

"Because Merrick Capital wasn't a Ponzi scheme, that's why. It's insulting. Madoff's operation was amateur hour. Everyone knew what he was doing. It was blatant. Note that not one of the major Wall Street firms invested a single cent with Madoff. A little peculiar given that Madoff only reported four down months in twenty years, no? That's like a baseball player hitting .900 for a season and still not getting signed by a major league team. The only reason Madoff wasn't caught sooner was that the SEC had its head up its incompetent, underfunded ass. They investigated him six times. *Six!* They should have had him in '99 when Harry Markopolos blew the whistle on him, but the SEC never bothered to confirm his accusations with the Depository Trust. So, yes, I'm offended to be lumped in with that hack."

She started the digital voice recorder in the center of the table. "Merrick Capital was so different?"

"Merrick Capital was a work of art. Our investment strategies were entirely legitimate, and our returns to investors unprecedented."

"Merrick Capital began falsifying returns as far back as 1998."

He could feel the blood pounding in his ears. "My clients still got rich."

"Not in 2008, they didn't. You lost a fortune betting on nickel in Western Australia."

"Ah, yes, the crash," said Merrick. "If only the American people knew how to pay their mortgages on time."

"It's the American people's fault you got caught?"

"You're damned right it is. If the crash hadn't caused the price of nickel to tank, then my bet, as you call it, would have paid off."

"Well, that's certainly a unique perspective," she said, leaning in. "But it was still an all-or-nothing bet. You must admit at least that much. Economists have called it one of the most irresponsible gambles in modern finance . . . with or without the crash. Yet here you sit, confident of a different outcome. How can you justify such certainty?"

Some part of Merrick knew, even then, that he should have checked himself.

Instead, he answered her question.

CHAPTER TWO

A one-hit shutout was no way to hook your kid on baseball. A lesson Gibson Vaughn was learning the hard way, pitch by masterful pitch. The Nationals starter had superb control today, mowing down batters like milk bottles at a fairground. Meanwhile, the Braves rookie was a two-pitch flamethrower—mid-nineties fastball and a breaking ball that dropped so far off the table that if you wanted a taste, you'd be eating off the ground.

Ordinarily, Gibson would have been a happy man, basking in the April sunshine along the first base line, watching what was evolving into a great early-season matchup. This was why Sundays existed. But not this Sunday. This particular Sunday, he was rooting for the game to turn into a sloppy home-run derby. Anything to get his daughter excited about the game, because so far Ellie Vaughn was not exactly riveted by the American pastime, and conveying the intricacies of a brilliant pitchers' duel to a seven-year-old hadn't been covered in any parenting book he'd ever read.

Another frustrated Braves batter stalked back to the dugout after strike three nicked the inside corner. *Just throw it over the damn plate,* Gibson willed telepathically. What was one loss against the prospect of making a lifetime fan? Not very loyal of him, but the tickets had cost him an arm, a leg, and the better part of his ass. For this kind of money, he was entitled to be a little selfish.

His ex-wife, Nicole, would kill him if she knew what today had cost. He'd been job hunting for the last six months, and between child support and the mortgage, his savings were just about exhausted. A sullen knot had lived in his chest since the new year. As the weeks passed, it felt like someone had put first one, then both feet on his chest, until it was a struggle to draw breath. It had been hard to keep going, but it would all be okay after tomorrow. The two rounds of interviews had been smooth sailing, and now he had an honest-to-God job offer on the table—contingent, of course, on passing a polygraph in the morning. Since he'd taken plenty of polygraphs in the military, the test didn't worry him. He would be working by the end of the week. Real work. Real money. The kind he'd expected to make when he'd left the Marines.

So, sure, maybe it was a little premature to splurge, but he expected to be buried for the next few months until he got up to speed with the new job. After that, he would start looking for a new apartment, one with a bedroom for Ellie, and maybe a dog. He'd really love to have a dog. Something big enough to run with him and sweet enough to let Ellie climb all over it. Gibson smiled into the sunshine. That was a dream for the future, the kind of dream that Benjamin Lombard's vendetta had long made an impossibility. Well, as of tomorrow, those days were over, and today was a present to himself. He'd been looking forward to taking Ellie to her first game for a long time—the first of many father-daughter days at the ballpark.

He looked over at Ellie fidgeting in her seat.

Somewhere his dad was laughing at him.

Duke Vaughn had had four loves: diners, driving, baseball, and driving to a diner while listening to baseball. When Gibson had been Ellie's age, Duke had shuttled him regularly between Charlottesville and DC, where Duke had served as chief of staff to then senator Benjamin

Lombard. Listening to the Orioles on the radio had been a staple of those drives. To Gibson's seven-year-old self, it had been incomprehensibly boring—listening to something you couldn't see. What was the point? And of course there was his dad lecturing him on the history of the game.

"El, did you know DC used to have a baseball team called the Senators?"

Ellie stifled a yawn.

No one would ever accuse the Vaughn men of learning new tricks.

Gibson wished his dad could be here; Duke had always been good at coming up with silly games and contests, and kids had always loved him. Gibson caught himself. Since learning the truth about his father's death last year, he'd become a nostalgia factory. It was nice being able to think about his dad without the memories being drenched in bitterness, but he also had to be wary of indulging in too much wishful thinking. Whatever else might be true, Duke Vaughn was still dead.

Not that Ellie was having a bad time. She was the kind of kid who always found a way to entertain herself. He admired that about his daughter. But it would be nice if it had anything at all to do with baseball. She had become fast friends with two boys her age in their row. The three children had invented a game with rules so convoluted that none of the fathers could follow, but which resulted in a lot of conspiratorial whispering and giggling.

So far the highlight of the day had been the Presidents Race. A mainstay at Nationals games since the team had moved to DC from Montreal, it was a promotional event featuring five runners in oversized foam presidents' heads. During the fourth inning, George Washington, Abraham Lincoln, Thomas Jefferson, Teddy Roosevelt, and William Taft ran from center field to first base. Shenanigans ensued. For years, it had been an inside joke that Teddy Roosevelt never won. Teddy finally broke his winless streak to celebrate the team clinching the playoffs in 2012. Since then, the Rough Rider won periodically, but mostly Washington, Jefferson, Taft, and Lincoln ganged up on him.

Ellie didn't know that. So at the start of the race, she scampered down to the edge of the field to cheer on Teddy—her favorite president since playing him in a school pageant. Things were looking good, and Ellie's man led the whole way. She was pogoing up and down—her gleeful shrieks carrying back to Gibson. But in the last ten yards, Lincoln tripped Teddy, and George Washington took it at the tape.

Ellie came back despondent and threw herself into her seat. "Daddy, he cheated!"

"It's just a race, El."

"He cheated. I hate him. Abraham Lincoln is a cheater."

"That's exactly what Jefferson Davis said," one of the fathers deadpanned.

"It was close," said Gibson. "Maybe Teddy will win next time."

She perked up at that. "Can we come again? Please?"

Gibson pretended to think it over, milking the moment.

"Please," she begged and smiled an exaggerated, too-cute-for-this-solar-system smile.

"I suppose it might be possible."

Ellie squealed and threw her arms around him. He hugged her back, ignoring for a moment that he'd manipulated her enthusiasm. *You just social-engineered your own kid,* he thought. *Not cool, slick.* But he didn't care. He needed it. He'd begun to have his doubts about the kind of father he was becoming. This dad-at-a-distance routine felt false. Being a father didn't happen by appointment, no matter what the custody agreement said. Being a parent happened in the day to day. Not at baseball games and special events every other weekend. He feared that was how Ellie was beginning to see him. As the guy who came around every so often and took her places and conned her into hugging him. He needed to find solid ground with her. Soon. For now, Ellie was forgiving. If he didn't figure it out, he had a bad feeling that he'd spend the rest of his life looking in from the outside at the rest of hers.

"Want me to teach you how to keep score?" he said, holding up the scorecard enticingly.

"I gotta go to the bathroom."

"Okay, maybe after."

Ellie shrugged noncommittally.

Gibson steered his daughter along the concourse past several food vendors. He was getting hungry. Ben's Chili Bowl was over on the third base side. But if he got a half smoke, Ellie would want one, and a chili dog was way too advanced for her now. He loved her, but she could make a mess of eating an apple.

They found a ladies' room; the line stretched almost out the door.

"I'll be right here," he said.

"Okay."

"You're all right by yourself?"

His seven-year-old daughter rolled her eyes at him. "I'll be fine, Dad."

He chuckled and walked across the concourse where he could stand, back against the concrete wall, and watch for her. He got uneasy when Ellie was out of his line of sight; he didn't want to smother her, but at the same time he didn't give a damn if it meant knowing she was safe. It had gotten worse over the last six months, and he was afraid his paranoia would only accelerate as Ellie got older. As she got closer to the age at which Suzanne Lombard had disappeared.

Gibson lifted the beat-up Philadelphia Phillies cap off his head, swept the hair off his forehead with his free hand, and settled the cap back in place. It looked well loved, but the wear and tear was anything but love. It was Suzanne's cap, and Gibson wore it to remember her. If he had learned one thing last year investigating her disappearance, it was that the margin for error in guarding your children was absolute and unforgiving.

"Excuse me, Mr. Vaughn. May I have a word?"

A slight man in an open-collared pink polo shirt and khakis stepped into Gibson's line of sight. One of those men who had somehow gone through life without developing a single muscle and looked like he'd been made on a taffy puller. Gibson looked him over. Boat shoes—check. Whale belt—check. Requisite pair of Ray-Bans hanging from the V-neck of his shirt—check. Half man, half preppie flamingo. Gibson took a step to his left to keep the restroom in view.

"Can I help you with something?" Gibson said, making no effort to mask his irritation.

"Mr. Vaughn, my name is Christopher Birk. I was hoping for a minute." The Flamingo looked to be in his early thirties, although his thinning blond hair had mostly surrendered the fight and retired to the barbershop floor.

"Are you serious right now with this? I'm at a game with my kid."

"I'm aware, and I sincerely apologize for the intrusion. It couldn't wait."

"Maybe you've heard of e-mail? It's pretty snappy these days. Faster than following a guy to a baseball game."

"We'd prefer to keep this off the record."

Gibson gave the man a sidelong glance. "Now I'm really not interested. Enjoy the game."

A second man stepped aggressively into the conversation. Gibson had seen him earlier but hadn't connected the two men on the busy concourse because, apart from both being white, they could not have been more different. The second man was an inch or two shorter but looked hard where the Flamingo was soft, contemptuous where the Flamingo was conciliatory. He looked quick and wiry strong—a fighter. His DNA was missing the gene for growing an actual beard, but, undeterred, he had let a patchwork scruff grow in that gave him a trashy, feral look. A swirling tattoo emerged from his black T-shirt, ran up his neck, and disappeared behind his left ear. He looked like a broken shard from a shattered glass, the one you missed after sweeping up and found only with your bare feet in the dark on the way to somewhere else. Not a man that Gibson wanted around Ellie, and he hoped to be done with these two before she finished her business in the restroom.

"Just give this prick the envelope," the Shard said.

"Let me handle it."

"So handle it."

"I would if you'd let me."

The Shard shook his head and rolled his eyes but held his tongue. The Flamingo pretended not to notice and turned back to Gibson.

"Would you take a look? I think it will clarify things."

Gibson looked at the envelope in the Flamingo's hand. "What is it?"

"A request—"

"Not interested."

"Just read the damn thing," the Shard said.

"Who are you exactly? His secretary?"

The Shard locked eyes with him, head cocked to the right, arms hanging away from his sides, as he inflated the way small men did before a fight. "Yeah, I'm his secretary, bitch. Now read it before I feed it to you."

Gibson would lay money that the man had done time. Not for anything major. Enough to get thrown in with the hard cases but not enough to earn their respect. He'd had to fight to earn that. Gibson knew the type, had known them in jail and in the Marines. Man-boys with the simmering fury of someone with nothing to prove except how few fucks they gave about anything. As if not caring itself were an accomplishment.

"Cool it," the Flamingo told his partner.

"Where'd you do your bid?" Gibson asked the Shard.

"Buckingham," he replied with the same pride that another man might announce his alma mater.

Gibson's eyes went to the bathroom door, but Ellie still hadn't emerged. *Good.*

Buckingham was a level-three prison west of Richmond. Not a nice place, and now he really didn't want his daughter anywhere near these men. When it had looked like his trial would end in a conviction, Gibson had passed the time educating himself about Virginia state prisons. To give a name to the nightmares that plagued him at night in his jail cell. It hadn't helped.

The Flamingo held out the envelope to Gibson. "Please."

Gibson looked each man in the eyes before snatching it away. Not because he cared what it said; they had followed him to a baseball game, and he wanted to know why. He glanced down at the pale-blue envelope and felt a jot. He had a stack just like it bound with a thick rubber band back at his apartment. It had been seven or eight years since the last one had arrived, but he would've recognized the monogram anywhere: "HBD"—the *B* twice the size of the other letters. Gibson slipped a single sheet of stationery from the envelope and read the familiar, ornate handwriting. It was signed Hammond Birk.

Gibson glanced up at the two men.

"What did you say your name was?"

"Christopher Birk," said the Flamingo.

"Son?"

The Shard smirked at the question.

"Nephew," the Flamingo answered.

Ellie ran up and grabbed his hand. "Daddy, I'm hungry."

"Just a minute, El. Go pick out a hat, okay?" He pointed to a nearby stand. "I'll be right there." Gibson turned to Christopher Birk. "Where?"

"Back of the letter."

Gibson flipped it over. It was an address near Charlottesville.

"Can you come tomorrow?" asked Birk. "It's time sensitive."

Gibson shook his head. "I have a thing tomorrow."

"What thing?" the Shard demanded.

"A none-of-your-damn-business thing."

The Shard stepped forward, but Birk put a cautioning hand on his shoulder. "The judge would be very grateful," he said to Gibson.

Gibson knew he should say no—everything about this felt wrong—but he also knew no wasn't an option. Some debts you paid when they came due. He'd have a few days after he passed the polygraph before work started; he'd drive down to Charlottesville and talk to Hammond Birk. See what he wanted. It was the least that he owed the man.

"Maybe I can come out on Tuesday?" Gibson said, making it a question, not a promise, although that was exactly what it was.

"That would be terrific. Thank you."

"Maybe."

"Cute kid," the Shard said.

It was Gibson's turn to lock eyes with him. "Don't. I'm only going to tell you the once."

The Shard laughed. "What? You gonna start something here in front of all these nice people?"

"Yeah. Right here in front of them if you talk about my kid again."

The Shard moved his jaw soundlessly, testing a reply, but smiled instead. "Relax, Pops. Just saying."

"Get him away from me," Gibson said to Birk.

"Of course. Thank you for your time." Birk tried to lead his companion away, but the Shard twisted back to Gibson.

"See you Tuesday."

Gibson stood on the concourse, watching them until they were out of sight. *Hammond Birk.* After all these years. What might he want? It wasn't for old times' sake, that was for certain. Gibson's sunny mood was nowhere to be seen. He went to see if Ellie had picked out a cap, suddenly uneasy with the symbolism. Maybe she'd like a jersey instead.

CHAPTER THREE

The offices of Veritas Preemployment and Polygraph Services were located on the third floor of a nondescript office building in Ashburn, Virginia. Veritas was one of more than thirty private firms that contracted with the Office of Personnel Management to conduct federal security clearances. Secrecy was a growth industry in Northern Virginia.

Gibson arrived early and checked in with the receptionist—a drab, polite woman who asked for his driver's license and directed him to have a seat in the drab, polite waiting room. Abstract swirls of muted corporate art decorated the walls. It felt like a doctor's office, and no one looked particularly happy to be there. He sat beside an anxious man mainlining coffee. For the stranger's sake, it had better be his normal intake—an uncharacteristic dose of caffeine could confuse the machine, which might necessitate a retest. And you didn't want that—a full-scope polygraph took eight hours to complete.

No, thank you, and no, thank you very much. Gibson had taken multiple polys in the military, so he knew the drill all too well. Once would be more than enough. To be safe, Gibson went back through his paperwork, confirming that it was all in order—it ran to sixty-three pages plus attachments and covered his entire life. Most of it anyway.

Nowhere did his paperwork mention the name Suzanne Lombard, his role in the death of her father, Vice President Benjamin Lombard, or the promises that he'd made to Suzanne's mother, Grace Lombard. After Lombard's death in Atlanta, Grace and he had agreed that it would be safer if they severed contact except in an emergency. No one could know the real story behind Atlanta. So his paperwork glossed over the true nature of his consulting work for Abe Consulting Group, stating only that he'd helped identify network vulnerabilities. Technically true, and hopefully it gave the examiner no reason to ask specific questions.

His paperwork listed Jenn Charles as his supervisor at Abe Consulting. That was also technically true, although she would probably have a more colorful description for their working relationship. Not that anyone could fact-check it, since Abe Consulting had ceased to exist overnight, and the owner and founder, George Abe, had been missing since August. Jenn Charles had gone looking for him after Atlanta, and Gibson hadn't heard from her since. He regretted letting her go alone. *Letting her . . .* as if he could have stopped her. Still, he should have tried harder to talk her out of it. It had just been a strange time in the immediate aftermath of Atlanta, and Gibson, Jenn, and Hendricks had fled each other on journeys of their own.

Dan Hendricks had returned to California, where he was lying low and teaching tactical driving. Gibson checked in with him every two weeks, but Hendricks didn't know any more than he did. Assuming Jenn and George were still alive, they were both well off the grid. Gibson was good at finding things that people preferred remain hidden, and he hadn't turned up so much as a whisper. The fact was, Jenn was ex-CIA. If she didn't want to be found, she wasn't going to be found. He kept looking, all the same. It ate at him. Not only the guilt. He also found himself missing her. That was unexpected. They probably wouldn't be friends if they'd met under any other circumstances—they might not be friends now—but they'd been through something together, and it would be good to see her.

Absently, Gibson ran his fingers through his beard, touching the raised scar on his neck that ran from ear to ear. A souvenir from his investigation into Suzanne Lombard's disappearance. It was an ugly mark. One he never wanted Ellie to see. What would he say to her about it? He'd grown the beard as camouflage, but his fingers sought it out when he was distracted or lost in thought, running back and forth along the knotted length. He caught himself doing it and jerked his hand away.

The unmarked door at the back of the reception area opened; a woman stepped into the room and read his name off a clipboard. She gave his hand a businesslike shake and introduced herself as Amanda Gabir. He handed over his paperwork, and she rechecked his driver's license before ushering him down a corridor and into a polygraph suite. She talked him through the procedure as she wrapped a blood-pressure cuff around his biceps, put a pneumograph around his chest to measure breathing, and slipped galvanometers over his fingers to record electrical activity. He had to hand it to her, she made it sound as if she were fitting him for a suit, but it was impossible to feel like anything but a lab animal.

"Are you relaxed?" she asked.

"Is this part of the test?"

She smiled clinically at his joke and patted his arm, which didn't help to put him at ease. He felt solidarity with the fetal pigs of the world, pinned helplessly to high-school dissection trays. *Do your worst,* he thought, and shifted around, seeking a less painful position in the straight-backed metal chair where he'd be spending the better part of the day. All for a job he knew nothing about. But that was how top-secret SCI worked.

SCI, or sensitive compartmented information, was a control system that "compartmented" employees, who would never have access to an entire project. An employee might be assigned to develop a particular subsystem while having no idea of the full scope of the larger endeavor.

In theory, it made espionage much more difficult. It also meant that Gibson had interviewed for the job blind and wouldn't find out the exact nature of the work until his clearance was approved. Only then would he be officially read in. It hadn't mattered. Five minutes into the interview, he would have run through traffic for the job based simply on the hypotheticals they'd posed him. The guy who'd recruited him for the job, Nick Finelli, warned him it would be this way.

"Take the interview," Nick had advised. "Trust me, you'll want it."

Nick Finelli was a buddy from his days in Intelligence Support Activity. ISA, or the Activity, as it was affectionately known, was the military's version of the CIA and provided tactical support to the military's Special Operations Command, particularly Delta and DEVGRU. Serving in the Activity made you mighty attractive to defense contractors, and after Nick cycled out, he'd immediately landed a job with Spectrum Protection Ltd., which specialized in computer systems and cybersecurity. Exactly the kind of employer Gibson thought he'd have lining up for his services when he left the Marines.

The Activity should have opened doors in the private sector. Gibson had been something of a star in his unit. But whatever doors it did open, Vice President Benjamin Lombard had slammed shut again. Lombard hadn't taken it kindly when Gibson had hacked his computers and turned his files and e-mails over to the *Washington Post*. It hadn't mattered that Gibson had only been sixteen at the time, or that he'd gone on to serve his country with distinction. When Gibson left the Marines, he'd learned the hard way what it meant to be on the business end of the vice president's blacklist.

It had been a hard couple of years, and he'd had to scrounge for work. It had cost him his marriage and very nearly the dream house that he'd intended for his family. Bought at the height of the market before the financial collapse, the house had teetered on the edge of foreclosure for several years. It was Gibson's nightmare, losing that house. He might not ever live there again, but nothing mattered more to him than his daughter growing up there. It was safe. Good schools. Pretty back-yard with a canopy of elm trees. Gibson smiled. It was finally within reach. With Lombard no longer in the picture and a job with Spectrum Protection on the table, he could, for the first time since he'd left the Marines, envision a future in which Ellie's childhood at 53 Mulberry Court was secure.

Maybe that explained how badly things went from there.

The polygraph was going smoothly in hour three. Gibson was start-ing to anticipate the break for lunch at noon. Ms. Gabir's questions flowed steadily, punctuated by his staccato yeses and nos. His read-ings fed into a laptop, and she paused periodically to type a note, but otherwise they were making good progress until the knock at the door. Amanda Gabir excused herself and stepped out into the hall. When she returned, Gibson saw a pair of security guards behind her.

"What's going on?" he asked.

"I'm sorry. The polygraph has been terminated."

"What? By who?"

She didn't answer but set to unstrapping him.

"By who?" he said, voice rising.

One of the security guards stepped into the room. "Sir, please lower your voice."

He took that as an invitation to yell. "Who?"

"At the request of Spectrum Protection," Amanda Gabir said. "I'm sorry. I don't know why. Please don't ask me any more questions."

Unwilling to sit still and be unstrapped like a child on a fairground ride, Gibson ripped the blood pressure cuff off and threw it to the ground.

"Easy there, friend," the guard said.

Gibson chose not to be easy, and by the time he was hustled out the back into a service corridor, they weren't friends anymore either.

"Get the hell off me," he shouted to the empty corridor as the door slammed shut.

Traffic was a typical Northern Virginia quagmire. It took forty-five minutes to drive the fifteen miles to Nick Finelli's offices at Spectrum Protection. Security was there waiting for him. Five of them. Solid men in matching blazers. They saw him coming and formed a wall; Gibson didn't even get through the front door. He made his scene, and they let him rage for a while. He mistook their restraint for timidity and made a lunge for the door. They threw him to the ground and threatened to call the police.

"Go on home," the oldest of the five said. "You had a bad day. You want to top it off with a night in jail?"

Gibson dusted himself off and thought about whether or not he did. He knew he wasn't thinking straight, but he was in one of those states of mind in which knowing better wasn't the same as doing better.

"What's it going to be, friend?" the guard asked.

That made Gibson laugh. "I'm everybody's friend today."

"I'm trying, but you need to go home. There's nothing in there for you."

That was becoming abundantly clear. Gibson walked back to the street and turned around to stare at the building. Was Nick Finelli staring down at him? Did he feel like a big man hiding up in his office? How many times had Gibson covered his ass? Debugged his elementary-school coding? He tried Nick's number. It rang until it went to voice mail. Gibson hung up and dialed again. The fourth time, the phone rang once and a prerecorded message told him that the number he was dialing was unavailable. Nick had blocked his number rather than give him an explanation. So that was how it was going to be. They'd see about that.

Nick Finelli's white Lexus pulled into his driveway a little before seven that night. It was a large, modern house in a development in Fairfax. Bigger by half than Gibson's ex-wife's house. Toys littered the deep-set front yard, and Gibson watched Nick tidy them up. He'd had time to cool off, and the urge to wring Nick's neck had passed. Whatever was happening wasn't Nick's doing.

Gibson crossed the street and called out.

Nick did not look happy to see him. His old friend unbuttoned his jacket and ever so slightly turned his right hip away from Gibson. "What are you doing?"

"I tried to talk to you at the office, but your five secretaries said you were in a meeting."

"You can't be here."

Gibson looked at the ground for confirmation. "And yet here I am."

A car passed, and Nick watched it until it was out of sight. "I can't talk to you. You know how much trouble I'd be in? I have a family too, you know."

"So? You know where this leaves me."

Nick put his hands on his hips and nodded his head glumly.

"Why'd they pull the plug on the polygraph?"

"I don't know."

"Don't lie to me."

"I don't know. They didn't see fit to enlighten me."

"Who?"

"My boss. His boss. Christ, the CEO called personally."

"And that's unusual?"

"Are you serious? My boss has six bosses between him and the CEO. He's never even been on the same floor as the CEO. So, yeah, it's unusual as hell."

"What do you think happened?"

Finelli looked up and down the street. "All I know is, I'm in my supervisor's office. We're talking when the phone rings. He answers it and sits bolt upright like it's Ronald Reagan's ghost. Goes sheet white."

"And?"

"Cease all contact. That was the word that came down."

"With me?"

Nick Finelli nodded. "I don't know what you're into, but for the CEO to call down personally and halt a routine hire? Christ, I've never even heard of such a thing."

"What the hell is going on?" Gibson asked no one in particular. Lombard was gone. This blacklisting was supposed to be a thing of the past.

"I don't know, but you're radioactive. We can't touch you. I doubt anyone will, whatever this thing is."

"Find out for me."

"No can do, man."

"You owe me," Gibson said. "You know you do."

"Yeah, I do owe you. But there's a line, Vaughn, and you're not at the front of it," Nick said and gestured toward his house and the family inside. "So I'm just going to have to keep owing you for now. I'll understand if you need to hold that against me."

"This isn't fair."

"I don't imagine it is." Nick put a hand on his shoulder. "I'm sorry, man. I truly am. I know how bad you needed this."

"Yeah."

"Now be a friend and get off my lawn."

The day wasn't a total wash—everyone wanted to be his friend.

Monday nights were slow at the Nighthawk Diner. Gibson sat at his regular booth in the back and pushed food around his plate. His phone rang. Nicole, calling to ask how the polygraph had gone. He let it go to voice mail.

What was he going to do now?

It was a simple question, but one that he thought he'd answered at long last. Now that he knew that he hadn't, he didn't think he could face Nicole. The prospect of having to start all over, of needing to find a new answer, frightened him. The struggle to get himself to this day, to that interview, had been enormous, and, at this moment, he didn't know that he had the will to keep fighting. He felt only defeat. His hand shook as he took a sip of water. He couldn't get it to stop.

With Lombard out of the equation, this was all supposed to be over. Yet, clearly, the CEO hadn't terminated his hire on a whim. Someone with influence had reached out to Spectrum Protection, salted the earth, and put the fear of God into its CEO. But who? Gibson had no idea. And that was what scared him. Benjamin Lombard's crusade against him had ended in Atlanta. But someone out there was still keeping score, still determined to make him pay. One name leapt to mind— Calista Dauplaise. She was the most obvious suspect, but while she certainly had motive, he couldn't see it. Everything Calista Dauplaise did had a purpose, calculated to advance her agenda. In a strange way, a personal vendetta seemed beneath her; she'd have considered it a waste of valuable political capital. And frankly, it would be in her interests for him to get the Spectrum job. It would have given him something to lose and taken him off the board—now, he was an angry loose end. No, this was someone else. But who?

How could he fight an enemy he couldn't even name?

He took up his fork, started to take a bite, and then pushed his plate to the edge of the table instead. He sat brooding out the window until he saw Toby Kalpar's reflection. Toby owned the Nighthawk Diner with his wife, Sana. After separating from Nicole, Gibson had rented his apartment as much for its proximity to the diner as anything else. He'd adopted it as a second home in the months before the divorce became final, when he just hadn't wanted to be around people. A meal at the diner forced him to leave his crummy apartment.

Toby and Sana had adopted him in return.

Gibson pointed at the seat opposite. Toby sat and their eyes met. Toby nodded to his friend; Gibson nodded back. After that, they sat in silence as men do when talk seems a wearying proposition. Gibson was grateful for the company and grateful that Toby knew not to ask about the polygraph. Toby's given name was Taufeeq, but he had gone by Toby ever since emigrating from Pakistan.

"Are you still seeing that woman?" Toby asked, steering wide of the abortive polygraph.

Gibson had been on two dates with a woman from his gym. On the second, he'd made the tactical error of bringing her to the Nighthawk and now was all but engaged in Toby's eyes.

"Didn't work out."

"Why? She was a nice woman."

Because she has a roommate, and I'm embarrassed of where I live. Well, he could forget moving out and finding a better place now. No dog. No bedroom for Ellie, so no weekend visits. Gibson stopped himself there. If he kept working his way down this checklist, he was going to flip out again, and he'd only just calmed down. Not thinking about it seemed the safest option for the time being.

"It just didn't work out."

Toby smiled and nodded patiently—the way only men who have found their place in the world can to men who have lost theirs. Sana called for her husband to help her. He stood to go but hesitated.

"Gibson," Toby began, finally getting to the point of his visit. "I know you have much on your mind, but . . . there was a man here today."

"Who?"

"He was asking questions. Taking pictures. He knew a lot about you."

"What kind of questions?"

"About Atlanta . . . he wanted to know if you were in Atlanta last summer."

A chill raised the hairs on Gibson's neck. He'd told no one about Atlanta. Not even Nicole, although he'd desperately wished that he could. It wasn't safe for her to know, and he'd made a promise to Grace Lombard to keep silent and to stay away. Far away. A promise that he intended to keep. Anyone asking questions about Atlanta was not a friend.

"What did you tell him?"

"What could I tell him?"

Toby took out his phone and showed him a photograph. "He did not like it," he said with a shrug, "but if you take pictures of me, I take pictures of you."

It was true; the man in the photo did not look happy. He also didn't look anything like Gibson expected. Instead of being a clean-cut, po-faced suit, the man looked like a refugee from a Hacky Sack convention, with a garrulous, good-natured face framed by a receding hairline and a scruffy ponytail. The sweater vest he wore over a Henry Rollins T-shirt hung down below his hips, stretched long by swollen, overstuffed pockets. He was no one to Gibson, but Gibson was not no one to him. He asked Toby to text him the photo. He could see his friend biting back the impulse to ask what was going on and appreciated not having to lie to him.

"I should see what Sana needs," Toby said, excusing himself.

Gibson's phone vibrated, and he studied his new ponytailed admirer. The cherry on top of his day. If he'd been feeling needlessly paranoid after Nick Finelli's warning, now he didn't feel paranoid enough. It was a lot of chickens coming home to roost all at once. The Spectrum disaster. Judge Birk's letter yesterday at the ballpark. Was that a coincidence too? Gibson took the blue envelope out of his messenger bag and read it again. Maybe it was connected, maybe it wasn't, but it was a starting point: an answer to the question of what to do now. It would at least keep him moving, not necessarily forward, but moving. That was enough. Because he knew if he let inertia overcome him now that he might never move again.

Gibson checked the time—it was only seven p.m. on the West Coast. He dialed the number and let it ring.

"Hear from her?" Dan Hendricks had never been one for small talk.

Her. They never spoke or wrote Jenn Charles's name. Whether because of superstition or paranoia at who might be listening, Gibson couldn't say.

"Was just going to ask you the same thing. No, nothing."

"Then what do you want?"

That marked the end of the pleasantries. Neither one of them wanted to be the first to give voice to what both feared. That the months were ticking past, and the chances of Jenn Charles or George Abe being alive were dwindling. Gibson heard the strike of Hendricks's lighter.

"How are things out west? You noticed anything unusual?"

"Should I have? Why? What's up?"

"I don't know. Nothing. I didn't get a job."

"And what's unusual about that?"

Ouch. Gibson wanted to say something biting back, but he'd left all his fight back at the polygraph suite.

"I just have a bad feeling."

Hendricks became serious again; he had a cop's inbred respect for hunches and bad feelings. "No, everything's everything. All quiet. What's going on?"

"Someone came around the diner today, asking about Atlanta."

"Government?"

"I don't think so. Toby took his picture. I'll send it your way."

"Do that."

The two men fell silent.

"Gotta go," Hendricks said at last. "Appreciate the heads-up. Let me know if you get any more bad feelings. Or if, you know, they surface."

"Will do. Talk to you in a couple weeks?"

The line was already dead.

He paid the check but lingered at his booth. The prospect of facing his sterile, desolate apartment depressed him. Instead, he opened the blue envelope and reread the judge's letter. It didn't say much—not like the judge he remembered at all—and it made Gibson long for a little of the judge's wisdom. Wisdom felt in very short supply right about now.

CHAPTER FOUR

Next morning, Gibson was on the road south. He'd slept fitfully, given up around five a.m., and gone on his morning run rather than stare at the ceiling. Most mornings, he alternated between a five-mile and an eight-mile loop, but today he'd run them both, back to back. Still, no matter how hard he pushed himself, he couldn't outrun Nick Finelli's words.

You're radioactive.

We can't touch you.

Radioactive.

It was hard not to see fate moving the pieces around the board. Moving him south on Route 29 toward Charlottesville, Virginia—the place of his birth. He'd grown up there, buried his father there, been arrested and tried there, and by all rights should have been sentenced there. Instead, at the proverbial eleventh hour, Judge Hammond Birk had offered him a deal—the Marines instead of prison—in open defiance of then senator Benjamin Lombard. In doing so, Judge Birk had salvaged Gibson's life from the slag heap. At eighteen, Gibson would have been chewed up by prison, and God only knew what kind of man would have walked out the other side. The judge had saved him from finding out.

The first blue envelope had arrived unexpectedly the day before he'd graduated from Parris Island. He remembered sitting on his bunk, turning the letter over in his hands, only his third piece of mail in thirteen weeks. Family Day on base was a lonely time for a kid with none. Trying but failing not to resent the rest of his platoon as they guided proud mothers and fathers around base. The judge's twenty-page letter, warm and wise, helped him feel less alone in the world, congratulating him on becoming a Marine but also exhorting him to be still better.

New letters followed every few months, expansive, ranging in topic and tone, but always a needed tonic. The judge's letters had been the bridge for Gibson's transition into manhood—philosophical questions, well-timed advice, and encouragement at discouraging times. Gibson answered every letter; it felt good knowing there was someone out there who cared if he lived or died. Eventually Nicole filled that void, but for a time it was down to Judge Birk alone. He often wondered if the judge wrote to all the young people he granted a second chance.

The judge's letters continued for several years, but there came a point when they arrived less and less regularly, finally stopping altogether. It was about the time that the judge had stepped down from the bench at the end of his last term. Judgeships were voted on in the Virginia General Assembly, and the newspapers had been vague about why Birk wasn't running again. Gibson had always worried that the decision to defy Benjamin Lombard had cost Birk his career—and that losing his judgeship embittered Birk and caused him to stop writing. As the letters tapered off, Gibson kept up his end, but by then he was married and Ellie was on the way. After four or five letters went unanswered, life overtook him, and he consigned their correspondence to the past.

Until Sunday at the ballpark.

Gibson felt a reverential sense of duty toward the judge. Ironic that they had only ever had the one face-to-face conversation, because he loved the man dearly. The judge had maneuvered him into the Marines instead of prison, but truth was, Gibson had viewed the Marines as a prison itself. It had been the judge who had counseled him to make the most of his time in the Corps. The judge who had helped an angry, troubled kid get his feet under him and find purpose in life.

Nick Finelli might not believe in repaying his debts, but if it were within Gibson's power, he would do it for Birk. Whatever the judge needed. Unless, of course, he was being set up. The timing of the judge's letter, Spectrum's about-face, and the stranger asking questions at the Nighthawk came precariously close to the definition of impossible coincidence. Something was way off here; he just didn't know what. Gibson would keep an open mind, but he hoped that the judge had nothing to do with his losing the job. That would sorely test his faith in human nature.

When 29 hit Culpepper, he followed Route 15 toward Orange. He was in farm country now, and traffic thinned out. He split off onto Route 20, a winding two-lane, and drove until he realized he'd missed his turnoff and doubled back. From the road, the turnoff for Longman Farm was hard not to miss—just a small break in the trees, a worn yellow sign, and a gravel road that led away into the woods. Gibson followed it for a quarter mile alongside a wide field dotted with baled hay until he came to a rusted gate. He turned in and followed a rutted gravel road up to the big white house on the ridge. It was good land, but Gibson could see disrepair everywhere.

Christopher Birk came out the front door with a cup of coffee, his grass-green polo shirt clashing ever so slightly with his red chinos. He shook Gibson's hand like they were old friends.

"Thanks for coming," Birk said.

"Nice place you have here. How many acres?"

Birk looked around as if seeing the farm for the first time.

"Three hundred, all told. Should have seen it when I was a boy. We had more than double that. Dad sold off some to developers in '09."

Gibson heard a calcified bitterness in his voice.

"To develop what? I didn't see anything driving up."

"Well, that's the kicker. Developers went out of business in '10. The land's been tied up in the courts ever since. Now it just sits there, going to seed. Not sure there's anything sadder than land going unworked. Feels wrong, know what I mean?"

"You didn't strike me as a farmer."

"Because I'm not one," Birk said. "Doesn't mean I appreciate my family's farm falling apart."

A voice from around the side of the house: "That him?"

"Yeah, we're out front, Gavin," Birk yelled back.

The Shard pushed through a row of bushes that had once formed a neat hedge but had been left to run wild. He pulled off a pair of thick work gloves, smiled a caved-in smile, and pointed at Gibson.

"Told you he'd show."

"He's here."

"Told you," said the Shard again, like an older brother who couldn't not have the last word.

"I'm here. I think we've settled that. Gavin, right?"

"Nobody calls me Gavin. I answer to Swonger."

"He called you Gavin," Gibson pointed out.

"Yeah, and been telling him for fifteen years not to. College ain't what it used to be."

"Wouldn't know."

"That's right, you wouldn't. His uncle did you the Marines, yeah? Good on you."

Birk was getting impatient. "What's in the bag?"

"A little something for the judge," Gibson said. It had taken him three stops to find it. "Is he here? I didn't drive down here so you two could argue the fine points of where I am."

"Ain't no call to be talking out your neck." Swonger took an angry step toward Gibson.

"Who is this guy?" Gibson asked Birk. "I know you're the nephew, but what's Cletus here got to do with it?"

Birk sprang forward to block Swonger as he lunged for Gibson.

"My name's Swonger, you son of a bitch. Swonger."

Either Birk was stronger than he looked or Swonger allowed himself to be guided away, blustering at Gibson as he went. Gibson stood impassively on the steps while Birk soothed Swonger's ruffled feathers out in the driveway, then came back.

"Look. Swonger's particular about his name. So no nicknames, okay?"

Gibson shrugged. "Fine, but who is he?"

"Grew up with me. His daddy's the farm manager. The Swongers live a half mile up. And, yeah, they're a part of this."

"His dad runs the farm? So what does your dad do?"

"My dad? He drinks."

That ended the discussion. Swonger leaned against Gibson's car like he owned it, smoking a cigarette and still arguing some invisible argument. Watching him, Gibson felt slightly reassured. Whatever else was happening here, Birk and Swonger didn't strike him as part of any grand conspiracy. Perhaps the Spectrum timing and the nosy visitor to the Nighthawk were just coincidences after all.

"Look, I'm here to talk to the judge. Is he here, or not? I've got family in Charlottesville to visit if he isn't."

"You're here to *see* him," Swonger said with a smile. "No one said nothing about talking."

Gibson didn't know what to make of that.

"Yeah, he's here," Birk said. "He lives in the back house."

"He lives here on the farm?"

"Couple of years now," Birk said. "Come on. I'll take you out to see him."

Birk led Gibson around the side of the house and down a path between two fields. Thirty head of cattle watched their progress with a lazy pivot of their necks. Swonger, trailing behind, stopped to fix a section of fence that had collapsed.

The hedgerow on their left gave way, and they came up on the "back house." It was, in reality, an ancient single-wide trailer set on a cracked cinder-block foundation. Whatever color it had once been, it had long since sloughed off its paint like dead skin. Trash lay on the path leading up to the door, which Birk tried to sweep out of the way with an embarrassed foot. To the right of the front door, under a make-shift awning, three faded, folding patio chairs sat in the dirt around a ramshackle card table.

"He lives here?" Gibson tried to keep the surprise out of his voice.

During his trial, Judge Birk had cut a grand figure, imperious in his black robes, with a patrician bearing that overawed everyone in the courtroom. Gibson hadn't known much about courtrooms but knew a little something about power, and even he could see that the lawyers on both sides were intimidated by Birk. Gibson assumed the judge's family background would match it. His father had often warned against making assumptions about people based on too few data points. The farm, these people, this was far from the Virginia aristocracy. So who was Hammond Birk?

"Yep," said Birk in answer to Gibson's question. "Hold up here a second." Birk walked up to the front door but didn't knock. "Uncle Hammond? Hey!" Birk called. "Old man, you in there?"

Gibson heard movement from inside. A man appeared at the door in a filthy orange University of Virginia T-shirt and underwear that had once been white but now looked gray with age.

"Is it bath day?" the Honorable Hammond D. Birk asked, moving from foot to foot like a little boy who needed to pee. His long, unkempt beard swayed joylessly with him beneath eyes stained the jaundice yellow and red of a poisoned skyline.

It was hard to reconcile this man with the judge who had once silenced a packed courtroom with a single upraised hand. It had been more than ten years, but the judge's condition owed itself to much more than the passage of time.

"No, it's not bath day. Bath day is Wednesday. This is Tuesday. Now come on, I have someone here to see you."

"Who?" the judge asked.

"Gibson Vaughn. You remember. I told you he was coming."

The judge took a step back into the trailer, his expression uncertain.

"Come on, now. Don't make me come in there."

"I don't know . . ."

Birk caught hold of the judge's wrist. The judge tried to pull free, but his nephew was too strong and dragged him out the door.

Gibson didn't care much for bullies.

"Hey," he said. "Take it easy."

The judge stopped struggling and looked in Gibson's direction. At first, Gibson saw only confusion and fear in his eyes. Then, like smoke clearing, a distant awareness sparked, followed swiftly by shame.

"I should put on some trousers," the judge said.

"Yeah," said Birk, "I think that would be fine."

The judge disappeared back into the trailer. Birk and Gibson stared each other down while they waited. After a minute, the judge called for his nephew.

"Great. Now I got to go in there. Make yourself at home." Birk gestured to the card table and disappeared into the trailer.

From inside, Christopher Birk scolded his uncle the way an exasperated adult might upbraid a child. But more than that, an angry, loveless undercurrent colored the nephew's tone. It broke Gibson's heart. How had a man as vital and wise as the judge come to live here, like this? A pariah to his own family. The man should be in assisted living, not dying alone in a trailer.

It dawned on Gibson now why the judge had stopped answering his letters. It hadn't been out of anger over losing his judgeship; he simply hadn't been able. Was that also why he had defied Benjamin Lombard in the first place? Because he already knew he was sick and wouldn't be fit for another term on the bench anyway? Lombard had tried to play politics with a man whose diagnosis had transcended career aspirations. Life had a sense of humor to it, Gibson had to give it that.

Swonger wandered up from fixing the fence and leaned against the trailer just out of Gibson's line of sight.

"You work on the farm with your dad?" Gibson asked, not turning his head.

"It look like there's anything to work on around here?" Swonger said. "Nah, man. I help Pops out, but the Birks barely pay him anything anymore."

"So what do you do?"

"What do I do? Fuck you is what I do."

"Good talking to you as always, Swonger."

Swonger spat in the dirt. Nephew and uncle reemerged. Birk led his uncle to the nearest chair. Gibson stood and held out his hand to the judge.

"Hello, sir."

The judge glanced at his nephew.

"Gibson Vaughn," Birk prompted.

"Ah, yes. Thank you for coming," the judge said and shook Gibson's hand. His skin was the texture of muslin.

"You wanted to see me, sir?"

Judge Birk stared at him for a moment, then looked back to his nephew hopefully. "Is it bath day?"

CHAPTER FIVE

"Dementia," Christopher Birk said. "Runs in the family, so I got that waiting on me."

Gibson tried to catch the judge's eye, but Judge Birk avoided his gaze.

"He's a little anxious," Birk explained. "He gets like this around new people."

"I'm not new people."

"You know what I mean."

"Is he . . . is it always like this?"

"Comes and goes. Been not so bad lately, I suppose. Hit or miss on clothes. Has trouble with things that turn on or off. Just doesn't understand the concept anymore. Flooded the trailer three times before Swonger's dad shut the water off for good."

"He doesn't have running water?"

"Think that's what the man said," Swonger said.

Gibson swiveled in his chair and fixed a look on Swonger. "Why don't you come sit at the grown-up table where I can see you?"

Swonger didn't move.

"Bottled water's safer," Birk explained.

Gibson leaned in close to the judge. "You wanted to see me, sir?"

The judge still wouldn't look him in the eye.

"Did he even write the letter?" Gibson asked Christopher Birk.

"Nah, man," Swonger said. "He's got the tremors something fierce. Can't even hold a pen right. Looks like old Richter caught the big one, know what I'm saying?" Swonger made large jagged movements with his hand to demonstrate.

"You're a hell of a forger." Gibson thought he knew the judge's handwriting better than his own, but nothing about the ex-con's penmanship had raised a red flag. Swonger had talent.

"Sentiment was from the heart. For reals. Old boy's been wanting to see you bad."

"He doesn't seem like he wants to see me."

"Nah, he does. He's just confused."

"What Gavin wrote," Birk said, "is pretty much what my uncle's been saying. He really did ask to see you. Brought you up several times. *Several.*"

Gibson saw the angle. They'd trotted out the judge in all his pathetic glory so they could gauge how Gibson reacted, how affected he was by the spectacle. They wanted something from him, and the judge was the finger plucking at his heartstrings. Soften him up before they pitched whatever it was they were selling. Well, Gibson was plenty softened. In shock was more like it. And they'd exploit that weakness if he let them.

"Well, let's hear it," he said.

"Hear what?" Birk asked.

"You paraded him out here. Okay, I've seen him. I'm appropriately torn up. Now why don't you tell me why so I don't start feeling like I wasted a day for nothing."

Birk and Swonger glanced at each other. That wasn't how they'd expected it to go. They'd been following a script, but now that their mark was improvising his lines, they didn't have the experience to adapt.

Gibson found that encouraging. He didn't like being played, but it was a kind of comfort to know the actors were amateurs.

Birk shrugged. "Get him the magazine."

Swonger spat in the dirt again and went into the trailer. He came back with a copy of *Finance* magazine and tossed it on the table.

"UNREPENTANT," trumpeted the cover in block letters over a photo of a man in a prison jumpsuit who looked more like a Hollywood star than a convict. Maybe it was the mane of golden-blond hair flecked with gray. Or the man's smile, one part condescension mixed with two parts entitlement. But something made Gibson want to punch the guy out. He doubted he could be alone in that sentiment.

"Do you know the name Charles Merrick?" Birk asked.

"Not really. One of the Wall Street guys who went down during the crash."

"That's right. He's in Niobe Federal Prison over in West Virginia."

"Minimum security ain't prison," Swonger said.

"He's getting out in a little over a month—"

"Twenty-nine days," Swonger corrected.

Birk flashed an irritated glance at his partner, then asked Gibson if he knew how a Ponzi scheme worked.

"It's a financial con," Gibson said.

"It wasn't a Ponzi scheme," Swonger said, interrupting.

"Then why do they call him Madoff Junior?" Birk asked.

"'Cause they're idiots just like you?"

"Swonger—" Birk began.

"Then what happened?" Gibson asked.

"After Merrick's third fund flatlined, investors sued to get access to his books," said Swonger. "That's how they found out he'd been robbing them blind."

"Like Madoff," Birk said.

Gibson jumped in before the Ponzi-scheme debate could resume. "Let me guess. The judge invested?"

"Oh, yeah, he did," said Swonger.

"Well, that's sad for him, but what's it got to do with you?"

"Because the old fool talked my dad into investing with Merrick," Birk said. "Swonger's too."

A cloud passed across Swonger's eyes at the mention of it. "Stood in my kitchen and told my dad he was missing the boat if he didn't throw in. Talked down to him like he was a child." Swonger chuckled bitterly. "Old boy sure could talk."

"Thing is, my uncle convinced most of the family," Birk said. "We aren't rich, so the family pooled its assets to buy in. My uncles lost everything. My aunt had to sell her house. Dad was forced to sell half the farm; other half may not be far behind. Uncle Robert was going to retire from the Navy; that didn't happen."

"Old boy sure could talk," Swonger said again.

"Is it bath time, Christopher?" the judge asked.

Swonger leapt forward. "No, it ain't bath time. Shut the hell up already."

"Hey." Gibson stood.

"Don't *hey* me. This old bitch don't get consideration."

"That why you have him living out here in a field like an animal?" Gibson turned to Birk. "To punish him? He's your family."

Birk's face turned an angry sunset red. He was up and out of his chair, stabbing his finger in Gibson's chest. "Cain was family too. You hear me? Yeah, he's family. He's family. And we didn't turn him out like we could've. Should've. But nobody's got time to be taking care of him either." Birk was yelling now. "He's got a roof. Food. No, it isn't pretty, but pretty isn't on the menu, thanks to him. This is all there is. His quality of life isn't anyone's priority anymore. You hear me, you self-righteous son of a bitch?"

"Fuck his quality of life," Swonger agreed.

Gibson told himself to get out of there. He didn't move. The judge looked down at his lap, cowed by the anger in the air.

Get out of here, Gibson told himself again, but he still didn't move.

"Do you hear me?" Birk said a second time.

"Yeah, I hear you. What I don't hear is what I'm doing here. This is a sad story, but I've got sad stories of my own."

"You're here because of that." Birk pointed at the cover of the magazine.

"What about it?"

"Why don't you read it and tell us."

Gibson read the interview with Charles Merrick with a growing sense of awe. Not for Merrick himself, but for Merrick's delusional, self-important arrogance. It was the stuff of legend. His rant about the failure of his criminal enterprise being the fault of Americans who defaulted on their mortgages sounded like an obscene parody. And it only got worse from there:

> *Merrick: We took a chance on the American people. We offered them the opportunity to elevate themselves. Gave them the keys to their own home. And what did they do? They accrued credit-card debt they couldn't service. The banks opened a door for people to move out of the middle class, but the American people didn't meet us halfway.*

That should have been the showstopper, but Merrick was only warming up, each quote more jaw-dropping than the last. When Gibson finished, he whistled and pushed the magazine away from him like it caused cancer.

"Wow," Gibson said. "Just . . . wow."

"Right?" Swonger said.

"Who is he?" the judge asked.

"Gibson Vaughn," said Birk. "Remember?"

"What does he want?"

"You know. Charles Merrick. The interview."

The judge lost interest in the conversation and drifted away.

"I don't get it," Gibson said. "No argument, the guy sounds like a world-class prick, but you don't need me to tell you that."

"Last line, chief. Read it out loud," Swonger said.

Gibson gave him a look.

"Trust me."

Gibson flipped back to the end of the article and read:

> *Finance: What does the future hold for Charles Merrick? How do you plan on starting over?*
>
> *Merrick: Oh, don't worry about me. I'll be fine. I'm a man who knows how to invest his pennies.*

"Pennies," the judge repeated, shifting in his seat.

"Uncle Hammond," Birk said. "What does Charles Merrick say about pennies?"

"Save them. Always save them!"

"And if you do?"

"Real money!"

Birk and Swonger looked at Gibson like they'd just proved the existence of God.

Gibson stared back blankly. "I still don't get it."

Swonger was nodding. "Tell him, Chris."

"So Uncle Hammond was always repeating things this Merrick clown said like it was scripture. Merrick this, Merrick that. Well, Merrick had a motto. Went something like, a million dollars wasn't worth the paper it was printed on anymore because everyone's a millionaire these days. A million is the new penny, he claimed."

"But," Swonger cut in, "if you save your pennies, eventually you're talking real money."

"So save your pennies," Birk repeated.

"Pennies," the judge echoed.

They all stared at Gibson again, waiting for him to acknowledge the utter self-evidence of their discovery.

"You think Merrick's saying that he's got money the government didn't find."

"Damn right," Swonger said.

Gibson saw the appeal of the theory, but it sounded a little far-fetched. "Let's say that's all true. What does it have to do with me?"

"Help us get it," Birk said. "The money."

"Yeah, help us. Son of a bitch need to go down."

"We'll cut you in. Just name your price," Birk said.

"My price isn't the issue. The issue is, how am I supposed to do what you're asking?"

"Money's electronic now. If he hid money, stands to reason there's a digital trail. Uncle Hammond told us all about you, so I Googled you. Saw what you tried to do to Benjamin Lombard back in the day. What you did in the Marines. The other stuff."

"What other stuff?" Gibson asked.

"You know," Birk said with a wink. "Look, we need your computer expertise to track the money. Help us take back what belongs to us."

Gibson looked from one to the other. So that was what these people wanted from him. He hated to be the one to break it to them, but it was impossible.

"I can't help you."

"Why not?" Swonger demanded.

"A lot of reasons, but I'll just give you one. You point me at a network; I'll find a way in. I'm very good at that. But Merrick's accounts? His network? None of it exists anymore; his money's in a Swiss vault gathering dust. There's nothing to hack. No starting point. Even if there was a trail, it'd be, what? Eight to ten years old? I doubt I could track that. I don't know a thing about Merrick's world and even less about forensic accounting. But you know who does? The Justice Department. AFMLS." Gibson saw Birk's and Swonger's blank looks and explained.

"Asset Forfeiture and Money Laundering Section—I worked with those guys in the military. They are scary good at following money, and if they couldn't find Merrick's hidden stash when the trail was fresh, then I have no chance now. None." Gibson stopped to let it sink in.

Birk sat back and let out a sigh. "But he gets out in a month. After that, he'll be a ghost."

"Then he's a ghost. So is his money."

Swonger cursed and kicked the side of the trailer. "Well, this was a waste of time. Guess that's what we get for listening to this old vegetable."

"I'm sorry," Gibson said.

"Yeah, everyone's sorry," Birk said. "Uncle Hammond's sorry for flushing the entire family's life savings down the toilet. The rest of the family's sorry for being a bunch of lemmings and listening to this old faggot. Dad's sorry that Jim Beam bottles have bottoms. Swonger's dad is sorry he worked thirty years for a man who doesn't keep his word. Yeah, it's just a chorus of sorry around here."

"I'm sorry," the judge echoed.

"Hey. Screw you and your sorry," Swonger said.

"Take it easy."

"Don't tell him to take it easy," Birk said. "Our families are barely scraping by while Merrick is set to live the high life on some tropical island. Dad's gonna lose this farm. Been in my family since 1947. The Swongers'll be out on their ass. And the day that happens, I'm driving up to DC and dumping him on a street corner. You hear me, old man?"

Christopher Birk threw back his chair and stalked toward the house.

Swonger stood staring at the judge as if trying to make his mind up about something. "Show yourself out," he said and followed after Birk.

The judge watched the pair go, eyes rimmed red and sorrowful. Gibson flipped the magazine over so he wouldn't have to see Merrick grinning up at him. One more powerful man who had gamed a broken system, ruined lives, and lived to rub it in his victims' faces.

CHAPTER SIX

The town of Niobe sat on the West Virginia bank of the Ohio River. In the mornings after a long shift, Lea Regan liked to drink her coffee on the exterior stairs outside her apartment and watch the river make its solemn way southwest toward Cairo, Illinois, where it joined the Mississippi. It reminded her that the outside world was still waiting and that her two-year purgatory here in Niobe—self-inflicted though it might be—would be ending soon. One way or another.

Lea bartended nights at the Toproll, the bar directly below her apartment, which she rented from her boss. So more often than not, "morning" was code for early afternoon. Last call was two a.m., so she usually didn't crawl into bed until after four. At least it made for a short commute. She rested her coffee on the railing while she stretched and listened to her joints crack. Felt good but did nothing to loosen the golf ball–size knot between her shoulder blades.

A barge tramping upstream toward Pittsburgh passed between the two towers of the old Niobe Bridge, which loomed out of the water like CGI effects in some end-of-the-world summer blockbuster. The center deck had collapsed spectacularly on the Fourth of July, 1977, sending cars and families tumbling into the river as fireworks lit up the night.

The state legislature, in a decision that cemented Niobe's declining stature, deemed the bridge too costly either to repair or demolish. So the spine of the bridge rusted amiably in the sunshine, the unacknowledged symbol of a town on the far side of its heyday.

The citizens of Niobe had more or less adjusted to the inconvenience of driving north for an hour if they needed to cross into Ohio. But truth was, Ohio was an unfamiliar ambition for the many locals who lived within eyeshot of another state but never left West Virginia. Still, every so often, Lea caught Old Charlie, a fixture at the Toproll, in an expansive mood, and, for the price of a drink, he would recount the town's history and rail against the black mark on their honor.

It made her sad. She imagined that Niobe must have been a beautiful town once, but the money had moved on and left relics like the Niobe Bridge to remind people of their past. The people survived, if you could call it that, in hard-drinking bars like the Toproll, easing the pain of having been left behind as well. Most too young to remember the way things used to be but feeling their obsolescence deep in their bones like toxin absorbed from the groundwater. They were good people but quick to anger and held a grudge until it fossilized. In that way, she fit right in. In all other ways, she was an outsider and always would be if she spent the rest of her life in Niobe.

She pulled the rubber band off yesterday's mail and stood in the sunshine, sorting it. Mostly junk, but the magazine caught her attention. It was him. On the cover. That wasn't right.

"UNREPENTANT."

It was supposed to be only a short profile piece, not a cover story. At least that was what her source inside the prison had told her. Her heart lurched in her chest; Lea studied the photo of Charles Merrick, smiling proudly as if he were wearing a tuxedo instead of a prison jumpsuit. How did he manage to look smug? She tore the cover off, shredded it, and scattered Charles Merrick confetti out over the Toproll's back parking lot. She had a bad feeling, and coffee suddenly didn't sound nearly strong enough.

———————————

Lea sat at the bar of the Toproll and read Merrick's interview for the third time. She pushed the magazine away and reached for her beer, trying to decide what it meant. Merrick hadn't admitted to anything—not straight out—but it was all there, between the lines. If you knew him well, it was impossible to miss. Insane—the only word for it. Others would read it and glean what she already knew. Three years of preparation, and she might already be dead in the water. Everything was predicated on her, and her alone, knowing Merrick's secret. She wasn't equipped to fight a war. And it would be a war. They'd be coming now, circling like vultures the day Charles Merrick walked out of Niobe Federal Prison. The hell with taking him quietly at the local airfield. He might not make it ten feet out of the prison gate. He had beaten her. Beaten her without knowing or trying.

She texted Parker to set a meeting. A guard at the prison, Parker supposedly served as her eyes and ears. At least that was what she was paying him for, but getting blindsided by the full scope of Merrick's interview made her reconsider Parker's usefulness. Well, he was all she had, and she needed an update on Merrick so she could figure out what to do.

What *was* she going to do now?

Order another beer, to start. While she waited, she prodded her forgotten lunch with a fork until the fork got stuck. That's what you got for ordering fettuccine Alfredo at a dive bar in West Virginia. That being said, it was far from the worst bar food she'd ever eaten and not even close to the worst bar she'd eaten it in. One of the drawbacks of not knowing how to boil water was you wound up eating too many meals in places like the Toproll. Even when it wasn't your shift. Not that you could taste anything but the thick pall of cigarette smoke that hung in the air. There was no ban on smoking in West Virginia, and the citizens of Niobe took their smoking seriously. Only one p.m. and already it stung her eyes. After a shift, Lea changed clothes in the bathroom and tied them up in a garbage bag before heading back upstairs.

"You know you're not on the schedule until tonight," Margo said from behind the bar. Margo was her boss and landlord, a potentially dangerous combination, but they'd made it work.

Lea nodded.

"Just think it's kind of sad. I own the place, and even I don't hang out here on my days off."

That was a lie, but Lea let it go. "If I'm the saddest thing you see today, consider it a good day."

Margo nodded at the truth of it. "Well, it's your youth, babe. Just don't turn out like Old Charlie there."

Old Charlie had been drinking at the Toproll back when it had still been Kelly's Taproom. As the longest-tenured regular, he was treated with the lack of respect that such an accomplishment warranted. However, the position did come with its own barstool, a grace period after last call to order one more round, and the privilege of insulting Margo without Margo kicking his ass. Of those perks, it was definitely the latter that Old Charlie cherished most.

"Up yours," Old Charlie said without breaking eye contact with his mug of Budweiser or the shot of Jameson's keeping it company.

"Oh, hush up," Margo said. "You know I love your old wrinkled ass."

"Then come here and kiss it," Old Charlie said and belted back the shot.

"Exhibit A," Margo said. "Another beer?"

Lea nodded and pushed her empty across the bar top.

Margo had named the Toproll in honor of her first love, arm wrestling. Dozens of framed photographs of arm-wrestling greats decorated the walls: Duane "Tiny" Benedix, Moe Baker, Cleve Dean, John

Brzenk. For years, Old Charlie and his cohorts had amused themselves by hanging a framed picture of Sylvester Stallone and seeing how long it took Margo to notice. When she finally did, Stallone wound up on the curb out front and the game began anew.

Margo competed in the West Virginia women's over-forty division. She'd been runner-up to the state champ two years running, something Lea found hard to imagine. Margo was an obsessive CrossFitter; she rose at five a.m. every morning to drive to a Box over in Charleston and had biceps thicker than Lea's thigh. Her long blonde hair hung between her powerful shoulders in a thick Valkyrie braid. One time, Margo had demonstrated a toproll on Lea, and her fingers had ached for a week. Lea didn't much want to meet the woman who could beat Margo.

Lea couldn't imagine Niobe without the Toproll. It was better attended than church, and Margo was the pastor of its thirsty congregation. The Toproll was Margo's place, but if you asked her, she said it belonged to the bank. Then she'd smile, wink, and say, "But they've been nice enough to let me stay on until they find new management." It was about 20 percent joke, 80 percent truth. Like a lot of businesses in Niobe, Toproll was barely hanging on.

Lea decided to give the interview another read. Maybe she'd missed something. She adjusted her earbuds and clicked to the next song on *Mule Variations*. Tom Waits seemed tailor-made for West Virginia dive bars, although he'd have started a riot if she played him on the jukebox.

"Whatcha reading?" asked a skinny white guy as he slid onto the stool next to her.

Lea had been bartending at the Toproll for two years, and there weren't ever new faces, but she didn't recognize him. He was part of a group that had been drinking hard since before she'd arrived. He smelled stale, like a case of empty beer bottles, and a cigarette hung long from the corner of his mouth. It bounced as he talked. Not bad looking, all told: a young thirty or an old twenty-two. Chances were he was somewhere in the middle, like Lea herself. He wore a close-cut, sculpted beard that was clearly his pride and joy. On his head, a camouflage-style New York Yankees cap canted at a weird left-leaning angle. He'd been looking over at her for twenty minutes, trying to catch her eye, but like a fish that had been hooked once and released, Lea's eye was very hard to catch. She turned the magazine enough so he could see.

"*Finance* magazine," he read aloud. "What's it about?"

"Finance," she said and reopened the magazine to her page. She was fairly sure her body language was visible from space, but this guy was looking at her like she'd just put her hand between his legs.

"Cool, cool. That's really interesting. Listen, I'm Tommy. People call me Smokestack." He extended a heavily tattooed hand. "What's yours?"

So here she was, poised on a familiar precipice. Go on ignoring him and get called a bitch. Tell him she just wanted to be left alone. And get called a bitch. Or be her mother's version of a good girl, stop what she was doing, and invite the inevitable small talk with some guy who assumed the right to interrupt her because he was a man and she was a woman. And call herself a coward. None appealed.

She shut the magazine again, removed the earbud closest to her unwanted companion, and stared at him. "What?"

"I said, my name's Tommy—"

"I'm meeting someone," she said. It was technically true, just not today.

"Cool, so I'll just keep you company until they get here."

"Christ, Tommy," Margo snapped. "Girl couldn't be saying 'leave me alone' any louder if she had a megaphone."

"I'm just trying to talk to her."

"She's reading a magazine."

"It's a bar, Margo."

"What? Everyone comes to bars to talk to you?"

"Yeah, why not? Why else she here?"

"Maybe eat her food and read her magazine like she's doing?"

"What the hell?" he asked rhetorically.

"Come down the other end of the bar, and I'll buy you a shot."

Old Charlie perked up at the prospect of free shots, Tommy less so.

"Why you defending this stuck-up skank? I didn't do nothing."

There it was. She'd gone from girl he wanted to meet to skank in less than sixty seconds. All for the sin of reading in a public place. The bar went perversely, expectantly still. Lea could feel her temper wake and uncoil with reptilian malice. There was a good chance she was going to regret this, but she had no more give for the Tommys of the world.

"Hey, Tommy, tell me something," Lea said.

"Yeah? What?"

"What do guys with big dicks say in the morning?"

"Huh?" The question confused him. "What?"

Lea nodded. "Yeah, I didn't think you'd know."

She said it loud so everyone could hear, then swiveled slowly back to the bar and reopened the magazine. For its part, the bar let out a collective "oh" as it registered what she'd said. The ones that missed it asked their friends like they'd missed a line in a movie. There were a couple of ways this could go. Lea didn't see anyone leaping to her defense. One time in four, a friend would intercede and cool the situation down, but Lea knew better than to count on those odds. She'd been working here for almost two years, but she wasn't from here; these weren't her people.

Someone laughed. Could have been laughing about anything, but there was only one way Tommy would interpret it, and that would narrow his options considerably. Lea heard him curse and felt his fist close in her hair, wrenching her head back and up. She let out a yelp and stood up on her tiptoes, following his hand like a marionette. Anything to keep her scalp from coming off. The pain forced tears into her eyes, but it was the yelp that really bothered her. *Don't do that again,* she admonished herself.

A baseball bat came down hard on the bar and then pointed at Tommy.

"Don't make me come out from behind the bar."

"You hear what she said to me?"

"Do I look like *The People's Court*?" Margo asked. "I don't care what she said, or if it gave you diaper rash. I don't want to deal with the sheriff today. Do you? How long you been out anyway? Two days? You really miss a cell that much?"

"This is some bullshit," Tommy said.

Lea felt his fist tighten. She was right; she definitely somewhat regretted it, but this is what came of leaving her gun upstairs.

"Let loose of her," and when that didn't work, Margo yelled, "Thomas Edward Hillwicky, let my bartender go, or I will knock your one good memory out of that dumbass head of yours."

Tough spot, Tommy. Back down from a woman, even one who would crush him like a beer can, and they'd still be joking about it in his eulogy. That was how it went among men.

Tommy did the only thing he could that wouldn't land him in the ER and would also save face. He pitched Lea forward. Not hard enough to hurt her, but enough to let her know it was only by his good graces that she had all her teeth. For good measure, he picked up her beer and shattered it across the floor, then set to cursing Margo at the top of his lungs. Margo, for her part, just stood with the baseball bat lying across the bar and stared him down. Finally, one of Tommy's friends stepped up and tried to talk sense to him. Tommy used that as his excuse to be done with the lot of them.

"The hell with this dump," he said, then told his friend where he could go and told Margo the same for good measure. On his way out, he pointed a predatory finger at Lea. "Bitch, I'll be seeing you."

When he was gone, show over, the bar returned quickly to life. Lea pressed her hands to her head and pivoted on her stool so she could see the door in case Tommy got any ideas about round two. His threat left her feeling queasy. He'd said something, she'd said something back, but this would end up her fault. She knew that. She was the outsider. Two years in Niobe didn't mean you belonged. It was how these things went, and she could feel the heat of angry eyes on her back. Good old Tommy, fresh out of jail and kicked out of his own bar. She could hear the narrative forming even before Margo finished mopping up the spilt beer.

"Do me a favor, hon," Margo said.

"What's that?"

"Next time you feel like reading, try a Starbucks."

As if Niobe had a Starbucks.

"Really? You let people talk to you like that?"

"No," Margo allowed. "But I'm not built like one of the Gilmore Girls."

"How about you let me fight my own battles?"

Margo stopped mopping and looked Lea up and down. Lea could feel Margo weighing her up like a butcher weighed ground beef. Margo had fifty or sixty pounds on her. All muscle.

"Well, look at you, the last of the hundred-ten-pound shit kickers," Margo said with a grudging smile. "Hon, you're a real pretty girl, but you aren't gonna be pretty for long fighting your own battles."

"No one stays pretty forever."

"Maybe, but there's no call to go rushing into ugly."

Lea shrugged.

"Well, you do as you like. I'll be over there pouring drinks and minding my own business if you decide to raise any more hell."

"I'll try not to disturb anyone else with my reading."

Margo shook her head and left her to her magazine. Down the bar, Old Charlie caught her eye and raised his glass to her.

CHAPTER SEVEN

It felt wrong to abandon Judge Birk. Not that sitting here with him helped anything, but it was a pretty day and he doubted the judge got many social calls. During Gibson's trial, the judge had kept a stocked minifridge in his chambers and had given him an RC Cola before offering him the Marine Corps option. It had been about the first human thing a stranger had done for him in over a year, and RC Cola would forever remind him of the moment his life stepped back from the brink.

Gibson reached for the grocery bag. It had taken calls to six different stores to find the glass bottles that the judge had favored back then. It seemed like a nice gesture at the time but rang hollow now. Gibson opened a bottle, tossed the cap on the table, tipped his head back, and drank. Warm from the drive, it tasted good all the same. He glanced over at the judge, who was staring intently at the bottle.

"Gibson Vaughn, are you going to offer me one of those, or are you here to torture me like my nephew?"

It startled him, and he jumped a little, then laughed at himself. "Offer you one, sir."

"Well, all right then. Make it a good one."

And like that, the Judge Hammond Birk that Gibson remembered was back in the saddle—tone and body language shifting more than a decade in the blink of an eye. Except that they were both a long way from his old judge's chambers.

"I remembered how you liked it. Not sure how cold they are. It was a drive."

"At this point, I'd drink one if it had been boiled on a stove." The judge studied him. "I take it since you're here that my nephew made good on his threat to involve you in his cockamamy scheme?"

Gibson held up the blue envelope, and the judge shook his head.

"Now that's not right. I'd give him a piece of my mind if I had any to spare." The judge smiled wanly. "Forgive the gallows humor."

Gibson handed a bottle to the judge, who held it up to the light like a fine wine before putting it to his lips.

"Now *that* is something else," the judge said, his eyes shining and happy. "You know, if it weren't for your father, I wouldn't be addicted to these things. Did I tell you about the fridge he kept in his dorm room? RC Cola—only thing he allowed in it. Lord, but those were good days."

"You did, sir."

"He was quite something, your father. Duke Vaughn." The judge said his father's name nostalgically. "Surprised me when he befriended someone like me. I didn't run with his crowd. Caused a bit of a to-do."

"I don't think he ever did it the way he was told."

"You're right about that. So, did I do anything embarrassing?"

"No, sir."

"Bullshit. Probably didn't have any pants on. Wish someone would explain what the hell it is with getting this way that pants become heretical."

"My daughter isn't a big fan of them either."

"You have a daughter?"

"Yes, sir. Name's Ellie. Seven years old."

The judge gave Gibson an appraising look. "And what about you, son? How did you turn out? Did I do the right thing there?"

"You mean saving my life."

"Well, that's a mite dramatic."

"I'd probably just be getting out of prison now if it weren't for you. I still have every one of your letters."

"Ah, well, apologies for being long-winded. Runs in the family, as you've probably gathered. But that makes me happy to hear. I'm glad things worked out for you," the judge said. "Married?"

"Ex-wife."

"I'm sorry to hear that. A good marriage seems like such a wonderful thing."

"Should've been. Were you ever married, sir?"

"Me? No. They didn't let folks like me marry back then. And now? Well, I'm not exactly a catch these days."

"I don't know, sir. You're still a pretty sharp dresser. Pants or no pants."

The judge stared at him for a moment and then smiled broadly. "You know, you sound just like him. Duke always did like to take the piss out of people, but always with a twinkle in his eye so they never quite got around to punching him on the nose."

"That runs in *my* family, I'm told."

"I do see him in you. Your mother too. Such a lovely woman. Well, good. Good. You seemed like a fine boy, but you can't always tell. I'm glad you didn't turn out to be an asshole."

"Jury's out on that."

"Son." The judge paused meaningfully. "It always is."

"Yes, sir."

"Take my nephew, for example. Now I know what you're going to say, but he's a good boy at heart. Family's hit on some hard times, and he's not taken it well. Not been at his best. None of us has. But I believe there's hope for him yet."

"He's a little prick."

The judge didn't argue. "He does like to kick me a little when I'm not all here."

"I don't care for it."

"Well, I don't remember it most of the time, and it's not like he doesn't have a right. I ruined my family by getting them involved with Charles Merrick." The judge gestured to his trailer. "As you can plainly see from my accommodations."

"I'm sorry, sir."

"Well, I made the money, and I lost it. So there's nothing to be sorry about. That's what freedom means in this country. I had the freedom to make something of myself, and I had the freedom to screw it up too. And I've done both. But getting the family involved . . . that's the thing I can't forgive." The judge sighed. "Despite the example my nephew might set, my family is good people. But ambition has never been in our DNA. Took everyone a little by surprise when I announced plans for law school, and I guess when they made me a judge it earned me a measure of deference among them. Poor bastards." The judge ran his hand through his beard and down his neck. "I meant well. I did."

"Your nephew said everyone invested."

The judge nodded somberly. "Hand me another."

Gibson cracked another bottle open for him.

"I have three brothers and a sister. My eldest brother, Christopher's father, inherited the farm from our parents. He invested heavily with Merrick. Another brother owned a small construction company in Charlottesville. He invested."

"Owned—past tense?"

"Past tense, I'm afraid. My sister is an accountant for a car dealership. She held out, but I got to her. Cost her the house. My youngest brother enlisted in the Navy, was set to retire when he had his twenty. He looked me in the eye and said, 'I trust you, Hammond.' I hear him say that often, like he's here with me. He almost has his thirty now and still can't retire," the judge said. "I was ruthless. Some of the extended family had more sense, but I talked them into it in the end. I was always a persuasive son of a bitch. You should have heard me. All but called them ignorant and small-minded. 'Think about your grandchildren,' I said. Christ, I was righteous."

The pain in the judge's voice broke Gibson's heart. This man who had done so much for him had no one to fight for his cause. By the end of the story, Gibson wanted to throttle Charles Merrick with his bare hands. The judge looked away and wiped under his eyes with the heel of his hand.

"I don't have a lot of time here, Gibson. This thing has a mind of its own . . . so to speak. So you'll forgive me if I get to it?"

There was no self-pity in him, which Gibson admired.

"Yes, sir."

"Don't do it."

"Sir?"

"Whatever my nephew asked. Just walk away."

"I don't know if I can do that."

"You can, and you will. You have a daughter. Responsibilities. I won't compound my sins by mixing you up in my family's troubles. Merrick may be a criminal, but stealing from him is still stealing. Christopher can't see that, but I didn't send you to the Marines to turn around now and ask you to break the law on my behalf. Can't do it. So please, I'm asking you, just walk away, son."

"Yes, sir. If that's what you want."

"I appreciate that you made the drive. I'm grateful for the chance to see you."

"Me too, sir. Should have come sooner. I guess I didn't—"

"Hush with all that now," the judge said.

So he did. The two men sat under the awning outside the trailer and finished the six-pack of RC Cola. Gibson told the judge the story of Suzanne Lombard and Duke Vaughn. The whole story. He told him about Atlanta and the promise that he'd made to Grace Lombard. He'd never shared it with anyone up until now, never felt safe. The telling of it was a relief, and he felt better with each word. Unburdened. Even though the judge wouldn't remember it. Probably *because* he wouldn't. When he finished, the judge sat silently for so long that Gibson feared that he'd gone away again.

"Is that her hat?"

Gibson took the cap off his head and handed it to the judge. The judge handled it delicately, pausing to inspect Suzanne's faded initials written into the brim.

"That's a hell of a thing," the judge said at last and gripped Gibson's hand. "You did good."

It shouldn't have surprised Gibson how good that felt to hear. Through his letters, the judge had filled the void left by his father. And as if the judge had read his mind, he continued.

"He'd be proud of you."

"Thank you, sir."

"Thank you, Gibson. Nice to know I did a few things right in my time. Now I need to ask you a favor."

"What do you need?"

"For you to go."

"Did I say something? I didn't—"

"No. It's been grand. But I'm on borrowed time here. And I want to say good-bye while I'm all here. Understand me? Like two men."

They stood and shook hands in the dirt.

"Try and remember me this way."

"I will."

"And take this with you." The judge handed him the magazine. "Throw it away. Burn it. I don't want to see his face again."

"Take care of yourself, sir."

"I'll do my best. Thanks for the RC." The judge winked. "And thanks for the company. Hit the spot."

CHAPTER EIGHT

Room SH-219 in the Hart Office Building was the most secure room in the US Senate. The walls were steel cased and RF shielded to prevent electromagnetic observation, and access to SH-219 was strictly controlled—nothing and no one came in or out that wasn't rigorously screened, right down to the room's dedicated HVAC system and electricity, which were double-filtered for electromagnetic radiation that might carry a signal. Despite the room's bug-proof design, those responsible for its security assumed the worst and swept it for listening devices constantly. It was an object lesson in pragmatic paranoia. It had to be.

Within SH-219's vaultlike doors, the Senate Select Committee on Intelligence heard closed testimony on America's intelligence activities. When called, emissaries from the seventeen elements of the intelligence community—a feudal patchwork of acronyms ranging from the CIA and the NSA to the INR and the TFI—briefed the committee and answered the senators' questions.

CIA deputy director René Ambrose found the entire process farcical. Explaining complex strategic operations to elected officials, most of whom he wasn't altogether convinced knew the difference between Indonesia and Malaysia, cast democracy in a dubious light. It irritated him, and he woke most mornings irritable to begin with. He didn't care for politics, and as a rule, he didn't appreciate being drawn away from Langley for this dog-and-pony show. But he was the deputy director of East Asia and Pacific Analysis, and his testimony on China and North Korea had become staples of the committee's diet.

To add insult to injury, briefings were scheduled for mid to late afternoon, which meant a commute in the thick of the DC rush hour. Traffic irritated him. He'd been screwing a congressional press secretary named Lily for a little over a year, often meeting her at the Hotel George after his testimony. It was a tired affair, the sex tame and predictable, but he kept it up because she was discreet, showed no interest in his work, and was flexible to his calendar. And because traffic irritated him that much.

There were thirteen members of the Senate Select Committee on Intelligence, nine in attendance to hear Ambrose's testimony today. Eight and a half, if one were honest about Bill Russert of Tennessee, who was losing his battle with consciousness across the table. *Good,* Ambrose thought. He had worked long and hard to cultivate a droning monotone when he testified—the one he used with his wife when she got onto the subject of redecorating the bedroom. Ambrose paused for a sip of water, and Russert's eyes fluttered opened momentarily. Ambrose fixed him with a courtesy smile until they drifted shut again. By legend, former director William J. Casey's mutterings were so purposefully inaudible that the committee had headsets installed in the hope of catching the cagey CIA director's testimony. Ambrose wasn't so blatant about it, but then he was but a humble deputy director and you could only push it so far.

"If you'll turn to page sixty-seven, table 8J projects China's Air Force capacity over the next ten years. As you see, the Chendu J-20 is projected to give them long-range stealth bomber capacity by 2020. However, we believe this project is significantly ahead of schedule, and our estimates place the operational date no later than 2018. We further believe that its combat capabilities have been significantly underestimated by—"

"Mr. Ambrose, if I may? A question," said Krista Washburn.

Senator Krista Washburn of Iowa was an insightful, principled lawmaker gifted with a brilliant mind. She had a reputation in the intelligence community as a policy wonk and a hard sell. She asked the right questions and recognized when the snow started to fall. She did not take kindly to the kid-glove treatment, and Ambrose admired her for it. Not that he trusted her; in fact, quite the opposite. Her competence made all their jobs more difficult. Ambrose paused his testimony and ceded the floor to her.

"Would you expand on how you've arrived at these estimates? This is not at all what we're hearing from other agencies. In fact, we've heard testimony that the Chendu J-20 is behind schedule and that 2023 is more realistic."

"We have solid intelligence that Chinese claims of setbacks are diversionary."

"And what is the source of your intelligence?" she pressed.

"Senator, our intelligence is a composite, and can't be sourced to a single asset."

That was a lie, but one that he'd been selling to Congress convincingly for the last eight years to everyone but Senator Washburn, who was becoming increasingly disenchanted with it. However, it would be a cold, wintery day in hell before Ambrose even suggested the existence of Echo in the presence of these vultures. An asset of this quality, placed inside the Chinese Politburo itself, was irreplaceable and could not be jeopardized to satisfy Senator Washburn's intellectual vanity.

"Over the last several years," Washburn continued, "you've been out of step with the majority of our Chinese intelligence."

"And have we been correct?"

"Remarkably so, but how? That is my question. How is it that you know so much better than your colleagues? What do you say to that?"

"You're welcome?" Ambrose suggested.

Senator Washburn sat back and crossed her arms, and Ambrose looked for a conciliatory gesture he could make that did not involve Echo.

"Sir," a voice whispered in Ambrose's ear. It was his assistant, Kiara Hines—a smart, humorless woman. "There's something you're going to want to see."

That was good enough for Ambrose. He apologized to the chairman and asked for a brief recess. Not waiting for an answer, he gathered up his leather, gold-trimmed, monogrammed portfolio and gave a curt nod to the committee and another to Krista Washburn, whose expression assured him this conversation was far from over. So be it. He followed Kiara out into the hallway of the Hart Office Building. She handed him the April issue of *Finance* magazine. Charles Merrick stared defiantly out from the cover. Ambrose felt a jagged fingernail drag across his ulcer.

"What the hell is this?"

"Page seventy-three."

He flipped to the page and read the highlighted passage. When he was finished, not believing what he'd just read, he went back and read the interview in its entirety. Just to be sure he hadn't imagined it. For anyone who knew to read between the lines, Merrick had just drawn a straight line between himself and Echo. A line that the CIA had spent years erasing. Ambrose closed the magazine and studied the man on the cover. Eight years in federal prison had been good to him. Charles Merrick was still a handsome son of a bitch—a little grayer perhaps, but if anything he looked fitter. There was no justice in the world. Certainly prison had done nothing to dim the arrogance in the man's eyes. The caption beneath the photo read, "Unrepentant." That was an understatement. Merrick had ruined thousands of lives and, based on a quick look at the article, had the audacity to blame them for it.

If only he had stopped there.

"Where is Damon Ogden? I mean, right this minute."

"Langley, sir. In a meeting with Krieger." Kiara checked her watch. "The car is ready. If we leave now, we can be back at Langley in forty."

Ambrose thought about the Tuesday-afternoon traffic. He had Lily this evening, and there was still the matter of his testimony. If he left now, the committee would reschedule around him, but they hated doing it and would hold it against him. They might be the Committee on Intelligence, but they found the actual business of gathering intelligence mightily inconvenient.

"No, he comes to me. Get his ass down here."

"Yes, sir."

"And, Kiara?"

She turned to face him.

"He'd better be here when I'm done in there."

———————

Bistro Bis was an upscale French restaurant attached to the Hotel George near Union Station. Its proximity to the Capitol had long made it convenient and popular for discreet meetings. Now in its second decade, however, it was no longer considered a hot spot. Exactly how Ambrose preferred it—busy but not too busy and with a staff that understood how to make themselves scarce while business was conducted. It was remarkable how much got decided over a meal in this town. One of the waiters, whom Ambrose remembered from the opulent Le Lion d'Or back in the eighties, knew more political lore than three-quarters of the members of the House. There was DC, and then there was old DC. It amused Ambrose when colleagues who had lived in Washington for a mere ten years talked about how much the city had changed—they had no idea what they were talking about. If you couldn't remember when Tysons Corner was largely farmland, then as far as Ambrose was concerned, you were still a tourist.

The maître d' led Ambrose past the bar and down the stairs to the main dining area. Even though the restaurant was in the lull between the lunch rush and the start of dinner, there was only a handful of empty tables. At the far end, through an opaque glass wall, he could see the kitchen staff hard at work. He'd requested one of the top corner booths that offered a view of the restaurant, and it irritated him to see Damon Ogden had had the presumption to take the banquette that afforded the best vantage. On the plus side, Ogden looked nervous. The young African American case officer had gotten too big for his britches the last few years, and it pleased Ambrose to see him teetering on his perch. Not that Ambrose had a problem with black people. Far from it. But there was the old CIA and the new, and Damon Ogden was the face of the new century. Many in the next generation didn't respect that the Agency had a way of doing things. That advancement took time. That there was a pecking order. Few were willing to pay their dues any-more—that was the truth of the new CIA. Ambrose knew Ogden had an eye on his job even though he was ten years from reasonably being considered a candidate. Hell, if Ogden had his way, he would appoint himself director tomorrow.

"Have you read it?" Ambrose asked, slapping the magazine down on the table and squeezing into the booth opposite Ogden, adjusting his belt until it sat comfortably beneath his paunch.

"Yes, sir. On the way here."

"On the way . . . ? Let me ask you a question. When exactly did Merrick talk to *Finance*?"

Damon Ogden cleared his throat uncomfortably. "Before Christmas."

"That was almost four months ago. How the hell am I just reading about this now? In a magazine no less? We're the CIA, Damon, not *Reader's Digest*."

"Sir, Merrick's been a model prisoner. We had no reason to suspect he'd do something like this."

"Well, as long as you had no reason to suspect."

"Sir, I am not tasked with tabbing Charles Merrick. I—"

"Don't. Just don't." Ambrose held up a warning finger. He couldn't believe the arrogant prick was taking a tone with him. Ogden had been the golden boy so long that he'd forgotten what it was like to be downhill from a squirrel fuck. Well, he was about to find out. "Just tell me how this happened."

"The impression my contact gave me was that the story wasn't supposed to be anything. Just a one-column 'where are they now?' piece buried in the middle of the issue."

Ambrose tapped his finger on Charles Merrick's face. "Does this look like one column to you?"

Ogden shook his head, composure slipping. Ambrose could see the younger man was just now recognizing the avalanche of shit that was headed his way. This was the CIA—even when it was no one's fault, it was always someone's fault. The only thing that rolled uphill in Washington was the credit. And if the wrong person read that article, there would be hell to pay. It was a career ender. Hell, it might end all their careers.

"So what happened?"

"Merrick happened," Ogden said, then added "sir" as a grudging afterthought. "Once *Finance* realized what they had, they bumped him to the cover and did a good job keeping a lid on it. They timed the release to coincide with his impending release."

"Maybe I should hire *them*," Ambrose said. "So . . . you know him best. What's Merrick playing at? He's so close to getting out. Why give the interview? What's his game?"

"I don't know."

"Well, that's reassuring. Myself, I find the timing of this extremely disturbing. When does he get out? Exactly?" Ambrose took up a menu.

"Twenty-nine days."

"And then he leaves the country?"

"That is the deal."

"He needs reminding of that fact."

"He's on the FBI's turf. Who do you want me to send?"

Normally, that would have been protocol, but Echo was too critical an asset to entrust to the Bureau, and Merrick had been on the Chinese's radar once before. Fortunately, the Ministry of State Security had never connected Merrick to Echo. Primarily because, at the time, the MSS hadn't yet suspected that they had a problem. Well, the Chinese damn well knew they had a security leak now, and a growing faction within the MSS believed it all traced back to a mole within the Politburo working with the Americans. Ambrose feared that Merrick's interview would hand them the missing piece of the puzzle.

"No, I don't want to bring the Bureau in on this," Ambrose said. "Merrick's name has already bounced around the MSS enough."

"That was before Merrick's arrest. Their analyst was totally discredited. Merrick isn't on the MSS's radar."

"So we've been led to believe, but what if we're wrong? And what are the chances that someone inside the MSS has read this interview?"

"Better than average," Ogden admitted.

"So if he's back on their radar, or worse, never left, then how will it look if the FBI descends on Merrick for a sit-down?"

"Like confirmation."

"Precisely. So, no, there can't be any unusual activity around Merrick. We can't be seen to react to this. It has to appear business as usual."

"So what do you want done, sir?"

"I want you to talk to him."

"Me?"

"Yes, you. Go in quietly, unannounced and undercover, and sort him out. You brokered his deal. He knows you moved mountains for him before; best if it's you who reminds him that those mountains can be moved back. There's too much at stake here to allow Merrick to jeopardize Echo. Make him understand the consequences of opening his mouth again."

"And if he doesn't?"

"Then he goes where no one can hear him open it," Ambrose said. "We're at a critical juncture, Damon. The Chinese already have their suspicions that they have a leak. Losing Echo would be a catastrophic intelligence loss. What's the MSS calling their mole hunt? What's their name for Echo?"

"Zhenniao."

"English, Ogden."

"Poisonfeather."

"Christ, I miss the Russians. Look, we need this contained. The Chinese cannot be permitted to connect Merrick to Poisonfeather. So until he's safely out of the country, I'm relieving you from Echo."

Ogden recoiled as Ambrose knew he would. Echo had been Ogden's baby since the day Merrick fell into the Agency's lap. Ogden's career and reputation had been built on its extraordinary success. Relieving him of control would be a devastating blow to his career. Even if Merrick were brought to heel without further incident, it would be difficult to justify reinstating Ogden. Certainly, Ambrose wouldn't go to any lengths to do so. Ogden would be fine. He had a bright future but needed to learn how the pecking order worked and where he stood in it. Ambrose didn't have the stones he once had, so he aimed to kill all the birds he could with the ones he had left.

To his credit, Ogden didn't put up a fight. The man had enough savvy to recognize an argument that he couldn't win.

"And once Merrick is on the plane, I'm back in charge?"

"Of course, Damon, absolutely." Ambrose smiled, now that the battle was won. "We just can't have loose ends. Merrick has to be contained. You've got to be my man on this."

Ambrose signaled to the waiter that he was ready to order. Ogden reached for a menu.

"That will be all. Get it done."

Ogden put down the menu and stood without a word.

"And, Ogden. You do understand the consequences, don't you? For all of us."

"I do, sir. Yes."

"I have every confidence. Drive safe."

CHAPTER NINE

Charles Merrick sat on a bench, basking in the warm April sunshine. He liked his little corner of the yard by the vegetable garden, tended by a collective of diligent old-timers. Lifers, no longer a threat to anyone, doing time digging in the dirt until it was their turn to be planted. It comforted Merrick to know he wasn't one of them. His time here was nearly done.

He finished rereading his interview. At this point, he could all but recite it from memory. Wisely, the magazine had abandoned the three-column profile piece and put him on the cover, where he belonged. Damn right they had—it was a showstopper. Vintage Merrick. And as a result, requests for interviews had been pouring into the prison ever since. Much to the consternation of Warden Meeks, who'd issued a media blackout.

Disappointing but predictable.

If Merrick had one quibble about the whole thing, it was that he wasn't altogether happy with his photo. The lighting was atrocious, but it served its purpose, he supposed. If he were being absolutely honest, he liked how it made him look just a little dangerous.

"Merrick! Visitor!" yelled a guard from across the yard.

Merrick looked up. "Who is it?"

Had Warden Meeks changed his mind?

"Your lawyer. Get your ass moving. I'm not your damn secretary."

The answer surprised Merrick. In the last eight years, his lawyer had made the inconvenient journey from Manhattan to Niobe, West Virginia, for a face-to-face exactly twice. Both times for intense strategy sessions that followed months of calls and e-mails. So the idea that Henry Susman had arrived at the prison unannounced made Merrick uneasy. Some kind of bad news. What else could it be? And this close to his release date? Very, very uneasy.

Merrick trailed behind the guard to the legal counseling rooms. The guard ambled along, thumbs in his belt, whistling tunelessly. From a step behind, Merrick glared at him to hurry up, his imagination concocting worst-case scenarios for his lawyer's visit, and by the time they arrived, he was sweating prison-issue bullets. The guard unlocked the door and ushered him inside. Henry Susman stood up from the table and buttoned his suit jacket. Except it wasn't Henry Susman. For one, Henry Susman was white, pushing sixty, and a paunchy five four on his best day. Not Henry Susman was black, midthirties, and a lean six foot.

"Charles, you look well," Not Henry Susman said.

Merrick took the compliment in stride. "Good to see you . . . Henry. Been too long."

The two men shook hands like old friends. The man who wasn't Henry Susman smiled expectantly at the guard, who took the hint and excused himself. They waited in silence until they heard the door lock behind him. Merrick turned back to Not Henry Susman, whose warm smile was fast melting from his face. Merrick didn't care for the expression that replaced it.

"I thought we weren't to see each other again."

"And we thought you'd keep your mouth shut," Damon Ogden said.

"Ah. So you're not here to congratulate me on my impending liberation? Damon, I'm disappointed."

"It's Agent Ogden. Now sit down and shut up."

"Don't be that way. How's life at the CIA?"

"Sit. *Down.*"

It came out as a whisper but hit like a roar. Ogden took one step toward Merrick, who dropped quickly into the chair, heart pounding, mouth dry. The agent checked himself, hands clenching and unclenching. Merrick sensed that if he spoke again, Ogden would hurt him. Hurt him badly. Even after eight years in prison, Merrick had never been in a fight, and the prospect scared him. He tried and failed to keep his fear from showing. Ogden sat on the corner of the table, one leg on, one leg off, smiling down at his humiliation. He laid a copy of *Finance* magazine down on the table.

"You have well and truly screwed the dog, Merrick."

"It was one interview."

"You had it made and still shit all over us."

"One interview."

"The only interview," Ogden corrected. He opened a legal-size file folder and slid a contract across the table, spinning it so it faced Merrick. He opened it to the last page.

"This your signature?"

"Yes," Merrick muttered.

"What's that? Don't go getting shy on me now."

"Yes."

"Have we lived up to our end?"

Merrick nodded.

"That's right. We have. Did we let you get sent to a medium-security prison for a hundred fifty years like your pal Bernie Madoff?"

"No."

"No, we did not. Did we stop Justice from cleaning out that last bank account? The big one?"

"Yes."

"Yes, we did. And in return, have you lived up to your end? Have you kept that huge oxygen-sucking mouth of yours shut like you agreed?"

"It was one interview, and, well, I didn't actually say anything."

Agent Ogden was shaking his head. "No, you didn't."

"So what's the—"

"And that's the only reason you're having this friendly chat and not in irons on the way to Leavenworth. Because you didn't *actually* say anything. But. *But*," Agent Ogden said again like he couldn't quite believe it. "But you insinuated like a bitch, didn't you? This nonsense about Chinese puzzles? What were you thinking?"

Merrick saw an opportunity to reassert himself. "You're being a little operatic, Damon. My lawyer—my actual lawyer—will carve this up. There's no way you can demonstrate that I said anything damaging."

Agent Ogden sat back and laughed.

"Lawyer? You live in a fantasy world, white man. Get this through your narrow little head—there are no lawyers. Not anymore. Not for you. This is a national-security issue, which means you are now in the making-Agent-Ogden-happy business. That's your job. Make me happy. Because if I'm not happy, if I get even the vaguest feeling that you're getting ready to say something stupid again, I will suspend your civil rights on national-security grounds, I will personally escort you to twenty-three-hour-a-day solitary, and I will see you spend the rest of your natural life there."

"You can't do that."

"See that . . . see that right there?" Agent Ogden pointed a finger in Merrick's face. "That's not making me happy. And you're wrong: I actually *can* do that. Can and will. What I *can't* do is go back to Langley with you doubting what I can and can't do. You signed an agreement with the government of the United States of America. And more importantly with the Central Intelligence Agency. That deal is unequivocal. And if you jeopardize my operation again, if you interfere with the security interests of this great country, by word or action or even implication, then I will disappear you from the face of the earth."

The two men sat in silence, but Merrick's ears rang . . .

Ogden's operation?

The CIA only had the operation because of Charles Merrick. He'd handed them the veritable keys to the kingdom. If anything, they owed *him*. A lot more than a stay in a minimum-security prison and the right to keep his own money. They should be building him a monument for what he'd delivered them.

"So what now?" Merrick asked, voice low. He wanted Ogden to think he was afraid of him, and he realized that he was, no act required.

"You have twenty-seven days left before you're released. Until that time, you will abide by every word of your incredibly generous deal, and then I want you off US soil. We all think that's for the best."

"I understand."

"I assume you've made arrangements for your release?"

"I have."

"Good. Walk me through them."

Merrick did.

Mostly.

CHAPTER TEN

It was a peculiar thing to feel you knew someone intimately despite never having met. Yet Guo Fa considered himself something of an expert on Charles Merrick, Merrick's fall from grace being so closely tied to his own. Fa had bought a copy of *Finance* mostly out of morbid curiosity. Eight years in federal prison had done nothing to dim the arrogance in the man's eyes in the cover photo, which perhaps explained the audacious madness of the interview. Particularly one specific answer. It had already been a combative interview when the reporter pressed him on how he could be so confident in his investment strategy despite the crash of '08.

> *Merrick: Are you familiar with Chinese rings? It's an ancient puzzle—nine interlocking wire rings on a looped handle. The solution requires hundreds of steps. Before you can hope to complete it, you must understand how the rings interact and affect each other. Not dissimilar to financial markets. When I met my ex-wife, she kept one on her desk. She said she would only go out with me if I solved it.*

Finance: And did you?

*Merrick: Good lord, no. I took it to an old man in Chinatown
and paid him to teach me.*

Fa pored over the interview until convinced that he wasn't simply
seeing what he wanted to see. That Merrick had really said it. Well, not
said, not explicitly, but it was between the lines—practically a taunt.
Of that Fa was certain. He closed the magazine, delicately, as if it were
the lid to a box of deadly snakes. A religious man might have prayed
for guidance, but Fa sat motionless at his desk, listening to his heart
hammer against his chest like a prisoner clawing its way to freedom.
He wanted to let out a triumphant yell but stifled the impulse. Chances
were, no one would hear. One of the meager benefits of his cramped
subbasement-level office was that he could set off fireworks without
disturbing anyone. But he was already viewed as an odd duck at the
embassy and didn't dare chance it.

His career hadn't begun in the subbasement. His descent to this
humiliating, windowless tomb had taken years. Each new office less
desirable than the last. Each move justified with a reasonable pretext.
Fa had accepted each without complaint, as was expected, and could
even admire his nemesis's cruel design.

It could have been worse. Zhi had wanted him transferred to the
embassy in Nigeria, but Fa's family connections had made that politi-
cally inexpedient. So Fa had remained in Washington at his plum posting, and Zhi had set to isolating him. Gradually excluding him from
meetings, reassigning his workload to others, and moving his office
farther and farther to the periphery. At this point, Fa really was, for all
intents and purposes, the lowly embassy drone attached to the Ministry
of Agriculture that his papers claimed, and not an agent of the Ministry
of State Security.

Now thirty-six, Fa saw his younger self with the clarity that only failure brings. Being accepted to the MSS had been the proudest moment of his life, and then, when his first posting had been the embassy in Washington, DC, it had fueled his belief that he was destined for great things. He'd arrived in Washington at twenty-five, a young, idealistic hothead who knew he knew better. Expecting full well to make section head before forty, he'd caught himself mentally redecorating Zhu Zhi's office.

A sense of personal inevitability can be a dangerous thing, and Fa had believed that his theory on Charles Merrick would be the key to fast-tracking his career. Government corruption had been a hot-button issue even in 2006, and Fa's instincts told him that there was more to Charles Merrick's success than financial genius. Merrick's first two funds, Merrick I and Merrick II, were simply too staggeringly successful. From 1997 to 2006, his funds' returns had averaged 28 percent and without a single down year. In Fa's opinion, no one invested with that kind of accuracy without the benefit of inside information. No one was that good.

So Fa had gone to work, and gradually he'd uncovered the genius of Merrick's strategy: he never invested directly in China. Anything that blatant would have been spotted by MSS analysts back in '96, when Merrick Capital's first fund—Merrick I—launched. No, what Merrick did was so much more sophisticated. Instead, he invested *ahead of* China. By 1996, the Chinese economy was booming, thanks to the introduction of the special economic zones. GDP grew by almost 10 percent that year alone. Growth fueled by raw materials from all over the world: oil from Angola, bauxite from Indonesia, copper from Chile, tin from Myanmar and Bolivia, and on and on it went. All flowing into the insatiable cauldron of Chinese industry. Yet somehow, with remarkable prescience, Merrick Capital managed to arrive just ahead of major new deals, buying up infrastructure and mineral rights and making a fortune when China's economic interests became a matter of public record and drove prices sky high.

To Fa, there had been only one possible conclusion—Merrick Capital had a source inside the Chinese government, funneling classified strategic planning to the American businessman. Fa's intelligence report, based on fourteen months of exhaustive research and analysis, had been unimpeachable. Its conclusions unassailable. Zhu Zhi had seen it otherwise, dismissing Fa's report on Merrick as the fanciful skywriting of an ambitious young agent whose imagination had gotten the better of him. Fa, in a disgraceful act of youthful arrogance, had attempted to circumvent Zhi and go directly to Zhi's superior. Circumventing the chain of command in the Ministry of State Security was an unforgivable act of disrespect, and it had been an all-or-nothing play.

Nothing, as it turned out.

Now, because of his arrogance, Fa remained sequestered in Zhi's bureaucratic limbo, performing demeaning clerical work for the Ministry of Agriculture. Zhi, a genius at torturing his enemies, had recognized that being underutilized would drive Fa mad. As a result, Fa had so few responsibilities that he was always weeks ahead of schedule. In the early days, Fa filled his time reading intelligence briefs, saturating himself with American politics, and keeping current with MSS operations. But as the months turned to years and it dawned on Fa that his banishment was permanent, a lethargic depression had crept into his outlook.

He felt with certainty something that he had never experienced before: that his fate had fallen out of his control. Today, his most realistic ambition was not to be the kind of person found sleeping at his desk in the afternoon. He filled his time with a purgatory of crossword puzzles and online chess. It gave Fa ample time to reflect bitterly on the ruins of his career. He had considered resigning, of course. He missed Shanghai; he missed home. But it would have embarrassed his father, and besides, he wasn't about to give Zhi the satisfaction. So he sat in his ever more depressing office, did his job, such as it was, and dreamed about his next fishing trip.

Fishing was the one real pleasure he derived from living in America. The rivers here were heaven-sent. And such fish. Fa had fished up and down the East Coast—the Willowemoc Creek, a personal favorite. He'd been fly-fishing in the Blackfoot and Bitterroot Rivers in Montana. Stood waist deep in the frigid Kenai River in Alaska as salmon thicker than his leg surged past him. His next grand excursion would be to Michigan to fish the Fox and Two Hearted Rivers. In preparation, he was rereading Hemingway's short stories that had made the two rivers famous. These trips were all that had kept him sane during his eight-year exile within the Ministry. In the interim, Fa had forgotten all about Charles Merrick, who ultimately had been arrested by his own government for defrauding his investors of hundreds of millions of dollars.

But now, all these years later, Fa knew that he had been right and Zhi wrong. Merrick's interview vindicated his theory. But what to do? His responsibility was to take his suspicions directly to Zhi. Unfortunately, Fa knew what Zhi would do. If it turned out now that Fa's suspicions about Merrick had been correct—about something like this—and it became known that Zhi had suppressed his report . . . it would mean the end of Zhi's career. Zhi would have no choice but to bury it and Fa with it. For good, this time.

And it would be easy to do, for while Merrick's interview subtly corroborated Fa's suspicion, it was far from the smoking gun that Zhi would demand. Merrick was ancient history, and Fa's theory regarding Merrick's source in Beijing had never seen the light of day: Zhi had ensured that. Zhi would never endorse Fa's hunch. It would be an enormous loss of face to admit that Fa had been right all this time. And Fa's credibility within the Ministry was nonexistent; no one would take his side over Zhi's, even if he were foolhardy enough to go outside of regular channels again. So what to do? Fa sighed and gathered up his materials. What choice did he have? This was the job. He would take what he had to Zhi, who would summarily reject it, and that would be the end of it. No doubt retribution would follow, but he'd have done his duty; he would sleep with a clear conscience and wait for Zhi's reprisal.

Fa rode the elevator up to Zhi's office and considered taking the rest of the afternoon off. Get out of the city before rush hour and go fishing for a few hours to clear his head. A reward for the undignified abuse he was about to receive. It was personal with Zhi, who called him "Fa Gao" behind his back—"the cupcake." Perhaps he should consider resigning after all. He had served the cause for twelve years; it would not be such a great humiliation for his family now. Would he really sacrifice himself to a losing battle of wills with Zhu Zhi?

Apparently he would.

Fa stuck his head in the antechamber outside Zhi's office, where Zhi's secretary worked. When he asked to see Zhi, she masked her surprise with a demure cough—Fa hadn't met with Zhi in nearly four years. She replied that he would be tied up all day in the weekly operations meeting. Fa had forgotten it was a Monday. A further reminder of his ongoing humiliation, since the operations meeting had once been a staple of his calendar. Fa could guess at the meeting's agenda. In the last twelve months, directives from Beijing had taken on increasing urgency over uncovering the identity of *Zhenniao*—the Poisonfeather bird.

Within the MSS, Poisonfeather was the code name for the theory that a series of well-documented leaks to the Americans was, in fact, the work of a mole within the Politburo itself. The theory had been rejected initially for political reasons but also because it lacked a shred of hard evidence. However, an influential cadre within the MSS had stubbornly championed the theory over the last eighteen months, and it was gaining traction within the organization.

Hence Zhi's obsession with being the one to unmask the traitor. Fa himself thought it highly improbable and considered Poisonfeather an apt name for the Politburo's hypothetical mole. After all, the Poisonfeather bird was an extinct and likely mythological bird that had supposedly populated southern China until the thirteenth century. Whereas the Politburo's Poisonfeather bird had come into existence only in 2009. Fa chuckled at his own joke. It was as unlikely as it was . . .

The thought withered as he looked down at Charles Merrick's magazine cover and felt the chill that sometimes accompanies insight. He did the math, trying to see how closely the chronology matched, oblivious to Zhi's secretary.

"Fa? Fa!"

He finally heard her calling his name. "Yes?"

"He has ten minutes on Wednesday. At two."

Fa no longer wanted an appointment with Zhi. If Merrick's remarks really implied what he now suspected, then Zhi would take credit for it. For the honor to be his, Fa would need Merrick himself.

What would the old Guo Fa have done? Either take back your life, or you really are a worthless cupcake.

"On second thought," he told the secretary, "I'll just put it in an e-mail. I don't want to waste his time."

"What about my time? This is an embassy, Fa. I have work to do."

But Fa was already gone.

Fa's only friend at the embassy, or rather the only person who remained friendly toward him, was his de facto boss—Wen Bai, the agricultural minister. Wen Bai was either immune or oblivious, Fa wasn't sure which, to Zhi's political clout, and as long as Fa got his work done, Bai didn't meddle in his affairs. He was a plump, congenial man with thick bifocals from another era. Fa found him in his office. His door was, quite literally, always open.

"Fa! Hello there."

The two men made small talk for a few minutes.

"So what can I do for you?"

"I'm thinking about getting out of town for a few days."

"Oh, that sounds nice. What about your report?"

"Check your inbox."

"Oh, very good," Bai said, reaching for his mouse. "Well, have a good trip, my friend. Where are you headed this time?"

Fa smiled. "I was thinking West Virginia."

"Big fish?"

"With any luck."

CHAPTER ELEVEN

Gibson spent two days lying to himself.

He owed the judge that much, since he'd looked him square in the eye and promised not to get involved. A few days of make-believe, pretending that he could live with it. Live with the memory of Hammond Birk cowering in that trailer doorway like a beaten dog. Knowing that the judge would die in that trailer. The man who had saved his life, pushed him to make something of himself, a voice of compassion and wisdom in a chaotic storm, would live out his days in neglect and squalor.

No, he couldn't live with it.

He'd meant what he'd said to Birk and Swonger—he doubted he could succeed where the Justice Department had failed, but he had to know for certain. So in the middle of the second night, he roused himself from bed and started a file on Charles Merrick. Gibson didn't know a thing about him, but the man had a name and a past—the only two things Gibson needed. Unlike the anonymous cowards who had snatched the Spectrum Protection job away. Perhaps it was precisely because Gibson's own problems seemed insurmountable that Charles Merrick quickly became a stand-in for all of Gibson's fury.

So he did what he always did when contemplating a hack—he crawled into Charles Merrick's life. Merrick's celebrity made it easier than it might otherwise have been. Libraries could be filled with all that had been written about Charles Merrick, and Gibson immersed himself in the minutiae of the man's life: pulling key words and phrases, compiling lists of biographical details, sifting through the data for the patterns and habits that defined Charles Merrick. Two books told the story of Merrick's financial downfall, and Gibson picked the better reviewed: *A Shark in Shark's Clothing: The Rise and Fall of Merrick Capital*. He wasn't sure what else it would tell him, because the man's life had been completely documented online and in the press, but it paid to be thorough. Piece by piece, Gibson built a time line and picture of the man's life. By the end of the week, he knew Charles Merrick's life backward and forward.

Perhaps what he ought to be doing was finding a job. That's what the judge would have wanted Gibson to do. But it simply was not in him. Like a runner who'd finished a grueling marathon, only to discover the finish line had been moved farther down the road, he didn't have the will to start the race again. He was exhausted, and besides, what was the point? Even if he landed another job, they would just snatch it from him like they had the Spectrum Protection job. Whoever *they* were.

He rationalized his decision by telling himself that Merrick was a small job, if it was anything at all—a few weeks at the outside. That it was something he needed to do for the judge. But the truth was that once the familiar adrenaline burn took hold, his vision became increasingly narrow and myopic. The world beyond Charles Merrick lost its ability to command his attention. Even his daughter's name, which could always galvanize him to action, had no effect. He was ashamed that it didn't, but even the shame couldn't deter him. Not now.

Gibson looked up at Merrick's magazine cover taped to the wall above his makeshift desk and smiled. In the last twenty-four hours, a detail from the *Finance* magazine interview had begun to bother him.

Gibson nearly dismissed it as nothing until YouTube finally connected the dots.

Prior to his arrest, Merrick had been in demand as a public speaker, and Gibson found an entire YouTube channel devoted to his speeches. The man was electric in front of an audience, charismatic and cocksure. He would have thrived in politics. And like a politician, Merrick tended to give variations on the same speech. Gibson watched several of them, hoping to get a read on his personality. Midway through the third, he reached for the magazine and flipped to the end of the interview. Rewinding the speech, he listened to Merrick reiterate his motto about pennies being the new million. Almost. There was one key difference. Gibson clicked through several different speeches—same difference in each one between his lectures and the *Finance* article. He reread the line in the interview. It was a small thing, possibly a typo. A small discrepancy that might be nothing or might mean that Charles Merrick's money wasn't in the proverbial Swiss vault. If Gibson's hunch was right, Merrick had remained in close control of his fortune from prison. That required a network of some kind. And networks were always vulnerable.

Only one person knew for sure—Charles Merrick. But Lydia Malkin, the reporter who had conducted the interview, would do in a pinch. Where are you, Lydia Malkin? Foot tapping excitedly, he Googled her, all thoughts of finding a job forgotten. It was only Merrick now.

Merrick just didn't know it yet.

His attempt at bluster fell flat, cornball and hokey in his ear. He was trying to pump himself up to do something that he didn't believe possible. More than that, something he knew better than to try. Was he really going to chase Lydia Malkin down about a single word in an interview? And if he was right? What then? Would he travel to Niobe Federal Prison despite the judge begging him to stay away? If those two knuckleheads, Birk and Swonger, had deciphered Merrick's boast, then how many others had reached a similar conclusion? How far was he going to push it?

He was afraid he already knew the answer to that.

He remembered an old framed map of the world that had hung in his father's office in Charlottesville. At its margins, far out to sea, the mapmaker had written, in ominous letters, "Here there be monsters." He'd asked his father what it meant, and his father had said, *Some lines you can't uncross, Gib. It means be sure.*

In the end, Gibson traced Lydia Malkin to an address in Queens, New York, through her food. She belonged to that curious segment of the populace who obsessively photographed their meals in restaurants and posted it online. Gibson didn't get it, but it definitely made her easy to find since she also hadn't bothered to turn off the GPS metadata that her phone embedded in each photograph. It was just a matter of triangulating her location based on the places she frequented regularly. She ordered from New Good One Chinese Restaurant at least twice a week and really had a thing for their dumplings. It turned out to be only a block and a half from where she lived on Astoria Boulevard; the delivery guy was more than happy to reunite Gibson with his "sister" for forty bucks.

He waited outside her building under an awning for two hours. Dumplings were starting to sound good. Across the street, Lydia Malkin finally came out. He watched her cross the street toward him; in person, she looked younger than he'd expected. Maybe it was the fact that she was barely five feet tall. She seemed taller on TV. Since the Merrick issue of *Finance* had hit the newsstands, she'd been a busy woman. Appearances on all the major cable news networks, interviews in which she'd acquitted herself ably. But while he'd been impressed by how assured she was on camera, she hadn't answered the question he needed answered.

He felt more than a little stalkerish tracking her down this way. He hadn't liked resorting to it, but his efforts to contact her using more conventional methods had been met with silence. Understandably so. Her star was in the ascendancy, and who was he? But he needed answers and didn't have any more time for social niceties. The clock was ticking on Merrick's release, and Gibson felt late to the party. Hopefully the price of a round-trip ticket to New York City would leapfrog him to the front of the line.

The seven a.m. Amtrak from Union Station had allowed him to continue his homework on Mr. Charles Merrick. And there was always more to learn. It was astounding how much press Merrick had received even before his arrest. Easy to see why, though. Merrick was an extremely quotable interviewee. Outspoken to the point of recklessness, the man had a knack for the controversial and seemed wholly unafraid of the media. There was a tactical flamboyance in the way Merrick spoke to reporters.

That was a good word for it. Gibson had stopped reading and typed "flamboyant" into the file he was creating on Merrick. Research was the cornerstone of any successful hack. Knowing your targets better than they knew themselves: their habits, the name of their high-school English teacher, the street they grew up on, their children's birthdays. Gibson compiled it all, because you never knew what would turn out to be the key to unlocking someone's personal security. Personal experience was most people's first point of personal security. Despite the howls of warning from security experts, people went on believing their memories were private. They weren't. An entire generation was conveniently compiling its personal history on social media websites. Convenient to people like Gibson Vaughn.

Charles Merrick's background seemed typically privileged. He claimed to be self-made, but Gibson didn't know how self-made you could be growing up in a wealthy enclave of Connecticut. According to his transcripts, Merrick had coasted through his elite education, attending high school at Groton, a boarding school in Massachusetts, followed by an undergraduate degree in history from Dartmouth and an MBA from Wharton. There he'd met his future ex-wife, Veronica Barrett-Hong, whose WASP and Chinese family lines had sired a tireless overachiever. Unlike Merrick, Veronica had graduated summa cum laude from Wharton to accompany her undergraduate degree in economics from Yale. They'd married the summer before starting jobs on Wall Street, Veronica again the more impressive of the two, so it came as some surprise when Charles Merrick announced the creation of Merrick Capital while Veronica segued into the role of socialite and mother. They were a formidable pair, and as Merrick Capital roared to success in the late nineties, they'd risen together—stars of the New York scene with a home overlooking Central Park, a summer house in Southampton, a spectacular apartment on the Île de la Cité in Paris, and, in London, a house in Kensington.

After his arrest, Charles and Veronica Merrick had endured an ugly and public New York divorce. Veronica Merrick's newly minted status as social pariah had not sat well with her. Her revenge consisted of scorching what little remained of her husband's reputation and sprinkling the ashes across the New York tabloids. A steady stream of unsubstantiated gossip about drug use, infidelity, and physical abuse flowed from unattributed sources as the divorce dragged through the courts. It took several years for the Justice Department to sort out whether there were any assets for Veronica Merrick to contest. In the end, she'd walked away with almost nothing. Before the arrest, the Merricks' net worth was estimated in the billions. Veronica Merrick had a little money left to her by her parents, but it was no understatement to say that her standard of living had taken an ungainly swan dive from the balcony of her old life.

Currently, Veronica Merrick resided in Miami in a rented one-bedroom condo, as reported by several articles gleefully describing her pedestrian lifestyle. America did enjoy a good comeuppance. There was no love lost between the former husband and wife, and at this point, she was probably a dead end for cracking Charles Merrick. Merrick seemed the sort who would need to celebrate his triumphs and erase his failures. Veronica Merrick fell in the latter category.

The Merricks had one daughter, Chelsea Merrick. Unlike her mother, Chelsea seemed a promising angle. The daughter had followed in her father's footsteps to Groton and had been accepted to Brown. Her college-application essay, leaked to Gawker.com, was an adoring paean to her father. Father-daughter photographs painted Merrick as especially doting, and Gibson found numerous mentions of her in his interviews. She'd been a beautiful girl, mixing the best from both parents. Her mother's delicate bone structure and her father's eyes and spectacular blond hair, which cascaded down her back. His third hedge fund had even been named "Chelsea" in her honor.

During the trial, his assets frozen, Merrick had quietly emptied his daughter's trust fund to pay his legal bills. Chelsea Merrick had never enrolled at Brown, and instead gone west to find herself, abandoning New York before it abandoned her. She'd worked for a spell as a waitress at a ski resort in Colorado before moving to Oregon. Gibson found her transcripts from the University of Portland, an incoherent assortment of courses but no degree. After that, a spotty job history in and around Portland before she dropped out of sight. Gibson had decided to continue looking; the memory of an adoring daughter would be something Charles Merrick would cling to in prison.

As soon as Gibson stepped out of the shade, he reached for his sunglasses. It was a brilliant, cloudless day, and Lydia Malkin moved quickly along Astoria Boulevard. She covered a lot of ground in a hurry for someone her height, and Gibson found himself trotting to keep up, afraid to lose sight of her on the busy street. He was skilled at finding people but not so good at following them. The Marines had taught him many skills, but tailing a woman through New York hadn't been among them.

Lydia Malkin stopped to look at something in a store window. Not knowing what else to do, Gibson did the same and found himself staring stupidly in the window of a take-out chicken joint. When he glanced up she had doubled back toward him. Not toward him—at him. When he met her eyes, he knew he was busted.

"Who are you with?" she demanded.

"What?"

"I'm not giving interviews. That's all got to go through the magazine. You have to talk to Peter Moynihan directly."

"I'm not a reporter."

"Then why are you following me? Please don't be a stalker. That would be so boring," she said, channeling her best Dorothy Parker.

"I need your help."

"With?"

"Charles Merrick."

She said, "Ha" in lieu of laughing. "Get in line."

He looked around. "Think I'm at the front of it right now."

She made a face suggesting it was a passably clever retort. "Why should I help you?"

"Goodness of your heart?"

"Aw . . . first day in New York, sweetie?"

"All right, how about you help me and I don't publicize the real reason you wanted to interview Merrick?"

That stopped her. She gave him a second once-over. "Well, you're a quick study. I'll give you that." She checked the time on a clunky sports watch on her wrist. "I've got thirty minutes."

"I appreciate it."

"You can have fifteen of them . . . insert name here."

"Ben Rizolli," Gibson said, naming a kid he'd known in elementary school.

They ducked into a grim railroad bar. Inside, they ordered drinks from a massive bearded bartender who looked at them like they were lost.

"Bombay Sapphire and tonic," Lydia said. "Three limes."

"What?" the bartender asked.

"To which part?"

"The Bombay part."

"You're kidding me, right?"

"No, I'm not kidding you, princess."

"A gin and tonic."

"Well, then say that."

"Come for the smell, stay for the customer service." Lydia rolled her eyes and left Gibson to pay and found a table toward the back. Gibson ordered the first beer he saw on the row of taps, tipped heavily, and went to join her. She sat back lazily in her chair, watching him and stirring her gin and tonic. He finished his beer in three long gulps.

"Prick forgot my limes."

"They don't have limes."

"Of *course* they don't," she said and changed the subject. "You know, you're the first one to figure it out."

"How much did they lose?"

"Everything. But only half to Merrick. The other half went to Madoff."

"No way."

She laughed. "Right? My parents, the two-time losers. Way to diversify your portfolio, folks."

"Where are they now?"

"Mom's surviving," she said, turning serious. "She's not having the retirement she earned, but she's surviving."

"And your dad?"

"My mom survives him too."

"I'm sorry."

"Yeah, well, what are you going to do?"

"That why you went after Merrick?"

She nodded. "Didn't think I'd get half of what I did, but the man has issues with women. Couldn't help himself. Almost felt bad, but I just handed him the shovel; he did his own digging. So what's your story? Your parents ride the Merrick express too?"

"This isn't about my parents."

"Not a reporter. Not personal. So what then? You some kind of private detective?"

"No, I think I established that with my crappy tailing."

"True."

"How did you spot me anyway?"

"I'm five foot nothing and live in Queens. My entire life is built around spotting men taking an unhealthy interest in me. I caught you not looking at me when I came out of the apartment."

"Damn."

"You're big; I'm smart. Only chance I've got." She tried her drink and put it back down. "Wow, that is literally the worst. Is this left over from a prohibition bathtub?"

"Get you something else?"

"No, but you can tell me what it is you want from me. This is your blackmail thing after all."

"I'm sorry for that."

"What're you gonna do?" she said again with a shrug. "*Finance* would not take kindly to those kinds of undisclosed conflicts of interest. I'm actually kind of surprised no one has called me on it yet. It'll come out eventually. Always does. Not like I tried to hide it."

"What happens then?"

"Depends on how the media reacts. The magazine will act to protect their reputation. Peter will have to suspend me. Maybe fire me."

"You're not worried about it?"

"I'll take a hit, but in the long run it will probably be good for my career. The Merrick interview got my name out there. Spin it right, and I might even come out the hero. Daughter sticks it to man who ruined her parents. Has a nice populist ring to it, don't you think?"

"So why are you talking to me?"

She shrugged. "Never been blackmailed before. Got to admit, you have me curious. Truth, I've always had a naughty blackmail fantasy, and you're kind of cute in a Chris Pratt sort of way. Buff Chris Pratt, not *Parks and Rec* Chris Pratt. Not really my type, but I can work with it. If you ever get around to telling me what you want, I mean."

It was all bull, but she was having a good time pushing his buttons, using her natural brashness to unsettle him. Gibson played along, dropping his head as though embarrassed, letting her feel in control of the situation.

"Are you blushing?" she asked. "No blushing. You are totally going to ruin this for me if you blush. You cannot be a blackmailer and be this easy to mess with."

"Sorry."

She stabbed at her drink in mock disappointment.

"Well, the moment, as they say, is over, so you may as well ask whatever it is you came to ask."

"Invest your pennies," he said.

"What of it?"

"At the end of the interview, you asked what Merrick would do when he got out. He said not to worry about him, that he knew how to invest his pennies."

"And?"

"Well, the expression is 'save your pennies.'"

"I'm familiar with the expression."

"So which was it? Invest or save?"

She sat back and stared at him. "Why?"

"Just a theory I'm working on."

She sat forward. "What theory?"

"It's not important."

"Obviously," she said and waited.

He waited back. There was no chance that he'd confide in Lydia Malkin. She was too smart and too ambitious to be trusted.

"You're really not going to tell me?" She sounded hurt; she wasn't.

"I'm afraid I can't."

"What about after? I tell you what you want to know now, and you give me the whole story after you do whatever it is you're going to do?"

"Can't do that either."

"You suck at negotiating."

"I can hurt Merrick."

She smiled, showing all of her teeth and none of her heart. "See? Was that so hard?"

He shrugged. "I suck at negotiating."

"He said, 'Invest my pennies.' And before you ask, yeah, I'm sure."

"Okay, so last question. In the interview, you repeated what he said, but how did he say it? Like what was his demeanor? His tone of voice? Do you know what I mean?"

"Yeah, I know what you mean. His demeanor? Smug. So unbelievably smug. He had this look on his face like he was dying to say something. Like maybe he'd thought of something funny but was worried he might offend me . . . and then he said it."

"Got it," he said as levelly as he could muster.

Inside, he was the night sky on the Fourth of July, but it wouldn't do to let her see. There *was* a way. One way or another, Merrick had been managing his money from prison. Which meant he'd unlocked the back door.

"I hope it helps," she said. "So . . . I have a question."

"Shoot."

"Those two guys by the bar that keep looking over here. Friends of yours, or do I look better in these jeans than I thought?"

Gibson looked over his shoulder. Birk and Swonger were leaning against the bar like they'd been drinking here for years. They looked at him and nodded. Gibson nodded back.

Christ, he thought, they'd done it to him again. When this was all over, he really needed to learn how surveillance worked.

CHAPTER TWELVE

Swonger spun a chair around and sat, resting his elbows on the backrest. He smirked back and forth between Gibson and Lydia as if this were middle school and he'd just caught them holding hands. Birk circled around and took the last chair at the table.

"Mind if we join you?" Birk asked.

"Lydia, you should go," Gibson said.

"Lydia should stay," said Swonger. "That cool with you?" He laid an oil-stained hand on her wrist.

If Swonger meant to intimidate her, he was going to need a new plan.

"Take your hand off me," she said as if asking for directions to the bathroom. She made no attempt to shake off his hand.

"What are you gonna do if I don't?"

"I'm thinking I'll scream."

"Maybe I like that." Swonger's grip tightened.

"Maybe you do, but my cousin? Not so much."

"Who?"

"Big fella behind the bar."

Swonger's eyes flickered, and he glanced back toward the bar. The bartender stared back.

"He hates screaming. His mother, my aunt, used to scream a lot. When he was fourteen he put his dad in the hospital for making her scream. You? He'll probably kill you."

She was lying, but it was a good lie. Told like it was an old story that she'd been telling for years. Felt real, and only the faintest tremor around her eye gave her away. Gibson wasn't sure he would have caught it if he hadn't been at the bar with her earlier. She was very, very good. He didn't know whether to duck or applaud.

Swonger licked his lips dryly and let go of her wrist. "I was just being friendly."

"We're going," Gibson said.

"Uh-uh." Swonger leaned back in his chair and lifted his shirt to reveal the black beveled grip of a pistol in the waistband of his jeans. "She can go, but you and us have some conversating to do. Unless he's your cousin too."

Gibson looked at Lydia expectantly, but she didn't budge. He didn't know why he expected Lydia to bolt for the door; he hadn't known her very long, but he already knew she wasn't the bolting type. She took another sip of her drink and leaned forward conspiratorially.

"So," she asked. "What are we talking about here?"

"What are we talking about, Gibson?" Birk asked.

Lydia caught Gibson's eye, and he saw something click behind hers like a sniper adjusting a high-powered scope trained on his head.

"Gibson," she repeated. "What a nice name, Ben."

"Who the hell is Ben?" Birk asked.

"You tell this nice lady your name is Ben?" Swonger asked.

"Just let it go, okay?"

"Ma'am, this here is Gibson Vaughn. Famous computer hacker and varsity asshole."

Gibson exhaled wearily. He glanced over at Lydia, expecting the third degree. Instead, she had fixed a shocked, confused, explain-how-the-world-works-to-me-you-big-smart-man expression on Swonger. It was a thing of beauty; her eyes had somehow grown three sizes until she looked like the most innocent babe lost in the most dangerous of woods. It was a hell of an act, one that would keep an attention whore like Swonger talking until the rapture.

"Who?" she asked meekly.

"Gibson Vaughn? Guess she hasn't heard of you, big shot. Look up the Benjamin Lombard hack. That'll catch you all up." Swonger winked at Gibson.

"That was you?" she asked Gibson.

He nodded. No point in lying now.

"I remember when that happened. You were an idiot."

"Still is," Swonger said.

Gibson didn't feel inclined to argue with either of them.

"Well, nice to meet you, Gibson Vaughn," she said and smiled at him. But behind her eyes, he could see her tallying up all the ways he was going to pay for not playing straight with her.

"What are you two doing here?" What he really wanted to know was *how* they had followed him to New York. Or had even known to. He hadn't told anyone where he was going, and when he'd left the farm he'd been pretty damn definitive that Merrick was a no-go. Had they compromised his phone? Could these two hillbillies have hacked him? His natural paranoia fanned from a spark into flame.

"What did you think? That I wouldn't catch up with you?" Swonger snorted. "Boy, you can't hide from me."

"No, he means, *why* are we here?" Birk said.

"I mean both."

"Oh, why? Why's easy. 'Cause you a backstabbing son of a bitch," Swonger said. "I wondered why you sat up there talking to that vegetable stand all that time. But then I couldn't find the magazine after you left. So I wondered, why would Gibson Vaughn take the magazine unless he was up to something?" Swonger held out both hands toward Gibson and Lydia. "And here we are. Are you selling us out to this bitch?"

Birk put up a hand. "You played us. It's very disappointing. This is my deal. I brought you in on it."

They sat back righteously and waited. For what? For Gibson to break down and confess his betrayal? Lydia was watching intently; he could hear her mental tape recorder running. It was irritating, and he was losing patience with all of them.

"So?" Gibson asked.

"So?" Birk repeated incredulously.

"So you work for us. That so what."

"Like hell I work for you, Swonger."

"I brought you in on it," Birk complained.

"No, the judge brought me in, and the judge is the only thing keeping me in. You mean nothing to me."

"I was going to cut you in."

"Oh, you were going to cut me in. After I did all the work. Why should I cut you in at all? What do you even bring to the table?"

"What do you mean, what do I bring? It was my deal. We figured it out," Birk said.

"Yeah, that was pretty clever of you. But you already told me everything you know. So, I ask again, what do you bring to the table now?"

"Oh, so you double-crossing us," Swonger said.

"Jesus Christ. I can't double-cross you if we never made a deal, dummy. You asked me to see the judge; I saw him. Don't yell at me because you talk too much. Piece of advice: if all you have is information, don't give it away for nothing."

"We trusted you."

"Well, it wasn't mutual," Gibson shot back.

Swonger's hand went to his gun, the expression on his face turning the malignant color of an old bruise. Lydia pushed her chair back, sensing the atmosphere over the table changing for the worse.

"I think that's my cue to be going," Lydia said.

She stood and paused, turning back to Gibson.

"Walk me out?" she asked.

Swonger pushed out his seat a few inches, chair legs grinding angrily over the linoleum floor.

Gibson shook his head. "Thanks for your help."

"Anytime. Ben."

She backed away slowly, turned, and left the bar quickly. She sure could cover a lot of ground in a hurry. Gibson hoped that was the last he would be seeing of Lydia Malkin. When she was gone, he looked at Birk and then Swonger in turn.

"So what now?" he asked. "You planning on shooting me in a bar full of witnesses?"

"If I have to. I'm about done getting scraped off people's shoes," Swonger said and lifted the gun halfway out of his belt.

"Look," said Birk, the voice of reason. "It doesn't have to be like this. I just have concerns about your intentions. The way you left."

Swonger looked at his partner pityingly.

"The way I left was I finished talking to the judge and then walked back to my car. Wasn't anything sneaky about it. You watched me go. And my intention is to catch the train back to DC."

"The hell you are," Swonger said.

"Our car is out back. We'll drive you," Birk said.

Gibson let out an unscripted laugh. "The hell you will."

"We can talk on the way. Sort this out like—"

Swonger cut in, way past being reasonable. "Laugh again." The gun was out now, flush against his thigh where the bartender couldn't see it.

He thumbed the safety off without looking down. "Laugh again, just once. Swear to God, I'm all kinds of done with how funny you think we are."

Swonger had been bluffing before; he wasn't now. He'd stepped over that threshold in the blink of an eye.

"Gavin," Birk said. "Let's just take a minute here."

"Shut up."

"We didn't agree—"

"Shut up. Let's go," Swonger said to Gibson. "Out back."

Birk led the way and kept glancing back at Gibson every other step. Swonger fell in behind, gun at his side, but smart enough to leave enough room that he could bring it up if Gibson had ideas about making a move on him. Gibson didn't.

The back door was at the end of a long hallway by the bathrooms. Gibson slipped on his sunglasses and hoped it hadn't gotten cloudy. He slowed slightly to let Birk gain a few feet on him. Birk glanced back one more time and then pushed open the door. His hand went up to shade his eyes from being blinded by the sun.

Gibson took a running start and drove his foot into Birk's back, launching him out the door. Birk took two dancing steps, trying to keep his balance before pitching forward into the cement-gray Scion parked in the alleyway. His face broke his fall, bouncing unnaturally off the curved edge of the hood. Birk was unconscious before he hit the ground.

Gibson let his momentum carry him forward and out the door. The door hit the backstop and slammed shut behind him. He had at most a second of silence, but it was strangely peaceful. It almost felt as if he were watching the world in slow motion.

The Marine Corps martial art was known affectionately as Semper Fu. It wasn't graceful or elegant. It did not teach respect for one's opponent or lead to a Zen-like oneness with the cosmos. Semper

Fu was economical, brutish, and devastatingly effective. And being a martial art designed by the military, much of it assumed one or both combatants were armed. So Ka-Bar knives, sidearms, and rifles were all incorporated into its close-quarters, hand-to-hand fighting scenarios.

Gibson had been a natural. Although he'd been given Intelligence as his military occupational specialty (an appropriate if ironic fit given what he'd done to get sent to the Corps), the Marines preached "every Marine a rifleman." Soldier first, specialty second. He'd taken special pride in going toe to toe with the infantrymen who sneeringly referred to him as a POG—person other than grunt. The sense of grievance and injustice he'd carried with him into the Marines led him to seek out the biggest, toughest Marines as sparring partners. Guys with forty, fifty pounds on him, who thought the idea of joining the Marines to work on computers was a waste of a perfectly good excuse to dead some people. Somehow getting his ass kicked repeatedly yet always coming back for more eventually earned their grudging tolerance. But it wasn't until he started to beat them that they accepted him. He hadn't used it in a couple of years, but the instincts were there, dormant in his muscle memory.

Swonger came through the door angry, gun raised—expecting Gibson to have taken off running in one direction or another. Guns conferred a lot of advantages, but they could also make you feel invulnerable if everyone else was unarmed. Make you reckless. And Gibson hadn't run. He was right there waiting for him.

The burst of sunshine blinded Swonger and bought Gibson time to close the distance between them. Gibson put one hand on the gun and jerked it sharply past his hip, down and away. That combined with Swonger's forward momentum dragged his face in line for a clean, quick punch in the jaw. Gibson uncoiled through the blow, snapping Swonger's head around like a flag in the wind.

Swonger had some fight in him, though, and held on to the gun with a pit-bull grip—understandable but a real bad idea. Off balance, his body followed dumbly where his gun hand led him. That momentum was all Gibson needed. He stepped into Swonger's path and planted an elbow on the bridge of his nose. A twist of his wrists, a hard hip pivot, and Swonger was on his back, gasping for air. Gibson didn't need to kick him in the head, but he did it anyway. Then he did it again. He wanted Swonger to have something to think about on the drive home.

It was all over in five seconds.

Gibson dragged the two men over and slumped them against their car. While he waited for them to shake it off, Gibson unloaded Swonger's .45 into the storm grate, listening to the bullets rattle down the pipe to the sewer below. He considered taking the gun but vetoed the idea quickly. Who knew where this gun had been or *what* it had done? Swonger had done time for something. Instead, he disassembled the .45 on the hood of the Scion and pocketed the firing pin and the stop. If it ever came to it, it would be good to know Swonger was not a threat. Unless Swonger knew his firearms, and Gibson bet he didn't, then he wouldn't know anything was amiss until he pulled the trigger.

The gun reassembled, Gibson fished the car keys from Swonger's pocket and started the Scion. He wasn't surprised that it worked— the Scion, a patchwork of Bondo, had been sanded and primed for a paint job Swonger couldn't afford yet was tricked out with an oversized aftermarket spoiler and racing tires. Exactly the kind of car that he imagined Swonger would drive. The Marines attracted its fair share of gearheads, and the Scion was popular among cash-strapped tuners because the base model was cheap and the aftermarket options were almost limitless.

Gibson shoved the gun under the passenger seat. A six-pack of beer spoke to him from a cooler in the backseat, and he helped himself. It tasted better than cheap beer had any right to taste and helped cut the adrenaline from the fight. He thought about leaving Birk and Swonger in the alley to fend for themselves, catching his train, and putting some miles between them. But what good would that do? They would just follow him. Turn up again when it was least convenient. He was already zero for two and didn't rate his chances of spotting them the next time. He drank another beer and pondered what to do about his stalkers. He was still pondering when Swonger came around. Gibson offered him a beer, which Swonger held gingerly to his jaw. Birk was slower. He had really taken a shot to the head and was likely concussed. When he finally stirred he moved like a man who'd been dipped in wet cement. It would be a few days clearing those cobwebs, and Gibson was all right with that.

"Where's my gun at?" Swonger asked.

"What gun?"

Swonger's mouth opened, shut. He eyed Gibson hatefully.

"You with us there?" Gibson asked, snapping his fingers at Birk, who nodded, rolled away from Swonger, and threw up against the tire. When he sat back up, his eyes had cleared slightly.

"All right, now that I have everyone's attention, let's get a few things straight."

They waited for Gibson to go on, but he didn't know what to say to them. Nothing that would get them to do what he wanted anyway. Birk might be reasoned with, and if Birk was really running the show, then Gibson might expect him to keep Swonger on a leash. But Swonger was the real threat. Gibson hadn't seen it clearly enough at the ballpark or at the farm. Sure, he'd seen the prison tats, the missing teeth, heard the busted English. He'd written Swonger off as just another ward of the American penal system. But beneath the ignorance, bluster, and dubious personal hygiene, a carnivorous intelligence lurked in Swonger. Birk thought he was in charge only because Swonger let him think it.

Nothing Gibson could say would get Swonger to trust him, get him to go back to the farm so Gibson could take his run at Merrick without constantly looking over his shoulder. A kick to the head hadn't dimmed Swonger's determination any. Whatever else you could say about Gavin Swonger, there wasn't any quit in him. Swonger was a relentless, angry tide that would just keep coming.

He didn't like the options that left him.

"I'll drive," he said.

CHAPTER THIRTEEN

They crossed the George Washington Bridge in silence, the gloom of the lower deck matching Swonger's mood as he brooded in the passenger seat over whom to blame for the face-shaped dent in his precious Scion. That left Gibson to reach back every few minutes and shake Birk, who was definitely concussed, to keep him from falling asleep. The Scion was a two-door, so Birk had to lie sideways across the narrow backseat. Gibson accelerated around a lumbering pickup, and felt the car leap forward powerfully. Swonger had been tinkering under the hood as well.

The silence held until exit 9 on the Jersey Turnpike.

"Want my gun back," Swonger said.

Gibson ignored him. Swonger folded his arms and waited until exit 6.

"Where's my gun?"

After that it was every exit, like a kid demanding to know if they were there yet. At Baltimore, Gibson relented and told him it was under the seat. Swonger fished around between his legs and cleaned the gun off with the hem of his T-shirt. He popped the magazine and saw it was empty.

"Where the bullets?"

"At the bullet store."

Swonger thought about it. "This is some unconstitutionality right here. We got amendments."

"That's not what that means."

Gibson reached back and shook Birk's leg again, and Birk raised himself up to see where they were, didn't recognize anything, and tried to make himself comfortable.

"One thing I can't figure out is why . . . ," Gibson began, articulating a question that had nagged at him since the farm.

"Why what?" Birk said.

"Why Merrick would say anything. About pennies. About any of it. I mean, think about it. He went to jail, served his bid, kept his mouth shut for eight years, then all he has to do is drift away quietly. But now, inexplicably, months from release and getting away with it clean, he goes and broadcasts it in a national magazine. I just don't get it. What's his angle?"

"I don't know why he said it, but he said it," Birk said.

"The hubris," Swonger said, still looking out the window.

"Hubris?" said Birk.

"Yeah, man, the hubris. The Greeks were all into that shit. Defiance of the gods. Like my man, Prometheus. Tipped man to fire after Zeus told him to stand down. Zeus was pissed. Chained his disobeying ass to a cold rock and let this giant, crazy bird eat on his liver. But Prometheus is immortal, see? So every night, the liver? It grows back. Next night, that bird's back, chowing down like it's his job. Forever, man. That was Prometheus's punishment: forever. The gods don't take nothing light, and Prometheus? Prometheus had nothing coming, dog. And the kicker? Prometheus knew it. Knew Zeus would pink-slip his ass, but Prometheus did like he do anyway. Couldn't help himself. Because of the hubris. Had that hubris real, real bad."

"What the hell are you talking about?" Birk asked.

Gibson shook his head in amazement. About the last thing he'd have bet on was a dissertation on Greek mythology from Gavin Swonger.

"Merrick, man, he got the hubris too. Read that interview again. He was busting to tell someone. Thinks he's smarter than the gods. Thinks he's all tricksy with his little code words and such. Probably got himself a righteous little Merrick boner over how clever he is. Thinks he's smart and we're dumb. But he ain't. He's just like my cousin Cole."

"Cole-in-prison, Cole?" Birk asked.

"Cole-in-prison, Cole," Swonger agreed and turned to Gibson. "So my cousin Cole is serving a ten-spot up at Keen Mountain for armed robbery and assaulting a clerk. 'Cause why? 'Cause after this dumb mook robbed the place, he goes out drinking. Same night. Tells every girl in the joint how he a badass John Dillinger. Well, guess what? Someone dimes him out to the cops. Busted while he's paying his tab with bills from the robbery. Still had the gun on him too. Know what Cole says to me? He says getting away with it was the easy part. Hard part? Not telling nobody about it."

To his surprise, Gibson knew the wisdom of what Swonger said. He remembered when he was a teenager, after hacking Benjamin Lombard and turning the senator's files over to the press, how he would go online and come within a keystroke of bragging about it in the forums. Not even to hackers he knew well, just randoms he struck up conversations with. He'd get as far as typing, "you know that senator who got hacked?" His finger would hang over the return key until beads of sweat formed on his brow. Common sense stopped him, but there had been some close calls.

It had been madness, but ego wasn't afraid of prison. Ego wasn't afraid of anything accept being ignored. Swonger was right about that much. Gibson only hoped he could make Merrick pay for his.

"Excepting that Prometheus got eternity," Swonger said ruefully. "Merrick only got eight years. You believe that? Eight years."

"Doesn't seem like enough, does it?"

"We got crime and punishment all wrong in this country."

"How's that?"

Swonger sat up. He'd clearly been thinking about this topic for some time. "Say a mook hold up a liquor store. Say he pockets a couple bills, say he use a gun but don't fire one shot. If they catch him, he gets ten years in one of the worst places on earth."

"Cousin Cole?" Gibson asked.

"Yeah, cousin Cole. Now take a different mook. This one's clever. Goes to work on Wall Street and robs thousands of people, but he use a pen and uses every drop of ink in it to ruin lives, steal hundreds of millions. Well, this fella gets eight years, and the prison ain't even nothing but summer camp."

"Guns are dangerous," Gibson said.

"And I ain't saying they ain't, but why's that the only basis for punishment?"

"You got an alternative?"

"Yeah. Net worth."

"Net worth?"

"Yeah, look here. Cole was broke when he robbed that liquor store. I ain't saying what he did was right. Cole took what weren't his. It's a crime, no doubt. But I get it, know what I mean? Why he did it. Desperation. At least, I comprehend that shit. Now say you worth a hundred million, and you steal another hundred million? Now that shit's incomprehensible to me. Far as I can see, you a monster with no redeeming value. You belong in solitary for a long, hairy-ass time 'cause you a goddamn menace."

"Sentences inversely proportionate to your bank account?"

"Word. You got more money than God, all the power that come along with it, and you still feel the need to ruin other people's lives to get more than you could ever spend? Your ass needs to be removed from circulation."

"Interesting theory."

"I've got more."

Gibson believed him.

"So you really think you can get your hands on the money for us?" Birk asked.

"Let's get something straight—I don't work for you, and I don't owe you anything."

Birk started to argue.

"Let me finish." Gibson cut him off. "I do owe your uncle something. Everything, actually. So I'm going to go home, get a few things, and head down to West Virginia and see about Merrick's money. See if I can set things right for your uncle and your family. Don't know if I can yet, but I have an idea about how it might be done. Will you let me do that?"

"Sure," Birk said. "I just want to know what it is."

A tricky question because Gibson only half knew himself. His epiphany from the interview was simple: Merrick hadn't parked his money in a bank somewhere. No, somehow, some way, Merrick's money was in play. Working. Appreciating. *Idle money is wasted money.* A direct quote from a Merrick interview in '04. Gibson had found similar sentiments throughout the man's public-speaking career.

Another thing Gibson knew: if Merrick was investing his money, his ego would never allow those investments to be managed by others. Not for the last eight years. In these volatile markets? Not a chance. It also did not seem like something he could do from inside a federal prison. That meant Merrick had a confederate on the outside, someone to mind the store. They'd be in constant contact somehow, and that, ladies and gentlemen, constituted a network. It didn't matter whether they communicated via smoke signals or encrypted e-mails . . . if Gibson could find it, he could hack it.

If he could find it.

And that was his big problem—he couldn't even start planning the hack until he knew what kind of network Merrick was using. And that would take time, which, with Merrick's impending release, was not on his side.

Gibson laid out the situation to Birk and Swonger. To his surprise, they bought it.

"What do you need from us?" Birk asked.

"Okay. First thing, you're going to have to scrape together a bankroll."

"I've got four thousand dollars," Birk said, producing a roll of bills wrapped in a rubber band.

"That's it?"

Birk looked hurt. "Unless we sell some of the farm equipment. It'll take time, but I could raise more."

Underfunded and on a clock—things were getting off on stellar footing. Still, Gibson told him to hold off; he didn't like the idea of crippling the Birks' farm on a hunch. He gave Birk instructions on setting up an offshore bank account. If they got lucky and Merrick really did have money they could find, then they'd need somewhere to move it.

Swonger had sat silently stewing, but couldn't hold his peace any longer. "Ain't no way I'm riding the bench while you take our money."

That wasn't exactly a surprise to Gibson. A thought occurred to him. A horrible one, but it might be a solution. Take Swonger with him to West Virginia. Christ, were there really no alternatives? He glanced over at Swonger, who was eying him suspiciously. Well, at least this way he'd see him coming. Keep his enemy closer, isn't that how it went?

"If we go together . . . you think you can behave yourself? Let me handle things?"

"Long as you do like you say you will. I'll let you do your thing."

"All right, then," Gibson said.

"What about me?" Birk asked.

"I'll take you as far as Union Station. After that, you're riding the rails."

Birk began feebly to protest.

"Or the bus, I don't really give a damn. Look, this isn't a package deal. One of you can tag along. The other one goes back to the farm and looks after the judge."

"What? I'm supposed to go babysit the old man?" Birk said.

"Yeah. Between now and when I find that money, Hammond Birk better be living like a damn king. You know what that means?"

"What?"

"It means every day is bath day."

CHAPTER FOURTEEN

The Scion pulled into the parking lot of Gibson's building in the late afternoon. Gibson didn't plan on staying long; he needed to make arrangements to be gone for a few weeks. He wanted to get down to Niobe, West Virginia, and take the lay of the land. Merrick had twenty-three days left on his sentence, and Gibson would need every minute of every day if he were to have a chance of pulling this off.

"Make yourself at home," Gibson said, flipping on a light switch.

Swonger looked around. "Damn. How you living?"

Gibson shrugged, realizing that Swonger was the first person that he'd let see his place. A depressing thought all on its own. He knew his apartment was bare bones. He'd moved in after the separation and never expected to stay this long, buying used or broken furniture on Craigslist and refurbishing it. Nothing hung on the walls. No decorations or plants. It kept him dry when it rained. That was the best you could say for it.

"Did Goodwill charge you for any of this stuff?" Swonger shook his head. "They got more comfortable chairs in the joint."

"Take it easy."

"No, man. Respect. Take a special kinda guy to live like a bum but still act like a condescending prick all the time." Swonger opened the nearly empty refrigerator. "I think someone broke in and robbed your icebox."

Gibson handed him a spare set of keys.

"There's a grocery store a couple blocks north if you're hungry. I'll be back in a couple hours."

"Where you going?"

"See my kid. That okay with you?"

"Yeah, it's cool. Wait . . ." Swonger was looking around with mounting panic. "You don't have no TV."

"You want a book?"

"You killing me, man."

"Well, if you get bored, you can follow me around some."

"Nah, I'll give you the night off. Good faith, right?"

Right.

———————

Gibson picked Ellie up from her after-school program and took her to a movie. A revival house in Ashburn was showing *Finding Nemo*. It was Ellie's all-time number-one movie. A bold statement for a seven-year-old, but she'd watched it until she'd worn a hole in the DVD. She was too young to have seen it on the big screen, and Gibson figured it was a safe bet after the baseball-game fiasco. Dory was her favorite character—a fitting role model for his easily distracted daughter. "I shall call him Squishy and he shall be mine, and he shall be my Squishy!" she screamed happily at the screen. Ellie was still mastering the concept that you had to sit quietly at the movies. Fortunately, it was a quote-along, so audience participation was encouraged. Pretty soon Gibson was laughing and calling out lines right along with her.

After the movie, he drove them to the Nighthawk, where they split a deluxe banana split—one scoop each of chocolate, vanilla, and strawberry; banana; whipped cream; chocolate syrup; nuts; pineapple; strawberries; and three cherries. Toby Kalpar delivered the towering pièce de résistance personally. Ellie was going to be in a sugar coma for a week. Gibson gestured for Toby to sit and watched his friend fold his tall, thin frame into the booth beside Ellie. Toby and Sana treated Ellie as if she were their own grandchild, and she was starting to think she owned the place. Ellie bounced up and down in her seat in anticipation.

"Where's Ellie?" Toby asked, looking back and forth blankly. "I brought ice cream."

Ellie giggled and made an exasperated face. "I'm right here!"

"It's too bad. I guess we'll have to eat it ourselves." Toby pulled the banana split toward him and aimed a marauding spoon at it.

"Guess so," Gibson agreed, reaching for the other spoon.

Ellie shrieked.

Toby clutched his chest in shock. "Where did you come from?"

"I was right here!" she said. "Dad! Tell him."

Toby smiled and presented Ellie with a spoon, which she snatched like she'd just negotiated the end of a hunger strike. No one was ever going to mistake his daughter for shy.

"What do you say, El?" Gibson said.

Ellie managed a muffled "Thank you" a millisecond before she wedged a fist-size spoonful of ice cream into her mouth, tipping her head back to keep it from running down her chin.

"El . . . No Bruce the Shark, okay? Regular bites."

"Yeash, Dahbd," she managed.

After a few bites, Ellie stopped and offered Toby her spoon.

He smiled and tousled her hair. "I've already had mine today."

"You are so lucky," she told him. "I want a diner like this one when I grow up."

Toby beamed at that. "Doesn't fall far from the tree, this one."

Diners had been hallowed ground to Gibson's father, and they had in turn become hallowed to Gibson. As he got older, he was realizing that he hadn't fallen far from the tree himself. Those things that his father had cherished, he found growing in significance in his own life. Being able to make peace with his father's death had only accelerated the process. Did he even love diners at all, or did he just like the way they made him feel because they reminded him of his dad? Could he even separate the two at this point? He wondered what he would pass on to Ellie that she would one day mistake for her own. Would he give himself the chance to find out?

While Ellie inhaled the rest of the banana split, Gibson caught up with Toby, whose daughter, Maissa, a graphic designer living in Palo Alto, had been laid off in a wave of corporate restructuring. Toby was worried about her. Sana was more circumspect about it, which made Toby worry all the more. There was no new news. Maissa was job hunting, and Toby wasn't sleeping. Sana was about ready to banish him to the couch because he was keeping her up too. Gibson had seen Maissa's work; it was very good. He couldn't imagine she would stay unemployed for long, but telling that to Mr. Anxiety was a lost cause.

Gibson worked up the nerve to say what needed saying. He wanted to test saying it out loud to Toby. See how his friend reacted. He lifted his cap off his head and ran his fingers through his hair. "I took a job."

Toby, busy making faces at Ellie, began to congratulate him, but something in Gibson's tone stopped him. Toby stared levelly at him. Although his friend wore glasses, there was nothing wrong with Toby's vision.

"What kind of job? Like before?" Toby didn't know the half of what Gibson had done to find Suzanne Lombard, but he knew enough to be wary.

"No, different. I'm just looking into something for someone," Gibson said, trying to keep the note of apology out of his voice.

"Oh, something for someone. Foolish of me not to have guessed. When will you start to do something for yourself?" Toby's eyes narrowed. "Is it the same people?"

Gibson shook his head. "No, it's just a little job. Might not be anything. I'll probably be back in a couple of days."

"Have you told Nicole?"

"I'm not married to Nicole anymore."

Ellie glanced up at her father. He winced and squeezed her shoulder reassuringly, but his daughter set down her spoon and looked away.

"Gibson . . ." Toby trailed off, but Gibson knew the rest. He'd berated himself with some version of it for the last couple of days—*what are you thinking?* So far he hadn't found an answer that mattered to him more than doing right by Judge Birk.

"I know," he said lamely, and when that wasn't enough, "I know."

Last year, during the hunt for Suzanne Lombard, he'd called Nicole in the middle of the night and sent her into hiding. It had been a precaution, but it had strained his already-fragile relationship with his ex-wife. When he came back, she'd waited for an explanation that he couldn't give—there was no way to tell her some without telling her all of it, and there were parts that he had sworn not to share with anyone. Too much was at stake. Nicole understood how important Suzanne was to him and hadn't pressed him on it. But she had made it absolutely clear that if he endangered Ellie again, there would be consequences.

Yet here he was.

Across the table, Toby spread his hands in a gesture that said, *I cannot help you if you will not help yourself.*

"I know," he said again.

"Then why?"

"Because I owe."

Nicole met him at the door when he dropped Ellie off at home. She ushered Ellie inside and told their daughter to go upstairs. That should have tipped him off to trouble, but he was too taken aback by the transformation in his wife. Ex-wife. Her fledgling catering business was starting to take off, and tonight had been an audition for a new client. It was the first time he'd seen her dressed for work. Gibson tried and failed not to stare. His ex-wife had always been effortlessly beautiful, never working too hard at her appearance. She was working at it now.

He couldn't remember the last time he'd seen her in heels. She wore an understated, elegant pencil skirt that flirted with her knees, topped by a tailored white blouse. She'd always hated necklaces, but a silver pendant sparkled on her breastbone. Her makeup, although subtle, made her features pop in a way that was new, framing her eyes and accentuating her high cheekbones. Since he'd seen her last, she'd changed her hair, which for as long as he'd known her she'd always worn below her shoulders. Now it was at least twelve inches shorter and fell in a sleek, styled line along her jaw. She looked sensational, but he felt strangely melancholic at the change. He felt a stab of irrational possessiveness—her hair looked great, but what was wrong with how she'd worn it when they were married?

He mustered up a smile for his ex-wife. "Your hair looks great."

She thanked him, her voice as despairingly barren as it always was when speaking to him. A studied indifference that she'd perfected in the time since his affair had ended their marriage.

"Any word about the job?"

He should have told her the truth. He could have brushed it off and said he was still waiting to hear. Lying to Nicole had always been a waste of breath—they'd known each other since high school and married while he was in the Corps. She was the one person he could never fool. Instead, he launched into a lie. A stupid, unsustainable lie. Spectrum loved him. The job was a go. How excited he was to get started. What a great opportunity it would be. Talked about how busy he was likely to be as he got up to speed, figuring it would give him cover while he was in West Virginia.

"Maggie called," Nicole interrupted.

That stopped him dead in his tracks, and his mouth went silent as if she'd reached out and snatched language from him. Maggie was Nick Finelli's wife. She and Nicole were friends from back when he and Nick were in the service together. Gibson could tell from her eyes that Maggie had told her everything. A fragile second passed. Caught in a lie, the smart thing to do was own it. Nicole was angry, but it was still salvageable once everyone cooled off. He could have pled humiliation and embarrassment at being thrown out of the polygraph. All of which was true. Instead, he went the other way, picking the fight that often grew out of the faulty logic of liars after they'd been caught out: Nicole had played along with his deception, encouraged him, so if you really thought about it, it was *her* fault. She'd *made* him lie to her, which seemed in this blind moment to be the more outrageous of the two deceptions.

"Oh, what the hell, Nicole?" he exploded at her. "You knew? And so what . . . you're trapping me now? Is that what this is? That's such bullshit."

Nicole didn't take the bait, her voice striking an even more neutral, dispassionate chord. The tone that always infuriated and then broke him. "So now it's my fault that you're a liar?"

"Fuck you."

"Were you in Atlanta last summer?"

"What?" He tried to stop the question leaving his lips. There was no sloppier admission of guilt to a hard question than feigning momentary deafness. It was the question that he'd been steeling himself against ever since the Suzanne Lombard investigation. He just hadn't been expecting it now, on top of everything else. Nicole should have been a boxer.

"What have you done?" she asked.

"What?" he heard himself say again.

"Goddamn it. Were you in Atlanta? Is that why I had to go into hiding?"

"Why are you asking me this?"

"Because a man came to my door tonight asking about Benjamin Lombard and Atlanta."

No doubt the same man who had questioned Toby at the diner. But coming around where his daughter lived? Gibson thought he'd like to have a conversation with this man.

"Are you going to tell me?" she asked.

"I can't. I'm sorry."

Nicole stood in the doorway a long time, studying him.

"You *can't*? Were you always this person?" she asked rhetorically. "God, I'm such a cliché."

"Nicole . . ." His voice a pleading teardrop.

"No. I have wasted so much of my life on you. There's something not right about you."

For a moment, in the white-hot vacuum that followed, the only sound Gibson heard was the martial pounding of the blood in his ears. He felt a finger graze an unforgivable switch, and whatever crossed his face shook his ex-wife. Her hand went to the doorknob, a tremulous fear in her eyes. It broke him. *Is this what you are now?* He stumbled back from the door, down the walk to his car. He didn't dare look back to the house.

When he'd driven several blocks away, he pulled to the curb and screamed. His hands, bloodless on the steering wheel, tried and failed to rip it free.

Gibson slipped into his apartment sometime after one a.m. He'd driven around until he felt under control of himself, steering clear of the Nighthawk and Toby's disapproving glances. In a corner of the living room, Swonger snored quietly from the floor, a jean jacket draped over him for warmth. Gibson lifted a blanket from his bed and draped it over him. Then he took his laptop into the bedroom and shut the door—there was something he needed to check.

The drive had given him time to think about who had been nosing around asking questions, and something that Birk had said back at the farm nagged at him. Something about the "other stuff" that Gibson had done. Birk had winked at him when he'd said it. Gibson had been preoccupied at the time, but now it felt like he'd swallowed a red-hot cigarette lighter. He opened his laptop and did something that he hadn't done in years—he typed his name into a search engine.

Pages of results unfurled. Most of which fell into the ancient-history category: stories about the Benjamin Lombard hack, his arrest, and the subsequent trial. A few articles dated after Lombard's death mentioned Gibson in cursory fashion. He didn't care about any of these. He scanned down the list looking for something else . . . something out of the ordinary.

He found it on the third page of results.

A website called AmericanJudas.com listed Gibson's name in its citation. Gibson clicked on the link. The site, which was run by someone who called himself Tom Pain, trafficked in most of the stock modern-day conspiracy theories about 9/11, climate change, vaccines, autism, the origin of AIDS, and so on. The list went on and on, but only one topic stuck out to Gibson:

The Assassination of Vice President Benjamin Lombard

Gibson sucked in a breath and clicked through to that tab. Inside, Gibson found a rambling treatise speculating that Lombard's cause of death in Atlanta was anything but natural. Ironically, Gibson shared the same sentiment. However, the author's theories were hilariously off-target. Or would have been hilarious, if they didn't feature Gibson so prominently.

Exhibit A was a photograph of a page from a Secret Service logbook. As the website took pains to point out, the log bore the same date as Benjamin Lombard's death. And there was Gibson's signature halfway down the page, signed in to meet the vice president's wife, Grace Lombard. Why, Tom Pain demanded, would the man tried for hacking Benjamin Lombard have a private meeting with Grace Lombard? Why were there reports from staffers that Benjamin Lombard had assaulted Gibson Vaughn outside a conference room hours before the vice president rejected his party's nomination, hours before he died mysteriously alone in his hotel suite?

The site asked all the right questions, even if it had none of the right answers. *Yet*. He thought about reaching out to Grace Lombard; she should be warned. *No*. He'd promised to stay away, and she had people watching out for her. Most likely, they already knew more about American Judas than Gibson did. He shut his laptop and pushed it away.

His father had been right—there were some lines that you couldn't uncross.

CHAPTER FIFTEEN

You knew that the Toproll had crossed the tipping point from controlled chaos to plain old anarchy when there were more dirty glasses than clean ones. Nothing threatened a bar's delicate equilibrium like running out of clean pint glasses. It wasn't her shift, but Lea jumped up multiple times to collect empties and run the old Lamber glasswasher when Margo and her staff got too far into the weeds. It looked to be a long night.

Any regular celebrating a birthday was treated to round after round. The first by Margo, then the responsibility fell to an ever-widening circle of revelers. It was common courtesy. A birthday was a birthday, and that meant it got celebrated on the day of birth. None of this waiting for the weekend nonsense. That was weak-kneed hippie talk. Everyone has a job to get to, now take your damn shot. Lea had seen more than one fight over someone trying to duck out before closing time.

Lea threw her hip into the Lamber to shut the door, and the glasswasher rumbled to life. Someone passed her a shot over the bar. She tapped it on the bar before belting it back and got busy before someone handed her another. She had to get out of here before getting sucked into this mess. Where the hell was Parker? Niobe Prison was only a mile up the road. There better have been a damn riot to keep him.

"Remind me to start putting birthdays on the calendar," Margo huffed as she hurried past up the bar. She'd been saying that for as long as Lea had worked there, but it would never happen. That kind of planning was antithetical to the roiling mayhem that was the Toproll.

Lea finished restocking the glasses and turned around to find Parker standing at the bar. He was still in uniform; she'd never seen him out of it. Like most guards at the prison, he had a thing about wearing it around. The prison was one of the few steady employers left in the area, so the uniform carried some cachet. He gave her a nod and headed for the back room, where the pool tables were. He didn't play, but it was nominally quieter. He passed a table of four more guards, also in uniform. A lot of prison guards did their drinking at Toproll, gossiping and trading war stories. It was the main reason that Lea had taken the job.

Parker was sitting at a table, picking the pretzels out of a bowl of bar mix, when she joined him.

"Parker," she said by way of a greeting.

Parker didn't reply; he wasn't the chattiest of guys, which she thought ironic for an informant.

Parker was fifty-one and divorced, and lived alone. An ex-wife and teenage son lived in South Carolina; he hadn't seen either in years. He considered himself something of a movie buff and watched four-plus hours of television a night, more on weekends. One of those guys who could rattle off the movies on which Quentin Tarantino had done uncredited rewrites. His only ambition was working less and watching more. Exactly the reason that she'd chosen him. He would take the easy money and be happy. Double-crossing her would cut into his La-Z-Boy time. Plus, men his age tended not to take women her age seriously, and she found it useful to be underestimated.

"How was work?"

Parker shrugged as if the topic of his own day bored him. So much for a riot. She slid him his beer and laid a stack of napkins on the table between them. He took the napkin with the money folded in it, making a point of always counting it in front of her. She could understand how working around convicts all day might diminish your faith in humanity. His lips moved as he did the math, and when satisfied, he slipped the money into his jacket pocket and pushed several folded sheets of paper across to her.

She read through Parker's notes, which included a list of magazines and newspapers that Merrick received. She scanned it for anything anomalous, but it looked the same as every other week. Almost all were business related: the *Wall Street Journal*, the *Financial Times*, the *Economist*. The *China Economic Review* and *Journal of Asian Economics* headlined a long list of Chinese business periodicals. They puzzled her slightly. Merrick Capital had specialized in emerging markets but had never made an investment in China. Why the interest? Was China his destination after release?

Well, not if she had anything to say about it.

"How has he been this week?"

"Full of himself. Imagine James Cameron winning the Oscar for *Titanic*," Parker said. "Then multiply it by cocaine."

She shuddered to think what that might look like. "Any variation to his routine?"

Parker shook his head and took a sip of beer. "Same as always. Work detail. Little exercise. Reads in the library or out in the yard. Watches an hour of TV. Dinner. Plays cards with a couple of guys. Reads until lights out. You could set your watch by the guy."

"Then why haven't you ID'd his man in there?"

Merrick had a guard in his pocket. Lea was convinced of it. Someone acting as courier between Merrick and his contact on the outside. She needed the identity of the contact, now more than ever.

It was the key to everything, but so far Parker hadn't been able to flush him out.

"The man is careful, what can I tell you? I got it down to one of two. I'll know next week."

"I'm running out of weeks. He gets out in less than a month. And with this magazine interview . . . I need a name, Parker. Yesterday."

"Next week."

"You're not stringing me along, by any chance?"

Parker's expression darkened. "It's either Slaski or Leonard. But I can only be in one place at a time. I'll have it next week."

"That's good, because if I don't get what I need, then there's no payday at the end of this rainbow for you. Understand me?"

Parker nodded. "I'll get it."

"Good."

"Why you hate him like you do?"

"My family."

"One of those," Parker said.

"One of those."

Parker nodded and picked a few pretzels out of the bowl and munched on them thoughtfully. Building up the strength to actually use his words.

"Lawyer come to see him."

"What lawyer? Henry Susman?"

"That's the one."

"Henry Susman was at the prison?" Lea sat back, dismayed. "When?"

"Couple days ago. Him and Merrick had themselves a sit-down. Your boy came out looking like he'd been shown pictures of his own mother in compromising positions."

If Susman had seen her . . . She didn't finish the thought. She saw now how complacency and overconfidence had crept into her thinking in the time since she'd landed in Niobe. She felt safe in Niobe, and that had made her lazy. Well, it stopped now. This was the homestretch, and with that damn interview in circulation, the situation had become dangerously fluid. It was time to tighten up her ship, and Merrick's phone was the first step. She wondered what had been urgent enough to bring Susman down from his perch on the Upper East Side. What could the two possibly have to discuss now?

"Any idea what they talked about?"

"Those rooms are private. All I can say is the lawyer didn't look none too pleased neither. I thought he was gonna wring Merrick's neck."

Wring his neck? Susman was a lot of things, but a neck-wringer wasn't one of them.

"What did the lawyer look like?"

"Oh, big fellow. About six two, two twenty. Brother filled out that suit."

"Susman was black?"

"There some other kind of brother?"

"And you're sure his name was Susman?"

"What it said on his ID."

Now she really was worried. Someone posing as Henry Susman had visited Charles Merrick in prison. A pretty brazen move, and confirmation that, as she'd feared, the interview was drawing flies. But then why hadn't Merrick blown the whistle on the imposter instead of going along with it? Could it have been the partner that she'd long suspected Merrick had? It had never occurred to her that they would be reckless enough to meet at the prison. Maybe the partner recognized how foolish the interview had been even if Merrick couldn't.

Nothing but conjecture, unfortunately. She didn't know a damn thing now except that she really needed Merrick's phone.

CHAPTER SIXTEEN

The visitation room at Niobe Prison reminded Guo Fa of the old Shanghai Railway Station of his childhood—yellow light falling to a stained floor that would never come clean again. The burnt smell of electricity. Fa sat at a narrow metal table and studied the inmates engrossed in quiet conversation with loved ones. He rarely thought of his wife, who lived back home, but he missed her now. A distance had sprung up between them after the miscarriage that had almost taken her life and had rendered her barren. When this was all over, he would call her more regularly. He was her husband and should do better, no matter how disappointed she might be with his career.

At the next table, an inmate cradled his son. Fa assumed it was a boy; he had trouble judging the sex of white babies, but Americans liked to color-code their children, and this one was swaddled in blue.

It was an interesting country. Some of his colleagues held a romantic fascination for its culture, but Fa kept it at an objective distance. China and the United States were rivals, not sweethearts, and it didn't pay to become enamored of these *laowai*. Despite their protestations to the contrary—their delusional American exceptionalism—there was nothing special about them. For sixty short years they'd mattered as a country. Perhaps in another five thousand they might have a case. Until then, they should remember that they were little more than children. Pompous children, at that.

The rear door of the visitation room opened, and Merrick came through. The devil himself. Fa had built this moment up in his mind for years, but all he could think was that Merrick was shorter than he'd expected. Yet every bit as grand as his portraits suggested. A guard pointed him to Fa's table, and Merrick's chin, tilted imperiously upward, turned in his direction. Fa saw Merrick hesitate, wondering at the identity of his visitor, then make his way over between the tables like royalty among lepers.

"Henry Susman, I presume." Merrick brushed off the seat of the chair before sitting opposite Fa. The Susman line seemed a private joke of some kind, so Fa smiled politely. Merrick smirked at his own cleverness.

Fa waited until Merrick was settled. It seemed an elaborate pantomime until everything was just so. Merrick looked up expectantly.

"Well?"

"Do you know the recidivism rate in this country, Mr. Merrick?"

If the question caught Merrick off guard, he didn't show it. "I've no idea."

"Sixty percent."

"That high?"

"Within the first year. Do you know why that is?"

"Why is that?" Merrick asked, leaning forward to read Fa's name tag. "Mr. Lee Wulff . . ."

"A felon such as yourself must declare his criminal record on job applications. And since it is not illegal to discriminate against convicted felons, few will hire them. What option does the criminal have but to resume a life of crime?"

"A tragic cycle," Merrick agreed.

"Certainly you will never be permitted to take the Series 7 exam, never be a stockbroker again."

For a moment, Fa saw regret in Merrick's face, but the man blinked hard, and when he opened his eyes again, the arrogance had returned. Still, it satisfied Fa to know that Merrick could be ruffled.

"I wonder to myself: What will become of Charles Merrick after he leaves this place?"

"What is it you want?"

"To help you through this difficult transition."

"To help me? And how would you do that?"

"Money, of course. A great deal of it."

"How much money?"

"Something in the seven figures, certainly."

"Hmm." Merrick studied his cuticles. "That's very generous of you."

An interesting reaction, to say the least. A starving man would dance for a dollar. For a million, a starving man would do almost anything. Even a man with a million dollars would sit up at the chance to double his money. But Merrick wasn't dancing, hadn't even asked what the money was for. The offer of a million dollars had barely registered, which meant two things, only one of which pleased Fa. First, it meant that Merrick wasn't a starving man at all. He had money. Enough that a million dollars hadn't tempted him, not even for a moment. That was problematic, because what did a man like Charles Merrick care about besides money? Second, it meant that if Merrick had money, then the American government had not seized all his assets as they had claimed. Why? And why had they lied about it? Fa thought he knew the answer to that but knew with certainty that he would learn nothing more from Merrick today.

He stood and thanked a stunned Merrick for his time.

"That's it?" Merrick asked. "What about this seven figures? Aren't you going to stay and tell me what that's about?"

"As if that would do any good."

"Well, you're the oddest visitor I've had, I'll hand you that."

"I'll see you again. Good luck upon your release."

Fa left Merrick at the table and went through the exit procedures. It was raining lightly when he left the prison, but he hardly noticed. The rain felt good, and he smiled at what he'd learned from Merrick's behavior. Without question, Merrick had traded something valuable to his government, and in exchange the Americans had permitted him to plead out to a lighter sentence and keep some of his assets.

It had to be Poisonfeather.

What else could that valuable "something" be? Fa could imagine how it had played out. Looking at twenty years in prison, Merrick had sold out his source in China's government to the CIA. And the CIA had made Merrick's mole their own. It would have been a simple matter for the CIA to flip Merrick's source, turning him into Poisonfeather. Selling strategic investment secrets to Merrick Capital would have earned the traitor a date with a firing squad. The very threat of such exposure would have ensured Poisonfeather's loyalty to the CIA ever since.

This was Fa's way back. If he learned the identity of Poisonfeather, not even Zhi could prevent Fa's return to grace.

Merrick would give him Poisonfeather's name. Not now, of course. First, Fa had to guide Merrick into a more agreeable frame of mind. Once Merrick was starving, he would dance. He would dance for Fa and sing him a pretty song in the bargain.

CHAPTER SEVENTEEN

Charles Merrick's impromptu sit-down with Agent Ogden hadn't rattled him until the visit from Lee Wulff. The man calling himself Wulff spoke with no discernible accent, but Merrick recognized him as a Chinese national. And that scared him. Suddenly Ogden's paranoia didn't seem quite so paranoid. Merrick had considered notifying Ogden directly but didn't trust the CIA agent not to overreact. If Ogden had any reason to believe that the Chinese were onto him, mightn't he make good on his threat to rendition Merrick? Why take the risk? No, better to handle this himself. Once he was free, he'd have more than enough money to protect himself.

All this fuss over one magazine interview. It boggled the mind. Still, Merrick allowed that perhaps the interview hadn't been the best idea. Although, it would have been fine if that witch from *Finance* hadn't goaded him. *There ought to be a law,* he thought sourly. But the situation was salvageable . . . if only he could make a phone call.

That was a problem, because it wasn't the sort of call that could be made from the prison pay phones. The prison didn't listen to every outgoing call, but you never could be sure. After his early-morning visitor, Merrick had passed word to Slaski and waited in the library until lunch, but the guard hadn't shown up, cagey about being seen together out in the open. Merrick knew why, but he still found it infuriating. They had a system and a schedule, and Merrick had never deviated from it. Until now.

Yes, it was a risk, but it was a necessary one, and Slaski could put on his big-boy pants and do as he was told. Yet here he was again, twiddling his thumbs for a second straight afternoon because Slaski was too cowardly to show his face. *Ridiculous.* Even after eight years in prison, Merrick chafed at being kept waiting. He snapped through the pages of *Starting a Business for Dummies* and did the only thing he could do—kept waiting.

Either by design or by accident, there was virtually no cellular reception at the prison. The guards complained about it all the time. Apparently, it was an issue in town too. Not a large enough customer base to warrant more cell towers to avoid dead spots. The prison was one such dead spot. However, it was generally agreed that the southwest corner of the prison library offered the best cell phone reception in the prison. A narrow blind behind a column offered a modicum of privacy. Inmates who had deals worked out with guards called it "the booth." But even the booth only offered two bars, and sometimes no service at all if the technology gods were in a fickle mood.

Merrick looked up as Slaski came in and spoke to the guard on duty. After a minute, the guard stood and left the library. When he was gone, Slaski huffed his way back to Merrick on his stout Polish legs.

Merrick stood and walked back into the stacks. Slaski went down the next aisle and stopped on the far side of the bookshelf. They talked through the self-help section in hushed tones.

"Where have you been?"

"This isn't our regular day."

"It's an emergency."

"I'm not scheduled to work library today. That's why we meet on Monday. People will want to know what I'm doing up here."

"Couldn't be helped."

"What do you want?"

"I need to make a call."

"No way," Slaski said. "That is not the deal. Text only."

"Give me the phone. I'll be quick."

"I don't have it on me. It's not our day," Slaski said stubbornly.

Merrick sized him up. "That's a shame. A bonus would have been in order."

"What kind of bonus?"

"Double."

"Triple," Slaski countered.

"Triple?" Merrick said. "I just need to make a simple call."

"If it's so simple, use the prison phones."

"Fine. Triple." Merrick held out his hand. "Just clear the library."

"You've got five minutes." Slaski slid the phone across to him.

Merrick palmed it and went on flipping through the book. When Slaski was out of sight, he slipped the SIM card out of the cheap flip phone and swapped it for one that he hid in the hem of his pants. A precaution in the event that Slaski decided to get nosy about Merrick's business or got caught by the warden providing a cell phone to inmates. He powered the phone up and dialed the number.

The phone rang once, less than once, as if a hand were hovering at the other end, waiting to pounce. Merrick cleared his throat to speak but didn't get the chance.

"Are you out of your mind, Charles?"

"Hello to you too."

"Have you read this?"

"It's a good photo, no?"

"You're not amusing."

"I think it captures me quite well."

"Interesting choice of words."

"I had a visit from Agent Ogden."

An arctic silence whistled from the other end.

"Are you there?"

"I can't say I'm surprised. You all but trumpeted the fact."

"I made a vague allusion."

"Is that what Ogden thought of it? A vague allusion?"

"Ogden is paid to be overly cautious," Merrick said. "But we'll need an escort to the airfield."

"Why do we need an escort? What's happening?"

"Nothing." Merrick saw no good in mentioning the visit from the Chinese national. "Ogden felt it was possible that interested parties might get the wrong idea from the article. I think it's wise to take precautions."

"Oh, you are such a fool. What were you—"

The line went dead. He pressed redial.

"Did you hang up on me?"

"No, West Virginia hung up on you," Merrick said.

"What kind of escort?"

Merrick described what he had in mind.

"That's going to cost a small fortune. It comes out of your half. I'm not underwriting your vanity."

Small fortune? Merrick smiled. To some, perhaps, but not to him. Not once he was on the outside. Still, it wasn't in his nature to give anything away for free.

"If I don't get safely to the airfield, neither of us gets a penny."

"'A penny'? Is that more of your wit, Charles? It wasn't I who gave that ridiculous interview."

No, he supposed it wasn't.

THE COLD ROCK

Hell is empty

And all the devils are here.

—William Shakespeare, *The Tempest*

CHAPTER EIGHTEEN

When Niobe Federal Prison limped into view, Gibson pointed for Swonger to pull over.

"So you just gonna go in and ask him for the money?" Swonger asked, letting the Scion idle. "That the plan?"

"Just want to look at the prison."

"That ain't no prison."

"I'll just be a minute."

"Dog, I need a toilet. Drop me at the hotel; you can sightsee all day, all night."

"In a minute," Gibson said again and got out of the car. He needed to stretch his legs and clear his head. Swonger drove with video-game abandon, and the trip to West Virginia had been a flickering strobe of tailgating and testosterone lane changes. After five hours of imminent death, Gibson felt exhausted. He'd never missed Dan Hendricks more.

"Where you going?" Swonger called after him.

"You're worse than my seven-year-old."

"I *need* a toilet. It's a DEFCON 2–type deal."

Gibson walked up the road until he couldn't hear Swonger anymore. His phone rang. Nicole. He stared at the phone, unsure whether to answer, until it went to voice mail. What she might say scared him. She called back immediately, but he still didn't answer. He put the phone away and looked down the road toward the prison.

There was a lot of beautiful country in West Virginia, but this wasn't any of it. Niobe Federal Prison sat at the end of a narrow dead-end road. One lane in, one lane out—sounded like a lost Johnny Cash record. The prison itself didn't look like much, a series of low-rise concrete slabs that fanned out behind a central hub at the main gate. Apart from the coiled barbed wire, the fences looked no more imposing than those found around a high-school sports field. More of a helpful reminder to stay put than an out-and-out deterrent. A failed escape attempt meant a one-way ticket to one of Swonger's real prisons, which was the only deterrent anyone should need.

It disappointed him that this was Charles Merrick's prison. The Charles Merrick that he had gotten to know was a grand, larger-than-life figure, and Niobe Federal Prison seemed wholly inadequate to contain him. Merrick deserved a more fitting jailer. Gibson took his own odd sentiment as a good sign. Hacking a target required understanding, and often a strange parasitic sympathy developed. Often, he wanted the best for his targets even as he prepared to unlock them.

Funny how that worked. And here it came, right on schedule. He had a feel for the man now—how the man thought, how the man would react under pressure. Gibson let his mind work back through the problem. This was, without doubt, a unique dilemma. He had exactly twenty-one days to separate Charles Merrick from his money. Tricky enough if he knew where it was, but he didn't. Pretty much impossible to rob a bank if you didn't know the whereabouts of said bank. So the first step was to find it. Correction, the first step was persuading Charles Merrick to show him where it was.

Shouldn't be too hard . . . the man had only concealed money from his investors since founding Merrick Capital in 1995. But Merrick had gotten sloppy. The interview was proof of that. Maybe it was being this close to the finish line, but after successfully lying low for all these years, the man had lost his self-control. The question was, could Merrick be goaded into another lapse in judgment? And if so, where would the money be? *Where would a man like that hide it?* Chewing that over, Gibson got back in the car, and Swonger swung the car around for the drive into Niobe.

The Wolstenholme Hotel had seen better days itself, but Lea had been in love with the place since arriving in town two years ago. Defiant in the face of decay, which only worsened if you ventured inside, the old girl had managed to keep her dignity, and that endeared her to Lea. A broad-shouldered brick building in the Queen Anne style, it had dominated downtown Niobe since the end of the nineteenth century, when coal money had flowed into the state. The hotel had been built by Clarence and Bessie Wolstenholme, wealthy eccentrics from Philadelphia with visions of establishing a cultural outpost in the wilds of West Virginia. Its long, slow slide into disrepair paralleled the town's own. It was also the only hotel for ten miles, so if anyone came into town, which they rarely did, they stayed at the Wolstenholme.

Rarely . . . except during the last few days. Unfamiliar faces had begun popping up around town, driving cars with out-of-state plates. Lea recognized the orange and black of New York plates on an SUV parked in the hotel lot. She assumed the worst: the cars belonged either to Merrick's victims looking for a little redress or else to opportunistic, mercenary raiders. Being a criminal himself, Merrick couldn't very well go to the authorities for protection. That made him the perfect mark, and unless Lea missed her guess, the jackals had already begun to circle. She wondered how many were in town already. How many more were on their way? Jimmy Temple at the Wolstenholme Hotel would know better than anyone.

At the top of the stairs, she had to put her shoulder into the heavy wood doors to push them open. The groan of the hinges echoed through the cavernous lobby. Jimmy Temple wasn't behind the front desk, but a friendly sign promised he'd be back soon. In addition to being owner and manager, Jimmy Temple was also the hotel handyman and spent his days making repairs to his hotel. His dreams of restoring the hotel to its former glory reduced to polishing brass on his own personal *Titanic*.

Lea rang the bell and called his name but got no response. As she leaned against the reception counter to wait, "Have Yourself a Merry Little Christmas" played over the lobby stereo, making her smile.

Jimmy had inherited the hotel in 1981, after his father passed. By that time, no one passed through Niobe anymore; after the bridge collapse, Niobe had become out-of-the-way overnight. With the hotel failing, Jimmy and his wife, Donna, had nearly sold out to an investment group in 1998. Jimmy and Donna had planned to move to the Florida Keys and watch the sunsets for as long as their eyes held out. But that winter, Donna came down with pneumonia. Christmas was her favorite holiday, and she held on until the twenty-sixth. Jimmy, who had no use for sunsets without his wife, put the kibosh on the whole deal. He sold their house, moved into the hotel, and ran it more or less on his own. Ever since then, Christmas music had played 365 days a year in the lobby of the Wolstenholme.

Jimmy Temple emerged from the back office, cleaning his hands on an old chamois. He always wore a suit, even when doubling as handyman. He was narrow of shoulder and white of hair, age taking its toll on both. His ruddy face brightened when he saw Lea. He never set foot in the Toproll—Jimmy Temple did his drinking in private—but he'd always had a soft spot for her. She liked him too.

Lea held up a gold watch by the leather strap. One of the last remaining artifacts from her old life. "Found this at the bar last night after we closed."

Jimmy whistled. "That real gold? Looks expensive."

You have no idea, Lea thought. "Doesn't belong to any of our regulars. Anyone check in recently?"

"Oh, yes, several, actually."

"Several?"

He smiled. "Must be my winning personality. They've been trickling in the last couple of days. And I've had calls for reservations for the next few weeks."

"They know this is Niobe, right?" she joked.

He laughed. "I didn't mention it."

"Seriously, that's great news. How many you got here now?"

"Well, let's see, four men checked in yesterday."

"Together?"

"Uh-huh, they did. Young fellows. Businessmen, I think. They were wearing jackets is why I say that. They weren't too chatty, so that's just me speculating."

"Anyone else?"

"Yep, two more this morning, and an Asian gentleman has been here for a couple of days, nice fellow. Fisherman. From Ohio, I think. Couldn't quite place his accent." Jimmy pointed at the watch. "But I doubt that's his. He was up at the crack of dawn. Headed over to the Elk River today, fishing trout. Doubt he's spending time at the Toproll."

"Well, ask around. It'll be behind the bar if they can tell me the inscription."

Although if anyone could tell her the inscription, that would frighten her to death.

———————

Gibson and Swonger drove into Niobe along Tarte Street, which ran parallel to the Ohio River. Niobe was one of those towns whose reason for existing had long since passed into history, and its century-long contraction had left a swath of shuttered, abandoned buildings to mark high tide. According to their map, this was the center of Niobe's historic district, but to Gibson most of the town looked like history at this point. Tarte Street was a stretch of brick buildings, some open, most closed permanently—windows bricked over like bandaged eyes. One bank, one hardware store, one drugstore. Three antique shops all in a row, possessed of a liberal definition of "antique" judging by the junk piled up in the windows. Four churches. A police station with one lonely cruiser parked in front. A dollar store and a Food Lion. A defiant liquor store called Niobe Spirits. Away to the right, the remnants of a bridge that once spanned the Ohio River rose into view, a grand old relic, beautiful in the way that American ruins could be.

A group of teenagers stood outside a service station that had been converted into a sandwich shop, not doing much of anything but waiting for someone to suggest somewhere else to stand. The lonely migration of small-town kids with nowhere to go and nothing to do when they got there. Swonger maneuvered around a beat-up mail truck double-parked outside what might be America's last surviving video store. The mail truck caused something to click in Gibson's head. The question wasn't *where* Merrick had invested his money; it was *how*. If Merrick was managing investments from prison, he would need a computer. Gibson didn't know if inmates had Internet access, but even if they did, Merrick couldn't risk the prison network, which would certainly be monitored. So either he had a computer . . . no, that was stupid. Where was he going to hide a laptop in a prison? Even a tablet would be next to impossible. Gibson thought back to his time in jail, awaiting trial—how many times did the guards conduct random searches? There were only so many places to hide things in a cell, and the guards knew all of them.

What about a cell phone? *No pun intended.* Maybe. It was smaller but still a huge risk to take, and Merrick had a lot on the line. In his mind, Gibson drew a question mark next to it, but until he had a very good reason to believe otherwise, he was discounting the possibility that

Charles Merrick had hidden a cell phone and charger for eight years without getting caught.

That meant Merrick had help. If Merrick couldn't manage his accounts from the prison, then someone on the outside was executing transactions on his behalf. So how was Merrick communicating with them?

When you thought about it, it was bin Laden but in reverse.

In fact, Charles Merrick and Osama bin Laden had a lot in common. Both were prisoners. The only difference was bin Laden had built his own prison. Like Merrick, bin Laden couldn't travel and couldn't risk using modern communications technologies. Instead, bin Laden had relied on a sophisticated, low-tech courier network to communicate with the outside world. The United States knew what was being communicated and with whom; it just didn't know how. It had taken years, but they had tracked bin Laden to Pakistan through those couriers.

In this instance, Gibson knew the location of his subject. Merrick was fixed and unmoving behind bars. That was the known. The unknowns were what was being communicated, with whom, and how. So who were Merrick's couriers? How was he getting information in and out? As with bin Laden, it was probably a low-tech human network. If Gibson could find it and break into it, he could trace it back to the money. He smiled to himself. In this case, the money was the "bin Laden." To find it, all he had to do was locate Merrick's confederate on the outside.

Swonger pulled into the parking lot behind the Wolstenholme Hotel and threw the car into park.

"What are you grinning about?" Swonger asked. "Oh, you having one of them epiphanies. Whatcha got for me?"

Gibson waved him off. "I got nothing for you," he said. "You're here strictly in an observational capacity. Understand?"

Swonger rolled his eyes and made a lemon-sucking face. "This where we staying?"

"It's where I'm staying. Did you make a reservation?"

"You an asshole, know what?"

The hotel rose five stories, but the dilapidated black fire escape that ran up the back of the building went only as high as the third floor. Gibson could see damage to the hotel's exterior wall where the top two levels of the fire escape had wrenched loose of their moorings and collapsed. How did a hotel pass inspection with half a fire escape? Well . . . safety first.

Gibson carried his bag around to the front of the hotel and looked up and down Tarte Street. He didn't trust a town without a diner. Across the street stood, or rather leaned, a windowless clapboard bar. Above its green door, a hand-painted sign read, "The Toproll." Out front in the parking lot, a woman with a weight lifter's build was having a serious heart-to-heart with a deliveryman. The deliveryman wanted no piece of her.

Inside, the hotel's lobby had the run-down feel of a neglected museum, but it must have been grand in its day. Gibson didn't know a thing about architecture, but even he could see that much. A vaulted ceiling soared twenty feet overhead, where a massive ceiling fan, like the propeller of a ship, chopped through the air. Crystal sconces glittered along dingy marble walls, although several were either cracked or missing entirely. Off to the right lay an oval sitting room, dark wood paneling the walls, with a fireplace, overstuffed chairs, and several chessboards. Through an archway to the left, he could see a shuttered dining room with chairs flipped upside down atop the tables. Somehow Gibson doubted his room included a complimentary breakfast.

Behind the counter stood an older man in a three-piece suit. He smiled in delight at the sight of them. Not even Swonger plopping the trash bag that served as his suitcase onto the counter could dampen his enthusiasm. He greeted them warmly and introduced himself as Mr. Temple, owner and proprietor.

"But call me Jimmy."

Gibson liked him immediately and shook his hand over the counter. The same could not be said of the young woman who had been talking to Jimmy Temple. As he'd walked in, Gibson had the impression that the two were wrapping up their conversation, but now she lingered at the counter, watching him with hard, unwelcoming eyes. He didn't much care for it and turned to face her. She didn't seem to care for it either and held his gaze. She didn't strike him as the kind of person who ever looked away first.

"Can I help you?" she asked.

"Was going to ask you the same thing."

Jimmy jumped in to intercede. "Ah, no, that would be my department. Lea, thanks for stopping by. I'll talk to you soon."

She didn't take the hint and instead leaned against the counter defiantly like she was planting a flag. One hell of a welcome committee. *And why is there Christmas music playing?*

Gibson told Jimmy that his reservation had been on the fifth floor and asked if he could be moved down to three.

"As it turns out, the fifth floor is entirely booked," said Jimmy. "We'll be happy to find you a room on three."

"All booked?" the hard-eyed woman asked. "Since when?"

"Just this morning. The four gentlemen. Isn't it fantastic?"

"They needed a whole floor to themselves?"

"Well, they needed peace and quiet, so they took every room on the floor. I think they're on some kind of retreat. They said some colleagues may be joining them. Whatever business they're in, I want in," Jimmy said with a conspiratorial wink.

"How long are they staying?" she asked.

"They left it open-ended but at least a week."

"Wow. That's great, Jimmy," she said, not sounding like she thought it was great in any way, shape, or form. She held up a gold watch as she turned to leave. "Let me know if anyone lost this."

Jimmy said he would and turned his attention back to his customers. "We have a nice room on two or three with a view of the river."

"Anything out back?" Gibson asked.

"You want to look at our parking lot?"

"If you have it," he said. "I like a sunrise."

Jimmy gave a the-customer-is-always-right smile and checked the leather-bound registry. No computer. Jimmy Temple was old school. Gibson didn't give a damn about a sunrise. But providing the remaining fire escape was still structurally sound, he liked the idea of having another way out. Just in case. Gibson checked in under the name Robert Quine and handed Jimmy an ID and credit card to match. After Atlanta, and with Jenn Charles still missing, it had seemed prudent to put together a scramble kit in case he needed to disappear in a hurry. They were quality fakes, and Gibson hated to burn them, but he wanted to leave as small a footprint in Niobe, West Virginia, as possible.

Jimmy Temple handed Gibson a key—an actual key, not an electronic key card. Old, old, old school.

"Does the hotel have Wi-Fi?" Gibson asked.

"Only in the lobby, I'm afraid. I've been meaning to wire the rest of the hotel, but you know how things are." Jimmy smiled brightly. "Enjoy your stay, Mr. Quine."

Lea left the hotel, her false smile melting in the sunshine. She was in trouble and knew it. At least seven new arrivals in the last few days, plus those two clowns checking in now. She couldn't be sure how many were here for Merrick, but those fifth-floor suits weren't here for a retreat. One thing was for certain: she might have started ahead of the pack, but they'd run her down now, and she was in danger of being left behind. Unless she adapted, scrapped her plans, and took a realistic look at the situation as it evolved. Beyond that, she needed to decide what she really needed out of this. What she could live with.

After two years in Niobe, planning and biding her time, she ought to know the answer.

So what does *she want?*

Across the street, Margo stood in the Toproll parking lot signing for a delivery. A full keg of beer weighed a hundred and fifty pounds, but her boss hefted one easily and walked it into the bar. Lea trotted across Tarte Street, picked up a case of longnecks, and followed her inside.

Margo looked back at her. "What did I tell you about hanging out at the bar in your free time?"

"I came to talk to you."

"Oh? Well, make it quick. Your boyfriend is stopping by in a few," Margo said. "Trying to get himself unbanned."

"Tommy Hillwicky? Are you serious?"

"He'll be sober so he'll probably say the right things, and then later when he's drunk again he'll say the wrong ones again."

"So why?"

"He drinks a piece more beer than you, flyweight."

Lea shrugged. "You own the place."

"Yeah, like the Indians owned Manhattan." Margo set down the keg and shook her arms out. "So what do you want to talk about? 'Cause you're not getting a raise."

"Remember what you said about fighting battles?"

"Vaguely."

"I might need your help with that after all."

Margo regarded her with curiosity. "What kind of help?"

"What do you owe on the bar?"

Margo's eyes narrowed. "Enough."

"What if there was a way to square yourself with the bank? Would that be something that interested you?"

"I'm listening."

CHAPTER NINETEEN

It was turning into an ugly night at the Toproll. A festering, hostile energy swirled through the smoky rafters. Lea had seen two fights already, and it wasn't quite nine yet. Reggie Weir and Cece James, the town lovebirds, had thrown down over nothing at all; Reggie had stormed out, leaving Cece in tears. Not much of a drinker, Cece was in the corner, aggressively nursing her third Long Island iced tea.

Everyone was drinking hard tonight, and that was saying something. Lea scrambled to keep up. She pushed four pints across the bar, took the twenty, and made change while scanning the bar for the next customer. The customer pocketed the bills and dropped the coins heavily, scattering them across the bar. Punishment for Tommy Hillwicky. The regulars had thought it over and found Tommy hard done by. They'd taken turns buying him drinks to welcome him back from his one-week suspension as if he were a returning war hero. Tommy hadn't seen this much love when he'd gotten out of prison and was three sheets in search of a stiff breeze. He stood at the end of the bar, talking loudly about missing high-school football and the license it gave to hurt people.

"People knew better than to come across the middle, boy," he said, eyes drifting to Lea. He clapped his hands together to suggest the violence of his collisions and called for another round of shots.

Lea had spent enough time in joints like this to know that bars had personalities, especially ones that depended on their regulars. Moods could take hold and spread from barstool to barstool like a bump in the back with no apology. No one was immune. The regulars were still a little on edge about Tommy, but the mood would have passed by on any other night. Tommy was a symptom rather than the cause.

The cause sat in the back room at Al Reynolds's regular table. Al Reynolds had hosted a poker game at the same table for eight years. It wasn't official, but everyone in town knew that come nine p.m., the table belonged to Al Reynolds. The same couldn't be said for the four strangers from the fifth floor of the Wolstenholme. They'd come in around seven thirty for dinner and sat at Al's table. The four ordered politely and weren't bothering anyone, except they bothered everyone. Maybe it was their healthy, square-cut features. Maybe it was that none drank anything stronger than Diet Coke. Maybe it was that now, well past nine p.m., they still hadn't reached for the check.

Lea could feel the room pressurizing, and normally, she would worry for four strangers in a bar full of hostile regulars, but something about the four men's bearing made her think that it was the regulars who would regret starting anything. The regulars felt it too and milled about, unsure what to do about the situation. The accustomed ebb and flow of the Toproll had been disrupted. The established hierarchy, so critical to the peaceful coexistence of a bar full of alcoholics, was under threat. Nothing was in its assigned place.

Earlier, Old Charlie had stuck his head in the door just far enough to see his stool was occupied, turned tail, and fled into the night. Might be the only wise thing that she'd ever seen him do. The men in Old Charlie's space were actually wearing suits. The first two suits she'd ever seen in the Toproll. One of them had ordered, and was actually drinking, a glass of white wine. His companion kept playing songs on the jukebox that Lea had never heard in here before, which was amazing because Margo hadn't put in a new CD the entire time Lea had worked there. He'd played about twenty dollars of music so far, and no one else's stuff was getting played. A small thing, but in the delicate, alcohol-fueled hothouse of a bar, way over the line.

The two waitresses stood at the service bar and traded war stories while Lea made drinks for their tables. One had served a group of three men who'd ordered in faint Russian accents, then waited in eerie silence. The waitress was spooked. "They don't say nothing. They just stare at each other like telepathy, you know? Weird."

Down the bar, Margo was watching her crowded bar with a smile borrowed from Jimmy Temple. The place was busier than it had been in a year, and they were on the way to their best night in a long time. Anger had a way of making people thirsty.

"Did I miss where we became a tourist trap?" Lea asked when they bumped into each other at the cash register.

"Hey, their money spends."

"'Nother beer, darling," Tommy Hillwicky drawled over the din, enjoying having Lea fetch him things.

Margo winked at her. "Make nice. Money is money."

Lea brought Hillwicky his beer as the door opened and more new faces entered. It was the two men who'd arrived at the hotel this morning. They were an odd pair, and given a hundred guesses, she'd never have put them together. The little one—with the trash bag for a suitcase—looked like he'd been drinking in the Toproll since birth. He studied the crowd as if he were sizing up tonight's first fight. Tattoos sprawled from his collar and sleeves, and she'd give odds that everything he wore came from Walmart. His partner, on the other hand, didn't belong, but she couldn't say why. He just didn't fit in, and she would have been hard-pressed to say where he would. He was a decent-looking guy with a neatly trimmed beard, melancholy eyes, and the blueprint of a cocky, just-read-your-diary smile. He met her gaze and held it. A flicker of something passed across his face that made her stomach flutter unpleasantly. *Knock that shit off,* she warned herself. Next thing she knew, she'd be clutching her pearls and fanning herself. She put her head down and got back to work. When she glanced up, the two had disappeared into the back room, looking for a table.

Over the next couple of hours, the bar picked up yet another notch. Lea and Margo poured beers steadily, and neither had time to worry about Tommy Hillwicky or any of the unfamiliar faces in the bar.

"What'll you have?" Lea asked, moving blindly to the next customer.

"Whatever. Beer."

Lea looked up, recognizing the voice. Parker stood there in his uniform. She poured him a fast beer, and he hooked his head toward the back. It wasn't their scheduled day, and Parker wasn't in the habit of going the extra mile, so whatever had dragged him away from his movies must be important.

Lea waited ten minutes before telling Margo she was taking her break. She dropped a fresh bowl of bar mix in front of Parker and slid into the booth opposite him. The poker game was finally under way, and tension had eased a little. Across the room, the mismatched men were locked in animated conversation. Lea would have loved to know about what. Instead, she turned her attention to Parker.

"Your cable out?"

"Slaski."

Lea felt her breath catch. "You're sure?"

Parker nodded. "I'm here, aren't I?"

He told her about Slaski clearing the library for Merrick so Merrick could use Slaski's phone. The only reason an inmate would need the library, he explained, was that it offered the best cell signal in the prison. Lea felt jubilation but hid it with a subdued fist pump under the table. Her mind raced ahead. How to get her hands on that phone, see who he'd been calling. Might be enough to give her back the edge. She would need to move quickly, but she felt optimistic for the first time since reading the interview.

"What?" Parker asked.

"Nothing. Surprised he was so careless."

"Had something to do with the visit he had yesterday."

"Not his lawyer again? Henry Susman?"

Parker shook his head. "Some fella named Lee Wulff. Didn't see him, but he rattled your boy good."

"Okay," she said. "Tell me everything you know about Slaski."

CHAPTER TWENTY

A pall of animosity more toxic than the haze of cigarette smoke hung over the bar. It took more than an hour to get food. The bar was busy but not so busy that it should take fifteen minutes before someone even dropped menus at the table. In the same time, Gibson watched the middle-aged waitress make three trips to the poker table and the group of Niobe Prison guards shooting pool. When she finally dropped off their menus, Gibson ordered a pitcher of beer in case she took her time coming back to take their order—Swonger was thirsty work.

"This is discrimination," Swonger groused.

"Don't start." But Swonger had a point; it was not the friendliest bar.

Gibson looked over each of the prison guards, all still in uniform. Scrutinized how they carried themselves and interacted with each other. He would need a set of eyes inside the prison, and guards' salaries should make them susceptible to a well-aimed bribe. Still, none of them felt right to him. Fortunately, the place was thick with off-duty prison guards, and there were a few more options in the front room. He'd take a closer look after he ate. Where was that waitress?

When the food finally came, they ate in hungry silence. Swonger drowned his burger in ketchup and mayo and ate it with an ex-con's wariness, head down and fast, like someone bigger and stronger might try to take it from him. Ignoring the French fries until he'd devoured the protein. When his plate was clean, Swonger pushed it away and fished around in a pocket for paper and a pencil. It was a list, and beside each item was a number. Swonger went over his columns, lips moving as he added the sums, making adjustments and additions as he went. An unfamiliar smile crept over his face as he worked.

"What are you working on?"

"Nothing," Swonger said, then, "You know. Just what I'm going to do with my share. Of the money."

Gibson was all too familiar with the fantasies of money to come. When the Spectrum job had seemed assured, he'd daydreamed about everything he would buy. All the ways that life would be better for his daughter. So he understood the impulse, dangerous as it might be, but that didn't mean that he wanted to listen to Swonger's plans to trick out his Scion. Instead, Swonger surprised him.

"Already got the plot picked out."

"Plot?"

"Only a hundred fifty acres, but good land. Me and Pops. Set things up right. Cattle. Sheep. Soybeans and corn. Sell to those locally sourced hipster restaurants. It'll be pretty sweet."

"A farm?" Gibson said. "Really?"

"Dog, that's all I ever wanted. Been working with Pops since I don't know when. Never had much use for school, but I can farm. Believe that. After Merrick, I'm gonna get my mom and pops away from the Birks. Do things right."

Gibson studied him and tried to reconcile this with what he already knew about Swonger. Peer through the swirl of anger and see the pain that anger protected.

Swonger felt it. "You scheming on kissing me?"

Gibson shook his head to show that he didn't mean any offense. He wanted to warn Swonger somehow but didn't know what words could penetrate the ex-con's hopefulness. Swonger had so much riding on Merrick, on his desire to avenge and simultaneously save his family. Gibson knew all about that fantasy as well. He realized something else that he should have seen sooner.

"How long?"

"How long what?"

"Until the Birks lose the farm."

"Oh, that 'how long.' Couple months. Pops hasn't even started looking for somewhere to live. Just keeps killing himself for the Birks. Like mending fences will make a difference. Man works so damn hard. Always has. But he doesn't want to know nothing about the world. Just wants to farm. I remember when the judge talked Pops into investing. Pops had never invested in anything more than a savings account. What's he know about hedge funds? Nothing. But here comes Judge Birk talking about me. About my future. How this was Pops's chance to jump our family ahead. Pops trusted the judge. Even after Merrick got busted. Hell, he still does. I don't. So here I am."

"Listen, Swonger. Go easy, okay?"

"I'm easy, dog."

"No, I just mean don't get ahead of things. Maybe there's money. Maybe there isn't. But even if there is, it's not going to be as much as you think."

"How you figure that?"

"Like I told you, the Justice Department is really, really good at finding money. So whatever money Merrick managed to hide away, it was small enough to fall through the cracks. So go easy."

Swonger considered this and shrugged. "Still more than I got now, dog. Know what I'm saying?"

Gibson knew that math all too well.

After dinner, Gibson tried and failed to catch the waitress's eye, his hand poised optimistically above his head to signal for the check. A new guard came into the back room and squeezed himself into an empty booth. It was ungainly ballet, and Gibson's hand dropped gently to the table as he watched the guard struggle vainly with the belt that pinned his paunch half in and half out of his pants. Failing to broker a truce, the guard glanced around surreptitiously before loosening his buckle several notches. That seemed to do it. Freed from the belt's constraints, the guard nursed his beer and picked at a bowl of bar mix. Every few minutes, he looked over his shoulder as if expecting someone.

A smile crept over Gibson's face. God, it was beautiful: middle aged, no wedding ring, a stain on his uniform that was at least a few days old. Impatient, lazy eyes. When he'd come in, none of the guards at the pool table had waved him over, and he hadn't so much as glanced in their direction. Yeah, he'd do, all right. Gibson just needed an approach. While he mulled that over, the young female bartender who had twice now given him the stink eye—once in the hotel when he'd first arrived and again when he'd come into the bar—entered the back room, made a haphazard lap around the other tables, and sat down with his guard.

Well, isn't that interesting?

Gibson couldn't make out what they were discussing, but it wasn't the casual chat between friends they wanted it to appear. Whatever their arrangement, she was in charge, even if the guard didn't want to acknowledge it. Her graceful, intelligent hands conducted the conversation at her tempo. She thought with her mouth, chewing pensively on a corner of her lip; he imagined that she would smile beautifully—nimble and expressive, although something in her eyes told Gibson that smiles were few and far between. He thought he'd enjoy listening to her talk even if the same couldn't be said for the guard. She had seen what Gibson had seen—the guard was weak, and she had exploited that weakness. But to what end?

He had the strangest feeling that he knew her from somewhere. Not just from the hotel this morning. From further back. But why would he know a West Virginia bartender? Maybe she'd been a Marine? He willed her to sweep her long brunette hair away from the side of her face so he could get a better look. Where did he know her from? Her features were hard to place too, and he could only guess at her ethnicity. Some Caucasian to be sure, but something else as well. East Asian perhaps?

A crazy thought occurred to him.

He took out his laptop and opened his research on Charles Merrick. He scrolled until he found a picture of Merrick with his family: ex-wife, Veronica, and daughter, Chelsea. It was an older picture, posed for an issue of *Hamptons* magazine—Chelsea Merrick's sixteenth birthday looked like it had been quite an extravaganza, and the family smiled brilliantly. Just two years before the roof fell in on her father's house of cards. His research into her whereabouts hadn't gotten past Portland, where she'd more or less disappeared off the grid.

Couldn't get much more off the grid than Niobe, West Virginia.

Chelsea Merrick would be what? Twenty-six now? Gibson glanced back and forth from the picture to the bartender across the room, trying to imagine the sixteen-year-old as a grown woman. In the picture, Chelsea Merrick was blonde like her father, hair piled in a chic swirl atop her head. Gibson didn't know enough about women's fashion to say for certain, but her flowing summer dress must've cost a small fortune and was a world away from the black sleeveless Joan Jett T-shirt and blue jeans that the bartender wore. Gibson shook it off—there was a passing similarity, but that was it. He'd started to close his laptop when the bartender leaned out of her seat to gaze through the doorway, checking on the bar up front. She gathered her hair up in one motion and tied it up in a ponytail. And like that, he saw her. Same jawline, same ears, and a small mole on her temple above her right eye.

Chelsea Merrick, in the flesh.

Bartending in a dive bar in Niobe, West Virginia.

He let that sink in. Bartender was a good cover, but what was she really doing here? Obviously, it had to do with her father. Was *she* Merrick's liaison with the outside world? Who else could it be? Whom else would Merrick trust with his money? And they were using this guard as their courier? It made sense.

"What?" Swonger asked.

"What?"

"You're smiling again. It's weird."

"I need you to do something in a minute."

"Oh, yeah? No can do, dog."

The two men stared across the table at each other.

"What?"

"Nah, man, see, I'm here in a strictly observating capacity. Think that's what you said." Swonger shrugged helplessly. "So, wish I could help you out, but . . ."

Gibson sighed. "Fine."

"Fine what?"

"I need your help."

"And you'll tell me what's going on and quit condescending at me?"

"That's a lot to ask."

"Then do it yourself."

"Okay, okay, it's a deal."

Swonger's attitude changed instantaneously as he sat forward. "So what you need?"

"Table across the way. At your four o'clock."

Swonger dropped his head and looked low over his shoulder. "One with the angry hot bartender at it?"

"Right. You see the guard?"

"The big boy? Uh, yeah. He ain't exactly stealth. What's the play?"

"You're so good at following me. Follow him instead. I need a name and an address. Where he lives."

To Gibson's surprise, Swonger didn't ask why but stood and drained the last of his beer. "Then what?"

"Then what, what?"

"After I got an address. What you want me to do then?"

Gibson wasn't sure. He hadn't expected Swonger to actually follow his lead, so he hadn't worked out the next part yet.

"Text me and sit on him until you hear from me."

"On it."

Swonger ambled out. A few minutes later, Chelsea Merrick left the guard's table and went back to work. The guard rebuckled his belt before heading for the door himself. Gibson hadn't seen him pass the bartender anything, so the message must have been simple enough to remember.

He'd have dearly loved to know what it was.

After Gibson finally pried the check from the waitress and settled the bill, he went to have a closer look at Chelsea Merrick. There was an empty seat at the bar where he could watch the Dodgers and Giants getting underway on the West Coast. An old man on the next stool contemplated a shot and a beer; he glanced in Gibson's direction as if his being there were a sin.

"Someone sitting here?"

"Aren't you sure?"

"No, I mean . . ." Gibson realized he was being messed with and sat down. The man introduced himself as Old Charlie, which Gibson thought an odd way to describe yourself.

"Robert Quine." They shook hands.

"So, Bob . . . you with these other out-of-town sons of bitches? Sitting in folks' seats, acting like you own the place?"

"Not with them. But I am an out-of-towner."

"Y'all here to cause trouble?"

"Not for you."

Old Charlie thought that over and pointed to his two drinks. "Which would you drink first?"

"The shot."

"Yeah, me too. But lately, I'm wondering to myself why. The order. Hard stuff first, easy stuff last. What kind of way is that for a man to do things? What if you never make it to the easy stuff? But you say shot first?"

"Shot first."

"From the mouths of babes," Old Charlie said and threw the shot back.

Last call in West Virginia was three a.m., but the bar crowd began to taper off around one. Gibson nursed a beer and watched the bartender work. Up close, there was no doubt: she was Chelsea Merrick. Although here customers called her Lea. For the price of a shot and a beer, Old Charlie confided that her last name was Regan and that she'd lived above the bar the last two years.

Gibson nodded, thinking that Charles Merrick was a bastard to pull his daughter into his world this way. She was risking jail to help him hide and manage his stolen money, but family was hard to outrun sometimes. Gibson understood that. Or maybe that apple had fallen and rolled right up against the tree. He checked himself—he shouldn't go and get sentimental about her just because she was tough and smart and took no shit from any of the men at the bar, all of whom stared openly at her ass whenever she walked by.

By one thirty, the empty seats at the bar outnumbered the occupied ones. The back room had cleared out except for one of the pool tables. *SportsCenter* played on all the televisions, and the muscular bartender—Margo—had disappeared into the office to do paperwork. Gibson guessed that Margo owned the place, the way everyone treated her. He didn't think he'd given away that he knew Lea's real name, but she definitely didn't like him sitting there. She kept her distance and served him quickly. Of course, just being in a regulars-only bar like this was enough to raise suspicion. Each time he finished a beer, she asked the same unfriendly question.

"Anything *else*?"

"I'll take another. Thanks."

Now his friendly tone met with a blank stare. "Don't you think you've had enough?"

To his left, Old Charlie snored peacefully, face on the bar, beside an untouched shot and beer. Gibson gave him a long look before turning back to Lea.

"Yeah, be a shame if anyone got overserved."

She slapped his bill down and left him to it. He chuckled to himself. There was no doubt about it—he liked her.

Swonger sat down beside him and ordered a beer. Lea served him, but grudgingly.

"I told you to text me," Gibson whispered.

"Been trying. It's like 1999 up here. Can't get a signal nowhere." Swonger gulped his beer before leaning into Gibson's ear. "Anyway, I got him. Jerome Parker. Lives up at a shitty little development twenty minutes east."

"Is he alone?"

"Only car his. But I didn't knock and take his particulars."

"Show me."

"My beer . . ."

"Finish it and let's go."

Swonger looked pained. "Dog, I been up in my car for three hours watching some mook's house while you been chillin' here eyeballing the talent? And I got to pay for my own beer? That ain't right."

Man had a point. Gibson threw an extra five on top of his bill, and they headed for the door.

CHAPTER TWENTY-ONE

Jerome Parker's place did indeed belong to a shitty little development. An aspiring real-estate tycoon had cleared a few acres of land and thrown up rows of narrow vertical town houses that alternated in color starkly between a neon custard and mud. It was a new enough development that the trees along Parker's street were only saplings, half of them brown and dying. Roughly one-third of the properties were unoccupied, and the wild, tangled lawns gave the neighborhood a desolate, uninhabited feel. Swonger pointed out a custard-colored townhome at the end of the block.

"Coupla vacant units back that way," Swonger said. "If you maybe looking to upgrade."

Gibson acknowledged the insult with his eyes and checked his phone. One bar. He tried making an outgoing call, but it wouldn't go through. Satisfied, he created a new contact on his phone, leaving it blank.

"Is there an outgoing message on your voice mail?" he asked.

"Just the phone-company one."

"Good. Put it on silent." He added Swonger's number to the new contact and saved it as "Lea Regan."

Gibson wondered how Swonger would react if he knew Merrick's daughter was tending bar in town. Could he be counted on to play things cool? Gibson didn't think he would take that bet, but beneath all the flagrant stupidity, Swonger was plenty smart. Gibson would be able to keep the truth from Swonger for only so long. Once Swonger figured things out for himself, their fragile truce would be shot.

"Let's go have a chat with our friend."

"Cool. What you want me to do?"

"Follow my lead. Back me up. Don't talk."

"Why you gotta be such an asshole?"

The gray-blue flicker of a television seeped out under the blinds of Jerome Parker's downstairs windows. Gibson rapped on the door hard, waited, knocked again, and when he heard the television go silent, took a step back. The door opened on a chain, and Jerome Parker regarded them through the crack.

"The hell you doing banging on my door?"

"Lea sent us."

"I don't know you."

"No reason you would. I'm Quine. That's Swonger."

"And I'm Danny Glover. How come I never heard of you?"

"What makes you think she tells you more than you need to know?"

That slowed Parker down. "So what's she want?"

"She said you came in tonight, yeah? Had a chat? Well, she got to chewing it over. Wanted us to follow up." Gibson decided to take a chance. A lot of men didn't like working for women, and misogynists always loved company. "You know how she gets. Pain in the ass."

Parker chuckled but didn't unchain the door.

Gibson pushed it a little further. "My opinion? She's only going to get worse, closer he gets to getting out. Know what I mean?"

Parker didn't confirm or deny but continued studying him through the crack in the door.

"Fine. Ask her yourself," Gibson said, reaching for his back pocket. The unmistakable sound of a hammer drawing back on a gun slowed him to a pantomime pace.

"Hey, now," Parker said. "Slow."

Gibson held up one hand and carefully withdrew his phone with the other. When Parker didn't shoot him, he dialed the fake entry he'd made for Lea's number and held it out so Parker could see the name. The guard made no move to take it, and in the West Virginia night both men listened to it ring. It rang three times before the signal cut out. Gibson cursed and redialed the number.

"You aren't going to get her out here," Parker said.

Gibson made a show of letting it ring until it died again. "Can you try her?"

Parker shook his head. "Won't make any difference. There's no service out here. That's why she sent you instead of calling." Parker was filling in gaps in the narrative on his own. A good sign that a lie was gaining traction. "I don't know what else I can tell you that I didn't tell her."

Gibson nodded in agreement but didn't reply. Parker grunted and slid the chain off the door. He led them into a den, offered Gibson a seat, and settled into a red leather lounger. Swonger stood away by the door. The room was lit only by a massive Sony flat-screen television, but Parker didn't move to turn on a light. On screen, a disdainful Humphrey Bogart cradled a black statue. An expansive DVD and Blu-ray collection spanned multiple bookcases.

"So what does she want now?"

Gibson shrugged. "Just felt like there was something she was missing. Wanted me to ask if maybe there was something you'd forgotten."

"Didn't forget nothing."

"Did he say anything else?"

"Who?"

"Merrick."

"He didn't say anything at all. He was just acting odd after he met with that lawyer. If he was a lawyer. Then when that other visitor showed up yesterday, he got plain spooked."

That was interesting, but Gibson nodded as if he already knew this part of the story. He wanted to know more about the lawyer who wasn't a lawyer, but the trick here was not to ask questions that he should already have answers to.

"Spooked how, exactly?"

"You mean besides making that damn phone call?"

"Who'd he call?"

"How should I know? Look, goddamn it, I gave her Slaski. I did my part."

Gave her Slaski? Gibson paused. Something was off here. Had he misread the situation and nearly blown it?

"I know. That's good. Just tell me everything you know about Slaski."

The disgruntled Parker didn't know much about his fellow guard, only that Slaski had cleared the prison library so Merrick could make a call using Slaski's phone.

Gibson realized he'd made a major miscalculation. Chelsea Merrick, or Lea Regan, wasn't her father's partner on the outside. It was whomever was at the other end of Merrick's phone call, and Chelsea Merrick wanted to know who that person was, the same as Gibson did. That spun the ball in a different direction. If she wasn't working for her father, then what was her angle? Was she going after the money herself? If she got to Slaski's phone first, then there was no chance he'd find Merrick's contact. Chelsea Merrick would control the board.

"She's going after Slaski?" asked Gibson.

Parker nodded.

"When?"

"Tonight, man." Parker checked his watch. "Right now. Guess I'm not the only one she doesn't tell everything. She's going after the phone."

"That won't work," Swonger spoke up.

"Why not?"

"'Cause there won't be no SIM card in it."

"What the hell's a SIM card?" Parker asked.

Gibson turned to Swonger. "How do you know it won't have one?"

"It'll have one. Just not the right one. That's how it worked at Buckingham anyway. The guards playin' Ma Bell had one phone for all their customers. They give you their empty phone for a price; inmates hold on to their own SIM card. Real tight. On their person, twenty-four-seven, so when there's a search, they can break it and flush it real quick. Guards can't give 'em up that way either. They didn't know nothing about no phone numbers."

"What's a SIM card?" Parker asked again.

"Subscriber identification module," Gibson said to shut him up. "A cell phone doesn't have a phone number without one. SIMs hold users' personal information."

If what Swonger said was true, and Gibson believed him, then Slaski's phone was worthless. The guard was just a mule and wouldn't know anything. Confronting him would only tip off Merrick, who would shut down entirely or else switch to a different system of communicating for his last few weeks in prison. Either way, unless he stopped Lea, Gibson would lose his only shot at finding Merrick's contact on the outside.

CHAPTER TWENTY-TWO

They drove like hell to Slaski's house, the Scion caroming across lanes on unlit back roads, headlights throwing meandering shadows that lit the way they'd already been. Swonger took the wheel while Gibson navigated from the crude map Parker had drawn them. It had been a long time since Gibson had been anywhere without GPS, and it cost them three wrong turns. He needed a damned sextant to make sense of this place, and Swonger's driving didn't help. The tension mounted each time they were forced to double back, losing still more time. Somewhere Dan Hendricks was laughing at him for his overdependency on technology. Hendricks's road-map brain would be damned useful right about now.

"Turn when I tell you to turn."

"Give me a little warning, then."

"Stop. Stop. What did that sign just say?"

Gibson craned his head back as Swonger slammed on the brakes, threw the car into reverse, and backed up the hundred yards to the sign. *What the actual . . . ,* Gibson thought. *How are we back here?*

"Turn around. We went too far."

Swonger pulled a U-ey, accelerated to eighty, then slammed on the brakes to make the turn that they should have originally taken. Gibson gripped the hand strap to keep from clattering into Swonger. Last call at the Toproll was three a.m. What time would that put Lea at Slaski's place? He checked the clock. Anytime now, really. If they were too late, then they might as well go home.

Swonger pulled up at Slaski's like the Road Runner stopping at the edge of a cliff, throwing Gibson forward into his seat belt. Slaski lived in a small white Cape Cod on a bare plot of land that had been mowed to within an inch of its life. On the side of the house, a vegetable garden, protected by more chain link than Niobe Prison, grew wild inside its enclosure. A solitary deer, gorging itself through a gap in the fencing, watched them while it chewed. *Dinner and a show.*

Across the street, Lea and Margo sat in a red pickup truck. Swonger had stopped directly between the pickup and Slaski's house—a move loaded with unfriendly symbolism. The two sets of passengers stared each other down. No one moved. Gibson hadn't really had time to formulate a strategy that didn't lead to bloodshed. The standoff stretched for more than a minute. Margo, in the driver's seat, turned and asked a question, but Lea didn't reply.

"Stay here," Gibson said, opening the passenger door.

"Oh, hell no." Swonger graced him with an adrenaline grin. "I got your back."

Swonger popped the mag on his gun, checked it, and slapped it back into place. For all the good it would do, since the firing pin was in Gibson's back pocket.

"Don't wave that around," Gibson said.

"Guns don't wave—people do."

Gibson had been impressed with how Swonger had handled himself at Parker's, but the drive had cranked him up and now he was writing his own little action movie.

"Just be cool."

He was halfway across the street when Margo stepped out of the pickup, baseball bat resting on her shoulder, an unseasonal ski mask pushed back on her head. Swonger hung back, keeping his distance.

"Little late for baseball, ladies," Gibson said.

"Hospital's open all night," Margo countered.

"Just want a word."

"Which one?"

Lea didn't look happy, and Gibson couldn't blame her. Strangers crashing your home invasion had to be disconcerting. But she wasn't panicked; she was calm and managing to seem unsurprised that they were there. A neat trick, given that Gibson was still a little surprised himself.

"Hello, again," he said.

"Something I can do for you?"

"I talked to Parker."

"Who?"

"The guy who drew me the map of where you were." He held up Parker's map and watched a lightning storm pass across her eyes.

"Did you hurt him?"

Gibson was encouraged that her first question was about the well-being of her man. It said good things about her. A soul was alive and well under her hard-ass exterior.

"He's fine. All we did was interrupt his movie."

"So he just told you where I was—"

"And why."

"—out of the goodness of his heart?"

"Well, I may have given him the impression that we work for you." He shrugged. "You didn't pick him for his independent thinking. Look, can we cut the crap? You're here for the phone Merrick used."

"And what? You and bunny rabbit there are going to take it from us?" Margo demanded.

Behind him, he felt Swonger take several angry steps forward. Gibson held up a hand. The footsteps stopped, but Swonger's shadow loomed on the asphalt.

"No," Gibson said. "We're not taking it."

"Damn right," Margo said.

"But neither can you."

"I knew you were an asshole at the hotel," Lea said.

"That might be, but you still can't take it."

"And why's that?"

He explained SIM cards and how Merrick would keep his own card on him, per Swonger's prison experience. Lea listened, working the corner of her lip between her teeth. She was taking him seriously, at least.

"The phone's worthless," he finished. "It's just a shell."

"You don't know that."

"If you go in there now, all you're doing is tipping Merrick off. He'll shut everything down, wait out his sentence, and disappear. You'll kill our only shot at breaking into his communications."

"Why? Because some white-trash ex-con says so?"

"Hey," Swonger said, stepping forward again. "I ain't afraid to hit a girl."

"You ought to be." Margo tightened her grip on the bat.

Gibson could feel the situation spinning away. If it were Lea and him, there was a chance of talking her into it. But Margo and Swonger knew only escalation, and they were headed to blows.

"I'm trying to help," he said.

"I don't need your help."

"Don't be this stubborn. You can't afford it."

Margo poked Gibson in the chest with the baseball bat. "You two need to get up out of here."

Gibson shoved the bat aside. There was a moment of silence, before the four of them set to cursing each other in the street. In the heat of the moment, they all forgot where they were, and as their tempers rose so did their voices. They were all exhausted. Maybe that explained their collective stupidity.

"Would you all shut the hell up!"

They all froze and then turned slowly toward the voice. Tim Slaski was standing on his front porch in a threadbare bathrobe, squinting in their general direction.

They fell silent and stared at him, openmouthed.

"I mean, it's four in the goddamn morning. What the hell is the matter with you?"

Gibson and Lea looked at each other. He shrugged as if to ask, *What's it gonna be?* She wouldn't even need to break in now—the lamb had come to the lion. He watched her calculate her options.

"Sorry," she called to Slaski. "Thought there was a party out this way."

"Ain't no damn party. It's four in the morning. Go on and get before I call the police."

"Say you're sorry," Lea hissed at all of them.

Sheepishly, they all raised a hand and called out an apology like a group of rowdy teens.

"Never mind that, just get," Slaski said.

"We need to talk," Lea said to Gibson. "Now."

"We'll follow you," Gibson said.

It was a relief when she agreed. He didn't like their chances of finding their own way back to Niobe at night.

———————————

It was a tense scene back at the Toproll. The darkest part of the night was over, and Lea could see the Wolstenholme Hotel coming into focus against the sky. She waited on the street for the two men while Margo opened up the bar. It had been a long night, and they'd all think more clearly in the morning. That would be the smart move, but smart moves seemed to be in short supply tonight. She shook her head at the yelling match outside Slaski's house. They'd all acted like clowns. She'd need to be smarter if she hoped to see this thing through. The best place to start was to learn these men's intentions before she let them out of her sight. They were still sitting in their car, staring at her, talking. Conspiring. *Get a good look, boys.*

"Are you coming?"

Inside the Toproll, Margo slipped into bartender mode and put on a pot of coffee. The bar wouldn't get mopped down until morning, and the stink of stale beer and cigarettes clung to every surface. Lea could tell Margo was still adjusting to the shift in the nature of their relationship. The boss had become the employee, and Lea wondered if she'd been wrong to mix Margo up in all this. She'd always had a gift for bringing people around to her point of view, and Margo's financial difficulties had made her an easy convert. But maybe this was one time that she should have left well enough alone. What had once seemed a complex but fairly linear puzzle was branching out of her control.

She watched two of those branches enter the bar. The skinny, tattooed one slipped behind the bar to pour himself a beer, but Margo shooed him away. He retreated grumpily to a barstool and sat staring at the row of taps. His companion stood silently at the door watching her, watching her like some microbe at the far end of a microscope. She didn't care for it.

"You really screwed us back there."

"I saved you."

She'd expected him to yell, try to intimidate her, but his voice was calm and considered; it surprised her, and that angered her still more.

"The hell you did. Slaski is burned. He saw our faces."

He shook his head. "Slaski wears contacts."

"Contacts? And you know this how?"

"He was squinting. When he came out on the porch, he was squinting because he couldn't make us out. We were blurs to him."

"Oh, bullshit."

"Hey," he called over to the bar. "It's a small town. Would Slaski know you if he saw you?"

"Yeah, he would," Margo confirmed.

"But he didn't. You're fine," he said, turning back to Lea. "So if you want to go back there later that's your call. Now, can we talk?" He looked at his partner, then Margo. "Just you and me, for now."

Lea led him through the back room to Parker's booth. Hopefully Margo wouldn't curb stomp his little friend in the meantime.

They sat across from each other. Up close, his eyes were beautiful and intuitive. In the middle of a fight, on a dark street, those eyes had seen Slaski squint and known why. It wouldn't do to underestimate him. She guessed he was no more than thirty, but he felt older to her. She wasn't sure why. Perhaps it was the beard. Or the tired lines at the corner of his eyes that no night's sleep would begin to erase. It was a kind face. Compassionate. But one thing life had taught her the hard way was that a face bore little relationship to the man beneath. He could be a saint or a serial killer: the face would be the same.

He was smiling at her.

"What?" she asked.

"The drive over here, I've been thinking of what to say to you. To convince you to trust me."

"And that's funny how?"

"About a year ago, I was in your exact position. Sitting at a booth with a man that I didn't trust. And he knew I didn't trust him but made his case anyway."

"Did you? Decide to trust him?"

"Not at first, no."

"But eventually?"

"Eventually."

"So how did he convince you?"

"Baited the hook with something I couldn't walk away from."

"You got something like that for me?" Lea asked.

"Nothing comes to mind."

"Tough spot. What to do?"

"Well, my first instinct would be to play you. Manipulate you. It's what I'm good at."

"But . . ."

"But it won't work on you."

"So maybe stroke my ego? Tell me how smart I am. Come clean about how you were going to run a game on me, but can see I'm just too gosh-darn smart for that? Something like that?"

"Like I said, that won't work on you."

"Tough spot."

"Tough spot," he agreed.

"What to do . . ." She studied him over the brim of her coffee cup. He wasn't wrong that she didn't trust him—the guy was a regular snake charmer with those dancing eyes of his. But the thing was, he also wasn't wrong that she might need to trust him. She saw now that her decision to move on Slaski had been born of frustration and fear. The fear that with all the recent arrivals in Niobe that Charles Merrick was slipping through her fingers. She'd reacted to the news about Slaski impulsively, trying to regain the upper hand. Instead, tonight had provided unequivocal confirmation of one thing: this wasn't her world. Everything she had done up until now was predicated on the idea that no one else knew about the money. A head start had been her only edge, and now that was gone. It had taken her a year to cultivate Parker as a source and for him to identify Slaski. While Mr. Dancing Eyes had made Parker and Slaski in one night. *One* night.

"How did you even know to go after Parker?" She watched him consider how to answer the question.

Finally, he pushed his baseball cap back and said, "Because you're Chelsea Merrick."

She hadn't heard her real name spoken aloud in five years. Her heart thundered in her chest. "My name is Lea Regan."

He ignored her. "I'll admit, at first I assumed you were working with your father, but you're not. Are you?"

"Who the hell are you?"

"Look, I appreciate you're angry. You knew about the money before the interview, didn't you?"

She gave no answer, but he carried on like she had.

"Slipped into Niobe quietly. What? Two years ago?"

How did he know that?

"Dug in, set up shop. Turned Parker—he was a good call, by the way. Probably had yourself a nice, simple plan for taking down your dad. But judging by all the new arrivals, nice and simple left town. It's got to hurt."

"It's my family's money."

"Well, that's convenient; your family has it."

"That man is not my family."

"It's stolen money, Chelsea."

"Lea."

"The thing about stolen money, *Lea*, is if it gets stolen, no one's going to the police. It makes your father a very attractive target."

She nodded grimly. "What are you proposing?"

"What do you think your father will do the day he gets out of prison?"

"Fly to a nonextradition country."

"So do I. Want to stop him?"

More than anything in the world. Truth was, she didn't give a damn about the money. She only wanted Charles Merrick to be penniless. The real kind of penniless. Destitute. It was a beautiful word. And she wanted Charles Merrick to know who had done it to him. She wanted him to know it was his own daughter. That she wanted more than anything. So if this guy was her best shot, then so be it.

"What's my name?" she asked.

"Lea Regan, far as I know."

"So what's yours?"

He took out a wallet and handed over a driver's license. It read "Robert Quine."

"My name is Gibson Vaughn," he said.

"Good to know you, Robert."

They shook hands over the table.

"Glad we got that settled," he said.

"So if Slaski's phone's worthless, how do we find out who Merrick's been calling?"

"I'm working on a plan."

"We don't have a lot of time."

"Give me until tomorrow morning."

She looked at her phone. "It is tomorrow morning."

"Pick me up at the hotel at nine."

"That's three hours from now."

"Like you said, we don't have a lot of time."

With that, he slid out of the booth and nudged his partner awake. When they were gone, Margo came back and took his seat. She looked pensive, not an expression Lea was accustomed to seeing from her boss.

"We need to talk."

Lea braced, expecting Margo to strong-arm her for a bigger cut. "What's up?"

"So I was standing in front of some man's house at four in the a.m. with a baseball bat and a ski mask. If those two hadn't stopped us, I would have gone into that house with you. Thank God they *did*, you know? Sorry, Gilmore, but I'm out. Can't do this. Maybe I hang on to the bar, maybe I don't, but I'll live with those odds. You know?"

Lea nodded. "Okay."

"You shouldn't either."

"What?"

"I don't know what all's going on here. Don't want know. But it's not going to end well. You have to know that."

Lea shrugged, too tired to have this conversation now when she'd been having it with herself for the last two years.

"Working for me can't be so bad you have to get yourself killed, can it?"

Lea smiled at that. "Thanks, Margo. I mean it."

Margo sat back and sighed. "Just lock up before you go."

CHAPTER TWENTY-THREE

It took Gibson and Lea a couple of hours to walk the perimeter of the prison. They kept to the woods and out of sight; it was public land, so they weren't breaking the law, but they dressed for a hike in case they were stopped. He used the bars on his phone to rough out a map of cell tower coverage around the prison. A signal meter would have provided a more accurate picture, but those cost three hundred dollars, and they needed to conserve Birk's meager four-thousand-dollar bankroll.

For probably the twentieth time since yesterday, he looked at the voice mail from Nicole. He still hadn't worked up the confidence to listen to it. Instead, he adjusted the cap on his head and scrambled up a berm to join Lea. It had been a long night, and they'd both spent the first half of the hike in a stupor, neither speaking more than necessary. Gibson was grateful that Swonger had been a no-show; he didn't have the energy for his chatter this morning.

At the top of the berm, Lea stood staring at the prison through the trees.

"When was the last time you saw him?"

She hadn't felt him standing there and flinched at the sound of his voice. She shot him a look like he'd caught her half-naked.

"I'm getting hungry," she said. "Give me the map."

She took over the mapping and jotted down his notes as he called them out to her. She also began peppering him with questions about his plan, which so far he had mostly deflected for the simple reason that he didn't have a plan. No, that wasn't entirely true; he had plenty of ideas, but none that didn't cost a hell of a lot more than the limited cash they had on hand. Sooner or later, though, Lea would want answers that he didn't have, and then she'd have no other option but to try her luck with Slaski in the hopes that Swonger was wrong about the SIM card.

It was past noon when they got back to her car. Gibson spread their map out on the hood and studied it. It confirmed what Parker had told them: cell coverage at the prison was thin at best. The nearest cell tower was off to the southwest, back toward Niobe, and the entire northern quadrant was one big dead zone. They'd stumbled across a clearing between the cell tower and the prison where he could set up shop and reasonably claim to be camping if discovered. It was perfect for what he had in mind. Unfortunately, what he had in mind required an exorbitantly expensive piece of hardware that wasn't available for civilian use, even if he could afford it. Lea asked him about the plan again, but he put her off with some vague allusion to needing to mull things over.

"So you've got nothing. Do you?"

He squinted at her over the hood of the car and chuckled. "Not unless you've got a half a million socked away somewhere."

"Are we partners, or was last night a con?"

"Partners," he confirmed.

"Then don't string me along."

He really did like her.

They were halfway back to town before Lea spoke again. "You know my grandfather was a surgeon? Chief of staff at a hospital in Connecticut. My grandmother founded four separate charities. They passed within a year of each other."

"Yeah, I read about them."

"Didn't have my parents' resources, of course, but they were well off. Put money aside in a trust to pay for my education. We didn't need it, but I was their only grandchild, and the gesture was important to them. I never really thanked them for it. I never thanked anyone for anything back then. Man, I wish I had."

"You were a kid."

"Yeah, well, anyway, they named my father the executor of the trust, and after the feds ceased everything, it was the only legit money left. He made this tearful plea. Swore he was the victim of a witch hunt, that he would be exonerated and everything would go back to the way it had been. But he needed the money. I loved him. I gave him my blessing. Felt proud to be able to help. Figured out later, he'd drained the trust weeks before he asked. It was all a lie." She pulled into the hotel parking lot and put the car in park. "So, no, I don't have a half million socked away anywhere."

Swonger, sitting on top of a dumpster with a Red Bull, hopped down and met them at the car.

"Something's up," Swonger said.

"Something good or something bad?"

"Well, it ain't Daytona. Them boys that booked the fifth floor? Got it on lockdown. Won't let nobody up there. Lot more than four of them now too. Two of them outside the elevator. Another in the lobby. Got those earpiece deals so they can talk to each other."

"Are they armed?"

"Oh, they strapped. Guarding somebody."

"Who?" Lea asked.

"Dunno. Came in through the loading dock. Never saw 'em. But they heavy. That the Sherman they rolled up in." He pointed to a massive black SUV with Texas plates.

Subtle.

"What are we gonna do?" Swonger asked.

"Take a shower to start."

"Y'all are pretty ripe," Swonger agreed.

They agreed to meet in Gibson's room in an hour.

Jimmy Temple stood behind the front desk and welcomed Gibson back to the hotel, but his smile was forced and thin. Gone was the twinkle in his eyes, which darted to Gibson's left. Gibson followed them to an intense Hispanic-looking man with a prominent jaw that lent him a near-permanent scowl. He wore his hair long on top, short on the sides, and slicked back in a gleaming black crest. The crease in the leg of his suit was freshly ironed, and his shoes glistened with a military attention to detail. Gibson recognized him from the Toproll last night. The man sat reading a newspaper. He closed it crisply and studied Gibson, who was glad to be dressed like a tourist back from a hike—even he wouldn't take himself seriously. At the elevator, Gibson glanced back. The man had moved to the front desk, where he paged through the guest registry while Jimmy Temple stood by silently with a look of embarrassment. It appeared to Gibson that the Wolstenholme Hotel might be under new management.

Up in his room, Gibson opened his laptop and used his cellular modem to log into Marco Polo, one of dozens of black-market sites that had sprung up in the void left by the Silk Road bust. Powered by Bitcoin and masked by Tor encryption, it offered anything and everything for sale: drugs, weapons, stolen credit cards. It was here that he'd purchased his Robert Quine IDs, but the tech he was after represented another order of magnitude entirely. But what other options did he have? So far, inspiration wasn't returning his calls. He left encrypted messages with the handful of vendors who might traffic in such high-end equipment and logged off feeling discouraged.

He took a long shower and contemplated the degree of competition they faced for Merrick's money. For most of the players, the general plan would be to take Merrick after he was released from prison. Which made it all the more important that Gibson beat them to the money and leave them to fight over Merrick. Which brought him back to the Stingray. He just couldn't think of another way to intercept Merrick's calls to his partner on the outside.

A knock came at the door. Gibson wrapped himself in a towel, let Swonger in, and went back to the bathroom. In the mirror, Gibson trimmed up his beard and cleaned away the stubble. When he was done, he spread his wet beard between his fingers and examined the scar on his neck. He hoped with time that it would fade, but beneath his fingers it remained livid: an ugly reminder of how close he'd come to following in his father's footsteps. He didn't care for the beard, but he needed to get used to it, because he still wasn't ready to bare his scars with anything resembling pride.

He heard the television in the next room. He dressed and found Swonger sprawled out on the bed, head propped on some pillows, surfing channels too quickly to see what was on.

"Get off my bed."

"What for? Maids are gonna change the sheets."

"Just get off."

Swonger thought about it, and then, with dramatic slowness, stood up and flopped down in a chair. Everything with him was a test of wills. It was the only way Swonger knew to navigate the world. Gibson understood where it came from—this inability to back down from any challenge, no matter how inconsequential—but it meant Gibson had to keep his thumb on him. If he let Swonger lie on his bed now, the ex-con would be that much harder to control when it counted. Such were the inconsequential details of manhood's pecking order.

Gibson laid out a new set of rules for them. "From here on out, we don't know each other. That means we eat separately. We stagger coming and going, never at the same time. Don't acknowledge me in public. We communicate by text only, except when we're sure we're in private. We meet here every morning. Go over things."

"That's cool. Very Sun Tzu."

"Sun Tzu?"

"What? I can read. *Art of War* only like sixty pages, dog. Old-timer in stir gave me his copy for a pack of Marlboros. 'Pretend to be weak, that he may grow arrogant.' Sun Tzu's the man."

Not for the first time, Gibson was taken aback at Swonger's more insightful moments. Another knock came at the door, and Gibson let Lea into the room. Her hair, still wet, was tied back in a hurried ponytail.

"So what do you have?" she asked.

Gibson laid out his plan. Lea and Swonger listened in rapt silence up until Gibson got to the sticking point.

"What the hell's a Stingray?" Swonger asked.

Gibson explained how it worked.

"Whoa, that even legal?"

"Not for civilian purchase. Government use only."

"And we need this thing?" Lea said.

Gibson nodded. "It's the only way, but there's no way we're getting ahold of one." He gave them the price tag.

Swonger whistled. "Dog, you don't think small."

"It would have been ideal, but there's just no way. We're just going to have to go back to Lea's plan. Figure out a way to take the SIM card off Merrick without him knowing. Maybe Parker could—"

"I'm telling you, ain't no way that's gonna work," Swonger interrupted. "Merrick will keep it close. Probably sewn into the hem of his blues so if he gets searched, he can snap it in half just as a precaution. Easier to get another one down the road. All this time and Merrick never been caught with it on him? Then he real careful."

"I agree with Gavin," Lea said. "There has to be another way."

Gavin? Gibson braced for the inevitable tirade from Swonger about his name, but none came. Instead, Swonger seemed pleased to have his opinion taken seriously.

"The only other way's the Stingray," said Gibson.

Swonger asked if he was absolutely sure the Stingray would work.

"Yeah. I'd need to make some modifications, but it'd work."

"Let me make a call," Swonger said. "Maybe I know a guy."

"Who?"

"My boy Truck."

"Truck?"

"Truck Noble."

CHAPTER TWENTY-FOUR

Seemed Truck Noble ran a crew out of Virginia Beach and wasn't much for crossing state lines without good reason—the best coming in stacks of green. Unfortunately, cash was in short supply, and Truck Noble wasn't interested in any kind of layaway plan. Appeals to his friendship with Swonger didn't do much to move the needle either. Still, Swonger swore he could convince Noble to meet them.

"I just need a little more time. Truck and me, we go back."

"Not far enough," Gibson observed.

"Hey, how about you go to hell?"

Gibson went back to combing through dark-net sites without any luck.

Their new routine was to meet in Lea's apartment above the Toproll every night after her shift to recap their progress. It didn't make for long conversations. They were getting nowhere but fed up. Lea and Gibson were both losing faith in the mythical Truck Noble. Instead, they spent more and more of their time trying to scheme ways to get Merrick's SIM card, which largely consisted of Lea and Gibson drawing up a plan to take it from Merrick in the prison, and Swonger shooting holes in it. Cue another argument.

But the real source of tension looming down over them all was the mysterious guest of the hotel's fifth floor. No one in town had the first idea about who was up there. Well, Jimmy Temple knew, but he'd made his deal with the devil and wasn't saying. However, his demeanor painted a grim picture, having turned jumpy, eyes red-rimmed, a white stubble settling across his jowls, as if sleep wasn't coming so easy these days. The look of a good man who knew more than he cared to know. Even housekeeping had been banished from the fifth floor. Meals were delivered by the phalanx of bodyguards, who also collected fresh sheets and towels each morning.

In a town devoid of juicy gossip, the fifth floor had become the lead story. There was a sense of personal affront that an entire hotel floor had been booked for one guest. That kind of excess served only to remind Niobe of its own perpetual insolvency, stirring resentment. Resentment and curiosity as the identity of the guest on the fifth floor festered in the imagination of Niobe. And, as any good horror-film fan knew, the human imagination was its own worst enemy.

Most nights at the Toproll featured drunken talk of confronting the bodyguards and demanding an explanation, but whenever the bodyguards came around, the tough talkers made themselves scarce. The bodyguards favored the booth by the door, and anyone sitting there would vacate spontaneously when they arrived, the bar muted and sullen until they departed. One more thing in town the visitors in Niobe owned.

Gibson wasn't surprised at the town's reaction: the bodyguards gave off a professional, not-to-be-messed-with vibe and were definitely not in the question-answering business. Gibson felt hostile eyes on him too and had stopped visiting the Toproll except after hours. He might not be from the fifth floor, but he also didn't belong, and, like white blood cells, the locals felt an indiscriminate need to excise any and all foreign bodies from their midst. Bottom line, the tension building in Niobe needed an outlet. There had been a steady uptick in the number of bar fights, petty theft, and domestic violence calls, and the drunk tank was standing room only most nights.

Niobe sheriff Fred Blake was a thin white man in his late sixties whose defining characteristic was a certain world-weariness. His default expression was the almost-imperceptible shake of the head of a man who couldn't quite believe the incompetence surrounding him. Despite being a sheriff's department of one, Fred moved at his own pace and of his own volition. If the town didn't like it, they could get off their asses and hire him some deputies. So far the town hadn't taken him up on his challenge. Thirty years in the Army as a transportation-management coordinator clearly informed his philosophy about law enforcement. His job was to keep the town running. Some town sheriffs resented outside interference, but according to Margo, Fred Blake was the first one on the phone to the state police on the rare occasions that something outside his typical purview occurred. Unfortunately, a full drunk tank didn't warrant a call to the staties. So what to do? The sheriff had gone so far as to contemplate an outright shuttering of the Toproll for a week until people settled the hell down. That had not gone over well.

"Instead of threatening us, who live here, you need to go on over to the hotel and—" Old Charlie began.

"And what?" the sheriff shot back. "Arrest them for pissing you off? For renting more rooms than they need? Conspicuous consumption isn't a crime, last I checked."

"What about the women?"

Gibson hadn't been the only one to note the steady stream of young working girls being escorted, two at a time, up to the fifth floor.

The sheriff shrugged at this too. "No law against that either."

"They're prostitutes. Everyone knows it."

"Everyone knows? Well, hell, if everyone knows, then I should probably go arrest them," the sheriff said with a patented shake of his head.

The tension in town continued to rise.

On the second day, Swonger lost contact with Truck Noble. A dozen text messages went unanswered without a word. It didn't surprise Gibson. Noble had grown either tired or suspicious of Swonger's insistence. Probably read it as desperate, which they were. Why would Noble risk exposure for a one-off deal that wasn't going to see him retire to an island? Gibson said as much and left Swonger and Lea to argue among themselves.

It was past two a.m., but Gibson didn't feel much like sleeping, so he walked down Tarte Street, hoping the night air would give him fresh eyes. He didn't see anyone on the street and liked having the town to himself. His evening stroll didn't last long, however, before Sheriff Blake's cruiser pulled alongside.

"Evening, Sheriff. Can I help you?"

"Come on and get in. I'd be appreciative if you spared me making this difficult."

The cruiser came to a halt, and Gibson heard the doors unlock.

"So don't ask you what this is all about or if I'm in some kind of trouble? Just get in the back?"

"Like I said, I'd appreciate it." Blake's hand rested lightly on the grip of his service weapon.

Gibson looked up and down Tarte Street, suddenly wishing for a little more foot traffic. Whatever Blake wanted, it wasn't official. Gibson felt curious to know if his suspicions were correct. He tried the passenger door.

"In back is good," the sheriff said.

Gibson did as he was asked, and the doors locked behind him. The cruiser made a U-turn and drove back up Tarte Street. They stopped in front of the hotel. He'd been in the cruiser for less than a minute. Long enough to rattle him, which he guessed was the point.

"Inside," Blake said as the doors unlocked.

In the lobby, a pair of men from the fifth floor patted him down and directed him to the oval parlor off the lobby. Gibson recognized the man at the chess table as the one who'd been reading a newspaper in the lobby the day he'd checked in. Gibson sat opposite, the board empty—not that they weren't playing a game.

"I wonder . . . Will we get off on a good foot?" the man purred in a soft Mexican accent. "My name is Emerson Soto Flores."

"Robert Quine," Gibson said.

"It is good to meet you, Mr. Quine. Due to the nature of our visit in Niobe, I've taken the time to familiarize myself with all the hotel's unusual guests. So many of them . . . One is tempted to hypothesize that Niobe must be very special to attract so many tourists at the same time. An exhibit or a festival perhaps. Or perhaps a celebrity. A man worth traveling a long way to meet."

"Perhaps."

"But such a famous man won't have time to meet with everyone. So it will come down to who most deserves an audience with this man. A difficult question to answer, hence my interest in the guests here at the hotel. And, if I am honest, most of them are undeserving, their interests too prosaic. This is why you are here, Mr. Quine. Because there *is* no Mr. Quine, and that concerns me."

With a disappointed flourish, the man placed a silver disk about the size of a hockey puck on the table. "Do you know what a rare-earth magnet does?"

Gibson's heart sunk. "Yeah. I do."

He'd stashed his real driver's license in his hotel safe. Rare-earth magnets were incredibly powerful devices that could break into the average hotel safe in about ten seconds. To illustrate the point, Emerson Soto Flores slid Gibson's driver's license across the chessboard.

"You have a very interesting history, Mr. Vaughn. I enjoyed reading about your exploits on the Internet. Especially Atlanta. However, I could not see any connection between you and Charles Merrick."

"Are you the fifth floor?" Gibson asked.

"No, but I speak for her."

"And what does *she* say?"

"She says that no one has come farther to see Charles Merrick. Anyone who attempts to interfere with her appointment will regret it."

"Does that pass for a threat where you're from?"

"Where I'm from we don't make threats, but this is the nature of women, don't you agree?"

"We must know different women," Gibson said.

"No. Women believe in nothing but talk. She hopes you will take her threat seriously."

"And what do you believe?"

"I believe I will have to kill you all," Emerson said with such casual conviction that Gibson's mouth went dry.

"So why bother delivering her message?"

Emerson considered the question. "Your parents are both dead, yes? Your mother when you were very young."

"Do you have a point?"

"Only that a man like you cannot understand my duty. I deliver her warning because I must."

They held each other's gaze like two wolves meeting in an ancient forest. Gibson said nothing but, realizing that this was a staring contest that he shouldn't win, forced his stare downward. He counted to five and glanced up again; Emerson was smiling. *Go ahead and smile,* Gibson thought.

"I'm glad we understand each other."

"Are we done here?"

"I sincerely hope not, but I think . . . yes."

Gibson stood to go.

"The elevator is out, so you'll have to take the stairs."

"What happened to it?"

"It's an old hotel." Emerson shrugged. "Things happen."

On the morning of the sixth day, Lea woke to a text from Swonger to meet him at the hotel. They'd all traded numbers, but until now she'd communicated only with Gibson. Curious, she threw on clothes and poured herself coffee to go.

As booked as the hotel might be, the lobby felt oddly deserted. A choral arrangement of "Good King Wenceslas" echoed eerily through the space. Two of the fifth floor's men in the parlor paused their chess match to look her over. One said something to the other that Lea couldn't catch, but she could guess from the smirk on his companion's face.

Jimmy Temple emerged from the office with a wrench in hand. "Looking for your friend?"

"Ah, yeah?"

"He's in the back. Come on."

Confused, Lea followed Jimmy down the hall, past the "Out of Order" sign that hung crookedly on the elevator, and into the kitchen. She gave Jimmy a puzzled look. Since shuttering the dining room five years ago, he had used the kitchen primarily for storage, and only housekeeping ever came back here to use the servants' staircase. Jimmy had taken her on a tour of the hotel once and shown her the stairs, which were a historic feature of the hotel that predated elevators. The stairs had concealed exits on each floor through which servants had once attended to their responsibilities out of sight of the guests.

They threaded their way among stacks of boxes and around a central prep table. Swonger's legs stuck out from behind the double oven, which had been pulled out from the wall. When he heard them, he sat up and grinned at Lea.

"What are you doing?" she asked.

"Been trying to help Mr. Temple get this stove working."

"I didn't know you two knew each other."

"We didn't," Jimmy said, handing Swonger the wrench. "But your friend introduced himself the other day, and he's been a godsend."

"Just needing to keep busy," Swonger said and disappeared back behind the stove.

"Is that a fact?" she said and looked bemusedly at Swonger's legs. "Well?"

"Well, what?"

"*You* texted me."

"Oh, right." Swonger sat back up. "Heard from Truck. We're on."

"We're on? Just like that?"

"I told you. Me and Truck go back."

———————

They all met later at Lea's apartment to discuss options. Truck Noble was coming to them, the meeting set for the next day at a state park on the Virginia–West Virginia state line. Lea expressed curiosity about Truck's sudden reversal, and Gibson feared walking into some sort of trap. Swonger, however, clearly felt vindicated and insisted it would be fine so long as they played it straight and kept it to two.

"Small is good. Small ain't threatening."

Swonger knew Truck and Gibson knew the tech, so it made sense for it to be the two of them. Lea agreed to stay in Niobe and keep an eye on the fifth floor. With that decided, Gibson fetched beers and offered a toast. Swonger clinked bottles enthusiastically, and Lea drank her beer, feeling more optimistic than at any point since reading her father's interview.

"How'd you get caught, then?"

"Behind some bullshit, that's how. This real pretty Porsche Cayenne. It was smooth—in and out in two minutes, no doubt. But some noodle-dick frat boy was railing a cheerleader in the backseat of a Tahoe down the way. Saw me jim the door and nine-one-one'd me."

"What happened?"

"State's attorney offered me a deal—St. Brides, if I gave up the crew." Swonger opened another beer. "But I ain't no snitch, so the DA sent my ass to Buckingham. The crew in Richmond hooked me up with Truck on the inside. Out of gratitude, you see, 'cause they knew I wasn't no rat. Truck was my stand-up."

"Stand-up?"

Swonger thought about how to explain. "Truck had my back. I was just a skinny fish, dog. Seventeen. Didn't have no gang. No rep. No sleeves. I would have been someone's bitch in under two minutes, no doubt. Truck showed me the ropes. Made sure my skinny white ass didn't get thrown off the tier. Aryans didn't like me hanging with a brother, but I ain't down with all that white-power shit. And nobody fucks with the Truck."

Swonger spoke the name reverentially. Nothing like the Swonger that Gibson knew. It made him wonder what was so special about Truck Noble.

Swonger saved him the trouble of having to ask.

"Yeah, so about Truck . . . he don't have the most philosophical of natures. He like a bull. He see someone waving something at him, he don't wonder why. He just gonna put you down for even contemplating that disrespect, know what I'm saying? So be cool and don't give him any of your usual lip."

"I'm hurt."

"Yeah, just like that. I'm telling you, he don't do so well with attitude. Especially from white boys. So maybe let me do the talking this

CHAPTER TWENTY-FIVE

Swonger and Gibson left early, hoping to arrive before Truck and scope out the meeting site. It turned out to be an abandoned forest station, a perfect spot for conducting business. *Isolated enough that no one will find our bodies for weeks if it goes badly,* Gibson thought cheerily. Swonger, seeming considerably less concerned, fetched a cooler from the trunk and cracked open a Natty Light. He offered one to Gibson.

"It's ten a.m., Swonger."

Swonger didn't see the relevance and hopped up on the hood of the car with his beer to wait.

Gibson asked him how he knew Truck Noble.

"We jailed together at Buckingham."

"What were you in for?"

"Grand theft. I was boosting cars up in Charlottesville and delivering them to this crew in Richmond. Easy money."

"They sent you to Buckingham for that? Were you carjackin them?"

"No, man, no need for all that. All them rich college mooks? Easier tail them home and take them while they slept. Lot of expensive engi in them campus parking lots. Lined up like Christmas. Nothing to it

time." Swonger looked Gibson over to gauge if he was being taken seriously. "You ain't racist, are you?"

"Not on purpose."

"Then we probably all right. But if you feel something racist bub-
bling up, just put a gun in your mouth. It ain't worth it."

"I'll do my best."

"His nickname's Truck. It ain't meant ironic."

"So he's big."

"For starters. But you know how when you see a big guy, you think,
well, at least I can outrun him? And that's sort of comforting. Yeah, well,
nobody outruns the Truck."

"Play football?"

"They wanted him to, but his moms wouldn't let him."

"How come?"

"Concussions. Mrs. Noble a nurse, so that was that. Coaches
begged on their knees every year. But she wasn't having it. No one
outruns the Truck, and no one moves Mrs. Noble, she don't want to be
moved." He dropped his empty in the grass. "Where the hell they at?"

Gibson checked the time. Noble was late. Swonger went to piss in
the bushes again, came back, and opened yet another beer. By the time
Swonger's phone finally buzzed with a text message, a pile of empty cans
littered the ground at his feet. The meet was still on, but at a new location about fifteen minutes away. The message gave them ten. Swonger
made it in seven.

"Why'd they move it, you think?" Swonger asked.

"Noble doesn't trust us. The first spot was just to see if we were
setting them up. They were probably watching us."

"Damn, that's cold."

It was a smart play by Noble. The new location was an overgrown
park trail that opened into a clearing. Gibson saw no one here either.
His bad feeling crept back up his spine.

"Come on," Swonger shouted, pounding the dash. "What I got to do to get some trust?"

As if to answer, a gray panel van pulled into the clearing behind them and rolled to a halt on their front bumper. If the meet went south, they were boxed in. A slight black woman got out of the van, maybe five foot and a hundred pounds. She couldn't have been more than twenty-one years old. After all Swonger's buildup about Truck, it was almost a letdown. She adjusted her oversized jean shorts, which stopped at her calves above worn combat boots. Her outfit was capped by an orange tank top with wide sleeve holes down to her hips that showed off an electric-purple bra. The sides of her head were shaved, and a tall, chaotic Mohawk was piled precariously atop her head.

"Oh, this is not good," Swonger said.

"That doesn't look like a Truck."

"That Truck's sister, Deja." Swonger had spoken respectfully of Truck; now he sounded plain scared. "What's she doing here? Remember what I said about Truck? She's worse. Way worse. Don't do nothing stupid."

"Well, come on, then. I ain't got all day," Deja said as though they'd been keeping her waiting.

They both eased out of the car.

"Heya, Deja. Where's Truck and Terry?" Swonger asked. "Thought we was meeting them."

Deja Noble adjusted her oversized sunglasses. "Couldn't make it. But when I heard this long-lost friend of our family, Gavin Swonger, wanted a meeting with my big brother? Well, that just warmed my damn heart. Couldn't pass up a chance to reminisce, could I? How you been, Swong?"

"All right, I reckon—"

"Shut up," Deja snapped. "Damn, you are too dumb for this world. Now . . . I know you're strapped. So go ahead and ease it out, throw it there on the ground."

Swonger started to protest.

"Boy, I'm not going to tell you again." Deja lifted her tank top to reveal a pistol grip. "I am a loving person, but bullets misanthropic, know what I mean?"

Swonger tossed his gun at Deja's feet.

"Your turn," she said to Gibson.

"I'm not carrying."

"That a fact?"

Gibson lifted his shirt and turned slowly in a circle.

Deja looked at him pityingly. "Show up for a meeting, you ain't even strapped? Like I'm Sears or some shit? You disrespecting me?"

Gibson felt himself being sized up. She looked from him to Swonger and back again, trying to make up her mind about something.

"You setting my brother up, Swonger?" she said. "Is that what this is?"

"What? No!"

Even Gibson didn't believe him. Deja took a step forward and drew her gun.

"There's no need for all that," Swonger said.

"Oh, there's need when small-time white-trash car thieves who knew my brother once in stir call up out of the blue, looking to make a deal for a major piece of hardware. And I'm not supposed to wonder what's what? Wonder if maybe my brother's trusting nature isn't being taken advantage of?"

"It ain't even like that. This is on the level. He needs it." Swonger pointed at Gibson.

"Oh, and I'm supposed to believe you two are friends?"

"Why not?"

"One thing, he's got all his teeth."

"We're not friends. Believe me," Gibson said.

"I got most of my teeth," Swonger said, hung up on the wrong part of the conversation.

"So, what . . . ? You just business associates?" she asked. "That what I'm supposed to believe? Please. Tell me a bedtime story. Tell me how you got rolled up stealing cars again and cut a deal to serve up the Nobles to save your narrow ass. And after what my brother did for you . . ." There was cold fury in her voice as she strode forward and pressed the muzzle to Swonger's forehead like the cold finger of God, forcing him to his knees.

She's going to kill him and I'm next. Gibson believed it beyond a doubt until he saw her staring at him, calculation and purpose in her eyes.

"You police?"

"No."

"Then how do you know this fool?"

"Hammond Birk."

"Judge that lost his mind?"

"That's the one. I owe him."

"Owe him how?"

"That's private between him and me."

"That a fact? And what's that got to do with Swonger here?"

Gibson shrugged. "Believe me, I've been asking myself the same question. I mean, you ever try and get rid of him? Can't be done."

"Hey!" Swonger said.

Deja's piercing black eyes narrowed for a moment before she burst out with a laugh. "Well, that's the damn truth."

"Hey!"

Deja let the hammer down and stepped back. "Oh, don't be sore, Swong. Had to make sure. Go on and get up out the grass."

"I got my teeth," Swonger muttered to himself. He stood and dusted himself off, pale and shaken.

Deja slapped the side of the van three times, and a man in camos emerged from the woods with a scoped hunting rifle. Pointed at the ground. Gibson took that as a good sign. The man strolled over and leaned against the van as if he'd just happened along and was taking a break before continuing his hike.

"Terry," Swonger said.

Terry nodded but didn't answer.

"So are we okay to do some business?" Gibson asked. "Or are you going to scare the piss out of Swonger some more?"

"Is he for real?" Deja asked Swonger.

Swonger shrugged. "Can't do nothing with him."

She gave Gibson another look. "Truth is, ordinarily we don't have time for this kind of thing, you understand."

"Swonger said the Nobles were the people to talk to."

"Well, I appreciate good word of mouth, but our business model is pretty straightforward. We like it like that. And your needs are kind of specialized. A goddamn cell-phone interceptor? You know what a Stingray costs?"

"About three hundred thousand," he said. "Give or take."

"Give or take if you're law enforcement, which we just established you ain't. Gonna cost you a half mil on the street, easy."

"That's what I figured. We don't have that much."

"That's all right. I don't have one to sell you."

"And yet here you are."

"Well, these are what you might call special circumstances."

"Special how?"

"An opportunity has presented itself to my family. Might be, we can help each other. You were in the military? Some kind of computer expert?"

"Something like that." Gibson glared at Swonger, who looked guiltily away.

"I don't have a Stingray, but I know who does. Owners aren't going to sell it to you, but you might be able to liberate it. If you're willing to cross the line."

"What line?"

"I need a little something; you need a little something. Your lucky day because so happens they're in the same place. Should be a cakewalk if you're as good as Swong says."

"What line?"

Deja slapped the side of the van three more times. After a moment, a second man stepped out of the far side of the clearing, also carrying a rifle. He moseyed toward them. Gibson wondered how many more guns Deja Noble had pointed at them.

"Starting to get hot," she said. "Let's go somewhere cooler and cut it up."

"What line?" Gibson asked for the third time.

He didn't like the answer.

CHAPTER TWENTY-SIX

12:57 a.m.

Three minutes until he crossed Deja Noble's line.

It had been a hectic thirty-six hours prepping her little job. That's what Deja called it anyway. Easy enough for her to say from the sidelines, but there was nothing little about the prison time they'd face if caught.

Gibson started the van and reached for his phone to send Swonger an angry text for running behind schedule. It had been tough to sell Deja Noble on his plan. She favored a far less subtle approach, but he'd made it clear that violence was not an option. No one would pay for his choices but him. Deja agreed and made it clear that any foul-ups would be on him, so a late start did not augur well.

As if on cue, Swonger roared to a stop in a black 2013 Mustang Boss 302 Laguna Seca, pelting the side of the van with gravel. The love Swonger had for that car was not wholly platonic, and he was already mourning her loss after tonight. The ex-con looked a full three inches taller in the driver's seat—truly a case of the car making the man.

Swonger grinned, a little too amped up for Gibson's liking, and gave a thumbs-up that meant Lea was in position and the alarms and cameras were down.

Most modern security was networked to off-site servers that stored camera footage and other data. A good system, in theory, but one that rendered it vulnerable to direct, simple hacks. Gibson had found the junction/relay box a quarter mile up the road. A drab, easy-to-overlook metal box. Tens of thousands like it spread along roadways throughout Virginia, millions across the country. Those boxes cobbled together the digital infrastructure of the country, yet few had security beyond a simple pin-tumbler lock. It had taken Swonger less than a minute to pick it.

Security tended to be a reactive profession, and basic principles predicted that there was only ever enough to prevent the last type of intrusion, not the next. Most businesses learned the hard way again and again and again. American banks, for example, had excellent security precisely because they had been targets ever since the first bank robbery in the 1860s. By contrast, the average Internet-facing business was vulnerable because they didn't think of themselves as potential victims. At least not until a hacker splashed their customers' credit-card data across the web. A state-police motor-pool depot in the middle of rural Virginia fell into the latter category. It, too, had a false sense of safety derived from its low profile. Since no one had ever thought to rob it before, it got by with a few fences, cameras, and rent-a-guards. It was sufficient because it always had been. Until suddenly it wasn't.

For the thirty-six hours, Gibson and Lea had toggled the network connection at the junction box off and on at irregular intervals for a few minutes at a time. Long enough for the outage to be reported but brief enough that by the time diagnostics were run remotely, the systems were up and running again. By now, it would have been logged as an ongoing issue, but a low-priority one since the outages were short and intermittent. No doubt, it lay near the bottom of the to-do list of some overworked technician. Tonight's outage would be interpreted as yet another inconvenient outage. It would be called in—*again*—but security wouldn't panic.

Gibson checked his phone. Time to go. He slipped off his latex gloves. He'd put them back on when he was through the security checkpoint. He dried his sweating palms on his shirt. He'd broken into a lot of places in his life but always from the relative safety of a computer. It was a whole other thing to drive up to the front gate, where an armed guard got a good look at your face. Unfortunately, though, this thing couldn't be done remotely. *Time to get your hands dirty,* he thought, and put those same hands carefully back on the steering wheel at ten and two. He would wipe the van down once they were inside the vehicle storage facility, but he didn't want to leave anything to chance. Thanks to his childhood indiscretions, the Virginia State Police were already intimately familiar with his fingerprints.

Swonger pulled out behind him, and together the two vehicles crested a small rise. Up ahead Gibson saw it: the Virginia State motor pool, which serviced and maintained police vehicles from across the state. Apart from the chain-link fence and barbed wire, it looked no different from your average auto dealer: At the center stood an operations building that was 90 percent maintenance garage but also housed offices and a waiting area. Hundreds of vehicles fanned out across the two-acre lot. Row after row of white-and-blue Dodge Chargers and Ford Interceptors—the backbone of the force. Mobile command posts. Heavily armored BearCats and other specialized SWAT vehicles. A fleet of pickup trucks. In addition, out of sight on the far side of the garage, the facility housed an impound lot for seized vehicles. Inside of which lay Deja Noble's prize and the price for her support. The line she needed Gibson to cross.

They rolled toward the front gate.

"Are you really going to do this?" he muttered to himself. How many laws was he about to break? *Turn around. Turn around now, call it off, go home.* But his inner voice sounded distant, no real conviction behind it, and he pushed his doubts away. He would do it for the judge. And if he didn't do it, then Deja Noble would, and then people would get hurt, or worse. On some level, he recognized it as hollow rationalization. Nicole's words came back to him from their fight at the house: *Were you always this person?* He wasn't as sure of the answer to that as he once had been.

They'd chosen the midnight to eight a.m. shift because of the skeleton crew. A team of two security guards rotated between the front gate and the main building every two hours. Vehicles came and went at odd hours, so the depot never technically closed. The overnight mechanic who handled off-hours intakes would be asleep on a cot in the garage.

Gibson pulled up at the gate and watched Bill Michaels rouse himself from his chair, find his clipboard and hat, and slide open the door to his hut. Having done his homework, Gibson knew quite a bit about the man. Michaels had graduated from Norfolk State with a degree in criminal justice. He was an ex-cop and a deacon at the First Baptist Church in Amherst, Virginia, and had recently purchased a used Sea Ray pleasure boat. Gibson knew Michaels's wife's and children's names. He had learned enough about Michaels that Deja Noble's plan to take the depot at gunpoint had been a nonstarter for him. There were lines he would cross and consequences he would bear, but putting Bill Michaels in harm's way wasn't ever going to be one of them.

Deja had sneeringly called him soft. Actually, that was the Sunday-night version of what she'd called him, but Gibson had insisted on no guns. The current plan, Gibson's plan—if it worked—would see them in and out with no one the wiser. The depot wouldn't even know a crime had been committed. That part had appealed to Deja, and she'd grudgingly agreed to let him do it his way, but with one parting caveat.

If you go in there unarmed, and they roll you up, that's on you. That's your time to do. Now, you start making out like we know each other to reduce your time, and I'll be sure to introduce you to some folks inside who really know me. You hear?

He heard.

Bill Michaels slid open the glass door of his hut and offered an amiable smile. He took Gibson's paperwork and scanned the name off the Robert Quine ID.

"Heya, Robert," he said, flipping through the yellow sheets of Gibson's counterfeit paperwork, making notes on his clipboard as he went.

Deja swore it would hold up, but Bill Michaels was no rent-a-guard with a GED. He was ex-Bureau of Criminal Investigation with numerous commendations and had cashed out on a disability retirement because of chronic back problems. He'd been a good investigator, and a bad back wouldn't have dulled his instincts. In truth, this was the riskiest moment of the whole job. The depot had only one layer of security with the cameras disabled. They should have no problem once Michaels waved them through.

"How's the back?" Gibson asked.

"Manageable. Started a yoga class."

"Yoga?"

"Yeah, it's helping, I think. Me and fifteen girls my daughter's age. They think I'm adorable." Michaels sighed. "I may be the class mascot. But you gotta do what you gotta do."

Michaels's brow furrowed, and he started flipping back and forth between pages. Gibson's heart climbed his throat as if it wanted to get a better look.

"Problem?"

"These forms are out of date. We switched over in January."

"Sorry."

Michaels shook him off. "You're in good company. Half the stations are still on last year's." Michaels crossed out a box and made a correction. "We sent three memos, but you know cops, never throw away a damn thing. Pain in my ass."

"I'll pass it along," Gibson said.

"Appreciate it. So, you dropping this old tub off?" Michaels slapped the side of the van.

"Yeah, it's way past overdue. Afraid it was going to die on me on the way over."

"Careful." Bill winked. "Still gotta make it over to intake. Aldo'll be pissed if you wake him up to get out the pickup to drag it the last hundred yards."

Gibson chuckled agreeably—good old Aldo—and put a finger to his lips. The guard tore off two pink copies and handed the yellow originals back to Gibson.

"Who's that?" Bill asked, pointing to Swonger's car with his pen in between checking boxes on his clipboard.

"My ride back."

"Good man. You better be buying his drinks. Sign here." Michaels held the clipboard up for him to initial. "You know where you're going?"

"Like I live here."

"I heard that," the guard said and took out his phone. "All right, last thing. I gotta take your picture."

"Really?" That wasn't standard.

"Damn security keeps crapping out, so I'm keeping a photo log of everyone coming in until they get around to fixing it."

Damn, damn, damn. Normally you could count on lowest-common-denominator thinking, but leave it to good old Bill Michaels to blow the curve. Gibson had shut off the security, and Michaels had found a sensible, outside-the-box solution. Man deserved another commendation. Unfortunately, Gibson couldn't see a way around it.

"Yeah, whatever," he managed through a forced smile.

Michaels stepped back, lined up his camera, and took a photograph. "All right, see you in a few."

"Few as I can manage."

The gate swung up, and Gibson pulled forward to wait for Swonger to be checked through. He slipped his gloves back on while watching in the rearview. He wasn't sold on Swonger's ability to play any part but his own, but Swonger talked his way through and the gate went up.

They were in.

If everything else went as smoothly, they'd be on their way in twenty minutes. They started toward the intake lot at the back of the garage, but once they passed beyond Bill Michaels's line of sight, they killed their lights and arced instead toward the impound lot. Based on Deja Noble's map, the first vehicle would be in spot 562. Gibson breathed a sigh of relief when he saw the 2013 black Mustang that was the identical twin of the one Swonger was driving.

Swonger got out of his car livid. "Guard took my picture."

"He took mine too. Now's not the time."

Swonger started to say something else.

"Not now. Stick to the plan."

That temporarily stifled Swonger, who moved to the driver's door and took out a power amplifier that cost all of eighty dollars. Ordinarily a car's keyless fob needed to be within a few feet to automatically unlock the doors. The amplifier extended that range to a hundred yards. Swonger turned it on, and the impounded Mustang's fob, locked somewhere inside the depot garage but suddenly in range, opened the Mustang's doors helpfully. Swonger got in and set to work on the ignition. The Mustang roared to life before Gibson could switch vehicles—Swonger was every bit as good as advertised. He backed it out, and Gibson parked the replacement Mustang in the spot, wiping it down before exiting. The impounded Mustang had been used in the commission of a crime. That much Gibson knew. He also knew that when trial time came and the VIN didn't match, the car would be rendered inadmissible as evidence, gutting the case. And that would put Deja Noble's crew in very good standing with someone it paid to be on good terms with. Deja hadn't shown a lot of interest in divulging much beyond that. For the sake of Gibson's conscience, it would have been nice if they'd committed only a simple moving violation, but that was wishful thinking.

The line kept receding into the distance.

"How are we looking?" Lea asked in his ear.

He looked back toward the front of the lot. It seemed quiet. Apart from the candid photography, everything was going as well as could be hoped.

"One down, one to go. How's it looking out there?"

"Oh, you know, just a girl on the side of a road at one in the morning, waiting for Ted Bundy to stop and offer roadside assistance."

"Get a selfie with him if he does."

"You're not funny."

Gibson got back in his van, and their motley caravan made its way to the second stop on their itinerary. The Mustang was for Deja; they'd come for a van. It was waiting in spot 354, exactly as Deja had promised. It seemed Virginia had quietly purchased a Stingray a few years back and mounted it in a black panel van. All had been peaches and cream until the *Richmond Times-Dispatch* had written an exposé that forced the governor to explain why the state police had been capturing the public's cell-phone data without a warrant. *A very good question,* Gibson thought, *and hard to answer.* The resulting scandal had seen both the chief of police and the Stingray put out to pasture. The chief had retired to Boca Raton while the Stingray quietly lived here in spot 354, undisturbed for eighteen months now. Swonger and he would trade their van for the van housing the Stingray, and with a little luck it might be years before anyone even noticed. Even when they did, the police might not be in any hurry to admit that they hadn't disposed of the Stingray as promised.

Police vans didn't come standard with keyless fobs, so Swonger had to jimmy the door the old-fashioned way. While he worked on the ignition, Gibson swapped the two vans' plates. They were identical in every other way except for the four antennae on the roof. He would roll the dice that Michaels wouldn't notice them in the dark. Gibson slid open the side door and climbed in back to make sure everything was there.

A built-in desk ran the length of the driver's side wall. Gibson sat at the flip-down desk chair and scanned the racks of communications gear until his eyes alighted upon the Stingray module itself. A good start, but fixed to the end of the desk, the docking station for a laptop sat empty. Gibson's heart nearly stopped. The Stingray module was no more than an expensive doorstop without the laptop that ran its software. Desperate to know he hadn't crossed the line for nothing, he rifled through the equipment drawers under the desk. He eventually found it and breathed a heavy sigh of relief when the laptop snapped neatly into place. They were in business.

The van's engine flared to life, and Swonger took that as a signal to start yapping about Bill Michaels and the photographs. Gibson stayed silent, hoping Swonger would talk himself out, but instead Swonger built himself a head of steam.

"We gotta do something," Swonger said.

"We're not done yet. Let's go."

"I'm serious," Swonger said but got back into the Mustang.

They pulled around to a door on the far side of the main building, out of sight of the front gate. The last item on Deja's to-do list. As long as they didn't dawdle, Michaels shouldn't be a problem.

The door was locked, but with security off, it was simple work for Swonger. He could open a lot more than cars.

"I need ten minutes," Gibson told him at the door.

"Need to deal with that guard," Swonger said.

Gibson didn't answer him. He didn't want to get dragged into an argument here. "Stay in the blind spot until I get back."

"We're not done talking about this."

"Fine, but later," Gibson said and slipped inside; Swonger relocked the door behind him.

Gibson toggled his radio. "Lea, turn everything back on."

"Done," she said in his ear.

He listened to the building, for the jackboots coming for him, but the only sound was the hum of the fluorescent lights overhead. With nowhere to hide anyway, Gibson made his way down the hallway like he belonged there. As long as he didn't act suspicious, there was always the chance that someone might buy that he was just looking for a restroom. Ideally, though, the mechanic would be asleep, and Bill Michaels's partner would be up front.

Deja's map of the interior, like everything she had provided, was top-notch, and Gibson found the office without incident. He let himself in, sat at the desk, and tapped the space bar to wake the sleeping desktop computer. It was an old machine and warmed up slowly, but eventually the screen flickered to life and a Virginia State Police log-in prompt greeted him.

Gibson didn't understand the point of having a log-in if you weren't going to encrypt the hard drive. Funny thing about computers, people were so concerned about hacks from the Internet that they didn't stop to consider how vulnerable their machines were to a hacker with physical access. Gibson checked the back of its tower. No USB port, but there was a CD drive. Fortunately, he'd brought one of each. He inserted his CD and powered the computer back up.

The CD contained a modified copy of the Linux operating system designed to break Microsoft encryption. So standard that Gibson had downloaded it from the Internet. So simple that if you could follow a series of simple prompts, you could break into an unencrypted Microsoft hard drive in about a minute. Back when he'd been sixteen, he'd looked down on such tactics as pathetic script kiddie hacks. Now all he cared about was efficiency, and if Microsoft couldn't be bothered to try a little harder, then neither could he.

It appeared the Virginia State Police were still operating on a hopelessly unpatched version of Windows XP. Not that it would have mattered. Windows stored passwords in a database called a "hive." Cute name. Gibson didn't know the reference, didn't care. He just knew what it did and how to defeat it. When active, the hive had layers of security, and its passwords were encrypted. But only when it was on. When it was dormant, as it was now, so was its security, rendering it defenseless.

Using the Linux boot disk, Gibson dug down to the passwords, which were still encrypted; however, for reasons that escaped him, usernames were not. The machine had three usernames: Ramsey.T, Administrator, and Guest. He chose Administrator because his tampering wouldn't be noticed until an administrator attempted to log in, and judging by how out-of-date this machine was, that could be years from now. He deleted its encrypted password and left it blank. When Gibson let the computer restart normally, the computer would trust that the new password was correct, because its operating system trusted the hive natively. The computer didn't have the ability to question why one password wasn't encrypted. What the hive said went.

Gibson removed the CD and rebooted the computer. The prompt reappeared. Beneath it, a banner read "Local Mode/Cached Copy."

Perfect. The entire operation took fifty-seven seconds.

As planned, the constant disruption of Internet access to and from the depot had forced the central servers to adjust. Normally, changes to files on this computer would be made automatically to the state DMV servers. However, the state servers required a second set of log-in credentials. Credentials that Gibson didn't have and didn't have time to acquire. But in local mode, he could make changes to files on the depot's local database, and because the network was in "local mode," they would be automatically uploaded to the DMV, overwriting whatever data was stored there. It would do his job for him.

Gibson typed in the case number Deja had given him.

The Mustang belonged to one Borya Dvoskin, a twenty-year-old Russian national who had been pulled over in Virginia Beach. A search of the vehicle had yielded drugs, guns, and $57,000 in cash. His trial was scheduled for the end of the month. Reading Dvoskin's sheet didn't make Gibson jump for joy, but it could have been a lot worse. Thinking about Judge Birk and Charles Merrick while entering Deja's changes to the arrest report made it a little easier. The changes were nothing major, just enough that nothing matched, creating a pattern of inconsistency that a good defense attorney would spin into gold.

Thanks to him, Borya Dvoskin would be back running drugs in a few weeks. That felt good to know. What would Nicole have to say about that? Gibson logged off and radioed Lea to kill the network again. He gave the room a once-over to be sure he'd left nothing behind, and exited the building a little bit less of a man than when he'd entered.

Back outside, Swonger leapt angrily off the hood of the Mustang. He'd had time to work himself up and wanted to know what they were going to do about Bill Michaels. Gibson told him to drop it.

"I'm not going back to prison because some old bastard took my picture."

"Keep your voice down," Gibson said, thinking back to their near-disastrous argument outside Slaski's house. They would go down in the annals of dumb criminals if they got arrested because of a yelling match.

"Deja ain't going to like it. She'll want something done."

Deja hadn't impressed Gibson with her delicate touch so far, and he didn't care to think about her solution to the Bill Michaels situation. Gibson couldn't have that on his conscience, although he doubted Swonger would have any such qualms. Instead, he appealed to what he knew Swonger feared most.

"What do you think Deja will do? Kill the guard and risk being caught? No, she kills the guy and frames *you* for it. You ready to go down for murder one?"

Swonger hesitated, and Gibson took the opportunity to argue that if they left now, no one would know a crime had been committed. When it was eventually discovered, Michaels wouldn't even connect them to it. They just had to leave the way they'd planned.

Swonger was shaking his head. "Can't do it." He drew his .45 from the back of his pants.

"I said no guns."

"You also said the cameras would be out."

"They are out."

"We take it from him now."

"Swonger, *think*."

But Swonger had about thought himself out. The .45 came up level with Gibson's heart, safety off, finger on the trigger.

"We take it from him now."

Gibson moved without hesitation. Sidestep, hands moving together from opposite sides, one around Swonger's wrist, the other coming across the pistol itself, snapping it out of his stunned hand. In one smooth motion, it was pointed at Swonger's eye. Gibson had learned that disarm in the Marines, but was a little surprised at how flawlessly he'd executed it. Now, if the .45 had still had a firing pin, he doubted his hands would have been anywhere near as steady. But Swonger didn't know that, and Gibson was happy to leave him in awe.

Swonger's hands went up. "Hey, man, I'm sorry. It's just . . . you know . . . I can't go back inside."

"I feel like we're on kind of a steep learning curve here, you and me."

"I just lost my head."

Gibson held the gun on Swonger a moment longer, letting Swonger contemplate what options he might be considering. He dropped the gun to his side. "Get in the car. We're leaving."

"Cool. It's cool."

"And listen to me good. Not one word at the salvage yard about this, or I walk. I'm done with this whole mess, and good luck figuring out how to work a Stingray."

"Jesus, all right, I get it."

At the gate, Gibson slowed to a halt. Michaels looked at the van with confusion. "Forget something?"

"You're never going to believe this."

"What?" Michaels asked, ready not to believe it.

"I brought the wrong van."

Now Michaels looked very confused.

"We have three of these. One of them needs servicing, but they gave me the wrong one. I just wasted half the night driving over here in the wrong van."

Michaels gave him a long look and burst out laughing. "I'm sorry, man. That's a raw deal."

Gibson pretended to see the humor in it too.

"I guess I'll see you tomorrow night."

Michaels shook his head. "Not me. Tomorrow's my day off."

Gibson knew that, of course, but wanted to close the narrative loop in Michaels's mind. Didn't want him wondering later why that guy had never brought the right van back.

"Ah, well, then. Take it easy."

"You too," Michaels replied as his eyes started to drift to the top of the van.

"Hey. Want a suggestion about your yoga situation?"

Michaels looked back at him.

"They have videos on YouTube. You can just do them in the privacy of your living room."

Michaels nodded thoughtfully. "You know, I might just do that."

CHAPTER TWENTY-SEVEN

Despite the mission going like clockwork, it had still been the longest thirty minutes of Lea's life. She'd sat with her back against the junction box in the dark and listened for the sound of sirens—the inevitable unraveling of Gibson Vaughn's plan. So when the van and Mustang finally pulled up, she felt a giddy relief that shot through her like whiskey in December.

She greeted Gibson and Swonger excitedly but got only grunts in return. They started the security system and relocked the junction box, neither one talking, which she wrote off as coming down off an adrenaline high. Some men needed to go off alone to process things, so she left them to their moody silence, although she didn't know what they had to be so gloomy about—Gibson's plan had worked. It was unbelievable. While she hadn't been any great fan of Deja Noble's full-frontal assault, Gibson's proposal had sounded like wishful thinking. But she'd be damned if he hadn't sweet-talked his way onto police property and driven away with a half million in high-tech equipment. Ironically, she had never stolen anything in her life. Now, here she was, an accomplice in a heist. Was that the right word for it? *Heist.* She liked the sound of it—a daring heist. She grinned to herself. It was a rush unlike anything she'd ever experienced.

Of the two vehicles, the Mustang was by far the nicer ride, but she didn't entirely trust Swonger behind the wheel of the muscle car. As if to prove her point, Swonger peeled out as she got in the passenger seat of the van. Thankfully, Gibson made no effort to keep up. A bored cop might wonder why a van and Mustang were caravanning across Virginia in the wee hours of the night. The two vehicles would stay in visual contact but give each other a safe cushion.

"You think he'll cry?" she asked.

"What?"

"When we destroy that car."

Nothing. Not even a smile.

"Were there any problems?"

He shook his head, a million miles away.

"So no snags?" Still unconvinced.

"What?" he asked, a faint trace of annoyance in his voice. "No, we got it." He hitched a thumb toward the back of the van as if she'd lost the power of sight.

She looked in back, but it didn't look like much. Hard to believe it might be the answer to their problems, but she would give Gibson the chance to prove it. He'd earned it. If she were honest, what she'd read about her new partner online hadn't exactly bolstered her confidence, but tonight had earned him some leeway in her book. He'd talked a big game, but he'd also delivered, so she would go another round with him.

When they reached Dette's Auto Wrecks, Swonger was waiting for them, Mustang idling outside the salvage yard's gate.

"Wasn't going in there alone. Spooky as hell," Swonger said.

Lea couldn't say she blamed him. Beyond the gate, the junkyard was pitch-black. They drove in cautiously, headlights casting medieval shadows off canyons of rusted cars. A vast wasteland of amputated vehicles stretched out of sight on both sides—trunks and hoods all open, scavenged for doors, hubcaps, windshields; carcasses picked over by crows. As they approached the main office, a pair of Belgian Malinois appeared from the shadows and trotted alongside. Powerful-looking dogs with black muzzles that accentuated curved ivory teeth. Gibson pulled up behind the Mustang and killed the engine but left his head-lights on. The dogs, positioned between the office and the vehicles, watched them speculatively. Not hostile but not nearly welcoming enough for Lea to open her door. A whistle split the night, and the dogs retreated under the covered porch of the office.

"You can come out now," a woman's voice called. And when they didn't move fast enough for the voice's liking: "Well, come on, now. I got things to do."

Floodlights lit up the junkyard, and Lea's hand went up to shade her eyes. Up on the porch sat an older African American woman, matri-archal and stern, with stately gray-white dreadlocks that swirled above her head like a nest of snakes. She set down an e-reader, took off her glasses, and rubbed her eyes. Nearby, a shotgun and a sledgehammer leaned side by side against the doorframe. The dogs flanked her, one by each knee, and as the three visitors approached the porch, the animals tensed and showed their teeth. The woman touched each dog's head gently, and they crouched, obedient but alert.

"They don't mean nothing by it," she said. "Not used to company this late is all."

Lea didn't entirely believe that and lingered at the bottom of the stairs, feeling like a rib eye hanging off the edge of a kitchen counter.

The woman looked them over. "The name is Claudette Noble. This is my place. You must be Swonger," she said as if she'd just found some-thing stuck to the bottom of her shoe.

"That's right."

He stepped forward, but Claudette's attention had moved to Lea, ignoring Gibson altogether. "Come up here, girl. Dogs won't bother you 'less I tell them. This here the Mustang?"

"Yes," Swonger said.

"Hush, boy, no one's talking at you," Claudette snapped.

Lea took a step up. "It is, yes."

"Look me in the eye and tell me these boys didn't bring back the same Mustang, thinking they'd put one by on old Claudette?"

"No, this is the car," Lea said, glancing over at Gibson and Swonger for confirmation. Both men chimed in that it was.

"Well, all right, give me your arm and let's go take a look. Just us girls. What do you say?"

Lea helped her up, wincing under Claudette's iron grip, uncertain whether she was helper or hostage. Certainly, the old woman needed no help standing or walking. Claudette gestured at Swonger and Gibson to stay put, and the dogs came forward to the edge of the porch and sat on their haunches.

Claudette opened the Mustang's driver's door to read the VIN off the frame. Never loosening her grip on Lea's arm, the old woman produced a knife—Lea couldn't say from where—and pried at the VIN, testing to see whether it had been tampered with. Satisfied, Claudette shut the door; the knife disappeared from her hand, and she took Lea back up to the porch.

"Good. Looks good. Everything smooth, I trust?"

"Like clockwork," Lea said.

A look passed between Gibson and Swonger that she couldn't interpret. Swonger looked away while Gibson nodded confirmation. It gave Lea a bad feeling, and the junkyard fell silent in solemn agreement.

The old woman sat back down and looked them over. "All right, then," she said finally. "On your way. I'll pass it along."

They mumbled a good-bye and backed away. Halfway back to the van, the office door opened. "A word," Deja Noble said and stepped out onto the porch.

Lea didn't know the kind of pistol, but it looked enormous and lethal in Deja's small hand.

"Aunt?" Deja said, the muzzle tapping her thigh inquisitively.

"Niece," Claudette replied. "There a problem?"

"Yeah, there's a problem. Swong, my aunt asked you a question, but she didn't hear an answer. Asked if everything went smooth. Now what've you got to say to her?"

Swonger's mouth started to open.

"It went fine," Gibson cut in.

Deja looked back and forth between the two men. "That was good. His mouth opened, your voice came out. Magic." Deja mimed a shiver of excitement. "How'd you all do that? Let me try another. Swonger, where's Terry at?"

Swonger looked sick to his stomach. "Out there."

"That's good. And what's he doing out there?"

"Got a rifle."

"Where's it pointed?"

"Come on, we really gotta—"

"Where's it pointed?" Deja asked again, patiently.

"My head," Swonger moaned.

"Got it in one. Now go ahead and throw down your piece like before. Then we can get back to the question at hand."

"I ain't—"

"We didn't bring guns," Gibson interjected. "Wasn't part of the plan."

Deja considered this, and Swonger, with interest. She made a twirling gesture with her finger for Swonger to lift his shirt and do a three-sixty. When he was done, Deja shook her head.

"Not getting the whole pacifist thing, but that's you all's call. Now, Swonger. My aunt asked you a question, and all of us up here want to hear your answer. Not his. Not hers. Just yours. Auntie?"

"Did things go smooth?" Claudette repeated her question.

Swonger didn't answer but glanced in Gibson's direction again.

"Quit looking at him," Deja said.

"Nah, it's all good," Swonger said. "Went like he said."

"We got the Mustang you needed. What's the problem?" Gibson demanded. "We held up our end."

Deja cast her eyes on Lea. "That your story too?"

Lea nodded, her bad feeling metastasizing. She was on the hook for something but had no idea what. It didn't give her a lot of options.

Deja studied them all with her relentless gaze. "Truck. What do you think?"

A towering man came out of the office, stooping as he passed through the door. When he stood upright again, his head grazed the porch roof. He was the largest human that Lea had ever seen. Massive biceps and forearms strained the sleeves of his black button-down. Despite his size, he moved with a balletic grace that few large men possessed. His physique was perfectly proportioned apart from his head, slightly too small for his body, which only accentuated his otherworldliness.

Gibson looked astonished.

Swonger looked like the second coming himself had just ducked out onto the porch. "Hey, Truck."

"What do you think?" Deja asked.

Truck shook his head.

"Yeah, me too. Frustrating. Know what I mean?"

Truck nodded in solemn agreement.

"I understand them two lying," she said. "They don't know us. What are we to them? But my heart's broken over Swonger here. After all you did for him. And he's lying to us."

Deja looked disappointed by this troubling development. Disappointed in life. Disappointed in humanity. Lea didn't get the sense that this was a family that dealt with disappointment well. Her elation at pulling off the job was gone, replaced by the dry-mouthed certainty that she would not leave this junkyard. If this went bad, it was going to go bad their way. Like anyone, she'd tossed around the word "afraid" all her life. Now she understood what it was to be afraid. Afraid that these were the last faces she'd see.

"Want me to ask him?" Truck asked, speaking at last, his voice surprisingly high and sweet for such a large man.

"Would you? I can't seem to get through to him."

Truck picked up the sledgehammer and hefted it lightly over his shoulder. It looked like a toy in his fist. He started down the stairs. "Come here, Swong."

Swonger turned the white of a fried egg. "Hey, dog. Hey. Come on." The nonsensical words of a man with no defense save hope for a mercy that wasn't coming.

"Don't make me come over there."

"Please," Swonger said quietly, all masculine posturing forgotten. He fell to his knees.

"The guard at the front gate took our pictures," Gibson said loudly.

Everyone stopped at that and looked at him. He said it again. Truck looked back at his sister.

"I thought you boys took security down," Deja said.

"We did. That's why he took the pictures himself. On his phone."

"That's it?"

"That's it."

Whatever internal lie detector Deja thought she possessed accepted that answer. "Well, hell, that ain't even a thing. Why are you all making me sweat? Swong, you can't go appealing to my baser instincts this way." Deja said it like this had all just been a misunderstanding over nothing.

Swonger smiled weakly and apologized. Lea took a deep breath and realized she'd been holding it.

"Which one was it?" Deja asked. "We'll take care of it."

"No," Gibson said, punching a finger in Swonger's direction. "Don't you say a word."

"You know," Deja said, "for a fella that's unarmed, you're giving a lot of orders."

"It doesn't matter who it was."

"Does matter if those pictures lead to you, because you lead to my family here. That guard is a loose end. What did I tell you? You should've gone in hard, with masks."

Gibson protested, and Deja shouted him down. Lea listened to them argue back and forth, voices rising, echoing across the junkyard, Gibson becoming more and more animated.

Again, Deja shut him down. "Both you boys got records," she said. "They find you, they find us. Can't have that. Told you that up front. So now this thing needs tying off."

"Not happening."

"Really not going to tell me, are you?"

"Can't do it."

"Even if Truck beats old Swong to death with that sledgehammer? Even then?"

Lea prayed that was a rhetorical question. At some point, the shotgun had made its way into Claudette's hands. Underscoring the importance of every choice made, every word uttered from here on out. The only thing she knew for certain—she wasn't about to let Gibson Vaughn act out whatever morality play he planned on staging.

"You don't get it," Deja told Gibson. "We talking about risk. It ain't worth the risk to me."

"What would be?" Lea said.

Everyone turned to look at her.

"What would what be?" Deja asked.

"What would make it worth the risk?"

"To leave that guard alone? What you got?"

"Ten percent of my end."

"Ten percent of what end?"

Lea hesitated, unsure how to answer since she didn't know how much there actually was to offer. She guessed at a number. "A million."

Deja Noble came down the stairs to search Lea's eyes. "What are you all into?"

"What do you think the van's for?" Gibson asked.

"What's the job?" Deja clarified.

"This isn't an interview. We're not hiring," Lea said.

Deja froze and then burst out laughing. "Oh, shit," she said. "Listen to this bitch here. Not hiring, she says."

"Ten percent."

"You pay us a hundred thousand to leave that guard alone?"

Lea nodded. "As Gibson said, we got away clean. So as long as we don't raise further suspicion, the guard will delete the pictures once security is back up and running and things get back to normal. But as your partner, I can see your concern and that you are assuming a measure of risk here. I think it's only fair to compensate you for managing that risk on my behalf. Insurance, if you will."

"If I will?" Deja was smiling and shaking her head in amused disbelief. "Getting all MBA up in here. All right, well allow me to counter—we, the undersigned, do accept your offer of one hundred thousand, but not contingent on the success of the heretofore mentioned 'job.' You owe now. One hundred thousand, regardless. Do you stipulate?"

"We go free and the guard doesn't get hurt?"

Deja glanced to her brother, who pursed his lips and arched an eyebrow.

"Yeah, I believe that buys you a ticket on my ride."

CHAPTER TWENTY-EIGHT

Margo lived in a thumbprint of a house on the outskirts of Niobe. She hadn't seemed especially happy to see them, but she agreed to stash the van in her two-port garage, which was almost as large as the house itself. Gibson knew she and Lea had ended their business partnership after the incident at Slaski's house, but the two women embraced in the driveway, and a relieved Margo slapped Lea's back before letting her go. Gibson backed the van into the garage. He didn't expect a hug.

For the most part, it looked like an ordinary panel van; however, four small antennae arrayed across its roof might draw unwanted attention. Swonger had said he might have a solution and, after measuring the roof of the van, left and hadn't been back all day. Having them both out of his hair suited Gibson fine; he had work to do, and the show-down with the Nobles had left everyone rattled. The delicate ecosystem of their alliance had taken a serious hit, and some time apart would do them all good. Hopefully when they reconvened, Lea and Swonger would have figured out that last night was a net win. The proof of which was parked right here in Margo's garage.

Margo stuck her head in to say she was going to work. She looked around at the mess he was making.

"Y'all make sure you red up after you're done."

Not knowing what "red up" meant, he gave her a silent okay sign without breaking away from the screen. Margo lingered by the door until he removed his earbuds and looked her way.

"Was it worth it?" she asked.

"What?"

"Almost getting killed."

"What do you want me to say?"

"That you know if it is or not."

He shrugged, put in his earbuds, and turned away. He didn't have time for bartender philosophy. His thoughts were already elsewhere. He got this way when deep in a project, zoning out for eighteen-hour stretches while the real world passed by out of focus. He had never seen a Stingray, and the Virginia State Police hadn't been considerate enough to leave a user's manual, so Gibson was learning how it worked by trial and error. Charles Merrick walked out of prison in eleven days, so it needed to be more trial and less error.

He couldn't say for certain how long it was before the knocking at the side door made its way down to his conscious brain. He threw open the door with an apology, expecting Swonger. Instead, it was a trim Asian man with a doughy face and short-cropped hair, uniformly black apart from a small, perfect shock-white circle above his temple. He wore blue jeans and wading boots; a frayed fishing vest with a dozen densely packed pockets hung heavily over a green plaid shirt. Gibson recognized him from the hotel. They'd passed in the hall a few times, but the fisherman smiled at Gibson like they were the oldest of friends.

"Mr. Vaughn," he said in a clipped, inflectionless cadence. "Have I come at a bad time?"

Mr. Vaughn, not Mr. Quine. That did not bode well.

"I'm sorry, who are you?"

"A friend. Perhaps an ally. May I come in?"

Gibson couldn't place the accent, but if he had to guess, it would be somewhere in the mid-Atlantic. Or maybe midwestern? The man's accent kept drifting.

"I'll come out," Gibson said, conscious of the half million in stolen equipment behind him.

The man put a gentle hand on his chest. "Better that I come in. Trust me, I've seen a Stingray before."

The mention of the Stingray knocked Gibson sideways. This man knew his name and his business here in Niobe. His immediate reaction was fear, anger fast on its heels, panicky questions piling up on his tongue. But he also felt admiration for the man's ploy—a threat painted as reassurance and framed with a smile. Gibson knew the role he was expected to play here and held his tongue, unwilling to play defensive or nervous. Instead, he stepped aside and invited the fisherman inside.

"If I'd known you were coming, I'd have put out cookies."

The fisherman shook his head. "No. You're overdoing it. Less is more."

"Fine, why don't you just feed me my lines?"

"May I?" The fisherman indicated the van.

"Be my guest," Gibson said with a tired wave of his hand and watched him poke around in the back of the van. The man wasn't law enforcement; beyond that Gibson had no idea.

"I admired your work at the police yard. It was well executed."

"Are you with Deja?" Gibson asked and regretted it immediately. It was a stupid question that did nothing but give information away cheaply. He'd get none in exchange.

The fisherman winced in mock sympathy at Gibson's slip. "I'd like to offer my help."

"You want to help me? How?"

"You have a Stingray—that's good—but there are more cell phones in Niobe Prison than you've been led to believe. Do you know when Charles Merrick uses his? Because otherwise, think about the time and effort it will take to sort through all the background noise to pinpoint

Merrick's number. A week? Two? Does your schedule have that kind of leeway? Charles Merrick will be released in eleven days."

Gibson knew it didn't and had been fretting over this exact issue. "What are you offering?"

"The day and time."

"Just like that? That's a generous offer, but I already have a lot of partners. What exactly do you want in return?"

"Only your success, Mr. Vaughn."

"Again, very generous. What's your interest in all this?"

"That is between Charles Merrick and myself."

Call him a cynic, but Gibson didn't believe in selfless acts, and he didn't like not knowing the agenda behind this generosity. What did Merrick have that was more valuable to this man than money?

"Who are you?" Gibson asked.

"I'm the gift horse," the fisherman said. "Let's leave my mouth out of it, yes?"

"Fair enough."

"Do you want my help or not?"

"And if I say no?"

Knowing when to expect Merrick's call would be a huge corner to cut, saving them at least a week. Gibson didn't trust that this man had a generous bone in his body, and he didn't like how much the fisherman knew about him or how little he knew about his new patron. It did underscore how unpredictable Niobe had become. They needed to get out of town as soon as possible.

"You're not going to say no."

Gibson knew that to be true. "When?"

"How soon will you be operational?"

"I need a couple of days to really master the software. It's not overly complex, but I'm not ready to run it in the field yet."

"That is unfortunate, because the next opportunity will be tomorrow. After that, Merrick's schedule is murky."

Gibson stared over at the Stingray and did some mental calculations. "Morning or afternoon?"

"Afternoon. Between two and four. Can you be ready?"

It would be cutting things close, very close, but it was feasible. It had to be done, so it would be done. Although it meant letting certain basics, such as eating and sleeping, go by the wayside.

"Then I won't delay you any further. If I can be of any further assistance, hang a 'Do Not Disturb' sign on room 103."

The door had hardly closed when there came a second knock at the door. Gibson expected the fisherman had forgotten something, but it was Lea with a paper sack of burgers and fries. His stomach rumbled at the sight of it. He hoped she was just dropping it off—he had no time for social calls—but she seemed intent on staying. They sat on the open back of the van and ate while he talked her through his progress.

"I should be ready to go by tomorrow, so I think we're in good shape," he said.

"I saw Jimmy Temple drinking at the bar in the Toproll."

"So?"

"Jimmy never comes in. Never. No one went anywhere near him, like he was contagious. Looked like he'd stopped eating. Suit didn't fit. Lost ten, maybe twenty pounds," Lea said. "I asked him, was he okay. He said they just keep checking in. He didn't sound happy about it either. He knows something bad is coming down. The whole town does."

"And they're right."

"I think someone got to the sheriff. Margo said he's been in and out of the hotel the last few days. It's getting tense out there."

"I know, Lea. I know. What's your point?"

"Last night can't happen again," she said. "I don't know what kind of deal you have with Swonger, but don't play hero with my life again. You want me to back you again, don't leave me in the dark like that. Does my hundred thousand buy me at least that much?"

"Is that why you did it?"

"Does it?"

"It won't happen again."

She studied his face, a picture of sincerity. "All right, then. I'll leave you to it."

After Lea left, he realized it hadn't even occurred to him to tell her about the fisherman.

The third knock didn't come for another few hours—this time it really was Swonger. Gibson opened the door for him and went back to work. Neither man spoke. Swonger dragged a Thule roof box into the garage and laid it out on the floor. He worked diligently on his solution to the antennae problem, cutting four slots into the roof box that the antennae would fit inside. Gibson helped secure it to the roof, and then the two men stood back and admired it. The only question it might raise was why a van would need rooftop storage; otherwise it worked well. Gibson was impressed.

"Nice work." He held out the .45 to Swonger.

"Thanks."

Gibson put a hand in his back pocket and touched the firing pin and stop. "I have another job for you."

"Yeah?" Swonger sounded surprised, maybe even a little hopeful. His default cockiness hadn't returned since Truck Noble had almost used him as a croquet ball. Gibson didn't mind that at all.

"You seen the fisherman staying at the hotel?" Gibson asked.

"Asian dude? Yeah, once or twice."

"I need to know how he's spending his days."

"You mean besides fishing?"

"Yeah," Gibson snapped back. "Besides fishing."

CHAPTER TWENTY-NINE

While a Stingray could mimic a cell tower, it wasn't one. So once a phone connected, it would take only a few seconds for the phone to realize it couldn't make contact with its service provider, disconnect, and move on to the next strongest signal. But that was all the time it took for the Stingray to capture a phone number. It was an outstanding if highly controversial law-enforcement tool for tracking down a suspect's phone. In earlier generations, that was as far as it went. Police hadn't been able to listen in on conversations, because cell-phone data was encrypted at the source and could be decrypted only by the intended recipient.

That was no longer an issue.

With FishHawk and Porpoise, the latest generations of Stingray software, during the brief connection, the Stingray would record a phone's unique encryption key. Later, when that phone connected to a real cell tower and placed a call, the Stingray could listen in to calls or read outgoing texts. After the complications at the junkyard, Gibson hoped that capturing Merrick's cell-phone number would be exactly that simple. Or at the very least, that no one would point a gun at them. That would be nice. He hadn't had nearly enough sleep for more of that.

The cell tower nearest the prison sat on a hillside at the northern edge of town. The prison lay at the outer edge of its effective range, accounting for the generally piss-poor reception. The clearing that Gibson and Lea had scoped out on their hike was only a quarter mile from the prison, ensuring that the Stingray's signal would be by far the more powerful. Cell phones always hunted for the strongest signal as a way to conserve battery life, so every phone at the prison would jump at the Stingray as soon as it came online.

Gibson managed to get them set up in the clearing in plenty of time for the fisherman's window of opportunity in the afternoon. That allowed him to practice using the Stingray's software to capture calls. Really, it was a one-person job, but trust was at a premium since the junkyard, and Lea had insisted on spectating. Since he still had not told Lea about the visit from the fisherman, Gibson went through the charade of Parker shadowing Merrick to alert them if Merrick went anywhere near the library to make a call.

"Where's Swonger anyway?" Lea asked.

Swonger had made himself scarce since Gibson had tasked him with keeping tabs on the fisherman.

"Running errands."

"Is he all right? Hasn't seemed himself."

"I couldn't tell you."

Lea shook her head. "What's your deal? You two friends?"

Gibson realized that Lea had no idea of the nature of his relationship with Swonger.

"I wouldn't go that far."

"How long have you known him?"

"Including today? Three weeks."

"That's it? Would have gotten that one wrong."

"How's that?"

"You act like brothers."

"Brothers? Are you incredibly high right now?"

"Oh, come on. The guy worships you."

"Now I know you're high."

"He'd wear a Gibson Vaughn mask on Halloween if they sold them."

"Is that why he keeps pulling a gun on me?"

"Keeps? That wasn't the first time?" Lea pondered that tidbit. "Well, sometimes bad attention is better than no attention at all. Trust me. Maybe pointing a gun at you is the only way he knows to get it."

"Well, it's not working."

Swonger's Scion pulled into the clearing alongside the van, which brought a welcome end to the conversation and allowed Gibson to get back to work.

A few minutes after three, Parker texted that Merrick was on his way to the library. Lea let out a scream, and Swonger's feet came pounding back to the van. There was general high-fiving while Gibson pretended to be surprised that they'd gotten lucky on their first day. He powered on the Stingray and watched numbers scroll down the laptop as phones within range began connecting. The fisherman hadn't been wrong—close to five hundred phones attempted to connect within the first sixty seconds. Not all could be from the prison, of course, but the Stingray couldn't differentiate, so Gibson started by eliminating all the numbers that had connected so far, narrowing his search parameters to more easily spot Merrick when he inserted his SIM card into the guard's phone.

"He's in the library now," Lea relayed from her phone.

They crowded around the screen. Over the next few minutes, seventy-two new phone numbers connected and then disconnected from the Stingray. On a second window, Gibson watched to see if any of them made calls. One did to a West Virginia number, which was a very good sign. It was a text:

```
5616.kl B10K@MKT;4398.kl B50K@MKT;3675.
kl S150K@LMT160;2212.kl B100K@MKT;4536.
kl B200K@MKT;2301.kl S75K@MKT;1320.kl
H100K;1102 H250K;2424.kl H50K;6676.kl
H75K;1506.kl H210K
```

It went on and on like that, line after line, fifty-six texts in all. The Stingray enabled them to read only Merrick's outgoing texts, so any replies were lost.

"What is that? Some kind of code?" Swonger said.

"No," Lea said with a grin. "It's stock notation—'.kl' means he's trading on the Bursa Malaysia. Those are buy and sell orders. The four numbers is the stock. *B* is buy. *S* is sell. Not sure about *H*. *MKT* is market price; *LMT* is a limit order. Ten thousand shares at the market price. And so on."

"Wait," Gibson said, the hairs standing up on the back of his neck. "So he's selling one hundred fifty thousand shares of whatever *LB* is at a hundred sixty dollars a share? How much is that?"

"Twenty-four million," Lea said quickly.

"Holy shit," Gibson said. "How much money does he have?"

"If it's dollars," Lea cautioned.

"Been saving his pennies like a boss," Swonger said in an awed whisper.

"Why Malaysia?" Gibson asked.

"Malaysia went dark," Lea explained. "It doesn't share financial information with the United States. Perfect for someone who needs to invest without our government interfering."

"Gangster," Swonger said.

"Can you send all that to me?" Lea asked. "I want to figure something out."

Gibson nodded as Merrick sent a final text:

```
Confirmed. This will be our final
communication prior to my release. When
I reach secure location, I'll send for
you. Sit tight but be ready. Stick to
the plan. You've done well.
```

And that was it. Merrick's number vanished from the Stingray's list. They all sat back in relief and disbelief.

"Is that it?" Swonger asked. "We've got it?"

Gibson nodded that they did. The question was what to do with it.

"West Virginia ain't Texas, but it ain't your backyard either."

Swonger had been arguing about the relative size of West Virginia for a while now. After their success at the prison, they'd returned to Lea's apartment above the Toproll, where a debate raged about what to do now. All three had strong opinions about next steps, and with no one willing to roll over, they were at the stage of an argument where they simply reiterated earlier points at ever-increasing volume. This is how her parents had always fought, neither budging an inch, and it made Lea uncomfortable to be a part of it. She looked over the table of empty beer bottles that pointed to the growing futility of continued discussion.

In the bathroom, she splashed water on her face. This was getting them nowhere.

It boiled down to this: Charles Merrick's contact used a West Virginia cell phone, but that didn't mean he was in West Virginia. The phone could be in Barcelona for all any of them knew. But why get a West Virginia cell phone if you weren't local? And hadn't the last text said to "sit tight"? Didn't that suggest that whoever it was had to be close? Most likely, but it might also mean they were meeting somewhere else—like Barcelona. And so the debate raged on regarding whether or not to call the number. Gibson agreed it might be possible to social-engineer the person at the other end, perhaps get them to give them something that would narrow their search. But he also cautioned it could go the other way, that they could spook their targets and cause them to shut down for good. They'd get only one shot at it.

Swonger ran out of steam, which meant it was Gibson's turn again. For what seemed like the thousandth time, he argued that the safest solution was to play the odds that the phone was in state, create a grid map, and comb West Virginia with the Stingray until it registered a hit for the phone number that Merrick had texted. Then the Stingray could triangulate the signal and lead them to its owner. But that led Swonger back to his argument about the relative size of West Virginia.

"Dog, there are seventy thousand miles of road in West Virginia." Swonger had Googled that figure and felt committed to his research. "If it's even *in* West Virginia."

Lea listened to them bicker from the bathroom. A thought occurred to her.

"Will the Stingray work if the target phone is off?" she called into the other room. She heard silence in return and went out to find Swonger staring at Gibson expectantly.

"Does it?" she asked.

"No," Gibson said. "The phone would need to be on."

"Well, what if whoever it is keeps the phone off except when Merrick is scheduled to make contact?"

Gibson made a face that said it hadn't occurred to him.

"So shouldn't we make sure it's on? It's a pretty state, but we have better things to do than sightsee for the nine days. Don't you think?"

Gibson nodded.

"See?" Swonger said as though he'd won the argument. "That's what I was saying."

Once Gibson was on board, she watched him snap into action. He laid out a pretense for the call and started crafting a script to get something useful out of whoever was at the other end of the phone. Again she was impressed at how his mind worked.

"Is it a man or a woman?" Gibson wondered aloud.

"A man," Lea said without hesitation.

"Why?"

"Women at Merrick Capital only answered the phones. And after the divorce, I don't think trusting women is high on his list."

Gibson smiled at her.

"What?" she asked.

"You'll make the call. You used to act, didn't you?"

"Yeah, but why me? Isn't this what you do?"

"If it's someone Merrick trusts, then it's someone who thinks like him. Someone who doesn't take women seriously. All you have to do is play the sweet girl. Lull them. Can you do sweet?"

She held up her middle finger.

"Perfect. You're a natural."

Together, they honed Gibson's script until Lea felt comfortable with it. Then he had her practice with him until she knew it backward and forward.

"I'm ready."

Gibson checked the time.

"No, too soon. These guys always call at dinnertime."

They got something to eat themselves and reconvened in Lea's apartment at seven o'clock. When she was ready, Gibson played a recording of the background noise of a busy call center. The burbling sound of ringing phones and dozens of voices filled her apartment. She dialed the number. It rang six times and went to voice mail—a mechanical voice recited the number and gave instructions for leaving a message. She hung up, and Gibson killed the soundtrack.

"Should I call back?"

"Wait an hour. We don't want to be too eager."

The time passed in silence, heavy like they were waiting for news on a loved one in surgery. Swonger turned on the TV and found an old *Simpsons* episode. She went to the bathroom and threw up her dinner. The way she always had before an audition. It settled her down, and she felt better. She called again at eight. This time someone picked up but didn't speak. Lea listened to the hypnotic static until Gibson's snapping fingers spurred her to speak.

"Hello. Good evening. I'm calling on behalf of the governor's office. How are you this evening?"

Silence on the other end. She made a frightened face at Gibson, afraid whoever it was had hung up. Gibson made an exaggerated smile and spun his finger for her to keep going.

"Hello?" she said cheerfully. "Is anyone there?"

"Who is this?" A young adult male voice, wary and soft.

"Oh, I do apologize, sir. This is my first day. My name is Annie Silver. I work in the governor's office here in Charleston, and we're taking an informal survey on a proposed bill to fund West Virginia public schools—"

"Wait, who is this?"

"Annie Silver from the governor's office?"

"Oh, yeah, look, I don't vote."

"But you are a resident of West Virginia, aren't you?"

"Well, yeah, but I'm . . ."

Gibson pumped his fist and began tapping the list of questions that they'd written to help narrow their search area.

"Still, we're interested in all our citizens' opinions. May I ask you our survey questions? How do you feel about the redistricting that's—"

"I told you I don't want to answer any questions." His voice hardened, but he didn't hang up. Gibson pointed to a different question on the list, but Lea knew if she asked it, he'd be gone.

Instead, she said, "That's okay. I don't really like asking them, to tell you the truth."

She was completely off script now. Gibson mouthed, "What are you doing?" She held up her hand and turned away so she could concentrate on the voice at the other end of the phone.

"Yeah?"

"Yeah, only my third call. I'm not really good at it."

"Oh, no, you were okay."

"Really?" she said, allowing her voice to brighten.

"Definitely. Politics just isn't my thing."

"I appreciate that so much. I feel like I don't know what I'm doing here. I just moved to Charleston for this job, and I don't know anybody."

"Yeah," he said. "I know how that is. But maybe it'll get better?"

"You're really nice. Do you live in Charleston?" She held her breath.

"No, I'm about two hours away."

"That's not so far. Maybe you could drive in some time?"

"Wish I could, but . . . how did you get this number?" Changing topics on a dime's edge. He sounded completely different, paranoid and unhinged, like a madman had snatched the phone away.

"Oh, uh, I don't know. They just give us a call sheet, and we're supposed to go down the list."

"What's my name?"

Lea didn't expect the question and drew a hard blank, almost said "Gibson Vaughn" because he was in her line of sight, and spluttered out the author of the book she was reading.

"It says, Thomas Piketty."

The line went dead and her face went cold. She looked at Gibson. "I'm sorry."

He put his hands on her shoulders and squeezed. "You killed it," he said with a huge grin. "You really are a natural."

"Yeah," agreed Swonger. "You seemed like actually nice."

"But we still don't know where he is."

"We know so much," Gibson said, spreading a map of West Virginia out on the table. With a pencil, he drew a circle around Charleston.

"He's only a couple hours away. That eliminates the eastern and north-ern corners of the state. Plus we know he's in state, so the Ohio River cuts down our western area."

"Also cuts out everything right around Charleston," Swonger chimed in.

"Exactly."

"So we just have to search a band that's a 'couple hours' from Charleston."

"You did it," Gibson said. "We have a shot."

"So now what?" she asked.

"Now? Now we wardrive."

CHAPTER THIRTY

Wardriving dated back to the early days of wireless networks, when few routers came with encryption already enabled. Most people, too lazy to follow instructions, just plugged the router in, factory settings enabled, and left themselves exposed to the world. Big cities became all-you-can-eat buffets of wide-open Wi-Fi that software such as Netstumbler or InSSIDer could exploit. Often it was simply to "borrow" free Wi-Fi, but open Wi-Fi presented many less adiaphorous avenues if one were so inclined. Many hackers were, driving the length and breadth of a city, mapping all its unprotected access points. Nowadays, commercial routers defaulted to passwords, so wardriving was less prevalent than it once had been.

Lea's performance on the call had significantly narrowed their search parameters, but Gibson knew they still had a lot of roads to cover and not a lot of time to cover them. To have a chance meant driving twenty-four hours a day. The plan called on them to drive in shifts, stopping only for gas, food, and bathroom breaks. A fold-down cot in the back of the van would serve as a communal bed. They would drive until they found the cell phone or time ran out. Either way, Gibson didn't see returning to Niobe. This was his shot, and if he missed, he wasn't fool enough to mix up with the predators now circling the prison.

Emerson Soto Flores folded his newspaper and watched Gibson check out of the hotel. Two of his men sat in the parlor over a chessboard. Jimmy Temple looked tired and anxious. His once-spotless suit had a stain on the lapel, and a small black thread dangled from his sleeve from a missing button. Eartha Kitt vamped her way through "Santa Baby" over the lobby speakers as Gibson and Jimmy shook hands over the counter. Gibson thanked him for his hospitality. Jimmy accepted it with a careless shrug. He hardly seemed the same man.

"Good luck, Jimmy."

"Drive safe."

Emerson met Gibson at the counter and escorted him across the lobby. "Don't be hard on yourself; there is no shame in cowardice. Sometimes knowing your limits is all that keeps a man alive."

Emerson held open the door for him, and Gibson saw the van idling at the curb. Lea motioned to him from the passenger seat, but Gibson hesitated. Emerson felt it and faced him as his men emerged from the parlor.

"You have something to say?" asked Gibson.

God knows Emerson did, along with a bully's excitement at the prospect. His men pressed closer. The van honked, and Gibson could hear Lea calling him. He should go, but still he found it hard to be the one to look away first. His father, a shrewd political strategist, had always said, *Fight the fight, but never let them pick the venue.* It was good advice. Before Emerson could speak, Gibson broke away, descended the front steps, and threw his bag in the van. He turned back to take one last look at the Wolstenholme Hotel. Emerson watched him from the front doors, an amused expression on his face. Gibson climbed in back, gave Emerson a lazy two-finger salute, and slammed closed the sliding door. He'd be happy to leave Emerson, the hotel, and Niobe in the rearview mirror.

"Ready to go?" Swonger asked.

"As I've ever been."

Lea piped in with an exuberant English accent. "Engage!"

That broke the tension. Even Gibson cracked a smile as he pointed the way forward. And that set the tone for the wardrive, all smiles as they left the poisonous atmosphere that had settled over Niobe, West Virginia. They had reason to feel confident: the job at the motor-pool depot, their good fortune to capture Merrick's cell number on the first day (only Gibson knew the truth), Lea's artful handling of Merrick's partner . . . they were on a roll, and what's more, they had the edge. Sure, tracking down Merrick's partner might be a long shot, but they shared the belief that things would break their way. Plus, it felt good to leave the competition sitting on their hands back in Niobe.

It wasn't until they'd spent a few hours on the highway that the magnitude of the task dawned on Gibson. On the map, the wide band circling Charleston that needed to be swept looked comfortingly small, at least compared to the entirety of West Virginia. However, to be effective, the Stingray couldn't move faster than about thirty-five miles an hour. It also required line of sight, and West Virginia wasn't the flattest state in the Union. Clearing a grid would mean combing back and forth over every road, from highway to dirt trail, before moving on. Gibson kept his reservations to himself—morale was high, and he wanted to keep it that way for as long as possible.

As the days wore on and they made their meandering way across West Virginia—the Stingray resolutely and defiantly silent—a strange thing began to happen. Gibson expected tempers to fray and the close quarters to breed contempt and short fuses. Especially between Lea and Swonger, who couldn't have had less in common. She of the Upper East Side pedigree and prep-school education, and Swonger of Buckingham Correctional Center. Instead, it brought them together.

It began over music during one of Lea's shifts behind the wheel. The first rule of wardriving—driver controlled the music. She took great pride in her eclectic taste in music, and she deejayed her shifts, one hand on the wheel while she scrolled through her music library for the next track. An odd, discordant, synth-heavy song began. Swonger looked up questioningly at the speakers, and Gibson braced for the inevitable explosion. From his time in the Scion, Gibson knew Swonger took a dim view of anything not rap, but to his surprise, Swonger slid into the passenger seat and asked Lea the name of the song.

"'Ashes to Ashes,'" Lea said. "David Bowie?"

"Who's he? It's cool."

With the breathless, intimate pleasure that comes from introducing someone to a favorite musician, Lea spent the next several hours playing Bowie for Swonger and answering his questions. Then she moved on to Iggy Pop, Lou Reed, and Talking Heads. Perhaps that's how "Life During Wartime" became the wardrive's official theme song. When it was Swonger's turn to drive, Swonger returned the favor and educated Lea about the underground rap scene: Action Bronson, Danny Brown, Vince Staples, Westside Gunn, Schoolboy Q. Swonger was an encyclopedia on the subject.

From the cot in the back, Gibson recognized only one song in ten, which made him feel hopelessly out of touch. An old man at twenty-nine. His childhood had skipped the part where he developed his own tastes. His music collection belonged to his father, to the Marines, and to Nicole. He didn't know why it mattered, but it made him a little melancholy. Up front, Lea and Swonger were howling over some private joke, and just like that, Gibson had become the third wheel. When it came time for his next shift behind the wheel, Gibson opted for silence.

Lea took a growing interest in Swonger and peppered him with questions. Swonger, suspicious at first, gradually opened up and told her about his life, his father, and the bleak future of the Birk farm. He told it straightforwardly and with none of the false machismo that Gibson expected. She seemed mightily affected by it and grew increasingly pensive as Swonger railed against Merrick. Finally, Lea turned to Gibson.

"Does he know?"

"Not from me," Gibson said.

Lea looked at Swonger and told him her real name.

It took Swonger a long time to speak. "Why are you telling me this?"

"Seemed right."

"Stop the van," said Swonger.

Gibson pulled over, and Swonger got out and walked into the woods along the road. Lea and Gibson watched him until he disappeared from view, then looked at each other. Gibson shrugged.

"What do I do?" she asked. "Go after him?"

"Let him work it out."

"I thought I should tell him." She had a thought. "Is he armed?"

"In a manner of speaking," Gibson said, but he didn't explain about Swonger's .45. "I wouldn't worry about it."

They waited in silence. Finally, Swonger emerged from the woods. He climbed back in the van and slid the door shut.

"He named the third fund after you . . . ," Swonger said, his words pitched halfway between a question and a statement.

"Yes, he did." Lea had turned all the way around in the passenger seat to face Swonger.

Swonger's eyes studied the floor. "That why you're here?"

"Something like that. I'm sorry."

"Wasn't you," Swonger said. "Let's go."

They didn't talk about it again after that. In her downtime, Lea continued parsing through Merrick's text messages, hoping to decipher all of his instructions. She made notes in pencil, keeping a running tally when she wasn't researching stocks on her phone. Slow going, but she made steady progress, becoming more and more excited as her list grew. Gibson and Swonger were both dying of curiosity, but Lea seemed content to let them die. It was Gibson's shift when Lea finally finished her calculations.

"Oh my God," she said. "Oh my God."

"How much?" Gibson asked.

"Yeah, how much?" Swonger asked.

"One point two seven billion. US."

Gibson caught a glimpse of Swonger in the rearview mirror and saw the exact moment that his brain fused to the top of his skull. Swonger began to whoop and drum the roof of the van with his palms.

"No. Your math has to be wrong," Gibson said.

"I'm telling you, I did it five times. One point two seven billion." Lea held up her worksheet for him to see as if he could check it while driving.

"There is no conceivable way that the Justice Department missed one point two seven billion," Gibson said. "It's just not possible."

"Maybe it wasn't that much when they arrested him?"

"Maybe Justice just ain't all that?" Swonger suggested.

"Or maybe they didn't miss it," Gibson mused under his breath. He had been wondering how Merrick had pled out to such a short sentence. Could there be more at play here than a Wall Street crook with a big mouth?

"You think he made some kind of deal?" Lea asked.

"It would explain a lot."

"What could he have that the feds would want?"

"You're asking us?" Gibson said.

Gibson didn't know, but assuming the fisherman knew as much as they did, he must have wanted something pretty important in order to pass up $1.27 billion. It made him question exactly whom he had gotten into bed with. He brooded on that as he drove on. Glancing over, Lea looked troubled about it too. Of the three, only Swonger seemed in good spirits about the news and babbled excitedly about it.

Lea's discovery changed the tenor of the wardrive instantly. The hypothetical had become a one followed by nine very real zeros. And now that the stakes were known, the pressure was on and the tension began to mount. No more music; they drove in silence, and every day that the Stingray remained idle brought more backbiting among them. Four days before Merrick's release, Swonger raised the idea of Lea calling the number again and digging for more information. Gibson shut him down. It was a nonstarter, as far as he was concerned; going back to that well would almost certainly spook their target. But the idea came up with increasing frequency as Merrick's release drew closer, and even Lea began warming to the concept.

Still, they kept crossing grids off their list, kept shrinking the remaining map. Gibson had lost track of the one-gas-station towns that they'd stopped in. Mostly because Swonger had a bladder the size of a leaky teacup. At one pit stop, they both had to go. In the empty restroom, Swonger sidled up to the urinal beside Gibson—in clear violation of every unspoken rule of men's room etiquette. Gibson glanced over at Swonger, who was staring down thoughtfully.

"You circumcised?"

"What the hell, Swonger?"

"I am. Strange thing to do to a kid, know what I'm saying? I mean it's weird. Like who was the first dude to look at a baby and think, yeah, I'll just take a little off the top? What's that about? And it was a long-ass time ago. Like BC. So weren't no scalpels. They were taking like flinty rocks to their baby boys' business. No Bactine neither. Nobody even knew there was such a thing as a germ until like the nineteenth century. I mean, it's hard enough out there for a baby in olden times without dying over some infected junk. And for what? Ain't no purpose to it."

"What is your point?"

"Just saying. People can talk themselves into almost anything being a good idea."

"We'll find him," Gibson said, sounding far less confident than he'd intended.

The day before Merrick's release, Gibson drove nonstop for ten hours, exhausting the largest remaining grid. That left only nine more grids to cover, but when he turned the steering wheel over to Lea, it was already past noon. Gibson calculated that they had time to cover only four of the remaining grids before Merrick walked free. Not great odds, but they would ride this bet out to the bitter end. He climbed onto the cot, put in a pair of earplugs, and was asleep before the van left the gas station.

Gibson's body felt the van come to a stop and woke him from a guilty dream about his daughter. The van doors slammed shut. He sat up and stretched his aching back. Nighttime—how long had he slept? He climbed out of the van to find himself in front of Margo's garage back in Niobe. Lea and Swonger stood together at the top of the driveway, watching him.

"What are we doing back here?"

"It's futile," Lea said. "We agreed."

"Oh, did we? Did we agree?"

"You were being unreasonable, so Gavin and I took a vote."

"While I was sleeping."

"Majority ruled, dog."

"I'm not your dog, *Gavin*. This was still our best chance."

"Less than fifty percent isn't much of a chance," Lea said.

"What's our alternative?"

"Not sure there is an 'our' at this point," Lea said.

And like that, their alliance came to an end.

"And what about you?" Gibson said to Swonger.

"Sorry, dog," Swonger said with a shrug. "Wasn't happening."

"I'm sorry," Lea said. "Facts are facts."

"So you came back here? You know what you'll be up against at the prison when Merrick walks through those gates? Do you even have a plan?" When neither spoke up, Gibson snatched his bag out of the van. "You screwed us good here. I want you to remember that. This was the way."

He started down the driveway toward the street.

"Where are you going?" Lea asked.

"To the hotel. I need a shower. Park the van out of sight."

They called after him to come back, but Gibson kept going. The walk was the most exercise he'd had since they left Niobe. It felt good to stretch his legs, and it gave him time for his anger to dissipate. Well, not to dissipate but at least to spread evenly throughout his body and stop his temples from throbbing. He came up Tarte Street and saw the hotel on his right but instead walked down to the river and looked out toward Ohio. The river was beautiful by moonlight, and the ruined bridge seemed almost dignified. The road down to the bridge still stood, although it was blocked off by orange barrels and sealed at the mouth of the bridge by a plywood wall. *What a strange thing to live with,* he thought. How could anyone imagine a fresh start with the ruined bridge reminding them of what had been? Knowing your history was one thing, but living in it? That was a cage.

Gibson pushed through the door into the Wolstenholme Hotel. One of Emerson's goons sat in Emerson's chair, watching the lobby; at the sight of Gibson, he spoke into a radio.

"Big day tomorrow," Gibson said. "Shouldn't you be getting some rest?"

The goon smiled, uncrossing one leg and crossing the other, shifting in his seat as he did. Tomorrow was coming fast, and Gibson had a bad feeling that not everyone would live to see another. He wondered if Merrick had any inkling of the tempest waiting to fall upon him.

A disheveled Jimmy Temple appeared from the back after Gibson rang the buzzer several times. He didn't look any too happy to see Gibson.

"I need a room."

"Are you sure about that?"

"Something facing out back."

Jimmy handed him a key. "How long will you be staying?"

"Just the night."

"Good."

Up in his new room, he'd barely put his bag down before a knock came at the door. He engaged the chain on the door before opening it.

The fisherman stood on the other side and smiled through the crack. "Welcome back."

Gibson acknowledged the greeting with a faint nod, in no mood for the fisherman's particular brand of vague. Wary too of what his real interest in Charles Merrick might entail.

"Will you invite me in?" the fisherman asked.

Gibson shook his head.

"Were you successful?"

"No. Too much ground to cover."

The fisherman thought it over. "That is a shame, but it was a lot to hope. I'm sure you did your best."

Gibson expected a "but." There was none; instead, the fisherman started away down the hall.

Gibson stopped him. "What do you think will happen now?"

The fisherman considered the question for a moment. "In Mandarin, the word 'crisis' is composed of two characters. One represents danger and the other represents opportunity."

"Is that true?"

The fisherman shook his head. "No, not exactly. It is just something that John F. Kennedy repeated because it sounded inspiring."

"Then why did you say it?"

"Because he said it, and people believed him."

"I don't understand."

"You will." The fisherman inclined his head toward Gibson and left him to his thoughts.

In his bathroom, Gibson ran the shower until it was hot enough to strip paint and stood under it until he couldn't feel the van on him anymore. By the time he stepped out, he knew he didn't want to be in Niobe come morning. The fisherman—he still didn't know the man's name—was right: something bad was coming. Call it a crisis, call it an opportunity, call it what you will—it would be bloody, and he didn't trust the fifth floor to exhibit much trigger control.

Gibson climbed into bed, wrestled with the covers until he was comfortable, and then got up again. Satisfied it looked like the bed had been slept in, he put out the "Do Not Disturb" sign, repacked his bag, and climbed out the fire escape. He dropped down lightly onto the parking lot, listened to the night, and disappeared into the shadows.

CHAPTER THIRTY-ONE

In the morning, Gavin was gone. Lea had lent him a pillow and a blanket, pointed him toward the couch, and promptly passed out in her clothes. When her alarm went off at five a.m., she felt stiff, as if she hadn't moved a muscle all night. She poked her head out her bedroom door to check on her guest; the pillow and blanket were stacked exactly where she'd left them. No note or indication of where he had gone, but the message was clear enough—she was on her own now. To her surprise, she found she missed Gavin. She didn't quite know what to make of that—missing people wasn't something she did anymore.

The wardrive had been devastating for her, but she felt grateful for the clarity it had brought. Up until now, her father's victims had been an abstraction, a meaningless number. So to meet Gavin and learn firsthand of the damage done by her father made her ashamed not to have understood the true impact of his crimes before now. So intent on her own personal revenge that she'd made her father's crimes all about her. What a child she had been. The memory of telling Gibson that the money belonged to her family made her cringe. The money belonged to the Swongers and the Birks.

Could there still be a way?

Lea made coffee and took stock of what needed to be done. Partnering up had been a bust—time for plan B, or rather, the old plan A.

It took her only twenty minutes to pack her things. She opened a suitcase and a garbage bag. When she was done, the garbage bag was stuffed to overflowing, while all her worldly possessions totaled only three-quarters of the suitcase. It made half of her sad to be such a vagabond, the other half proud that life had taught her economy. Her life was a Bob Dylan lyric. What little else remained, she left for Margo's next tenant, if there ever was one. People weren't exactly flocking to relocate to Niobe.

A single garment bag hung in her closet. She unzipped it and laid the yellow dress out on her bare mattress. She remembered the way her father had surprised her with it, draped casually over the back of her chair when she'd come down for breakfast that morning. His nose in the *Wall Street Journal*, pretending not to hear her squeals when she discovered the jewelry box where her breakfast should have been. The necklace inside had taken her breath away. What a lucky girl she'd felt that morning to have such a generous daddy. *Poor, spoiled, foolish Chelsea Merrick.* The dress matched the tie he'd worn that day. She'd thought that a wonderful touch but now saw what she'd been—an accessory to complement his big moment. They'd driven into his offices together, and she'd stood proudly at his side while he'd announced the launch of Chelsea—his third and final fund, named in her honor. The one that had spelled his downfall. She smoothed the dress with her hand and plucked a stray black hair from the sleeve. She'd worn it only that once, a lifetime ago.

She got to work in the bathroom—not bothering to read the instructions on the bottle; she'd been dying her hair for years now. Afterward, she took her time putting on her makeup and went through a roll of toilet paper before she was finally satisfied. Her seventeen-year-old self would have been horrified at the results, but it was the best Lea could manage now. It had been years since she'd worn anything but lip gloss.

The dress still fit, snug in the shoulders and hips, but not so anyone would notice. She'd been tall at nine and average by fourteen, never growing another inch. She checked herself in the mirror and wondered at the ludicrous girl looking back. Had she really once dressed like this on purpose? The pretentious ballerina collar, the cinched waist, the overly structured skirt—she felt like someone else's idea of a princess. Which, she supposed, she had been. Someone really ought to have slapped some sense into that girl. The whole getup was way, way over the top . . . and hence, perfect. After all, over the top was Charles Merrick's lingua franca.

But not if she looked like a war refugee . . . She forced a tight, jagged smile that wouldn't do much except scare small children. *Not attractive, Chelsea,* she heard her mother's voice say. She didn't want to be Chelsea Merrick again, but she would this one last time. For him. She practiced in the mirror until the smile radiated warmth and love. Her parents had fought over her acting classes when she was in high school. She'd harbored fantasies of becoming an actress, performing someday at the Public, Cherry Lane, Minetta Lane. Her mother, never the warmest of women, considered it a foolish, impractical hobby, but her father encouraged it. Clearly, he'd always been playing a part himself—upstanding member of the community, charitable donor, loving husband, doting father—so perhaps he saw the value in it. Or maybe he knew it would bedevil his wife.

Lea still didn't have a relationship with her mother. Veronica Merrick had struggled with pills and alcohol in the years since the scandal. They'd had a disastrous reunion in Miami six years ago, and since then Lea had stayed away. But she'd never forgotten her father's words the day of his arrest, on the phone with one of his shady accountants, moving money around in an effort to hide it from the government. And his family, as it turned out.

The bitch gets nothing.

Lea slipped the thigh holster into place. Hopefully, her father would appreciate her performance today. At least up until the third act. In the mirror, she studied the rigid swing of the skirt; its structure had one advantage—the holster was invisible. She checked her Walther PPK .380 one last time. The men at the gun range had spent the last year trying to convince her to upgrade to something with more stopping power and a larger magazine. But she valued its small size, which made it easier to conceal. The .380 felt comfortable in her hand, and her groupings were tight out to twenty-five feet. If she needed more than eight shots, then she was dead anyway. Plus her father had always loved James Bond movies; she hoped he would appreciate the homage.

A little before noon, Lea left the apartment above the Toproll for the last time. She locked up, went down the back stairs, and loaded her suitcase into her trunk. Then she walked up to Tarte Street. The hotel parking lot was mostly empty for the first time in weeks. It was checkout time at the Wolstenholme. Two men in dark suits stood on the steps of the hotel. One of the men ignored her entirely, his eyes fixed down the street, but the other watched her from the moment she turned the corner until the moment she went into the Toproll. Not the leering way a man ogled a passing woman, but a cold assessment of her threat.

Inside, Margo stood behind the bar, restocking the reach-in coolers. Old Charlie, alert at his post, stared down his first beer and shot of the day, communing with whatever voices that wouldn't let him be. Margo did a double take when she saw Lea. Old Charlie gave her the once-over, saw nothing that interested him, and went back to the matter at hand.

"Didn't know it was Cinderella day," Margo said.

"Hi, Margo."

"Look at you, you really are a Gilmore Girl."

"You know, I've never actually seen that show."

"Oh, it's really good; you'd hate it. So what's with the hair? Since when were you a blonde?"

"It's actually my natural color."

"I don't like it. People will be confusing us now."

"Take more than hair to confuse y'all, you evil harpy," Old Charlie muttered and threw back the shot.

"Did you bust up with your partners?"

"Have you seen them?"

"No, but one of them came and got the van last night."

Lea smiled. Gibson . . . pain in the ass didn't know how to quit. Well, she hoped he found what he was looking for. She put the apartment key on the bar top. Margo looked at it and came out from behind the bar, wiping her hands on a bar rag.

"Is it in good shape? I'll take it out of your security deposit if it isn't." Margo's voice was thick with feeling.

"Better than when you rented it to me." Lea handed Margo two envelopes, one for her and one marked "Parker." "I'm sorry it isn't more. Things haven't gone the way I'd hoped."

"It'll do." Margo tossed the envelopes onto the bar. "You sure about this, Gilmore? You know you could just let whatever this is go."

Lea's felt her own throat tighten, and her eyes felt heavy and wet. She remembered why she'd stopped wearing makeup in the first place. There wasn't time to redo it now so she couldn't afford tears, but then Margo drew her into a fierce hug, and Lea knew it was a lost cause.

"Let it go," Margo repeated.

Lea choked back a sob, shook her head.

"All right, then," Margo said, conceding defeat. She let go of Lea and took a step back.

"I need a damn drink after all that," growled Old Charlie.

Lea agreed entirely.

Merrick lay in his bunk and thought about the future soon to come. He rubbed his coarse blanket between his fingers and dreamed of four-hundred-thread-count sheets. Of course, they made sheets with thread counts in the thousands, but that was just a marketing gimmick for rubes who thought more meant better; counts of more than four hundred meant using thinner, weaker thread to fit it on the loom.

He would sleep well tonight.

When the lights finally came on, Merrick waited by his bunk while the guards took the morning count. He expected one of them to pull him aside, but the guards passed by without a glance and blew the whistle that signaled inmates were free to move around. He asked a large white guard with more tattoos than most of the inmates if there was somewhere he should go.

"Out my sight would be a good start, inmate." The guard refused to make eye contact. "Don't know nothing about no re-lease."

Perplexed, Merrick got in line for the showers and then headed to chow as if it were any other morning. He accepted his daily dose of breakfast and took his tray to an empty table, where he picked at it moodily. The table soon filled up around him with inmates talking among themselves. No one spoke to him or even acknowledged his presence. He'd never exactly endeared himself to his fellow inmates, and they were happy to see the back of him. There would be no congratulations or fond farewells.

A tall black guard came into the cafeteria and scanned the room for someone. Merrick made himself tall in his seat and looked his way.

"Merrick! What are you doing just sitting there?"

The room fell silent, then the guard continued before Merrick could answer.

"Get your ass moving, or did you go and fall in love? I can come back in another year, you need more time."

That elicited much merriment from the assembled congregation, and Merrick heard wolf tickets being thrown his way. That he was soft.

That he was a punk. That he was a stuck-up bitch. *Maybe I am,* he thought, *but this stuck-up bitch is going and you're staying.* He hustled over to the guard and apologized profusely. The guards were ontologically incapable of mistakes, so it was always safer to act sorry. Merrick followed him back to the dormitory.

"Collect your shit," the guard said and stood aside while Merrick gathered his possessions, such as they were, in a plastic tub. The guard was still angry about earlier and muttered under his breath. "Making me look for *you* like it's my job."

Shit collected, the guard escorted Merrick to a holding cell and cuffed him to a bench alongside two other inmates, each with tubs filled with their possessions: priceless artifacts on the inside, worthless junk in the real world. His compatriots passed the time engaged in the time-tested ritual of good-natured one-upmanship, trading stories about where they were headed, first meals, first drinks, the parties, and all the fine, fine ladies they had lined up. They tried to include Merrick, but he ignored them. He'd spent eight years humoring idiots like these two, but those days were behind him.

After an hour, a guard came and collected one of the inmates. A few minutes later, a replacement inmate was led in with his plastic tub, as if three were the room's maximum occupancy. Another hour passed before they came back for the next inmate. Then another. By the time it was Merrick's turn, his stomach was growling for lunch, and he was sorry he hadn't eaten more of his breakfast. He was taken to an office, where a guard filled out his release paperwork while Merrick answered questions. They asked if he wanted anything from the tub; he said no. Then they searched it for contraband anyway and tossed it in a dumpster. He was ordered to strip for a cavity search.

"Do you seriously believe I plan on sneaking anything *out* of prison?"

"Shut up, inmate. Spread 'em and cough."

Long is the way, and hard, that out of hell leads up to light, reflected Merrick as he assumed the position, heard the snap of the latex glove, and squeezed his eyes closed and thought of sandy beaches.

With that indignity complete, he was permitted to dress and wait in a different holding cell, where he rejoined his compatriots. They shared a pitiful lunch—a granola bar, a cup of water, and a brown banana. For entertainment, the two inmates treated him to a graphic replay of how they would celebrate their impending releases, only with more steak, more parties, and many, many more hot women who just couldn't resist a penniless ex-con.

Merrick put his head back and dozed.

————————————

Gibson pulled the van to the side of the road and spread the map out on the steering wheel. It was noon, and in the last twelve hours, he'd covered the smallest two remaining grids. Hungry and tired, he felt as though he'd driven every highway, byway, and alleyway in West Virginia. So it was discouraging to see how much of the state remained.

He looked at the map again, studied the remaining grids without a red cross through them. There were no more educated guesses left to make. It would be dumb luck or nothing at all. Quitting seemed a reasonable option. Merrick might already be a free man for all he knew. He hated to fail the judge, but he'd taken this thing as far as could reasonably be expected. Far past reason, if he were being honest, but honesty lay bleeding in a ditch a ways back.

So pick another grid, and get back on the road.

But which?

CHAPTER THIRTY-TWO

It was late afternoon before a guard finally came for Merrick. He felt half inclined to complain. Should it really take this long to let a free man go free? A ludicrously inefficient system, but he bit his tongue and followed the guard. It would all be behind him shortly. At a steel-caged door, he signed for his belongings. He changed into his suit and returned his prison blues. As he suspected, the suit needed to be tailored—loose at the waist, tight in the chest and shoulders. It offended his sartorial sensibilities, but at the same time it pleased him. As if it might come apart at the seams if he flexed. He looped his tie in the supercilious full Windsor that he favored and plucked a piece of lint from his lapel. He was already feeling more himself. Perhaps the clothes did make the man.

The custodian returned his wallet, a fountain pen, and the cheap Rolex knockoff that he'd been forced to wear in court—his Vacheron Constantin Tour de I'lle having long since been confiscated. God, how he missed that watch, but the knockoff would suffice until he got where he was going and could find a suitable replacement. He asked the time, then wound and reset it. It was almost five p.m.—*how is that possible?* He flipped through his leather billfold, empty apart from an expired driver's license. He slipped it into the breast pocket of his suit nonetheless. Squared away, he moved to a final station, where he attempted to sign his release papers with his fountain pen, but its ink had long since desiccated. They handed him a bus ticket for New York City, twenty dollars in cash, and a check for fifty-seven dollars and twenty-three cents—the remaining balance on his commissary account. He endorsed the check and slid it back.

"Keep it," Merrick said. "You need it more than I do."

It felt right to tip them, and he wished he had more to give. The average man tipped to show his appreciation; the exceptional man over-tipped to remind the world of its insignificance. After eight years, if Merrick had learned anything, it was that insignificance was the defining characteristic of everyone associated with this place. Imparting that lesson to them felt, in a small way, like repayment for all their many kindnesses. The guards looked dumbfounded, so he thrust his hand out and shook each one's hand, clapping them on the shoulder as he did—a formality perhaps, but that was what one did at the conclusion of a business transaction.

"Farewell, gentlemen," he said with a wave.

And with that, ten-plus hours after his exodus had begun, Charles Merrick finally stepped through the doors of Niobe Federal Prison and walked to the front gate, a free man.

———————

For the last hour, each new road had been categorically the absolute last Gibson would drive. This was it, he'd tell himself, and then turn the corner and start down another. He was talking to himself at this point, an incoherent monologue about futility and stubbornness. Merrick was probably already out by now. But he didn't stop. He drove leaning forward now, to rest his chin on the steering wheel. He would finish this one road, pull into a parking lot somewhere, and sleep in the back. After this one last road.

In a moment of perfect metaphor, the Stingray alarm sounded as he pulled up to the crossroads of a small town with a McDonald's and a service station at its center. Gibson craned back in his seat to stare at it with the look of a man who flies halfway around the world only to bump into the guy who terrorized him in elementary school.

"No . . . ," Gibson said. "Way."

Then he did a happy dance in his seat that resembled an upright seizure more than anything and punched the steering wheel in celebration. The car behind him interrupted, honking for him to get a move on. Gibson made a right, pulled into the service station, and heard the signal diminish in intensity. Good—the four antennae spread across the roof of the van were already doing their jobs, triangulating the signal and pinpointing its direction. The alarm was telling him this wasn't it, which left two possibilities. He scrambled back to the laptop in its dock, his exhaustion forgotten in an adrenaline surge, and scrolled through the data.

There was the phone number, pinging away.

The Stingray led him out of town, such as it was, down a long featureless road. He followed it for a mile until the signal began to weaken, then doubled back and crawled along the side of the road with his hazards on, listening to the tone of the alarm and looking for a turnoff that he might have missed. There wasn't one; he saw only solid woodland in both directions. But the signal was definitely coming from the east. He consulted his map and found a road that ran perpendicular to the one he was on. He went to the crossroad and took a right.

The signal was stronger now, and the Stingray chirped away happily. The homes here all had a healthy footprint, with driveways spaced out every hundred yards or so. He pulled up at a plain white ranch-style home. A unmowed lawn, but otherwise it looked unremarkable. He checked the laptop. No mistake. The cell phone was inside.

Gibson stared at the house, trying to decide what to do now. He'd been so focused on finding the house that he hadn't considered what to do if he actually did. Nothing wrong with the direct approach, he reckoned, so he went to the door and knocked. He waited and then knocked harder. He rang the bell. Finally, he went back down the walk and made his way around the side of the house, checking the windows, which all had the shades drawn. Around back, he came upon an elevated deck. At the foot of the stairs, a dead bird lay peacefully in the tall grass. He stepped over it and went up slowly, pausing by a rusted grill to look for movement through the sliding glass door. Nothing. The only other furniture on the deck was an old aluminum chaise longue with green-and-white webbing. A metal bucket that might once have held a citronella candle was now an overflow of crushed-out cigarettes. Mixed with rainwater, over time the butts had stained the deck a soggy yellow. Empty beer and liquor bottles lay nearby where they'd been discarded.

Cupping his hands to the glass, Gibson peered into the dark house. The room was a combination kitchen and living area, divided by a kitchen island. In one corner sat a desk and an office chair with a computer and precarious stacks of papers. In the center of the room stood a wide leather armchair, and in the chair, a pasty white man in boxer shorts stared blankly at an enormous flat-screen television. The television was off. The man was emaciated, bones propping up his skin like an abandoned circus tent. Gibson rapped on the glass to get the man's attention but saw no movement apart from a slow, steady blinking.

Gibson tested the door, found it unlocked, and slid it open. A rancid, flatulent smell stung his eyes. He asked if he could come in but got no answer. He weighed his options. Everything about the man unnerved him, far more than if it had been some burly thug with gun. He felt a superstitious tickle at the back of his neck, as if he were trespassing in a graveyard. But he'd come a long way for this, and he commanded himself to get it together.

"I'm going to come in," he announced and stepped across the threshold. Still no response. If the man in the chair had a gun, Gibson would be a dead burglar. It wouldn't take a jury an hour to exonerate his killer. He left the door open for ventilation and as a potential escape route.

"So how are we doing today?" he asked, not expecting an answer but needing to fill the vacuum.

He worked his way slowly around the perimeter of the room, giving the man in the chair a wide berth. Despite the smell, the place was remarkably tidy. Not clean—a layer of dust and grime coated every surface—but tidy. More than tidy, it was bare essentials and no more. Nothing hung on the walls. No plants, no decorations or personal touches anywhere. It reminded Gibson of his own apartment. A depressing thought. In the kitchen, he found the source of the smell—a half-dozen trash bags, full to spilling over, sat propped against a wall in a row. The man had taken the time to empty his trash but not to walk the trash out to the curb for pickup. A stalagmite of empty pizza boxes suggested it had been some time since he'd ventured outdoors at all. Gibson checked the chair again, but the man remained statue still.

What little Gibson knew about drugs, he knew from the movies and a guy in his unit who'd been court-martialed for a heroin addiction, but the kitchen counter looked like Amsterdam at Christmas. In the center stood an ornate green bong. Arrayed around it, like presents for all the good little addicts, were little Baggies of pills, powders, and crystals. A glass pipe with a bulb blackened from use listed on its side. Razor blades, matches, a crooked spoon—the man hadn't missed a trick.

At the desk, Gibson tapped the space bar, and the monitor flickered to life. Amazingly, there was no password prompt, and it took him to a portal page for a brokerage account on the Bursa Malaysia—the Malaysian stock market. Lea had been right on the nose. *The barbarians are at your gate, Charles.* Gibson tapped the space bar again idly while he stared at the blinking cursor prompting him for the username and password for the brokerage account. It wouldn't be stored on the machine locally, so he couldn't change it the way he'd changed the password at the Virginia State motor pool. There wasn't anything remotely like enough time to hack the Malaysian brokerage, so if he couldn't find it written down somewhere, that whittled his options down to one: pry it out of the man in the chair. But how was he going to manage that? He'd never social-engineered a zombie before. Instead, he started with a quick search of the desk—under the keyboard and through all the drawers—in case it was taped somewhere helpfully. The hacking equivalent of flipping down a car's visor and having the keys drop into your hand. Wishful thinking, but of course it wouldn't be that easy. He set about a more thorough search of the desk.

The desk was a treasure trove of junk and meaningless papers, no semblance of order. Behind the monitor, Gibson found two picture frames facedown on the desk. Based on the archaeological quantity of dust, they'd been back there for some time. Gibson lifted each up to the light. The first was a picture of a younger Charles Merrick sitting on a sofa, a small boy balanced on his knee. The boy looked determined to squirm free, but Merrick had a firm grip on him. Only Merrick's mouth smiled; the rest of him looked prepared to flee. The second photo showed five young white teenage boys in suits and confident smiles posed in front of the Merrick Capital logo. One of them held a placard that read, "Summer Intern Team."

They were the only personal artifacts in plain sight, so Gibson flipped them over and removed the pictures from the frames to check the backs. The intern photo was blank, but on the back of the other, written in a woman's hand, was "Marty and Charles—2nd Birthday." He'd hoped for a password, but this piqued his interest. Gibson looked over at the man in the chair. His head still faced straight ahead, but the man's eyes were on Gibson now. Pupils dilated so wide it looked like an eclipse had moved permanently across the iris; the broken whites of his eyes stained red. Gibson thought it might be him. The second intern from the right in the other picture. It might be the man in the chair, but it was hard to say for certain.

"Are these supposed to be you?" Gibson asked, holding up the pictures.

The man's head canted in Gibson's direction. As if there'd been a delayed reaction, and it was only now getting its marching order from his eyes. His head wobbled slightly on its stalk as he looked at the pictures and began, softly, to giggle.

CHAPTER THIRTY-THREE

Lea watched yet another car pull into the visitors' parking lot outside the prison. She sank a little lower in her seat; there had to be at least thirty now. The parking lot was already full, and like the other late arrivals, the car circled the turnaround outside the prison gates and pulled over along the road leading to and from the prison. The crowd reminded her of the press and protestors that had clamored outside her father's trial, but these people weren't here for sound bites or a good cause.

It was strange, but in all the time she'd been planning on taking down her father, she'd never once felt so much as a twinge of sympathy for him. Now, though, she felt strangely protective. It was like insults and families. Family members could say what they wanted, but watch your mouth otherwise. So she felt a little conflicted at these strangers jostling for position to be the ones who would take Charles Merrick when he walked through those gates. Which should have been some time ago . . . she checked the time again. It was already five p.m. Maybe he had seen what was waiting for him beyond the gates and opted for another eight years instead. It would be his first smart move in a decade.

What about her? Did she have a smart move in her? Was she smart enough to throw in the towel and get out while there was still time?

She started her car, changed her mind, and threw the key up on the dashboard. Who was she kidding? Gibson would have something smart to say right about now. It felt comforting to imagine him roaming around West Virginia in that van. And what about Gavin? She hoped he'd gotten far, far from here. Not that she believed it. Gavin was like her. Now that he had his teeth into this thing, he'd hang on until it broke his neck.

Lea felt a change in the atmosphere of the parking lot like a storm coming in. The parking lot had gone absolutely still, every head turned as one toward the front gate. There stood Charles Merrick, one foot in and one foot out of the prison. Even at this distance, she could see his fear. The desire to protect him leapt in her again. *No,* she thought. *That man doesn't deserve your pity.* She dredged up the memories that always worked to stoke her bitterness and used them to fight back any instinct toward charity.

Her legs wobbled when she stepped out of the car. She could feel predatory eyes on her. Wondering at this woman in the formal yellow dress. Was this how Little Red Riding Hood felt when she stepped off the path? She forced herself to take a step toward him, then another, and another. By the time she'd crossed the parking lot, she was smiling. *You're happy,* she reminded herself. *So happy to see him.*

Make him believe.

From the windows of the prison chapel, one could look out over the front gates and down the road that led away to the real world. Charles Merrick had owned homes in the most beautiful cities on earth, with views worth millions, but none stirred him as did the view from the chapel. In truth, it was an ugly, lonesome road, but he loved it, loved it enough to endure the daily services for the chance for five minutes at the window, daydreaming about the moment he walked free. In eight years gazing out the window, he'd seen maybe a handful of cars. Even on the holidays that drew more families, the modest visitors' parking lot was never more than half-full.

Well, it was full today.

Up until the moment Charles Merrick stepped through the small door at the gates, he'd held to the belief that all the fuss about his interview was nothing but mountains from molehills. But the scene that greeted him outside Niobe Federal Prison lent him some sorely needed clarity. Merrick had never seen anything like it. Vehicles lined the circular turnaround in front of the prison. He searched them for a friendly face, but every set of eyes he met burned cold and hungry. Where was his transportation? Where was Damon Ogden?

"Friends of yours?" the guard asked.

From the roadway, a horn sounded, and Merrick flinched.

The guard smirked at him. "Guess not."

"I don't want to be a burden, but would it be permissible to wait just inside? Just for a few minutes?"

"Permissible? Jesus. No, it would not be permissible. Only guards and inmates beyond this point, and you, Sunny Jim, are a free man."

"I . . . I want to visit a friend."

"Nice try. Visiting hours are over."

"Please. Just five minutes."

"Well, ain't you a greedy one? We gave you eight good years, but that's not enough for you. But there's no pleasing some people."

"Call the police," Merrick said and held out the twenty he'd only just been given.

"Call them yourself."

Merrick contemplated punching the guard. Not in anger but because they would have to take him back inside the prison. As little as the idea appealed, he feared the parking lot far more. The guard swung shut the door before he could make a fist, and he listened to the guard's muffled laughter through the gate, took a deep breath, and

turned to face the road. Some men had left their vehicles and were leaning against them, watching him patiently. He didn't know them, but
they knew him. It reminded him of a nature documentary about seals
trapped onshore, returning to the ocean despite the sharks that circled
just beyond the breakers. Merrick marveled at the instincts it took to
take that chance. Were they too stupid to know better? Or was it simple
necessity that gave them the bravery to swim that gauntlet of blood and
death to reach open waters?

Well, he wasn't an animal. He didn't have to make a run for it. He
would just stay here by the gate. It was safe here; the guards couldn't
make him leave. He'd sleep here if necessary. Those men in their cars
weren't brazen enough to take him in full view of the prison. But what
if the guards had been bought off? Merrick knew exactly how easy that
was. Making a break for it might be his best option. He judged the tree
line to be fifty yards away. Suddenly his suit became a liability, and he
wished for a solid pair of running shoes. Even if he did make it that far,
these men would run him down in the discreet shadows of the forest.

"Dad?"

Merrick spun in the direction of the voice and watched his daughter walk from the parking lot toward him. She wore a bright-yellow
dress like something out of a dream.

"Chelsea?"

"Hi, Daddy."

"Why are you here?"

"To see you. I've been waiting for you."

Merrick tried and failed to make sense of it. He hadn't seen
his daughter since before the trial. She'd taken his arrest . . . badly.
Unforgivable things had been said. And after, when prison had given
him time to regret his words, either no one knew, or no one would tell
him where she'd gone. He blamed his ex-wife for poisoning her against
him, although Veronica claimed not to know where their daughter was
either—as if he'd believe her. It had always been his intention to spare

no expense to find his daughter and to send for her. But only once he was safely out of harm's way. Not now.

"I brought your watch."

She held out his Vacheron Constantin Tour de I'lle; it felt surreal to see the watch sparkle in the sunlight, since he'd only just been reminiscing about it.

"How?"

"I didn't want the government to take it, so I hid it."

"All this time?"

"Of course. For you."

He put on the watch: even more beautiful than he remembered. Just like his daughter, who had grown into a stunning woman, made more so against the ugliness of the day. She tried to embrace him, but he took a step backward.

"Don't touch me," he whispered.

"Dad?"

"They'll know. If they realize you're my daughter . . ."

Her eyes widened. "Why do these people want to hurt you?"

"Because of—"

"It doesn't matter," she said, cutting him off. "I have a car. In the parking lot. We can go anywhere."

She took his hand as if to lead him away. His little girl wanted to save him. He beamed down at her and briefly considered it—whether her presence would shield him from what was waiting. He knew it wouldn't. These animals wanted what was his, and he shuddered to think what they would do to take it. He should send Chelsea away now, before they got tired of waiting. Before they saw her as a weakness to exploit. But he was afraid to let her go, to be alone here. And it wouldn't make any difference. His little girl wouldn't leave him no matter what he said. She loved him too much to abandon him again. They'd face it together as a family.

A vehicle crested the far end of the road and came up fast on the prison. As it neared, Merrick realized that it was in fact four separate vehicles driving in tight formation. He felt a burst of relief. It was going to be all right. He was safe. The SUVs roared recklessly into the turnaround, circled, and pulled crisply to halt in front of him, blocking the entrance to the prison. A door in the lead SUV opened, and a stout, professionally dangerous man in a suit stepped out. He approached Merrick.

"What's playing today?" Merrick asked.

"*Wall Street,*" the man replied and shook Merrick's hand. "I'm Bo Huntley, Mr. Merrick. We're here to escort you out of here."

"How do we look?"

"Well, there's a lot more traffic here than we'd anticipated, but we'll be fine."

"She's coming with me."

"Sir, she's not part of the contract."

"Then amend the contract. I'll pay."

"Yes, sir. Let's get you squared away and be on our way," he said and ushered Merrick and Chelsea toward the third vehicle, a stretch Escalade.

"Come with me," he told Chelsea.

"What about my car?"

"I'll buy you a dozen."

At the Escalade, the man held the door for him. It had been a long time since someone held a door for Merrick, and he enjoyed the familiarity of it. The man's suit jacket fit too snugly across the chest to button because of the Kevlar vest, and through the gap Merrick saw a shoulder holster. He found it reassuring.

Inside the stretch limo's spacious interior, Damon Ogden was taking in the crowded scene in the parking lot. He began to say something, but the sight of Chelsea caused him to reconsider. *Good.* Merrick wasn't in the mood for another lecture. He took his seat beside the brittle, severe woman facing Ogden. He patted her knee.

"Cutting it a little close, weren't you?"

"Would you rather I left you entirely?" the woman snapped back, removing a pair of oversized sunglasses to study her offended knee as if calculating where to begin the amputation.

"Look who I found," he said casually, as though they'd all just bumped into each other at Bergdorf's. As he reached over to help his daughter into her seat, the two women froze—Chelsea balanced, half in, half out of the vehicle, Veronica Merrick staring, mouth agape. A truly priceless moment, and Merrick did not feel one bit bad for savoring it.

"Mother?" Chelsea sounded dumbfounded.

Veronica Merrick slipped her sunglasses back on and adjusted them on her nose with a surgeon's precision.

"Hello, dear. What have you done to your hair?"

CHAPTER THIRTY-FOUR

The giggling tapered off, but it left Gibson with a bad case of the cold creeps. He would hear that laughter in his nightmares—low, joyless, and lunatic. The creature in the chair stuck out a hand, which opened and shut reflexively like that of an infant demanding something that it didn't yet have a word for. He wanted the pictures. Gibson handed them over, and the man in the chair clutched them to his chest.

"Stay there," Gibson said, as much to give himself the illusion of control as for any expectation that the man might obey.

A search of the living room turned up a wallet with seventeen dollars, a credit card, a Manhattan gym membership, and an expired driver's license that belonged to one Martin Yardas, twenty-six years old, of Montclair, New Jersey. No slip of paper with a username and password, but the picture on the license confirmed the identity of the man in the chair . . . if Gibson squinted and used his imagination. The Martin Yardas who had stood for this picture was a plump, rosy-faced kid. There were two kinds of people in the world: people who smiled in IDs and people who didn't. Martin Yardas fell into the former category. At least he had six years ago. Contrasted with the gaunt ruin of a man in the chair—face pitted and charred, teeth yellowed like pit stains on an old white T-shirt—the driver's-license photo and intern photograph formed a cautionary time lapse of the brutal toll that drugs took on the body.

What other story did the pictures tell? Why was Charles Merrick bouncing a two-year-old Marty Yardas on his knee? Did Merrick have a son whom he'd kept off the grid all these years? His ex-wife's legal team had thoroughly excavated Merrick's life during the divorce, and she wouldn't have hesitated to use something this damning had it been discovered. After all, Martin Yardas was roughly the same age as Lea, which meant Merrick had been stepping out while Veronica Merrick was pregnant with his daughter. That took a special sort of person, and Charles Merrick was certainly special.

But it also appeared that Merrick had remained involved in his son's life . . . to a point. He'd bounced Martin on his knee, at least once, and arranged an internship at Merrick Capital. Would that be enough to manipulate an eighteen-year-old into being his accomplice? Convince a kid to be his lackey while he served an eight-year prison sentence? Gibson knew the answer to that. It was if the son worshipped him. If the son craved his acceptance and respect. A son like that would risk just about anything. And from Charles Merrick's point of view, it certainly made practical, if cruel, sense—who else would Merrick have entrusted with his money? Who else but a young, estranged son desperate for Daddy's approval? Gibson glanced at the pitiful remains of Martin Yardas.

Look what loyalty earns you, he thought.

"CharlesMerrick119070&," whispered Yardas.

Gibson nearly jumped out of his skin. Unwittingly, he'd imagined himself as alone in the room.

"What did you say?"

Yardas repeated the string of characters.

Gibson entered it into the username field and looked expectantly at Yardas. "What's the password?"

Martin Yardas stared sullenly past him at the monitor; his lips moved silently. Gently, Gibson prodded him for the password, but Yardas said nothing more.

Then why give me the first half? Just to mess with me?

Gibson didn't think so. Yardas wanted to tell him, but he needed permission.

"I won't tell him that you told me. I promise. It'll be our secret."

"Our secret?" Yardas repeated.

"It's not his money. You know that."

Giggles burbled up again from the cracks in Martin Yardas as if Gibson had unwittingly told a profound joke. Gibson saw tears coursing down his cheeks.

"Why don't you tell me?" Gibson asked. "What's the password?"

The giggling faded to silence, and Gibson watched Yardas struggle to his feet. The man wasn't well, but he wasn't as weak as he looked. He shuffled over to the computer, leaned over Gibson's shoulder, blocking Gibson's view, and quickly typed a long string of characters. Yardas hit enter and drew back to show Gibson.

He was laughing and crying again.

It must have been a strange sight: this ragtag motorcade snaking its lazy way through West Virginia. Her father's rented security at the fore, pursued by God only knew who. If you could call it pursuit. Everyone driving responsibly below the speed limit, obeying all posted traffic signs—not willing to risk police interference. It lent the proceedings an illusion of peacefulness that Lea wanted desperately to believe, but she sat facing backward and in the gathering twilight could see the long line of cars come for revenge. There would be no peace today.

Not all the cars from the prison were behind them now—some had, no doubt, assessed the competition, calculated the long odds, and decided that dead was too high a price to pay for Merrick's scalp. Part of Lea wished that she'd been one of those, because judging by what she saw out the rear window, more than enough remained to see the job through. Didn't the hearse lead the way in a funeral procession? That's what this felt like—Charles Merrick's funeral. Because whenever they got to where they were going, the cars trailing behind planned on burying him.

Lea sat squeezed in between two men. To her left, a fearsome, heavily bearded white man made all the more intimidating by the military chest rig and combat rifle wedged between his legs. He had the kind of beard that food disappeared into, never to be seen again until the ants retrieved it. The man hadn't spoken or acknowledged anyone, his attention absorbed by the chatter coming in over his headset. To her right, a pensive black man with a troubled expression fidgeted with a cell phone, checking the time every few seconds. Lea feared he might see the Walther holstered between her legs; she crossed her legs away from him.

Her parents, on the other hand, sat comfortably side by side at the back of the limo and appeared entirely oblivious to the situation. They carried on as though this were Central Park and heavy traffic on the Sixty-Fifth Street Transverse were keeping them from the Metropolitan Opera. Lea squinted into the fading sun and studied the former husband and wife. Charles Merrick certainly didn't look like a man just out of prison, and eight years had done nothing to dull his shine. The years had been less kind to her mother, and it angered Lea to see her alongside him. She had always been a slight woman, but now she verged on a sinewy, self-inflicted gauntness. Her features had gone from sharp to severe, the tautness of her skin no longer a sign of youth but of will. Veronica Merrick had never lacked for that.

Lea also found it disquieting how familiar this all felt: riding in a limo while her parents bickered without ever quite fighting. Separated eight years, they'd resumed the tense cold war that had defined their marriage without missing a beat. It left Lea with a terrible feeling of emotional déjà vu that made it impossible to keep up her ruse that she was the sweet, naïve daughter just happy to be reunited with her father. She felt the pantomimed smile plastered to her face slipping.

"Is she all right?" her father asked her mother.

"She's upset," Veronica said.

"Oh, do you think?" Merrick said dryly. "Poor girl is obviously in shock. We should have told her a long time ago."

"Told me what?" Lea interrupted to no effect.

"You know we couldn't."

"Where has she been all this time?" Charles asked.

"I honestly don't know."

"I'm sure you don't."

"Tell me what?" demanded Lea.

She'd have bet money on all four Beatles reuniting before seeing her parents partnered up in any manner. Charles and Veronica Merrick despised each other. That was the bedrock on which Lea had anchored her worldview. The basis for all her decisions. Her parents' divorce had scorched the earth and laid ruin to any pretense of civility between them. Her father had betrayed his wife, humiliated his family, and left them all destitute. That was indisputable—the reason Lea had come to Niobe. To avenge her mother. To set things right and see her father punished. Yet here they were, discussing her as though she weren't there. A terrible thought occurred to her.

"Are you two . . . together?"

Her parents stared at her as though she'd just appeared through a wormhole. Her mother's face crinkled into one of her patronizing smiles that passed for laughter.

"Oh, darling, no. Absolutely not. Your father is still a disgrace."

"Thank you, Veronica," Charles said and turned to Lea. "Your mother and I have an arrangement."

"What arrangement? And who are these men?"

"Oh, where are my manners? This gentleman is a mercenary. I'm not sure of his name. Excuse me."

The beard looked in Merrick's direction.

"Yes. What is your name?"

"Smith."

"His name is Smith," Merrick said. "He's part of the detail I've contracted to escort us out of the country."

"*You* contracted?" Veronica asked, eyebrow arched.

"Well, I am paying, aren't I?"

Veronica allowed the point to stand.

Merrick gestured to the pensive man with the phone fetish. "And this is Damon Ogden of the Central Intelligence Agency."

For the first time, the mercenary took an interest in the conversation and looked Ogden up and down.

Damon Ogden glared at Charles Merrick. "Are you out of your goddamned mind?"

"What? She's my daughter."

"This is, without doubt, the most bizarre family reunion of all time." Ogden leaned across Lea to speak to Smith. "How much longer to the airfield?"

"Two mikes," Smith replied.

"What is he doing here?" Lea asked, indicating Ogden.

"Ah, well, Damon is central to our arrangement. He's sort of an impartial observer . . . in an unofficial capacity. I can't really say more than that, I'm afraid."

Lea didn't understand. "You made a deal with the CIA?"

"It's complicated."

"This is why we couldn't tell her," Veronica said. "She has no nuance."

"What does that even mean?" Charles asked.

"Nothing."

"Thirty seconds," said the mercenary.

"No. What does that mean?" Merrick continued, undeterred.

The man from the CIA cleared his throat and told them both, in no uncertain terms, to shut the hell up. Under other circumstances, Lea would have savored her parents' astonishment at being spoken to so rudely, but she was distracted by Smith's hand sliding nonchalantly down to his rifle's trigger guard. Such a small thing, but it brought the stakes into focus. Out the window, night had fallen; a wooden sign whipped by announcing "Dule Tree Airfield." They took the turn hard, limo barely slowing as it left the main road, and then Lea felt the punch of acceleration throwing her forward in her seat. They caromed up the unlit dirt road for a mile or two, climbing the entire time until, finally, the road leveled off and they passed through an open gate and the airfield spread out before them.

It didn't look like much—the airfield—just an open space on a wide, flat hilltop carved out of the forest. It consisted of a single runway, a clapboard office, and an open hangar where a handful of single props—Pipers and Cessnas—were parked behind a chain-link fence. Lea didn't see anything that resembled a tower, or a single light on in either of the buildings. Everyone had gone home for the day. The only light she saw came from a pair of aircraft parked side by side at the end of the runway. The limo left the roadway and made a beeline for them. Lea recognized them as Gulfstream G450s, the same model that had once ferried her parents around the world back at the height of their power.

"Why are there two jets?" Lea asked.

"One for each of us," her mother answered. "Once we've conducted our business, of course."

The limo came to an abrupt stop behind the two jets, and the three SUVs in their little convoy formed a tight semicircle between the limo and the entrance to the airfield. Doors opened in concert, and a small army deployed, fanning out along the defensive perimeter created by the SUVs. Lea watched a two-man team set up a machine gun. This was a war zone . . . or was about to be.

Smith tapped on the window before exiting. "It's ballistic glass. Doubtful anything will penetrate that, but heads down if it gets loud."

He slammed the door and hustled over to join his team. Lea found that far less comforting than he'd intended it to be. The four of them sat in silence, staring at each other.

They'd bought themselves a small head start with their high-speed ascent, but now Lea saw one and then multiple sets of headlights crest the rise. The lead vehicle, an SUV, veered off the gravel road and made straight for them, picking up speed as it came. Lea heard several hollow, faraway pops. The windshield of the oncoming SUV turned a mottled white, and she watched it turn drunkenly and slam into the fence surrounding the hangar. The cars that followed took the hint and peeled away, stopping a hundred yards away. More and more vehicles arrived, spreading out across the grassy field. Headlights went off, and Lea saw a bustle of activity outside the cars, but no more shots were fired, at least for now.

The limo door opened again. Bo Huntley joined them. He handed a camouflage-green laptop to Merrick. Its hardened case looked like it could survive a five-story fall without a scratch.

"All right, sir, just need to transact a little business, and we can have you on your way. Do you have a destination in mind?"

"I'll tell the pilot when we're in the air."

"Copy that. Your wife has our routing numbers."

"She's not my wife."

"Thank the lord." Veronica unfolded a crisp sheet of paper and cleared her throat, ready to read the numbers to him.

"I'm not getting a signal," Ogden said, holding up his cell phone.

"Not an issue. The limo has a satellite hookup," Huntley said. "So . . . CIA, huh?" Word had traveled fast.

Ogden sent a glare in Merrick's direction. For his part, Merrick glanced over the top of the laptop at Lea and smiled reassuringly at her. Lea somehow managed to return it. Ironically, she appeared to have won over her father with ease—it was almost insulting—but to see him sitting beside her mother now made her question what she thought she meant to accomplish. Had her parents conspired since the very beginning? If so, then she'd been played right along with the rest of the world. But what else could their "arrangement" be? She wanted to scream.

It might not be *nuanced*, but she would have some answers.

CHAPTER THIRTY-FIVE

1,490,201.12.

Million, not billion.

It lacked a very significant zero. Gibson stared at the figure, trying to understand. It might be more money than he'd ever had at one time, but it was pocket change to someone like Charles Merrick and certainly not start-a-new-life money. This couldn't possibly be all of it.

"Are there any other accounts?" Gibson asked Yardas, who only shook his head. "So where was the rest of the money? There's supposed to be a billion dollars here."

Lea's math had been correct; Gibson had doubled-checked it himself. He tabbed through the account's activity log, looking for signs of recent transfers. Nothing. No funds had moved in or out of this account in eight years. And what's more, the account was liquid and had been dormant for eighteen months. So what did those fifty-six text messages mean? Gibson stared at the screen, trying to make sense of what he read.

"Where were all Merrick's trades, Martin?"

Martin didn't answer.

Don't get greedy, he cautioned himself. With Merrick free, Gibson didn't have the luxury of solving the mystery of the missing billion. A million and a half dollars, while not as much as he'd hoped, was still enough to give the Birks and the Swongers the fresh start they deserved. Enough to improve the judge's quality of life. It was enough. *So don't get greedy.* He had come too far to leave empty-handed. Gibson keyed in the transfer and entered the routing number to Birk's account in the Caymans. His finger hovered over the enter key, stopped, and changed the amount before executing the transfer—it felt right to leave Charles Merrick a little something.

As Gibson transferred the funds, it didn't occur to him to wonder why Yardas had fallen silent. Gibson was preoccupied, wondering if maybe there was something that he'd missed. He reached for the keyboard again as a thunderclap struck. The monitor exploded, flipping off the desk like a popcorn kernel. Gibson stared stupidly at the shattered monitor, ears ringing. The thunder came again. This time two bullets slammed into the computer's minitower, and Gibson, with primitive understanding, threw himself to the floor.

He rolled over to see Martin Yardas holding a thick silver .357. Everything moved in that gauzy, oatmeal-slow way when his adrenaline kicked in. It gave him time to wonder about irrelevant things, such as how long Yardas had been wearing that underwear and where he'd been hiding that gun. Didn't matter. Martin Yardas was crazy enough to use it. Gibson put his hands up, but it was the computer Yardas wanted, not Gibson. The thin man went to the desk and put another round through it like a mercy killing. Then stood there staring at it, his lips moving mechanically. Gibson couldn't hear the words over the ringing in his ears, but when it subsided, Yardas was still saying "sorry." Over and over as tears rolled down his face.

"Where's the money, Martin?"

"It's gone."

"Gone? Where did it go?"

"Lost."

Gibson didn't understand what that meant. "What do you mean?"

"I lost it."

Then Yardas cursed at the top of his lungs, doubling over at the force of it—a mad howling cry like a demon fighting an exorcism. The demon was winning.

"Lost it how?" Trying to keep him talking. Keep him on the thin side of coherent.

Yardas's hand went white around the .357, and for a second Gibson thought he'd asked his last question, but the gun stayed pointed at the ground.

"I was supposed to invest it," Yardas said in a whisper.

"You did." Gibson had seen the old transaction logs on the broker-age site.

"Yeah. But I did it wrong . . . he would have been rich."

Gibson was missing a piece of the puzzle. "Start at the beginning. How much money did Merrick have when he went to prison?"

"Three hundred and seventy million dollars."

Much less than a billion, but Gibson still didn't see how Merrick could have hidden it from the Justice Department. It was impossible. That kind of money would have left a trail a mile wide.

"And you've been investing it for him? All this time. He's been sending you text messages with investment instructions. I saw the texts."

"Yes."

The story tumbled out now through the tears. A truth that Martin Yardas had been living with for eight years. It must have been a relief to say it out loud. To admit it to someone, anyone. A son's confession.

From the beginning, Martin Yardas had disregarded his father's investment instructions, which he found strange and out of touch with reality. So instead of filling Merrick's orders, Yardas had struck out with an investment strategy of his own. He'd lost half of Merrick's money in the first year.

"I thought, you know, he'd been through so much. And he was in prison. So I could help, right? I'm not stupid, you know?"

"But you lost it? Three hundred and seventy million dollars? How is that possible?"

Yardas explained how: in a panic, he had chased bad money with good. So desperate to cover his losses that he'd made a string of high-risk, high-reward investments. None of which had panned out, each leaving him in an ever-growing hole. All the while lying to his father that everything was on track.

"And you're telling me that Merrick has no idea that he's lost almost everything?" *Well, everything now.* "He hasn't seen any of the statements or documentation?"

"He's in prison. What do you think would have happened if it had been discovered? We couldn't risk it."

"So Merrick thinks he has a billion dollars?" No wonder Merrick had been so cavalier in the interview.

Yardas nodded in despair. "One point two seven billion."

Gibson was no expert on the stock market, but to his understanding, anything above a 10 percent annual return was considered an exceptional year. For Merrick to more than triple his investment in only eight years, it would have meant a miraculous run. And all from prison. Instead, he'd been swindled by his broker. Apparently there was room left in the world for poetic justice.

"So he just took your word for it all this time."

"I was his son."

Yardas put the gun to his temple and pulled the trigger. He did it so casually—the way a man might scratch an itch with the tip of a finger—that Gibson didn't know to react until Yardas lay bleeding on the ground. In shock, Gibson still didn't move as he struggled to make sense of what had just happened. But then he heard a spluttering, coughing sound. Somehow Yardas was alive, struggling to bring the gun back up to finish the job. Gibson scrambled to his feet and wrested the gun away, then knelt beside the dying man.

Martin Yardas breathed in sandpaper rasps. It was a grisly sight. The bullet had entered at the temple and pinged around the inside of the skull, angry for a way out, until it found its freedom through his left eye socket. Blood pooled around his head like a halo, and he looked up at Gibson with his one good eye.

"I was his son."

Not knowing what else he could do, Gibson took his hand. "I know."

"A billion dollars . . . I'm sorry, Dad."

"I'll call an ambulance."

"I was his son."

Gibson heard a crash and the sound of splintering wood from the front of the house. Footsteps pounded down the hall, and Gavin Swonger came around the corner, gun in hand. It said something that Gibson wasn't even surprised anymore that Swonger had turned up. Of course Swonger had followed him. Gibson would have kicked himself if he weren't still in shock over what had just happened. The look on Swonger's face told the story.

"Goddamn, dog, not playing anymore, are you?"

"Hey, I didn't shoot him."

"That's cool. Did you get it first?"

"What?"

"The money. You get it?"

"Swonger, listen. I know what Lea said, but—"

"One point two seven billion," Yardas croaked.

Swonger's brow furrowed. "What's he talking about?"

"Nothing. You have to listen to me. There isn't any billion."

But Swonger wasn't listening and wasn't standing still for explanations. Gibson could see how it looked: a dying man, the sting of cordite in the air, and Gibson kneeling over him with a gun. Swonger's native paranoia had already jumped ahead to the part where Gibson had stolen the money and killed Martin Yardas to silence him. No matter what Gibson said, Swonger would see only betrayal.

"Where's the money?" Swonger asked, raising his gun.

Gibson wanted to explain, but instinct brought Yardas's gun up in self-defense. It was a reflex but the wrong one. Swonger let loose, pulling the trigger indiscriminately, gun held sideways like a gangster. Gibson flinched even though nothing happened, knowing he'd be a dead man now if Swonger's gun had a firing pin. Swonger stopped pulling the trigger and looked down at his gun. Gibson pointed the .357 at Swonger's chest and cocked the hammer.

"Listen to me."

Swonger took two steps back and bolted for the front door. Gibson chased after him, more to make certain that he was gone than out of any desire to catch him. At the door, he heard the wailing shriek of tires as Swonger's Scion roared away.

Good. Let him go. It didn't matter now.

He went back inside to find that Charles Merrick's son had died. This wasn't a part of the country where people called the police over a few gunshots, but he wanted to be long gone just in case. It was time to go. He wiped off the .357 as best he could and dropped it near the body of Martin Yardas. Then he did the same to the computer, picture frames, and door. He'd come a fair piece to stand in this room with a man who had been dead a long time already. Gibson pitied the young man and felt a kinship with him. He had been a fool, yes. A lunatic by the end, almost certainly. But Gibson understood the influence that Charles Merrick had held over his unacknowledged child. How far the son would have gone to prove himself, and how far he had fallen in so doing. Well, it was over now.

And what about Charles Merrick's other child? Gibson hoped she was safe and hadn't done anything reckless. Although, in a way, she'd gotten her wish in the end. Perhaps not by her hand, but her half brother had done the job that she'd set out to do. Their father was finally penniless. Nearly anyway.

It was almost funny.

He only hoped that, wherever she was, she appreciated the joke.

———————

Charles Merrick stared at his account balance like an actor stumbling on stage and realizing that he'd learned the lines for the wrong play. He felt them staring at him and knew he should mask his horror, but for the first time in his life he couldn't hide his real feeling.

One penny.

He had one penny to his name.

Veronica looked over his shoulder and shrieked.

After that, things went to hell at an alarming rate. Bo Huntley snatched back the laptop and saw for himself. Then he snapped shut the laptop's case. Merrick recovered enough to try and fail to reason with him, forcing a laugh to remind everyone that he was still in control here. It took far more effort than he would have liked.

"This is preposterous," he said.

"Do you have any other available funds, Mr. Merrick?" Bo Huntley asked for the third time.

Merrick didn't see how that was relevant. He held a handkerchief to his cheek and dabbed at the blood. Veronica had scratched the hell out of his face and, judging by her torrent of threats, would do it again if Ogden let go of her arms. The veins on her forehead stood out impressively, and she'd screamed herself an unattractive shade of purple.

"Where's my money? How can there only be one penny in this account? What have you done with my money?"

Merrick wanted to shove his fist in her mouth, but she had a point. Where *was* the money? He needed a phone. What had that idiot bastard of his done?

"We had a deal, you son of a bitch," Veronica spat.

"Mr. Merrick . . . ?" Huntley prompted.

"Preposterous," he said again and felt his mind going blank.

"I'm going to need you and your family to exit the vehicle."

"You can't seriously intend to leave us here. My ex-wife put down a sizeable deposit."

"And we delivered you to the airfield as promised. That's as far as the deposit takes you. I ask again: Do you have any other funds?"

"They'll kill us."

Huntley had the look of a man sick of arguing with a five-year-old. He rubbed a spot between his eyes and came to a decision.

"All right, everyone out. You have ten seconds, and then we drag you out. You too, Ogden."

With that, Huntley exited the limo and began barking orders to his team. Ten seconds after that, the dragging out commenced in earnest.

———————

Lea walked up the runway, following the taillights of the two Gulfstream aircraft as they rose into the night sky until she lost sight of them among the stars. It was a beautiful, cloudless night, and the sky was awash with stars. Had there always been this many?

She'd known it was Gibson the moment her father went ashen at the computer. She didn't know how he'd managed it but hoped it was the van, because then she'd at least played a part. But it really didn't matter. Watching her father's meltdown in the back of the limousine was the most satisfying thing she'd ever witnessed. Goddamn, it was perfection. She smiled, and she felt strangely at peace—for perhaps the first time in her life.

Which was funny, because she also saw what a foolish, wasteful thing she had done. This revenge of hers, if you could even call it that, had been a mistake. A stupid, selfish waste of her time, and probably her life. Of all their lives. But knowing that now, as she did, she still would not have changed a thing. That was the thing about mistakes: often you had to make them to see them for what they were. And she wouldn't trade this feeling of clarity for anything in the world. There would be a high price to pay, but she would pay it gladly.

She slipped off her heels. She wasn't about to die with sore feet. At the end of the runway behind her, depending on one's perspective, a comedy or a tragedy was unfolding. Perhaps both. Pilots unpaid, both aircraft had departed, and her parents stood amid her mother's luggage, piled unceremoniously on the tarmac, arguing with the security team, who ignored them as they loaded back into their convoy of vehicles. Huntley offered Ogden a ride out of there, but the CIA man shook his head.

"I think I gotta stay."

"You sure?" Huntley asked. "Things are about to get loud."

"Yeah." Ogden didn't look any too excited about it.

"Your funeral."

Damon Ogden stood to the side as the convoy departed, cell phone in hand, still trying in vain to get a signal. For all the good it would do in the time remaining. They were in denial about what was coming. It didn't really matter. Acceptance was overrated.

Like Ogden's, her phone had no bars. She'd wanted to text Gibson good-bye. Thank him for everything. She doubted that she'd get another chance, so she wrote the text anyway. It wouldn't send now but would store in the phone's outgoing folder, and maybe someone, perhaps not her, would carry the phone within range of a cell tower. It would send then. Not like there was a rush, and it felt good knowing he might get it—her electronic message in a bottle. As an afterthought, she texted Margo a simple message:

    You were right.

There was nothing else to say.

Lea watched as the convoy crossed the airfield and disappeared down the hill. When they were out of sight, the scavengers that had been lying patiently in wait for the lions to abandon the carcass turned their attention to the Merricks. Lea walked back toward her parents. If they were to die, they would die together.

The first gunshot sounded like a handclap in the distance. The night quieted itself, curious to see what came next. Then another. And another. And then it was a string of fireworks, dancing in the street. Ogden crouched beside her father. Lea knelt beside her mother, who was using a suitcase as a shield. She thought about drawing her pistol, but at this range it would be like throwing pebbles into the wind. They huddled together behind the luggage and listened to the gunfire and breaking glass. It wasn't until the first screams drifted across the airfield that Lea realized that no one was shooting at her. They were killing each other over there. Whatever unofficial truce existed among them had run out the moment the security team left, and they were fighting it out for the right to claim the Merricks.

At this distance, it all seemed like an abstraction, the muzzle flashes oddly beautiful in the night. The entire skirmish ended in a matter of moments. A final volley and then nothing but the odd gunshot. A few stray vehicles fled. Men moved among the remaining cars and settled up with the wounded or the dying. Her mother tried to take her hand, but Lea wrenched it out of her grip. The time for pretending was over. Across the airfield, two vehicles separated from the pack and sped toward them.

The bill had finally come due.

THE GIANT, CRAZY BIRD

Don't you know about the praying mantis that waved its arms angrily in front of an approaching carriage, unaware that it was incapable of stopping it? Such was the high opinion it had of its talents.

—Zhuang Zhou

CHAPTER THIRTY-SIX

Time to get out of West Virginia. Get out. Get out. Get out. He'd thought of nothing else since Swonger tried to gun him down with his busted .45. *Get out, stay out.* First things first, though. Gibson needed to lose the van. He didn't want to take it back into Virginia. A bus stop in Morgantown behind the West Virginia University Hospital would be a good dump site. He could wipe it down, catch a Greyhound for DC, and put miles between himself and Niobe, West Virginia.

He drove as fast as he dared—seven or eight miles above the speed limit. With each set of headlights that came around the bend, Gibson saw Martin Yardas's ghoulish face pleading up at him for forgiveness or mercy. Whatever salve the dying believed would ease their final moments. The smell of that grim room clung to the roof of his mouth no matter how much water he guzzled. The sound of the .45's hammer falling, and the split second when he'd forgotten the firing pin in his pocket and believed his destiny lay beside Martin Yardas.

Go home. While there's still time.

Was there still time?

A bug the size of a small bird splattered off the windshield. Gibson jerked the steering wheel so hard the van wobbled into oncoming traffic.

He straightened out the van and tried to shake it off, forcing out a dead-battery laugh. Then he pumped wiper fluid onto the windshield until the bug was nothing but a streak at the edge of his vision.

Driving north and east, he felt the confusion of a pilot who'd fallen asleep at the stick and, emerging from a thick cloudbank to unfamiliar terrain, realized he was horribly off course. Far from home. He had no idea how he'd let this happen . . . except that wasn't the truth, was it? He knew exactly how it had happened. After all, he was the one who'd been on autopilot, and it was hardly the first time. That was the worst part—how familiar this all felt. Once again, he'd muted the responsible part of his brain, the part that understood consequence and in theory knew better. He'd done it as a teenager so he could go after Benjamin Lombard, again in Atlanta, and now, older and supposedly wiser, he'd done it yet again. Muted it so that he could do what he wanted. Well, it wasn't muted now, and it had a lot of catching up to do. So he drove along in silence while, in his head, he caught a damn good tongue-lashing.

Where to start? He'd fled his responsibilities at home to right a wrong for a man who had told him explicitly to stay away. He could dress it up as noble, but maybe he'd done it for selfish reasons. This was exactly the kind of father that he swore he wouldn't be. He saw that now. And for what? Nicole had probably run his visitation rights through a shredder by this point. No doubt exactly what she'd left the message to tell him—to stay away—and how could he blame her? He never had listened to it, but feeling masochistic, he hit play and held the phone to his ear. His ex-wife's voice was weary but calm:

"Figured you wouldn't answer. Listen. I shouldn't have said what I said. I'm not going to apologize, but I shouldn't have said it. And I didn't mean it. Not all of it. I was angry; I was frustrated. I couldn't take any more. Even if I know where it comes from. I know you. I know how you beat yourself up. I know how badly you wanted that job, and I know you think you've let us down. But we're okay. Ellie is okay. She doesn't care what kind of job

you have. So come back from whatever you've run off to do. It makes me nervous that even Toby doesn't know. Now quit being an asshole and come back before it really is too late."

The message ended, and Gibson threw the phone into the passenger seat. *Don't start,* he warned the voice in his head but then berated himself anyway, using language that would have made his drill instructors in boot camp proud. Thoughts of home pushed the van up to seventy-five, but he quickly took his foot off the gas. It would be the height of stupidity to get pulled over now. Getting home was the important thing, not how fast.

In the passenger seat, his phone vibrated, then vibrated again and again, signaling incoming text messages. Gibson drove a mile or two before snatching it up: "Lea Regan (3 Messages)."

"Nope, nope, nope, not my problem anymore," he said and dropped the phone back in the passenger seat. His show of callous bravado lasted less than two miles before he pulled to the side of the road. He stared accusingly at his phone, then, with a resigned sigh, picked it up.

```
I don't know if you can see the stars
where you are, but they're beautiful.
So many. Been here two years but never
noticed them before. Funny right?

I'm at Dule Tree Airfield with my
father. Just watched his plane leave
without him. It was beautiful. Don't
know how you did it, but it worked.
They'll be coming for us soon. Thank
you. Goodbye and good luck.—L.

If you're still in Niobe, get out.
```

There was a lot to digest in those three messages, and he read them through a few more times, trying to parse her tone—tone being the hardest thing to convey in a text message. Her words didn't read as scared, and she didn't seem under duress. That should have been a good sign, but he didn't like her good-bye one bit. It didn't sound like the Lea he knew. She sounded resigned. Fatalistic.

Gibson could see the chain of events that led to her messages. If she knew there was no money, then Merrick must have tried to access it. If his plane had left without him, then he had needed the money to get himself out of the country. But it wasn't there because Gibson had taken what little remained. That had left Merrick at the mercy of his many enemies, and frankly Gibson felt fine with that. Merrick deserved whatever he got. But how would Emerson and the fifth floor react? He remembered clearly what Emerson had said he believed. That he would kill them all. Well, Gibson had a bad feeling that Emerson might be making good on his threat.

Gibson looked up Dule Tree Airfield and let his GPS plot the fastest route. Then he spun the wheel and turned the van toward the airfield and muted his inner voice before it realized his destination. Around the first bend, he saw a familiar gray Scion idling on the shoulder. Of course, Swonger was still following him; he didn't know anything else. Gibson slowed to a stop in the middle of the road and rolled down his window.

"What are you doing?" Gibson yelled over.

Swonger stared straight ahead, both hands on the wheel. Maybe he thought that was how invisibility worked? Gibson didn't know what went on in his head.

"Swonger." Nothing. "You know I can see you, right?"

A car zipped between them, horn wailing. Swonger didn't so much as blink, stubborn as a two-year-old at bath time. Gibson waited, but Swonger looked prepared to turn blue before he'd acknowledge Gibson. So be it; he didn't have time to deal with this now. Gibson left Swonger to play statue, but a quarter mile down the road, Gibson saw the Scion swing around to follow.

Swonger made a point of riding the van's bumper all the way to Dule Tree Airfield. Gone were the days of following Gibson at a discreet distance. Gibson made no effort to get away; that would have felt foolish and been a waste of energy. He turned off the main road and climbed the dirt road to the airfield. The Scion followed. At the gate, Gibson killed his lights and coasted slowly toward the main office; he didn't see anyone, but that didn't mean they were alone. Behind him, at the front gate, the Scion waited patiently. Seeing no other apparent way out, Swonger seemed content to leave him to his reconnoiter.

Something had crashed into the chain-link fence surrounding the hangar. The impact had caved in several sections, and judging by the deep tire tracks, it had taken a lot of tire-spinning to dislodge whatever vehicle had been responsible. In the moonlight, Gibson followed the tracks out onto the field abutting the runway, afraid of who or what he might find in the tall grass. But apart from a torn-up field, Gibson didn't see any hint of Lea's whereabouts. It was a relief, but not much of one . . . something bad had happened here.

Gibson drove around the grounds, looking for anything out of the ordinary, but came up empty. Lea was right, though—there were so many stars.

Over on the far side of the airfield, a light in the trees caught his eye. It rippled among the branches, but he couldn't see its source. Curious, he drove to the tree line, which dropped away down a hillside. He grabbed a flashlight and walked to the edge. Thirty feet down, cars had been rolled off the edge and lay stacked on top of each other like models at the bottom of a kid's toy chest. A shattered pyramid of metal and chrome. Gibson also found the source of the light—one of the cars was wedged upright between two SUVs; it stood on its hind end, headlights illuminating the canopy above.

His sense of relief shaken, Gibson clambered down the hillside to an SUV that had rolled to a stop against a tree away from the main pileup. Other than a shattered windshield, it looked more or less intact. At least until Gibson played the flashlight over the SUV—someone had used the side panels for target practice. It looked like it had been flown in from a war zone. He shone the flashlight inside, but the SUV was empty. Something caught his eye, and he opened the driver's side door. Blood had pooled in and around the seat, shell casings glittering amid the gore. Someone had fought and died in this car. So where was the body? On a hunch, Gibson popped the trunk but found it empty too.

Gibson checked the other vehicles. Most had taken small-arms fire, and he found plenty of blood but still no bodies. Someone had won a decisive battle at the airfield, dumped the cars down the hill, and taken all the bodies. He wondered who had come out on top and had a sinking suspicion that he knew the answer to that one. Emerson looked to have made good on his word.

What he still didn't know was whether Lea was alive or dead, only that she wasn't here. And that left only one option.

Niobe.

CHAPTER THIRTY-SEVEN

Not long after midnight Gibson arrived back in Niobe. He powered up the Stingray and programmed it to sniff for Lea's cell phone. Then he rolled slowly up Tarte Street, looking for signs of life, but the town was as still as a held breath. At the liquor store, a tumbleweed dog aloof on its haunches watched him go. As the familiar outline of the Wolstenholme Hotel loomed up on his left, the Stingray began to ping, the signal strengthening as he passed the front entrance. Lea's phone was inside. He glanced up through the glass doors into the dark of the lobby. A figure in the gloom stepped back and out of sight, or it might have been nothing but a shadow thrown by his headlights.

The hotel's side parking lot was deserted. As were the five spots in front of the Toproll—a first in Gibson's experience. He parked in back beneath the stairs to Lea's apartment, tossed his baseball cap on the dashboard, and scratched his scalp hard with both hands. No sleep in the past twenty-four hours had him feeling like a tire with no tread left.

A cinder block propped open the Toproll's back door. He counted that as an invitation and let himself inside. Faint music led him through the kitchen to the swinging doors that opened out to a nearly empty bar. Peering out, Gibson saw Margo behind the bar and Old Charlie at his regular perch, keeping a lonely vigil over a shot and beer. He found the man a comforting sight.

Gibson took a seat, and Margo came down the bar to see what he wanted.

"Well, well. The prodigal asshole returns."

"Coffee," he said. "Please."

She poured him a cup. "Fresh pot."

"Sugar?"

She slapped a caddy down on the bar.

"Where is everyone?"

"No one came in tonight, so I closed early."

"How come?"

"You know how come."

"What's the sheriff think?"

"Ain't seen the sheriff all day. Jimmy Temple neither. Hotel's been shut up tight since the fifth floor came back from wherever they went. Then the phones went out—landlines and cell. Internet too. That was two hours ago now."

"Is that all?" Trying to buck himself up with a lame joke.

"And I'm stuck with him?" She pointed to Old Charlie.

"You never had it so good," Old Charlie muttered.

"Lea with them?" Gibson knew they had her phone, and that probably meant they had Lea, but he would love visual confirmation before making his next move.

"Lea quit and moved out this morning. She's long gone."

"You really believe that?"

"No," Margo said and warmed up his coffee. "She went to the prison."

Gibson filled Margo in on the rest. How from the prison she'd gone to the airfield with Charles Merrick. The text messages. He described what he'd found at the bottom of the hill.

"Why didn't you stop her?"

"I think there was no stopping any of us."

"Damn, but you're a bunch of fools."

Truer words had never been spoken; still, there was a silver lining. Gibson knew the fifth floor hadn't gotten what it had come for at the airfield. How could it? There was no money to get—Gibson having finished the job that Martin Yardas had begun years before. But Emerson wouldn't have taken Charles Merrick at his word. They'd have to interrogate him, and that would require time and privacy. Why else come back to the hotel at all? A town this size probably had a single trunk line that handled phone and data; knocking it out had put Niobe on an island. For one night, the fifth floor owned Niobe, and that was all the time they'd need to extract their mistress's pound of flesh. Gibson didn't like to think about what might be happening over in the hotel. Especially since Charles Merrick couldn't give them what she wanted.

He needed a plan.

"What are we gonna do?" Margo asked with a bartender's clairvoyance.

"Let me get a whiskey."

"Not sure drinking is a solution," Margo said.

"Actually, make it two. I'll be right back."

"Now we're cooking with gas," Old Charlie cracked.

Gibson went out through the kitchen to the back door, ready to win a bet with himself. Sure enough, the gray Scion idled beside the van. Behind the wheel, Gibson's faithful shadow glowered at him. Rather than glower back, Gibson smiled. He felt a sense of admiration for Swonger. A camaraderie that surprised him, especially given all the trouble Swonger had caused him. Whatever else there was to say about Gavin Swonger, there was absolutely no quit in him. Didn't mean that Gibson didn't want to throttle him, and strangely that gave him sympathy for all the people in his life who wanted to throttle Gibson. An insight into what it must be like to care about him. He waved for Swonger to join him inside and went back to his two tumblers of whiskey.

"You gonna drink both of those?" Old Charlie inquired.

"Don't know yet," Gibson replied.

After a minute, Swonger eased through the kitchen door and stood there warily. "What do you want?"

"Talk."

"One point two seven billion. Nothing else to say," Swonger said, but came over to the bar anyway.

"Then how about you listen?"

"Where's the money?"

Gibson considered the best way to answer. He'd get only one shot at convincing Swonger, who wasn't the easiest sell on his best day. And this had been no one's best day. It would need to be a big play if he hoped to sway Swonger. Something that would put Swonger in the frame of mind to reconsider what he thought he knew for certain.

"Give me your gun."

"What for? Don't work."

"I'll give it back."

Swonger gave him a funny look but popped the magazine before handing over the gun. Then he took a seat at the bar next to Gibson and fidgeted nervously with the magazine. Gibson slid one of the whiskeys over to him. Swonger didn't touch it.

"You've pulled this on me three times now," Gibson said and began to disassemble the .45. "First time, up in New York, I thought you were just dumb. You're not, though, are you? Not by a long shot. But that thing they say about first impressions . . . well, yours stuck. Longer than it should have. And I've been treating you like you're stupid longer than I should've. I mean, you don't make it easy, but still, that's on me. Second time, at the motor pool, I told you not to bring a gun, but you did anyway. That was kind of the last straw. I knew I couldn't trust you, but I didn't get rid of you. I just pretended like it didn't happen and kept going. Couldn't figure out why I did that. But I realized something today."

He paused and produced the firing pin and the stop from his back pocket with a street magician's flair.

Swonger's face went slack. "Son of a . . . When? How?"

"Queens."

Swonger did the math and didn't like the sum of what it implied. "I been packing a busted piece since New York? That shit's cold, dog."

Gibson shrugged and put the gun back together while he told Swonger what he'd learned from Martin Yardas. He told it carefully. It was a true story, but that didn't mean it sounded true. Especially to someone who would want so desperately for it to be a lie. Who wanted to believe that their winning lottery ticket was off by one number? He finished with Martin's suicide.

"And then you burst in," Gibson said.

"You expect me to believe any of that?"

Gibson took the magazine from Swonger's hand. Swonger didn't let it go immediately, but Gibson tugged it free without too much struggle. A good sign that maybe he'd gotten through to him. Margo looked on in mute disbelief as Gibson slapped the magazine back into place and racked the slide. He laid the gun on the bar and pushed it back to Swonger.

"Oh, I can't even with this," Margo said and retreated to the relative safety of her office.

Old Charlie lifted his shot in anticipation of what might come next.

Swonger stared at it skeptically. "What's that supposed to prove?"

"It's a grand gesture, Swonger. Have a little poetry?"

Swonger picked up the .45, feeling the weight of it, studying it in search of answers. Gibson could only wait to see whether Swonger was friend, foe, or executioner.

"Poetry, huh? I pull the trigger, it gonna fire?"

"It'll fire," Gibson said, the moment of truth slinking into view.

"You a conundrum, dog, know what I'm saying?"

"So I'm told."

"So what you realize today?"

Old Charlie tapped his shot on the bar and drank.

Gibson smiled at Swonger. "That I could have been you. Or you could have been me."

Swonger looked at him quizzically. "How you figure that?"

"If I have a billion dollars, what am I doing back in Niobe?"

"Why'd you come back if you don't?"

"Lea. The fifth floor took her at the airfield. She's up in the hotel."

Swonger paled, but before Gibson could elaborate, the doors to the kitchen swung wide and Deja Noble knifed through, Truck Noble tight behind her. Terry followed, along with seven men. All armed. All grim purpose and ruthless intent.

"Oh, no," Swonger said.

"What are they doing here?"

"I maybe called Deja." Swonger didn't look too happy about that decision now.

The men fanned out across the bar, checking all the doors and corners. Two disappeared into the back room and returned a moment later to take up a post at the mouth of the hallway. One of them tried the door to Margo's office, but the door was locked. The man listened at it for a moment and then moved on. Deja traipsed toward them, trailing her hand along the bar.

"This town, ah-ahhh, is coming like a ghost town," she crooned in a faux-English accent. She stopped so close to Swonger that she practically touched him. Humming the melody to the song in his ear like a lover. "What are you fixing to do with that gun, Swong?"

"Nothing," Swonger said, swallowing hard.

"That's cool, but what say you let your Deja hold on to it for you, then. For safekeeping."

Swonger handed it to her with far less deliberation then he had with Gibson. Not that Gibson could blame him. Truck Noble glided past like an iceberg, brushing against their backs, and took the stool beside Gibson. He lifted Gibson's whiskey, the tumbler no larger than a thimble in his hand, and held it up to his nose. His top lip curled disapprovingly, and he put it down out of Gibson's reach. Terry stepped up behind Gibson and searched him; down the bar, Old Charlie was getting the same treatment.

"He's clean," Terry said.

"After all this, you still out here working your MLK game?" Deja said. "Don't get you nonviolent types."

"It has its advantages."

"Yeah? I was always more of a Malcolm X girl myself."

"Deja. Fellow over there staring," Truck grumbled.

Old Charlie had finally found something in the Toproll more fascinating than his shot and beer.

Deja looked down the bar at Old Charlie. "Ain't nothing to see down here, old man."

For a half a second, Gibson feared he had something smart to say, but Old Charlie dropped his eyes.

"Better?" Deja asked her brother.

"Don't like being stared at."

Deja rolled her eyes at Swonger. "See what you got me dealing with here?" she said. "Got me back in West Virginia, and you know how I feel about that."

Swonger nodded. "Sorry, Deja."

"Don't fret none. You did right to call. So tell me . . . what's this boy done with our money?" Then directly to Gibson: "Where's our money?"

Gibson looked at Swonger. He'd been wrong about the moment of truth. This was it now. Swonger looked back at him. For a sickening moment, Gibson knew, knew without question, that Swonger hadn't believed a word that he'd said. That he was about to be fed to the sharks.

"No, not him," Swonger said.

Gibson couldn't have been more surprised if Swonger had burst into flame. He wanted to plant a kiss on the top of his pointy little head.

Deja's eyes narrowed. "On the phone, you said it was your partner."

"I know what I said." Swonger swallowed hard. "Meant my other partner."

"White girl double-crossed you?" Deja said. "Didn't think little miss had that in her. Where she at now?"

"Across the street. But she didn't double-cross us; she got taken. The people who took her have the money now."

The best lies traveled in the shadow of the truth, changing only the bare minimum to achieve that end. Gibson gave Swonger style points for his performance, as he unspooled a version of events that was 95 percent truth and 5 percent fantasy. In the lie, Martin Yardas ceased to exist. The money was still a reality, but the fifth floor had snatched the Merricks at the airfield, brought them back to the hotel, and were probably up on the fifth floor counting the loot right this very minute. It was an impressive yarn, and Swonger grew into the telling of it. Gibson saw Swonger's plan—set Deja against the fifth floor. Let the two battle it out. Best case, the two sides would decimate each other. Worst case, Deja took the Merricks and found out Swonger had played her. It was a dangerous play, but it bought them a window of opportunity. It wouldn't stay open for long.

"How much?" she asked.

Swonger finished baiting the hook that Deja Noble wanted desperately to swallow. "A billion dollars . . . Maybe more."

Easy, Gibson thought. Don't overplay the hand. He needn't have worried; Deja's ambition betrayed itself in her smile. She asked how many guns up in there, looking to Swonger, then Gibson.

"Hard to say," Gibson said and described the scene at the airfield. "Could be a few, could be a whole lot."

Deja looked over to her brother. "What do you think?"

Truck nodded meaningfully. "Risky."

"No doubt. But is it worth it? That kind of money, we level up. Won't need the Russians no more."

Truck thought it over. "Don't like Russians."

"Amen," Deja said and stood up. She handed Swonger's gun back to him. "You're coming with us."

"Why do I got to go?"

"You don't go, you don't get paid."

"This is my score," Swonger protested.

She looked at him pityingly. "Swong, the only thing yours is those hopes and dreams, but that's all they are. Now, are you my boy or not?"

Tight-lipped, Swonger nodded that he was, indeed, her boy.

"So what's the plan?" Gibson asked.

"They're going to give us what's ours, or we're going to take it. One or the other."

"You're going to storm the hotel by force?"

"We're in the real world now, baby. Force is all there is. Once you get past all your weak-ass mind games, it comes down to force and the will to use it."

"What about me?"

"You? You stay put, Dr. King. Have yourself a little sit-in. Truck, keep an eye on Mr. Computer Hacker here. He tries to go anywhere, learn him why Malcolm was right."

Her brother nodded and slid Gibson's whiskey back to him as a consolation prize. Deja gathered Terry and the rest of her team to the side and laid out the situation. Swonger stood with them. When Deja finished her speech, Swonger glanced over at Gibson, who saw fear in his eyes. Fear but also something else. Swonger had always talked a big game, but now he was quiet and looked calmer than at any time since Gibson had known him. Almost brave. Well, he would need to be. They both would. One of Gibson's commanding officers had been fond of quoting Patton: "A good plan violently executed now is better than a perfect plan executed next week." Gibson had also heard it put more bluntly—a bad plan is better than no plan at all. Well, this was both of those, and none, and it would turn violent sooner rather than later.

Deja led her people out the front door and across the street. Gibson finished his whiskey in two gulps. He pushed the glass away and reached over for Swonger's tumbler. He needed to get free of Truck Noble. Easier said than done. The man was the size of the Death Star. He doubted the old "I need to use the bathroom" bit would come off like it did in the movies. Although he kind of did need the bathroom, now that he thought about it . . .

Truck Noble didn't view Gibson or Old Charlie as threats. He found the remote and put on *SportsCenter*. The office door opened a crack. Gibson had forgotten all about Margo. Old Charlie saw it too. From his angle, Gibson couldn't see in the door, but Old Charlie could and was having a telepathic conversation with Margo. The two seemed to arrive at a silent agreement, and the old man turned to stare at Truck Noble. Truck didn't notice at first, but at a commercial he caught Old Charlie's stare and didn't like it, not one bit. Gibson doubted Truck had had to say things twice very often in his life. Certainly not to run-down old men in bars.

"Tell your boy to quit staring at me," Truck muttered to Gibson.

"He's not my boy."

"Tell him."

Gibson told him, but Old Charlie kept on staring.

"I've been drinking here since 1967. I'll look where I goddamn please," Old Charlie said imperiously.

That brought Truck to his feet. He shoved Gibson toward the old man.

"I'm already done with this town, now quit staring before—"

Truck didn't finish his threat.

Margo wrapped the baseball hat around Truck's head. At least that's the way it looked as the bat splintered against his skull. The meat of the bat spun through the air and rattled off a wall. Truck took a staggering step forward, absorbing the force of the blow. He wheeled on Margo. Blood poured down Truck's neck from a gash over his ear, but he paid it no mind. Judging by the look on Margo's face, she'd expected the fight to be over already. She dropped the broken handle of the bat and brought her hands up in time to partially block the snap right hook that Truck delivered like a comet to the side of her head. It sent her crashing face-first across a table, and Truck sprang forward, wrapping one hand around the back of her neck, pinning her to the table, while the other rained blows down on her kidneys. Margo was strong, but Truck held her down effortlessly.

Gibson hit him low, driving his shoulder into Truck's ribs, trying to force him away from Margo. Truck didn't budge, and Gibson felt sudden solidarity with the bug that had splattered on his windshield. Hitting Truck reminded him of wrestling with his dad when he was six or seven years old. Truck pivoted with a ballerina's grace and flung Gibson clear. Gibson tumbled to the ground, rolled, and found his feet.

At least he'd accomplished his goal—Truck had lost all interest in Margo. That was the good news. Bad news, he seemed intent on putting Gibson's head in orbit. Truck closed on him in the blink of an eye. A man that big shouldn't be that quick. Gibson anticipated the same snap right hook, ducked it, but that only delivered his chin for the lefty uppercut that lifted him clean off his feet. He landed on his back and listened to cathedral bells toll, wondering who'd died. *You, dummy, if you don't get moving.* His head popped up, but he couldn't get his legs or arms to cooperate. Truck loomed over him, took a step forward, and stopped. The big man swayed drunkenly and shook his head. A mighty dry heave, and then Truck Noble vomited through his hands.

"The hell?" he puzzled aloud and dropped to one knee.

Gibson's arms and legs came back online, and he scrambled backward as Truck Noble toppled forward. The three of them looked at each other. Gulliver down.

"What happened to him?" Margo asked.

"Baseball bat must've taken a minute to register."

"I need a drink," Old Charlie said.

Margo told him to help himself. She fetched rope, and Gibson helped her hog-tie Truck. Badly concussed, the big man passed in and out of consciousness. It took both of them to drag him to the kitchen and lock him inside the walk-in pantry.

"Go," Margo said. "I'll mind our friend."

"Thank you."

"Try not to get her killed."

Gibson left by the back door, still wobbly on his feet. His jaw felt dislocated. He walked up a block before circling around to Tarte Street. He could see Deja's men forcing open the front door of the Wolstenholme Hotel with a pry bar. Swonger stood among them but distinctly not of them. Gibson could hear raised voices but couldn't make out what they were saying. Whatever it was, it wasn't any too friendly. But it did make for a nice diversion. The back of the hotel might be unguarded now, but he'd need to hurry.

Gibson broke into a run.

CHAPTER THIRTY-EIGHT

From beneath her hood, every sound had taken on an ominous dimension—the rustle of a curtain, a man's cough from behind her head, the indistinct murmur of men's voices. The effect was disorienting. Lea thought she might be back in Niobe. Maybe. She'd lost track since the massacre at the airfield. When Emerson Soto Flores had introduced himself at gunpoint, she'd been prepared to die. But the sense of peace that had gripped her at the airfield had faded, replaced by a sensible terror. Perhaps not dying had brought her back to her senses. The clarity that comes only when death runs a finger along your neck. She wanted to live but wasn't certain if that was in the cards any longer.

The only thing she could be certain of was the ropes lashing her wrists and ankles to this chair. That and the compact Walther still strapped to her thigh. At the airfield, Ogden and her father had been thrown to the ground and searched, but she and her mother hadn't warranted such treatment. From the way Emerson Soto Flores spoke, Lea didn't believe he held women in high regard. He and her father had that much in common. She hoped for the chance to make both men reconsider their prejudices.

A door opened, and the room fell silent apart from the whirl of an approaching electric motor. An older woman's voice broke the silence.

"I send you for two, and you bring me four."

"I'm sorry, Mother. It seemed wise to let you decide for yourself."

Lea recognized the man's voice from the airfield. Emerson Soto Flores's words showed respect, but the tension in his voice suggested that son and mother did not see eye to eye.

"We will see. How many did we lose?" the woman asked.

"Five. Tomás will not see the morning."

"So many?"

"There were more than we anticipated. It was . . . difficult."

"That is disappointing. Make Tomás comfortable."

"He is."

"And their killers?" There was a silence. "Good. The airfield is cleaned up?"

"The cars will be discovered, but no one will make sense of what happened there. The bodies have been prepared."

"Good. Then let me meet the two extras you have brought."

A rough hand gripped the nape of Lea's neck as the hood was tugged free. She blinked and looked around, confirming her suspicion—she'd been returned to Niobe. She'd never spent a night at the Wolstenholme, but there was no mistaking the faded opulence of the presidential suite. On her tour of the hotel, Jimmy Temple had recited the proud history of the hotel and shared anecdotes about its many illustrious guests. She wondered now if, in the last century, there had ever been a gathering quite as strange as this one.

Her fingers were numb and had turned a light frostbite blue. She flexed them, hoping to coax blood back into them, but the knots that bound her to this chair hadn't been tied with her circulation in mind. Beside her, Damon Ogden groaned under his hood; he'd taken the worst of it at the airfield. Her parents completed the row—four fools tied to chairs.

She counted six armed men spread around the room, many of whom she'd served at the Toproll over the last few weeks. Emerson knelt on one knee beside a woman in an expensive wheelchair with a plush burgundy leather seat. The woman was a lion, a proud dignity to her posture. No jewelry. A conservative black dress fell to her ankles. Lea guessed her age as sixty, and thought she might once have had a kind, maternal face, but the thick scars that bloomed at the woman's throat, fanning up her jaw and across her cheek, had burned all that away. The woman's silver hair, drawn back in a modest bun, made no effort to hide the melted scab that had been her left ear. Lea saw no kindness in her eyes, no signs of empathy of any kind.

"It's rude to stare, girl."

"It's rude to tie people to chairs," Lea snapped back, before she thought better of it.

The right side of the woman's face smiled. "Who is she?"

"Mother, may I present Chelsea Merrick."

"That explains her manners. Welcome, my dear," the woman said, and gestured for the next hood to be removed.

The guard moved down the row like a hostess in a game show revealing the prizes. Off came Ogden's hood. A length of rope had been used as a crude gag. That interested the old woman, who held up a questioning finger.

"Why is the black one gagged?"

"It was either that or cut out his tongue."

"Who is he?"

Emerson whispered in her ear, and Lea saw her smile.

"CIA? Well, what an unexpected windfall."

The final two hoods came off. The Merricks looked around in a panic. There were standard questions that came with the removal of hoods: Where am I? Why are you holding me? But no one asked them. Charles and Veronica Merrick knew better than to open their mouths. If they thought to question why, they could always refer to the swollen imprint of a pistol barrel that ran along Damon Ogden's swollen jaw, across his left eye, and up to his forehead. An object lesson in who was in charge and how the rules had changed since the firefight at the airfield. Rule one: Charles Merrick wasn't blustering his way through this. Rule two: No one gave a damn that Damon Ogden worked for the CIA.

"Do you know who I am?" the woman asked Merrick.

Merrick shook his head, downcast eyes showing a deference Lea never thought she'd see. Apparently, it took a pistol-whipping to teach her father a little humility.

"That's not unexpected. My name is Lucinda King Soto. Although you never met face-to-face, my husband worked for many years to move your money out of the United States. I've come for that money and for the honor of my husband, Montel Soto Flores."

Lea didn't recognize the name, but her parents and Damon Ogden certainly did. The three of them looked at the older woman in shock and fear.

"That's not possible," said Ogden. "You died in Mexico."

"Yes," Lucinda said. "Thank you for that."

"How?"

"How what? How did I stay alive after you painted my husband as a government informant?"

"That's not what happened—"

"Isn't it? Charles Merrick didn't betray my husband to save himself? Your government didn't exploit my husband's connection to Merrick to make cases against the cartel and its associates? And to seize the money he laundered on their behalf? Until even an idiot could see that my husband was the common link to all the arrests and seizures? And the cartel is not run by idiots. They reacted exactly as you expected they would and did your dirty work for you." Lucinda paused, her scars pulsing in anger. "Deny it again and I *will* have my son remove your tongue."

Damon Ogden seemed to take the old woman at her word. Lucinda nodded and a smoke-trail smile drifted across her lips. Lea recognized that smile. They were all actors in a play that Lucinda King Soto had been scripting for a long, long time. This suite was a stage, and Lucinda already knew the ending. Everything that happened from now until the end had been rehearsed in her imagination, and Lea and Ogden were now being written into the final act. This was the face of revenge, and it was ugly to see in someone else. Was this what she looked like? Lea wondered. Was this what Dorian Gray saw when he glimpsed his picture?

A knock at the suite's door interrupted Lucinda's moment. She glared at the two men who were ushered inside. They conferred in hushed tones with Emerson, who cursed under his breath. Lucinda demanded an explanation, which her son again knelt to deliver.

"Go," she said. "Leave Hector and Rafael. Take the others and deal with it."

Her son stood and led his men to the door. Lucinda stopped him.

"Emerson," she said. "They do not leave the lobby. Yes?"

"It will be done, Mother."

When they were alone, Lucinda studied Damon Ogden thoughtfully. The next act of the play was about to begin.

"It's fascinating how little we understand the forces at work in our lives. Up until now, I thought I had a clear understanding of Charles Merrick's betrayal. But it is only with your presence, Mr. Ogden, that I see the entire picture. That I must ask myself why the CIA would care about Charles Merrick. For years, I considered his paltry sentence proof that he had sold out his money launderer to secure a deal. But now I see that the real prize lay in China, didn't it? My husband was merely collateral damage. We were nothing but pawns to be cleared from your board. You let the cartel do your dirty work for you and eliminate the only man who could connect Charles Merrick back to China."

Ogden said nothing.

"I appreciate you not insulting me with a denial. To answer your question, Mr. Ogden, the cartel took my husband and I in Chiapas as we prepared to flee into Guatemala. At the time, we didn't know who had betrayed us. Only later did I realized that Charles Merrick was our patient zero. The source of the infection. Then we could only guess that the cartel had some sort of doubts about us. But when they took us alive, we thought foolishly that we would have a chance to plead our case directly to the *patrón*. After all, my husband's loyalty had never been questioned. Had he not overseen networks that for decades had laundered billions in cartel money without incident? Instead, we were delivered to an abandoned warehouse. Water dripped from the ceiling. Humidity like a clenched fist. We were bound to wooden chairs. Hoods blinding us."

Lucinda signaled to one of her remaining men, who put the hoods back onto their heads while she continued her story.

"We lived there, side by side, for days and nights. Yet I never saw my husband again. I heard him, though. And he heard me. Man from the CIA—you asked how I survived? Well, you have to make a choice, you see. It isn't an easy one to make, but you have to choose to endure. To cling to sanity even as your face burns.

"We knew nothing, as you well know, so we had nothing we could tell them. No way to satisfy them. And since our guilt was beyond dispute, that made them very angry. I confessed a thousand times. I would have confessed to nailing Jesus to the cross, but since I could not tell them to what I was confessing, they would not grant me the death I craved. They had a man. A gifted man. One at a time, we were untied and dragged into the adjoining room to this man so that the other might hear the screams. You cannot know the powerlessness and the despair that brings. To pray for your own agony to begin again if only to spare the one you love."

Lea listened to Lucinda King Soto tell her story with a mix of revulsion and empathy. Under the hood, she cried silent tears. For Lucinda King Soto, for herself. She knew enough theater to know that this story was but a preamble to something terrible.

"They always gave us a few minutes' respite between sessions," Lucinda continued. "Time to whisper to each other pledges of love. Never did we speak of what was occurring. Always my husband told stories of our youth. How we met. Private moments to take us away from our misery. While the cartel men laughed and cursed us. Then it began again."

Far away, the muffled sounds of gunfire punctuated her story. Lucinda paused to listen.

"My husband was not a healthy man, and the strain was inhuman. Twice his heart failed. Twice they brought him back. Unwilling for him to die on his terms. The third heart attack came as I was returned from my time in the other room. In a panic, they threw me to the floor and carried my husband away. I lay there. Unguarded. How do you survive? You make a choice, CIA. A choice to abandon your husband of thirty years, accepting that to stay means you will die together. But if you abandon him to die with those animals, then you have the chance to avenge him. You must break your wedding vows and run. Crawl, truthfully, on broken legs. Through a jagged hole and across miles of swamp until you happen upon a shop whose owner is too simple or too noble to turn you in for the reward."

"I can't imagine what you've endured," Veronica said.

Lea recognized her mother's charity voice. The warm, deeply concerned persona she assumed when addressing the media about this or that noble cause. Her entire childhood, Lea had never once heard it behind closed doors, and it sounded as false now as it had when she'd been a teenager.

Lucinda seemed equally unmoved. "No, you cannot imagine. But fortunately, you won't have to imagine for long."

"Listen to me. I had nothing to do with that," Charles said. "If you want to torture someone, torture him. The CIA sold you out, not me. I was in jail."

"We couldn't have done it without you, Charles."

"Ogden, you son of a bitch."

"Calm yourself, Mr. Merrick. You're not going to be tortured," Lucinda said.

"Thank you—"

"You're going to listen."

"What? What does that mean?" Merrick asked, voice rising to a shrill note. "There is no money. What does that mean?"

"Hector," Lucinda said. "Begin with the girl."

Lea felt strong hands at her ankles and wrists untying her ropes. She knew now what part Lucinda had written for her. She had been cast as the sacrifice. The room exploded into chaos. Everyone yelling, no one listening. As soon as she was untied, Lea kicked out, fighting to get away. For half a second, she struggled free of one set of hands, and her heart soared with false hope. She was blind and outnumbered, and the two men easily overpowered her. They each seized an arm and cuffed them in front of her before marching her from the room.

———————

Merrick struggled against his ropes but could do little more than listen to his daughter scream. From the sound of things, she was putting up a hell of a fight. Over and over, he demanded that everyone stop and be quiet. He knew he could sort this all out if only they would let him call his son. He didn't know what Martin had done with his money, but there was more than enough to reach some kind of accommodation. If only this madwoman could be made to see reason. But no one paid him any attention. It was this damn hood. To his side, Veronica yelled for him to give up the money.

Far away in his mind, he realized that his daughter had stopped screaming. The room fell eerily silent, and Merrick heard the echo of gunfire like distant thunder from downstairs. It had intensified over the last few minutes, although it didn't appear to have drawn any closer. He didn't think he could endure his daughter's pain. Why had she come to the prison? None of this should be happening. Through a haze of hot, frustrated tears he demanded the opportunity to speak. His chair rocked back and forth as he strained against the ropes, and then crashed on its side. The fall winded him, and he lay there listening to Lucinda King Soto mock his pain. He howled out his despair.

"Rafael," Lucinda said. "Set this imbecile upright."

Merrick heard footsteps approach, and Rafael began to heft his chair upright. A single gunshot, immediate and deafening, froze Rafael in place. Merrick couldn't place where it had come from, but Lucinda called out in Spanish. He didn't understand her words, but he recognized her fear. Merrick's chair crashed back to the ground as Rafael swore in anger.

A hail of gunshots cut him short, and Merrick felt a thud near his head. The guard grunted three times in quick succession and then deflated like an old balloon, whistling in Merrick's ear.

Lucinda gasped. "No, please, no, no, wait—"

A single gunshot.

Lucinda cried out, then said nothing more.

Merrick couldn't follow the action but guessed someone had slipped away from the battle downstairs. But who? They'd been spared whatever fate this psychopath had planned for them, but he doubted this was a rescue. The only question was whether this was the frying pan or the fire. Whichever it might be, best to start on the front foot.

"Hello?" Merrick began. "Thank you. Whoever you are, thank you. She was insane. Please help us."

He felt his hood tug free. He blinked and looked up into the face of his daughter. In his shock, Merrick noticed for the first time how much his daughter resembled her grandmother. She knelt over Rafael, who lay on his side, left leg twisted beneath him at an unnatural angle. She rummaged through his pockets for the key to the handcuffs that shackled her wrists.

Behind his daughter, Lucinda slumped in her wheelchair—a puzzled expression on her face, eyes looking blankly to the heavens, as if someone had told her a terrible joke but botched the punch line. Merrick looked back at his daughter, noticing for the first time the pistol in her hand and the blood splattered across her. The answer was obvious, but he couldn't quite put it together in his mind.

"Chelsea?" he asked dumbly.

"I ruined your dress."

"What . . . ? It's all right. I'll get you another."

"I don't want another."

"Okay, that's okay," he said soothingly. "Now, listen. You need to untie us quickly. Before more come."

She put the gun down and reached for his left wrist. But instead of untying the ropes she unfastened his watch. She held it up for him to see, then brought her face close to his.

"Dad, I need to tell you something."

"What is it, honey?"

"It was me."

"What was?" He sought understanding in her eyes. "Untie us."

"I took your money. It was me. I wanted you both to know that when they come for you. Good-bye, Mother . . . you deserve each other."

Lea stood while he tried to make sense of what she'd told him. Damon and Veronica both began babbling in unison, trying to bargain with her, but Chelsea was already halfway to the door. Merrick held on to the preposterous notion that she was merely going to lock the door to give herself more time to free them. Only when the door clicked shut behind her did he understand.

He laid his head on the carpet and wept for himself.

CHAPTER THIRTY-NINE

The rear façade of the Wolstenholme Hotel could have been more forbidding. Sure, it was possible. Throw in a few gargoyles. Maybe a moat and fill it with alligators.

Gibson told himself it would be fine. Chances were, Deja and her boarding party had drawn attention away from the rear entrance. Unless the fifth floor were disciplined, which up until now they had been. He judged it to be about thirty yards. Thirty yards of open, well-lit parking lot between him and the hotel. All it would take was a single man with a rifle to ruin his night. Gibson wouldn't even hear the shot that put him down. He scanned the darkened windows again. Nothing.

It wasn't a comfort.

He broke cover and sprinted across the parking lot. No serpentine or zigzag nonsense; he put his head down and ran for his life. Thirty yards later, he threw his back against the hotel and strained to hear any indication that he'd been seen. So far so good. Now he needed a way in. Vehicles were parked in tight formation around the loading dock, so he didn't feel like rolling the dice there. Emerson wouldn't leave his escape route unprotected. Instead, Gibson hoisted himself up on a dumpster, where he realized the jump was a lot farther than it looked from up on the fire escape.

Don't be such a baby, he told himself; it's only a ten-foot jump from the top of a dumpster to an antique fire escape. In the dark. If he missed, he was going to break something. Hell, he might break everything.

"You can do this," he whispered to himself.

Gibson took a short run up, leapt, and reached for the bottom edge of the fire escape. Actually, the jump was the easy part. The hard part was absorbing his forward momentum with his shoulders and arms so that his lower body didn't swing him loose and let gravity slam him down onto the concrete.

To his surprise, he managed to hang on. He hauled himself up and rolled his shoulders in their sockets. A pair of gloves would've been nice; he wiped the blood on his pants and picked splinters of black metal from his palms, then climbed the fire escape to the third floor. He knew someone had been in his room, because the window was open, and the smell that greeted him made him gag. It reminded him of a latrine that had taken a mortar round when he'd been in the Marines. He remembered the sad bastards tasked with cleaning it. Not the kind of thing they put in the recruiting commercials. Gibson covered his mouth and nose with the collar of his shirt and climbed inside.

His room had a new guest.

Gibson stood over the body lying on his bed—fully clothed, on top of the covers. From the look of him, he hadn't been dead long enough to decompose, but he'd taken at least one round to the gut, which explained the terrible smell despite the window opened for ventilation. Gibson reckoned he'd found one of the second-place finishers from the airfield shoot-out, although why the body had been brought back here he couldn't guess. He doubted it was out of respect for the dead.

Time to move.

The door guard blocked the door so it couldn't close all the way. As if someone had just run down the hall for ice. Gibson slipped out into the hallway and made his way to the stairwell at the front of the hotel. Along the hall, every door was cracked open the same way. Morbid curiosity forced him to check all the rooms in turn. In every bed, another body. All strangely serene despite the brutality of their deaths. This was a morgue now, not a hotel. But so far he couldn't count Lea among the dead, and that gave him some small hope. Near the end of the hall, Gibson found the sheriff and Jimmy Temple; they lay side by side in a queen bed. They hadn't been shot like the others but were dead all the same. Gibson touched the scar around his throat, cursed, and left them as they lay. Emerson Soto King had a lot to answer for.

In the last room, he found the answer for why the doors had all been cracked open: a simple but effective bomb attached to a radio detonator, wrapped around two barrels of acetone that would act as an accelerant. By design, hotel doors swung closed to act as fire breaks, and propping the doors open would cause the fire to spread even faster. Now that he thought about it, the windows hadn't been opened to air out the rooms but to provide oxygen to feed the fire. He'd bet good money that he'd find a similar device on every floor. The old hotel would go up like a bonfire. It would cover the fifth floor's tracks crudely but efficiently. Investigators would spend years attempting to unravel what had happened in Niobe, much less be able to prove it.

Gibson knew better than to attempt to disarm the bomb himself. It wasn't his skill set, and simply because the bomb wasn't complex didn't mean it hadn't been designed by a pro. Good bomb-makers always anticipated attempts to defuse their work. His best hope was to find Lea and get far from here before it detonated. At the mouth of the main staircase, angry voices rose up from below, trading threats and promises of violence. Gibson slipped out onto the stairs, but heavy footfalls drove him back into hiding. He held his breath as Emerson led half a dozen men down the stairs. If they'd gone any direction but down, he would've joined Jimmy Temple for one final night's rest.

Below, gunfire exploded in an ugly cacophony. From the sound of things, Deja had her hands full. Hopefully she would hold their attention long enough for him to free Lea. Gibson glanced out onto the third-floor landing and saw that one man had been stationed on the landing to guard the rear. The gunman had his back to the wall with unobstructed views up and down the stairs. He would cut Gibson down before he took three steps.

A gun would come in handy right about now, and he was glad Deja wasn't there to tell him so.

———————

Guo Fa didn't know the new players down in the lobby, but they had his eternal gratitude. They'd drawn most of the security detail away from the presidential suite, and that presented a window of opportunity. Fate had smiled upon him, and he would not allow it to pass him by again.

At the airfield, he'd cursed himself for underplaying his hand here in Niobe and allowing Merrick to escape. But then the planes had left without Merrick, and the firefight for the right to claim Merrick had exploded the night—decisive and brutal. Fa had watched the chaos from the tree line, a knowing smile creeping across his face: Gibson Vaughn had proven more resourceful than Fa could possibly have anticipated. Well, he hoped the hacker enjoyed Merrick's money; he'd more than earned it. Meanwhile, Fa's prize lay at the end of the hall. He drew his gun, tightened the suppressor in place, and made his cautious way down the hall. Fa had to admit to being more than a little curious about the identity of the presidential suite's mysterious guest. It was the only piece of the puzzle that still eluded him.

As he neared the suite, he heard a shot from inside. Fa rushed forward, fearing Merrick had been executed before he could be questioned. More gunfire caused Fa to reconsider. Not an execution, a fight. But who? He hadn't seen anyone enter. As he pressed himself to the wall and crept forward, the door to the suite opened. A blonde woman in a yellow dress emerged. He recognized the dress from the airfield, although he'd been too far away to see who wore it. Fa assumed Merrick had arranged entertainment for his flight. It seemed an accurate assessment now, for she held a pair of heels in one hand and closed the door delicately behind her, as if she were slipping out quietly after a one-night stand. In the other hand, she held a gun, and when she turned, Fa saw blood splattered across her dress. He recognized her as the bartender from the Toproll. Not at all who he'd expected to come through that door, but she didn't give him time to puzzle it out. She saw him and her eyes went wide. Her gun jerked up in his direction.

Fa shot her.

The impact drove her back against the door, knocking the gun from her hand. The shoes flew into the air. Her legs buckled and she sat down hard, collapsing onto her side. Fa tsked under his breath the way another man might at finding a stain on a crisp white shirt. He hadn't intended to shoot her, but what alternative had she given him? He watched her crawl after her weapon. She had heart. He stepped over her and picked up the gun, then rolled her onto her back with his foot. Her dress shone black with blood. The bullet had struck her in the chest and could have missed her heart by only millimeters. Lucky to be alive. Not that she would last for long without medical attention, and there were no ambulances on the way to save her. He leveled his gun to finish it. She raised her hand to block the bullet.

She did have heart.

Something stopped him, and he looked at her more carefully.

Charles Merrick's daughter.

She'd been right under his nose all this time. He cursed himself for missing it. Obviously she'd dyed her hair since he'd seen her last, but that was no excuse. He hoped his blunder would not prove fatal to his plans. Chelsea Merrick might yet prove a useful lever, but he didn't have time to waste tending to her injury. Every second that ticked by saw his window sliding shut. Fa took her by an ankle and dragged her to the nearest room. She whimpered as he yanked her over the threshold. The rooms on the lower floors held bodies from the airfield, but not the fifth floor. Until now. Fa brought her the towels from the bathroom and pressed them to her chest. She would live or die on her own.

"Pressure," he instructed her.

She wrapped her arms around the towels and held them like a life preserver. She looked scared. She had good reason.

"Tight," he said and shut the door behind him.

At the suite's door, Fa paused to listen, uncertain what to expect on the other side. Certainly not the carnage he found. He cleared the room of immediate threats and counted at least two dead. Thankfully, Charles Merrick lay on his side tied to a chair and very much alive. A guard who lay dead near Merrick had cleared his gun from his holster but hadn't gotten off a shot. His killer had been firing wildly; he'd been hit in the shoulder, the gut, and the thigh. The last of which had clipped the femoral artery, judging by the blood loss.

Chelsea Merrick's handiwork, he presumed. She had heart but lousy aim . . . lucky but lousy. Fa took the gun and pressed a finger to his lips for Merrick to stay quiet. A near-catatonic Merrick made no answer.

To Merrick's left, two hooded figures sat tied to chairs. The first could be only Veronica Merrick. Fa could hear her hyperventilating. He couldn't guess who the man beside her might be. A bodyguard perhaps? A fourth chair, rope coiled around the legs and armrests, sat unoccupied. Chelsea Merrick's, no doubt, but how had she freed herself and gotten her hands on a gun? He had more questions than answers.

He didn't recognize the woman in the wheelchair, but apparently she'd been in charge. Hard to imagine someone so frail being the author of so much havoc. Perhaps she'd been more fearsome before Chelsea Merrick had put a bullet in her head. Judging by the star-shaped wound in her forehead, blackened by soot from the discharge, it had been done up close and personal. The woman's expression, a mix of outrage and disbelief, suggested that things had not gone the way she had envisioned. Fa retraced Chelsea Merrick's footsteps back to the inner room.

On the bed lay the tools of the modern-day torturer. The would-be torturer, splayed on the carpet, had taken a bullet to the throat. Clearly Chelsea Merrick had had other ideas. Fa regretted shooting such an impressive young woman. But the interesting part of the narrative was that, after freeing herself, Chelsea Merrick had abandoned her parents. Chelsea Merrick had worked hard to put herself in this room with her parents and then brushed by them like strangers. What had she said to him before leaving him to his fate? Judging by Merrick's stricken, tear-stained face, it would have been worth hearing.

Fa knelt beside the fallen man.

"Hello again, Mr. Merrick. Do you remember me?"

"Lee Wulff."

"Exactly right. Have you enjoyed your first day of freedom?"

Merrick craned his neck up to look Fa in the eye. "What do you want?"

"Not in the mood to spar with me today? The last time we spoke, you were intent on being clever. I was looking forward to a rematch." Fa shrugged. "Ah, well. Straight to the point, then. Last we spoke, I made you an offer. You weren't interested. I thought perhaps you'd had time to reconsider, now that your financial situation has changed."

"How do you know about that?"

"Who do you think pointed Gibson Vaughn and your daughter in the right direction?"

The head of the unidentified hooded man jerked in the direction of Fa's voice.

"Who the hell is Gibson Vaughn?" Merrick asked.

"A very rich man, thanks to me," Fa said.

"Why?"

"So that I could help you, Mr. Merrick."

"You're here to help me?"

"Yes, that's all I've ever wanted to do."

"What are you offering?"

"To get you out of here. To offer you a comfortable life."

"How comfortable?"

"More comfortable than dying in that chair when your captor's men come back."

"And what do you want?"

"The name of your Chinese collaborator. Merrick Capital had a source inside my country's Politburo. The real secret to your success. I want the name of the traitor you sacrificed to the Americans to save your skin."

Merrick's eyes narrowed. "Who are you? Really?"

"For God's sake, Merrick," the other man said from beneath his hood. "He's a Chinese spy. Shut your damn mouth."

Fa rose and pressed the muzzle of his gun into the hood. "Who is this man?"

"Damon Ogden. My CIA pimp."

"Your handler?"

"Not anymore."

Not that Fa had any doubt, but the presence of the CIA was final confirmation that Merrick knew Poisonfeather's identity.

Ogden's shoulders slumped in defeat.

"He hasn't done so well by you, has he?" Fa said.

"No. What are you offering?"

"An apartment in Shanghai overlooking the Huangpu River. The opportunity to be a stockbroker again with one of China's finest investment firms. Citizenship in the greatest country on earth. And of course a generous consulting fee."

"How generous?"

"Ten million. US."

"I want twenty."

Fa chuckled. Even tied to a chair in a room full of bodies, Charles Merrick wanted to negotiate. The identity of Poisonfeather was worth ten times that amount to his government.

Veronica Merrick interrupted. "I'll give you the name for nine."

That was an unexpected development. Fa pulled off her hood.

"How nice to meet you, Mrs. Merrick. You know the name?"

"Of course I know the name. Who do you think ran Merrick Capital? Charles? That would've cut into his mirror-gazing time."

"Veronica, what do you think you are doing?"

"Negotiating my release."

"What do you think *I'm* doing?"

"Negotiating *your* release. I learned my lesson eight years ago when you changed the passwords on our accounts. Do you think I'm going to sit idly by while you double-cross me again?"

"You want to talk about a double cross? Let's talk about the fact that we started Merrick Capital together, but somehow your name wasn't on a single document. You reaped the reward and left me to take the fall."

"Charles. You wanted to play the big man and cast me as the little lady. Well, big men go to jail."

Fa watched them in wonder. Despite being tied to chairs, despite the bodies at their feet, despite the surging gunfire, neither Merrick possessed any inkling of the direness of their situation.

"It's a package deal, or I tell him now for nothing," Veronica Merrick snapped. "I would have gone to the press before just to see you suffer. I'll do it again now."

The Merricks glowered at each other.

"Okay, okay, you win. A package deal." Merrick looked to Fa. "Get us out of the country, and *we'll* give you the name."

"This is treason, Merrick," Ogden yelled. "Do you understand that?"

Fa cracked the butt of his gun across Ogden's head, and the man went limp. He cut Merrick free as a crash in the hall caught his ear. Fa handed Merrick the knife.

"Cut her loose. Be ready when I get back. I'm going to check our exit."

Fa drew his gun and glanced out into the deserted fifth-floor hallway. Sporadic gunfire echoed up the stairwell; the battle had reached a stalemate. If the Merricks followed his instructions and kept quiet, there was still time to get away. He recognized the enormity of that *if*. He calculated the time to get the Merricks to his safe house and make arrangements for their exfiltration. He hadn't counted on phone service getting knocked out. That had set him back, but he had a satellite phone at the safe house.

That left Damon Ogden. Leaving him alive was a risk, but killing a CIA agent on American soil was an act of war. Even the identity of Poisonfeather couldn't justify an unsanctioned assassination. But if Ogden somehow managed to raise the alarm, it would complicate matters. Fa scratched the back of his head. Then again, the man was tied to a chair in a building rigged to burn. Sometimes the thing to do was to do nothing at all. These situations had a way of working themselves out.

In the hall, an upended planter led Fa to a thin blood trail on the carpet leading from the room where he'd stashed Chelsea Merrick. Somehow she was gone; a bloody handprint on the doorknob marked her exit. It didn't seem possible, but he saw no drag marks; she had gotten up on her own. His admiration for her continued to grow. Most people would have lain down and died, but not this woman. She didn't stand much of a chance, but Fa wished her good fortune.

Fa went back to the presidential suite to collect his cargo. Charles Merrick hadn't cut the ropes binding his ex-wife to the chair. It took Fa a moment to understand the blood on the knife. The blood everywhere. Merrick had put her hood back on. Had not looking into her eyes made it easier? Nonetheless, he'd made a mess of it, but he hadn't given up. American stick-to-itiveness at its finest. Merrick stood over Veronica Merrick's body; his shoulders shook, and he looked to Fa, eyes wide.

"Twenty million."

Fa raised his gun. "Drop the knife."

"I want twenty million."

"Twenty million," Fa agreed. "Now the knife. Put it down."

Merrick did as he was told and looked at Fa with sundown eyes.

"It's not the same, getting your own hands dirty, is it?" Fa asked.

"Twenty million."

How Fa despised these people.

CHAPTER FORTY

The tile floor felt cool against her face. She might be content to lie here forever, though Lea didn't imagine forever would be that long in coming. Still, the idea of dying facedown on a hotel kitchen floor didn't appeal to her any more than dying in an anonymous hotel room. With what strength remained, she raised herself to a sitting position and put her back against a wall between two stacks of boxes. Better. Not good, but better. A shaft of moonlight lit the kitchen in pretty blues it didn't deserve. All around, boxes stacked like haphazard skyscrapers formed a cardboard skyline that reminded Lea of the New York of her childhood.

What an odd place to die, she thought, but couldn't think of anywhere better. Not that it was up to her. Her legs could take her no farther. They hadn't been in a cooperative frame of mind, and the old, disused servant staircase, warped and uneven with age, had exhausted their patience. They'd gone out from under her at the top of the last flight, and she'd tumbled her way to the kitchen floor. Not that it had hurt. Strangely, nothing hurt, although her hands and legs felt terribly cold. Didn't seem right to die and feel fine. If she didn't look down, it was almost possible to forget that she was even shot.

Honestly, dying didn't sound so bad. Today hadn't given her the satisfaction she thought it would, but she'd done what she'd set out to do. She took comfort in the knowledge that this had all been her decision. That would have to be enough.

Strange the way it had ended, so close to getting away, only to take a bullet from a Chinese fisherman. He'd seemed irritated and a little sad about it. She hoped he didn't feel too badly; it all just struck her as funny now. The utter randomness of it. Except, of course, not at all. They'd all, for their own selfish motives, come to this godforsaken town, this godforsaken hotel. None of them were innocent. They'd all tallied the risks and chosen to stay out of greed or revenge. Or both. The very essence of human purposefulness in all its venal glory. So it was pure arrogance to think she would leave unscathed from this meat grinder. Lea could accept that now.

The gunfire sounded far away. Soothing in its way. Lea licked her lips. What she wouldn't give for a sip of water, but the kitchen sinks might as well have been in New York.

A stack of boxes blocking the dining-room door tilted and spilled across the floor. A figure squeezed through the opening and slunk toward her. Lea considered where she might hide, then realized the utter pointlessness. Whoever it was would be doing her a mercy.

Gavin Swonger stole into the moonlight, weaving his way toward the servant staircase. He paused a few feet away, almost close enough to reach out and touch. He hadn't seen her, and the dying part of her hoped he left her in peace. The living part thought that was about the stupidest thing it had ever heard. The living part won out. For now. Her lips spoke his name but couldn't muster so much as a whisper. Had she died? Become a ghost in her own silent film? He moved on, and an animal panic seized her.

"Gavin," she whispered in a voice filled with gravel.

Swonger looked back in her direction. A big goofy smile spread over his face that made her want to cry. She was too thirsty for tears.

"Been looking all over for you," Swonger said.

"Here I am." She waved weakly to him.

Swonger knelt beside her, smile dissolving when he saw the blood. "What happened?"

"Got shot."

"You think?"

"What's going on out there?"

Swonger shook his head. "Dog, it's bad. World War Four and shit. Bodies everywhere. How is it upstairs?"

"About the same. What are you doing here?"

"We're looking for you."

"We?"

"Gibson's back at the Toproll."

"You guys are idiots."

"Yeah, been feeling like that for a while now. So what's up with the dress, Duchess?"

"Shut up, Gavin." She took his hand and squeezed it; he squeezed back.

"Okay, the hell with this *Notebook* shit. Let's get you to a hospital, yeah?"

"Yeah," she agreed, not letting go of his hand.

"Swonger!" Deja Noble stood over them both, gun at her hip. "Saw you creeping off. Who you got there?"

Swonger moved aside so Deja could see. "Thought I'd try the back stairs. Found her here. Got to get her to a hospital."

"That's good thinking, but the only thing we got to do is get to the fifth floor while Terry has them boys tied up out front."

"I got to help her."

"Isn't any helping her. Bitch is dead. She just don't know it yet."

"She's not dead."

"Let's go."

"No."

"*No?* Say that again."

Swonger licked his lips.

"Give me your damn gun." Deja put her hand out expectantly. "Time to get gone."

Swonger pointed his .45 at her in answer. Deja stared at it. She almost looked proud. One of her men stepped into view, rifle trained on Swonger's forehead. Deja gestured for him to hold his fire.

"Sure this is your play?" Deja asked.

Swonger shrugged at her. "Only if it's yours." Gone was his bluster and cockiness; in its place Lea saw calm and determination. Deja saw it too.

"Give me the gun," she said, but her voice lacked the weight it had once had. She kept her own gun against her hip.

"Clock is ticking. This the conversation you want to be having?"

Deja glanced at the servants' stairs, then back to the muzzle of Swonger's .45.

"All right, then. I'll catch up with you down the road."

"No need for that."

"Oh, there's need. But you get your girlfriend to the slab on time. Tell me later, you think it was worth it."

With a disappointed shake of her head, Deja disappeared up the stairs. Her man pivoted and followed her up the stairs backward, rifle on Swonger until he disappeared from view. Swonger's arm fell to his side, and he let out a shuddering sigh.

"I thought I was going to die."

"Join the club."

Swonger snorted with laughter despite himself. "That ain't funny."

"It's a little funny."

"Forget that; you owe me. Ain't no dying now."

"Deal."

Swonger hoisted Lea to her feet and slung her arm around his shoulders. She could feel him shaking, not from fear but from the adrenaline throwing a house party in his chest. Together, they squeezed through the dining-room door and hobbled out through the lobby. Deja's men had fought their way up the staircase but at a terrible cost. Smoke hung over a lobby torn apart by small-arms fire. One of the double front doors lay across the floor, ripped from its hinges; the walls were splintered. Bodies lay contorted and mangled where they'd fallen, as if a child had scattered his action figures across an imaginary battlefield. These had been living men once. It was a haunting, ghastly landscape. Lea heard music: Jimmy Temple's eternal Christmas soundtrack had survived the carnage—David Bowie and Bing Crosby traded verses on "Little Drummer Boy."

Pa-rum-pum-pum-pum.

Out on the street, Swonger paused to adjust his grip. He looked at Lea with concern. In the last few minutes, sensation had returned, and a shrill squeak escaped from between her clenched teeth with each agonizing step. It had left her out of breath and bathed in sweat, but all she could manage were short, jagged gulps like a fish on a cutting board.

She managed a grateful grimace. "Didn't think I was going to ever be outside again."

"Me either. Feels like a dream," Swonger said. "Okay, just a little farther. Car's around back. You good to make it?"

Lea nodded as Margo's red pickup truck rounded the corner and stopped in front of them. Old Charlie rolled down the passenger window, took one look at Lea, and cursed with Shakespearean eloquence. Margo leaned across him, the left side of her face an archipelago of stippled bruises that would fuse into one large mass before long.

"Oh, Gilmore. What have they done to you?"

They propped Lea up in the backseat of the cab and used a seat belt to keep her from tipping over. While they worked, Swonger gave Margo the short version of events inside the hotel, and Margo told him about Truck and her baseball bat. She said that she'd waited as long as she dared but that it was high time to get to a minimum safe distance.

"Where's Gibson?"

"He went after you," Margo said.

Swonger looked back at the hotel. His expression changed.

"You sure?" Margo asked. "He's a big boy."

"Yeah . . . ," he said. "I gotta get my car anyway."

Margo reached a hand across Old Charlie, and Swonger shook it. He looked back at Lea.

"You owe me. Don't forget."

"See you soon," she promised.

"Now would be good," Old Charlie said.

Swonger stepped back off the running board, and the pickup leapt forward. Lea looked back and saw the spire of the Niobe Bridge in the moonlight, rising stoically above the Ohio River. It was a lovely old bridge, and she wondered if she'd ever see it again. As they left Niobe behind, Lea listened to Margo and Old Charlie argue the pros and cons of area hospitals. It was about the most beautiful sound Lea had ever heard.

CHAPTER FORTY-ONE

Plan B came in the form of Deja Noble herself. It took some time and sounded like it came at a horrible price, but Deja and her men were slowly but surely pushing the fifth floor back up the stairs. Gibson hoped that price didn't include Swonger. The changing tide of the battle drew the guard away from his post on the third-floor landing. The guard took two steps down from the landing to get a better view, which created a blind spot. Gibson took the opportunity to fly up the stairs, hugging the banister for cover. Deja to the rescue again. Good thing, since all of Gibson's scenarios ended with him dying in a hail of bullets.

He expected to encounter more resistance but reached the fifth-floor landing without anyone rising up to bar his way. The long hallway looked likewise unguarded. How many men must Emerson have lost at the airfield? At the door of the presidential suite, Gibson saw fresh blood on the carpet beside a pair of high heels. Something glinted at him from behind one of the shoes. He picked up an expensive-looking gold watch; the inscription on the back read, "Merrick Capital 1996–2006." What had happened here? He pocketed the watch and listened at the door. Not a sound. No movement. Nothing. Keenly aware of being unarmed, he slipped inside and inched through the entryway until he saw the living room. It locked his knees and took away even the idea of breath.

The presidential suite was a slaughterhouse. He counted four dead. Blood everywhere. Flecks of blood on the ceiling some twelve feet above, stretched away in a perfectly straight line. He marveled that amid the chaos something so orderly had been made. Beautiful in its way. A strange thing to think about, but it had been a long day into night since Martin Yardas had shot himself. Gibson's exhausted mind had absorbed all the atrocity that it could and had no room for the dead woman in her wheelchair. Or the dead guard riddled with bullets. Or the pair of hooded bodies slumped against the ropes that bound them to chairs—murdered in cold blood. But the truth was, he didn't have time for his mind to play the wandering philosopher. This was a blood game that could afford no witnesses. If anyone discovered him here, he would join the dead.

In the next room, he found another body amid an array of torture implements. He'd been shot in the back and died with his gun holstered without getting off a single shot. Other than the dead, the suite was empty—whoever had done this was long gone. An example he should consider following.

He went back to the sitting room and realized one of the seated, hooded bodies was a woman. Everyone else had been shot, but a bloody knife at her feet testified to the horror of the last moments of her life. *No, no, no,* Gibson whispered to himself. This was his fault. Gently, delicately, he drew back the hood. Veronica Merrick looked so much like her daughter that it took Gibson a moment to register. Her lifeless eyes stared past him at the ceiling, mouth locked in either a snarl or a prayer. Gibson dropped the hood and sank to his knees, guilty for feeling nothing for the dead woman except relief at her not being Lea.

Had Lea even been here? Had Charles Merrick? The two empty chairs suggested that they had. Had they escaped together? The body in the next chair shifted, groaned. Gibson didn't even flinch, his central nervous system way past the point of cheap jump scares. He asked the body its name; the body answered with another groan. Not helpful, body. Gibson yanked off the hood. Someone had given this man one hell of a beating. A wide cut in his forehead accounted for all the blood that had soaked through the hood. The man's eyes fluttered open, irises dilated and unfixed. But his first words were articulate enough.

"Where is Charles Merrick?"

"Not here."

The man's eyes gradually focused. "Who the hell are you?"

"I'm not tied to a chair, nice to meet you. My turn . . . where's Chelsea Merrick?"

"She's gone."

"Is she alive?"

"I *am* tied to a chair, so I would guess I have no damn idea."

"Then what good are you?" Gibson started to wrestle the hood back over the man's head.

"I'm with the government, and I need you to untie me. Now."

The man had the kind of voice that ordinarily would make people jump to it, but ordinarily he wouldn't have been tied to a chair. Still, it made Gibson hesitate.

"What part of the government?"

"You really want to have this conversation now? You do understand what happens if Lucinda King Soto's son comes back and finds his mother like that?" The man gestured with his chin toward the woman in the wheelchair.

So that was the woman at the center of the fifth floor. Emerson's mother. Gibson had a pretty good idea how Emerson Soto Flores would react. He cut him loose using the same knife that had killed Veronica Merrick. The man stood gingerly and thanked Gibson. A little premature, in Gibson's opinion, because the gunfire downstairs had stopped. Someone had won and someone had lost. They'd be coming now, and it didn't matter who: Emerson or Deja, neither would be happy to see him. The front stairs were no longer an option. With the elevator out, the only other alternative he knew was the fire escape at the back of the building. It went only as high as the third floor, but a two-story drop beat a five-story fall any day of the week.

"Give me the gun," the man said.

"You really want to have *that* conversation now?"

"I have training."

"I was a Marine, and you look like ground round."

The man gave him a hard look and ceded the point. "After you, then."

Gun drawn, Gibson led him down the hallway. Midway, Deja came around the far corner with one of her men. Her eyes widened at the sight of him, and they all came to a halt. An awkward bump-into-your-ex-at-a-wedding moment passed. No one seemed to know where to start, so Gibson put his gun on her. He wasn't much in the mood for Deja's "give me your gun" routine.

"Gibson Vaughn. Didn't expect to see you here."

"Deja."

"See you finally got yourself a gun."

"It was good advice."

"That's funny. You're funny."

"I've got no issue with you yet, so gun down, Deja. Your man too."

"My brother dead?"

"No, but if you see a drugstore on the way back to Virginia, stop for some aspirin."

"You put him down yourself?"

"That's right." He saw no need to bring Margo or Old Charlie into this.

"That boy's going soft."

The questions were a stall. She hadn't put her gun down and instead had taken a half step forward and to her left, blocking his view of her man. Gibson took a step to his left, matching her. Deja showed him her teeth and stepped back to her right.

"Now we just dancing. Why you dancing with me, Gibson? You wanting to fuck me?"

Behind him, Gibson heard rising voices. At the other end of the hall, Emerson had come up the front stairs with two of his men. He disappeared inside the presidential suite. Everyone else froze. A momentary, indecisive cease-fire. When it ended, and it would, they would be the meat in a very unhealthy sandwich, cut down in the cross fire. The government man knew it too and eased slowly toward the nearest door. An anguished howl came from the direction of the presidential suite. Gibson knew that sound intimately. The son had discovered his mother. It meant so many different things, but only one of them mattered.

The cease-fire was over.

Gunfire erupted once more in the Wolstenholme Hotel. The man yanked Gibson inside and slammed the door. The battle took on a different tone. Gone were the disciplined, tactical bursts of professionals. Now it was a son avenging his mother, and the gunfire sounded berserk and indiscriminate. The story of this family would end here tonight.

The man hopped on one leg to the bed. A bullet had taken a chunk out of his calf, but he gritted his teeth and used his tie to stanch the flow of blood as best he could.

"Find us an exit."

Gibson checked the window, confirming what he already knew—five stories down to a concrete alleyway. They weren't climbing down the side of the hotel, and the fall would kill them. The door to the adjoining room was locked from the other side. Gibson shot the lock out and forced his way into an identical room. It didn't gain them much more than fifteen feet, and it still left them squarely in the line of fire.

"Anything?"

Gibson came back, shaking his head. "I like the plan where you call in the cavalry, Mr. Government Man."

"Unless you have a satellite phone, we're on our own." The man lowered himself behind the bed for cover.

"Then we may be in last-stand territory."

The man nodded in grim agreement.

The battle was short and definitive, and the hallway beyond the door fell silent. Gibson wasn't sure who he preferred to have won. He joined Ogden behind the bed and took aim at the door as a fist hammered on it.

"Time to finish our dance, boy," Deja shouted. "You and your friend come on out. Only going to tell you once." Deja put a burst of gunfire through the door when they didn't answer. "Now."

Gibson had an idea and whispered to his companion. The man nodded that he understood and stalled for time while Gibson moved quietly into the adjacent room.

"Your friend's dead."

"How's that?" Deja said.

"Caught a bullet in the hall."

Deja didn't sound all that broken up at the news. Gibson cracked the adjoining room's door open. Deja's man was down in the hall. One more dead for no good reason. Judging by her mood, Deja seemed intent on adding at least another to the list. Gibson opened the door just wide enough to step out, and he closed the distance between them in four fast steps; she felt his shadow at the last moment and turned her face into his fist. He put it through her jaw and spun her like a top. Deja went down in a heap. Shooting someone in the back, even someone as dangerous as Deja Noble, didn't sit with him. He wasn't that kind of man. Although, apparently, he was the kind of man who coldcocked women. Still, he figured she'd appreciate it more than a bullet.

"Very charitable of you," the man said as he limped out into the hall.

They went back down the hall toward the presidential suite and the main staircase. Emerson lay in a tangle of his own limbs, his men both dead. His breathing was shallow, and his face was sallow and bathed in sweat. He didn't have long. Gibson saw the remote detonator too late. Emerson smiled as he triggered it. A series of dull explosions rattled the floorboards beneath their feet, and a moment later Gibson felt the oxygen in the hall being inhaled greedily down the stairwell.

"I told you I would kill you all," Emerson said as if the thought were a comfort.

Smoke poured into the hall, and even though they couldn't see the fire, they could feel it. The temperature spiked twenty degrees in a matter of seconds. Gibson looked up at the sprinkler heads when they didn't kick on. No alarm either. The dying man laughed at him and cursed them in Spanish. The man tugged Gibson's arm and dragged him back the other way, and one last time they hobbled down the hallway of the fifth floor of the Wolstenholme Hotel. At Deja Noble, Gibson faltered, stopped, and hoisted her up over his shoulder in a fireman's carry. He wouldn't be that kind of man either.

The drop from the fifth-floor window to the fire escape below left them bruised but not broken. Even after Gibson lowered the man out the window, it was still a fifteen-foot fall. The man clattered onto the fire escape and came up cursing, holding his wounded calf. Next went Deja, who Gibson dangled by a wrist.

"You've got to be kidding me with this," the man said, but to Gibson's surprise, he caught her. Maybe the guy wasn't as much of an asshole as he seemed. Gibson followed, and by the time they reached the safety of the parking lot, the fire roared through the Wolstenholme Hotel like a funeral pyre. Even from fifty yards away, Gibson could feel its angry heat. He laid Deja out on the ground while the man shuffled over against a wall to check his calf. All around, townspeople huddled together in groups to watch the old hotel burn. Bearing witness to the end of an era.

"She would have killed you," the man said, indicating Deja.

"I've stopped holding that against people."

"There's a hell of a story making the rounds about you at Langley."

"You're CIA?"

"And you're Gibson Vaughn. Your father was Duke Vaughn."

"And you would be?"

"Damon," he replied and paused. "Damon Washburn."

The man put out a hand. If that was his real name, Gibson would eat his hat, but he took the hand anyway.

"What's the CIA got to do with Charles Merrick?"

"That's not germane to this conversation."

"Germane?" Maybe he was exactly that big an asshole. "So what story?"

"Something about you and the vice president in Atlanta."

"Former vice president," Gibson corrected.

"Guess you saw to that."

"Had nothing to do with it."

"Just like you had nothing to do with this?" Washburn pointed to the hotel. "Just awkward timing. That what you're telling me?"

"Good luck with your leg," Gibson said and walked away toward the Toproll. There was still a chance that Lea or Swonger had made it out, and he wasn't much in the mood for Agent Damon Washburn or his accusations.

The man called after him. "Got to say, I was surprised to hear your name come out of a Chinese operative's mouth. Even with your track record, I wouldn't have seen that coming."

That stopped Gibson in his tracks. "The hell are you talking about?" But the answer came to him before he finished asking the question. "I had no idea he was Chinese."

"I'm sure that will fly when they try you for treason."

Nope, definitely an asshole.

"What do you want from me?"

"Your help."

Gibson pointed at the hotel. "You still haven't thanked me for the last time."

"Thank you for that. Now I need your help."

"It's been kind of a long day. Why don't you call in the big boys? I'm tired."

"I fully intend to do just that, but it's the middle of the night in West Virginia. By the time my people mobilize, Merrick could be out of the country. So call you my fail-safe."

"So other than falsely accusing me of treason, why should I help you?"

"The American way of life?" Washburn said.

"Oh, I already have one of those, trust me."

"What about Jenn Charles? You got one of those?"

At the mention of her name, Gibson felt his heart leap. He tried hard to hide it from Washburn, though. "You know where she is?"

"No. But the Agency does. George Abe too."

"Why is the CIA keeping tabs on Jenn and George?"

"Because you did a little more than burn down a hotel in Atlanta, didn't you? The vice president died. We pay attention to that sort of thing."

"So I help you, and you tell me where they are? That the idea?"

"That's the idea."

"Are they even alive?"

"Your Chinese associate—any idea where he might be?"

Gibson started to say no, but stopped. As a matter of fact, he thought that he might. "What's this all about? How is Charles Merrick mixed up with the Chinese?"

"It's classified."

"Good luck with that." Gibson started to walk away again.

"Merrick knows the identity of one of our assets inside China. A mole the Chinese call Poisonfeather. He . . . it's a long story. Bottom line: Merrick's gone over to the Chinese. He's made a deal with your Chinese friend to trade the name of their mole for a new life, since you stole his earlier today. In a way, this is your fault."

The pieces all fell into place. From the start, he'd questioned how Merrick had hidden money from the Justice Department. The answer was, of course, that he hadn't. Justice had simply turned a blind eye because Merrick had given the CIA something more valuable. Poisonfeather.

"Can you find them?"

"I'm not killing anyone."

"Believe it or not, that's not what we do. And I need Merrick alive. If you find him, bring him to Dule Tree Airfield. You know where that is?"

Gibson nodded. "How do I let you know?"

"I have a number; do you need to write it down?"

"No, just give it to me."

Washburn told him the number. "Text the letters *GV*. I'll have a plane there in sixty minutes."

"If you don't hear from me in a few hours, I'm probably not coming at all."

"I figured as much."

"What about her?" Gibson nodded at Deja's prone form.

"Unless she's a Chinese spy, I don't think she falls within the Agency's purview."

"Do all you guys talk like that?"

"Good hunting," Washburn said, neither confirming nor denying. The two men shook hands once more.

"What are you going to do in the meantime?" Gibson asked.

"Me? Find a working phone. Call the cavalry."

CHAPTER FORTY-TWO

The Wolstenholme Hotel fire burned for an hour and a half before the first fire engine arrived. In addition to cutting the phones and the Internet, Lucinda King Soto's men had disabled the alarms. By the time the nearest firehouse had responded to the scene, it was too late anyway. The hotel burned to the foundations while the town stood by helplessly and watched. The fire would have leapt to nearby buildings, but a group of seven devoted Toproll regulars rallied to the cause and doused the neighboring rooftops before the blaze could spread. For years after, whenever all seven convened in the bar, Margo would ring a bell and serve them a round of flaming shots to cheers all around.

———————————

Gibson pushed through the crowd gathered on Tarte Street to watch their history burn. A few recognized him as an outsider and eyed him accusingly, but none roused themselves from their vigil to confront him. The fire reflected off the river in beautiful golds and reds. From a safe distance, tragedy was life's most irresistible spectacle.

Back behind the wheel of the van, Gibson slipped his Phillies cap back onto his head and thought about how to find Swonger in this chaos. Was Swonger even alive? A car horn replied to his rhetorical question, and Gibson glanced in the direction of the gray Scion. Swonger sat in the driver's seat as if he'd been waiting on him, a sly smile fighting his best efforts to look steely. Gibson shook his head and laughed at the total absurdity of it. Where else would Swonger be but just around the bend, waiting for him? For the first time, Gibson felt happy to see him, and to his surprise, Swonger looked happy to see him too. Gibson grabbed his bag from the back of the van and joined Swonger.

Before Gibson could ask, Swonger launched into an account of finding Lea in the hotel kitchen, the confrontation with Deja, and escaping the hotel. "Margo took her to a hospital."

"Why aren't you with them?"

Swonger shrugged bashfully and patted the Scion's dashboard. "Couldn't leave my baby behind."

"Thank you."

Swonger nodded.

"You think she'll make it?" Gibson asked.

"I ain't no doctor. Surprised as shit she alive when I found her. He shot her in the chest, dog. In the chest."

"Who did?"

"The fisherman."

"About him. You remember where his fishing cabin is?"

"Why wouldn't I?"

"Show me."

Swonger started the car and then shut it off again. "You're not going to start some shit 'cause he shot her, are you?"

"When did you get so circumspect?"

"Dog, look at that," Swonger said, meaning the inferno that had been the Wolstenholme Hotel. "I know you don't believe in fate or nothing like that, but if ever the universe was trying to tell us something, this is that time."

"Yeah? What's it saying?"

"It's saying to get up out of this town. Go meet Margo and check on our girl. We just walked out of that mess, and you want to go start in again with some John Woo fisherman? Universe liable to take that the wrong way."

There was truth to what Swonger said. Gibson had pushed his luck every way he could in the last twelve hours, and eventually it would catch up with him. But he also didn't believe in fate; he believed in the cold mathematics of chance. Throwing heads ten times in a row didn't change the odds on the next. The last twelve hours didn't matter, only what came next; and if it had been about anyone but Jenn Charles, Gibson might have agreed. But this was Jenn and George. Even if it was only a 1 percent chance, he knew he would take it.

"There's something I have to do first."

Swonger started the car again. "All right. I tried."

They left Niobe in silence. For the first time since he'd known him, Swonger drove the speed limit. Ten minutes out of town, Gibson felt his phone buzz in his hip pocket. It had a signal; they'd rejoined the twenty-first century. Random news alerts and sports scores began popping up—dispatches from another world, another life. The battery was below 10 percent so he resisted the urge to check his messages in case he got lucky and needed to text Washburn. The Scion stopped along a lightless road. Dawn was still a little ways off yet. Swonger pointed to a dirt turnoff.

"It's down there," Swonger said. "About fifty yards. What's the plan?"

"I need you to do something for me."

"I'm listening."

"I need you to leave."

Swonger leaned back, dissatisfied. "That ain't right."

"I need you to go home. Make things right for your family. For the Birks."

"Thought there weren't no money."

"No, there just wasn't a billion dollars."

"You said—"

"You never let me finish."

"How much?"

"A million four."

Swonger looked to be at a loss for words. Gibson enjoyed the effect.

"And you're giving it to me?"

"I gave it to you yesterday. It's in the bank account Christopher set up. I tried to tell you, but you were busy shooting at me."

"Yeah, about that—"

"Take care of the judge. Get him in a home. Make him comfortable. Then we're square."

"My word."

"Thank you . . . Gavin."

"Why you got to be such an asshole?"

But Swonger was grinning at him. They shook hands. Gibson got out of the car with his bag. Damn, it was dark. On impulse, he took off the baseball cap and handed it to Swonger.

"Hold on to this for me?" Gibson said.

"Riding into battle without your crown? Don't know about that, dog."

"I'll catch up with you after."

Swonger held out his gun. "You might need it."

"It's okay. I have my own," Gibson said and showed him the dead guard's Glock.

"Deja'd be proud."

"Somehow I doubt that."

"You sure about this?"

The question alone caused Gibson's resolve to waver. Walking into the woods alone, at night, into God knows what, didn't exactly thrill him. But he needed to know Swonger was safely away. He'd come here for the judge, at what cost, he couldn't say yet, but he needed to know it hadn't all been for nothing.

"I'll call you if I need you."

Swonger looked at him funny. "Uh-huh."

"Tell Lea I'll check in on her."

"Better had."

Gibson watched the Scion until the taillights disappeared around the far bend. Then he picked up his bag and walked into the woods.

CHAPTER FORTY-THREE

Why rent a fishing cabin in the woods *and* a hotel room in town? That was the million-dollar question, wasn't it? At the time, distracted by the hunt for Charles Merrick's money, Gibson hadn't given it much thought. But now that he knew the fisherman was a Chinese spy, he was betting that he'd been prepping a safe house. Somewhere to stash Merrick off the grid until transportation out of the country could be arranged. In the darkness, Gibson stumbled over a rut and almost rolled his ankle. *Watch where you step,* he reminded himself.

The road crested a gentle rise. Down below in a dirt clearing stood a simple one-story cabin. It looked peaceful in the moonlight. Raised up on stilts, it overlooked a lazy bend of river, and log steps cut into the slope led down to a modest dock. No boat, but beneath the detached carport, Gibson saw an old Nissan Sentra—underwhelming as far as spy-mobiles went, but you couldn't beat the gas mileage. If it was even the fisherman's car. The naked bulb above the porch was off, but at the edge of the windows halos of light leaked from behind drawn shades. A shadow passed before the window. Someone was home.

Gibson knelt beside a stunted, dying sycamore that would never get enough sunlight to compete with the surrounding forest. Normally, he'd spend weeks prepping this kind of hack, but there wasn't the time. He reached up to adjust the hat that wasn't there. Instead, he rubbed his forehead and thought through his strategy. He drew the Glock and shoved it into the bottom of his bag under his laptop and among his dirty clothes. Then he walked down the slope to the cabin and up the stairs, and knocked on the front door.

The truth is your friend; lie as little as possible.

From inside, he heard a voice tinged with alarm. A second voice, calm and calculating, quieted the first. Gibson stepped back down the stairs, not wanting to crowd the door, and also to give himself running room in the unlikely event that the fisherman decided to shoot him as a precaution. Unlikely, because Gibson represented information, and the fisherman would have questions he'd want answered first. The way Gibson had it figured, that bought him maybe ten minutes before the fisherman dumped his body in the river.

The lights went out inside the cabin and the door opened. The fisherman stood in the doorway, a gun rested at his side. Most likely the gun that had shot Lea, Gibson reminded himself.

"Mr. Vaughn. You should not have come."

"I need your help." Technically true.

"How did you find me?"

"I had my man tail you after our first meeting."

"The hillbilly?" The fisherman sounded skeptical.

"I know, right? Surprisingly handy that way."

"Is he here with you now? In the woods with a rifle, perhaps?"

"I'm alone."

"Of course." The fisherman studied Gibson's face for clues he might be lying. The dance had begun. Seemingly satisfied, the fisherman stepped back from the door, a welcoming smile on his face. "Come inside."

An instruction, not an invitation. More instructions followed—Gibson shut the door and switched on the lights. The fisherman never allowed him closer than ten feet, his gun raised now.

"Do you have a weapon?"

"In my bag." Gibson hoped to establish his good intentions with overt cooperation.

The fisherman patted him down anyway and confiscated his cell phone, the gun pressed firmly to the base of his skull. As Gibson knelt, nose to the door, the fisherman searched his bag for the gun.

"There is blood on this gun, Mr. Vaughn. Were you on the fifth floor of the hotel earlier this evening?"

"Yeah, took it off one of the men you killed."

"I haven't killed any men tonight. You have Chelsea Merrick to thank for that."

Gibson didn't believe him but let it pass, wary of being drawn off script. He was a good improviser, but the chances of a miscue increased with each unforeseen topic. His host knew it too and would look to get him talking and keep him talking. Loosening him up until the truth slipped out. This was an interrogation, not a conversation. The fisherman stowed the gun and cell phone in Gibson's bag and pointed to an old rattan couch for Gibson to sit.

The small living space looked like it had been decorated by picking one piece of furniture at random from six different houses. Everything was second- or third-hand. A kitchenette the size of an airplane galley took up the far wall. Two closed doors led to bedrooms or bathrooms . . . and his new business associate, Charles Merrick. Between the doors hung a framed needlepoint that read, "Everyone should believe in something; I believe I'll go fishing. —Henry David Thoreau."

The fisherman stowed all of Gibson's things by the kitchenette and returned with a stool. Adopting a friendly, convivial tone, the fisherman asked him the same questions a second time, probing for inconsistencies. They could have been mistaken for good friends catching up after a hard day, and Gibson admired his host's illusion of nonchalance. It was false—the gun resting on his thigh attested to that—but it made for good theater. He wouldn't kill Gibson until certain that this location hadn't been compromised beyond Gibson and Swonger. So they talked in circles, despite that being the only question that mattered.

Gibson tried to steer them back to a topic that mattered to him. "Look, I have Charles Merrick's money."

"So why are you here?"

"Did you give my name to the CIA?"

"Why would I have any cause to speak to the CIA?"

"Well, someone gave Damon Washburn the impression that I worked for you."

"I don't know a Damon Washburn. In what capacity does he believe you work for me?"

There it was. If this were poker, the fisherman would have just raised Gibson all in. Gibson now had two options—fold or call. If he called, it meant showing all his cards, and if he did, the fisherman would never willingly let him leave this room alive. Gibson tried and failed to keep his eyes from drifting down to the gun pointed casually at him.

"Washburn thinks you're with the Chinese Ministry of State Security. He says Charles Merrick knows the name of a mole in your Politburo. Poisonfeather, I think you call him. That's why you helped me steal Merrick's money. So he couldn't leave the country without your help and would have no choice but to give you the identity of Poisonfeather. Which makes me a traitor. Thank you for that, by the way. You really fooled me with that accent."

"We had an arrangement. You're a very rich man now, thanks to me."

"What good is money going to do me? Where can I go that the CIA won't find me? Washburn accused me of treason. They're going to hang me."

"So what is it you want?"

"You need to get Merrick out of the country, yeah? That's the deal, right? You take care of him; he gives you Poisonfeather. I have a plane, fueled and ready to go. Take me with you."

"It's not possible."

Gibson did his best to look frustrated and desperate. Not that much of an act, really. "I'll split the money with you. One point two seven billion dollars," Gibson enunciated emphatically more for his audience in the back bedroom than for the fisherman. He needed to convince only one of them, and he wasn't getting anywhere with the fisherman.

"A very generous offer," the fisherman said and sat back thoughtfully, pretending to think it over. In fact, he was shifting the gun off his thigh. There'd be no final speeches; the fisherman would put him down with as little fuss as possible. Gibson's daughter's face flashed before his eyes. A face he'd been suppressing these last few weeks while he'd been on this fool's errand. These were the consequences of ignoring his better judgment. How many opportunities had he been given to walk away? How many times had he ignored the warnings?

One time too many as it turned out.

A second thought occurred to him, and this one was terrible. That his daughter was better off without him. Because, even now, he didn't think he'd do it differently if he had it to do over. He'd put the judge ahead of her, then Lea, and now Jenn Charles. Each of those choices felt right to him, even now. Maybe he didn't possess the bravery to live the quiet life that his daughter deserved. So how would he ever be the stable presence that she needed? He'd been fading from her life for years; better to pull the plug now than this slow dissolution. The fisherman saw it on Gibson's face—not the details but the awareness—and smiled at him.

"You can have it all," Gibson said.

"I know."

The fisherman wasn't taking the bait, but the same couldn't be said for Charles Merrick. It saved Gibson's life, at least in the short term. A crash came from the next room, followed by the sound of breaking glass. The windows in the cabin were narrow; a grown man wouldn't fit through without smashing out the upper frame. It sounded as if Charles Merrick was having second thoughts about their partnership.

The fisherman rose with a stark warning. "Move and I will shoot you."

At the bedroom door, he glanced back to make sure Gibson had stayed on the couch. His divided focus might have accounted for how much he underestimated Charles Merrick. The fisherman unlocked the bedroom door and hurried across the room toward the broken window. Charles Merrick stepped out from behind the door. He had something large in his hands. It was like watching a movie through a peephole. Gibson saw a red blur. The fisherman cried out and crashed to the floor.

Gibson scrambled across the room to his bag, unzipped it, and dug through it for his gun. He grabbed something metallic and yanked it out from among his unfolded laundry. Wrong end. He cursed. Two steps to reverse the gun in his hand. At one, a gunshot splintered the wall above his head. Gibson froze. Charles Merrick stood in the doorway with the fisherman's gun.

"So you're the one who stole my money."

CHAPTER FORTY-FOUR

In a predictable turn of events, the cabin didn't get the best cell service. Gibson's phone showed only one bar. He thought how funny it would be to die now because he couldn't reach Washburn. Merrick held the gun to Gibson's ribs and watched over his shoulder to make sure it wasn't a trick.

Sending . . . sending . . . sending.

Miracle of miracles, the text went through. After a short interval, a reply came back:

```
Confirmed. Plane inbound one hour. Thank
you for your business, Mr. Vaughn.
```

A nice touch. Just the thing to convince Merrick that Gibson's flight out of the country was real. They took the fisherman's Sentra, Gibson driving while Merrick kept the Chinese agent's gun trained on him from the passenger seat. Gibson kept his hands on the wheel and eyes on the road. The way Merrick tapped the trigger restlessly made him wince every time the car hit a bump. At least with the fisherman, if he had been shot, it would've been on purpose.

"I transfer the money back to you and you let me go?" said Gibson, projecting nervousness.

That was their deal, although Merrick seemed capable of anything at this point. The dried blood caked down the front of his suit made Gibson wonder what had really happened in the presidential suite. The fisherman had claimed that Lea had killed all those people, but Merrick's clothes told another, grimmer story.

"Just drive," Merrick said.

The car's clock read 5:56 a.m. when they turned onto the road that led up to Dule Tree Airfield. Somehow they bumped their way up the hill without Merrick accidentally shooting Gibson. Praise be.

Gibson drove out to the runway and parked. No plane. That fact wasn't lost on Merrick.

"It'll be here," Gibson said.

He hoped that was true.

Merrick ordered him out of the car.

To the east, the sky was rimmed in jaundiced yellows and reds, as if a burner, lit beneath the horizon, were bringing it slowly to a boil. Gibson watched it with a sense of gratitude. He was so close now. One last thing and then home. Improbable as it felt, he'd come through this night whole. He felt both alive and dead—a foot resting in both worlds.

He glanced back to Merrick leaning on the hood of the Nissan, Gibson's laptop beside him for the mythological transfer of a billion dollars once they were safely in the air and out of the country. Merrick looked gaunt and old. His eyes had the haunted distance of a man sobering up after a historic bender and remembering in painful clarity all his worst excesses. Gibson knew those kinds of memories—the ones that never faded but only became more lurid and disgraceful with each remembering. He consoled himself that the things he'd done had been for good reason; he doubted Merrick knew any such solace.

"One hell of a night," Gibson said.

Merrick flinched at having his mind read. "This plane—what's its flight plan?"

"Doesn't have one."

"Good. And it's not owed anything?"

"I paid in full."

"You mean I paid."

"I met your son," Gibson said, thinking of those who had truly paid.

"Martin?"

"You have other bastards?"

Merrick ignored the jab. "How is he?"

"He's dead."

Merrick absorbed that information. Gibson couldn't tell what the father felt about it one way or another.

"Did you kill him?"

No, you did. A part of Gibson wanted to tell Merrick how he found Martin Yardas. How guilt over losing his father's money had led to drugs, and drugs had led to madness. Or maybe that hadn't been the order of things at all. In Martin Yardas, Gibson saw a son unmade by his failure to live up to his father's image. But he knew that was simply the lens he saw the world through. Lea. Swonger. Martin Yardas. These were his people. His kin. Through what lens would Merrick see his son's suicide? Gibson decided he didn't want to know.

"Would it matter?"

Against the dawn, they saw the plane descending. Merrick stood up from the hood of the car to watch it take shape. He smiled over at Gibson, and for the only time, Gibson smiled back. They were both relieved to see the plane, albeit for different reasons. The plane touched down at the far end of the runway, braked hard, and taxied toward them. They stood well back as it turned around for takeoff. The engines powered down, and stairs lowered at the front of the aircraft.

Two pilots met them at the bottom of the stairs, each built like a linebacker. Merrick immediately began issuing instructions about their destination. A booming voice interrupted him.

"Hello, Charles."

The man who called himself Damon Washburn stood at the top of the stairs. A simple bandage had been wrapped around his wounded calf, but he looked like Caesar returning victorious to Rome. Merrick stared up at the CIA man. It took an endless second for him to grasp the situation and go for his gun. One of the pilots seized Merrick by the arms while his partner divested Merrick of the gun. Merrick fought them like an animal, writhing to get free, but it was futile. Gibson took a step back and raised his hands, just to be on the safe side.

Damon came gingerly down the steps, flanked by two more men in combat rigs, compact shotguns slung across their chests. They wore sunglasses even at dawn. Probably wore them to sleep.

Merrick's face morphed into a relieved smile. "Damon, I'm so glad you're all right," he said. "It was a terrible situation at the hotel."

"That's one way of putting it."

"Obviously it was pandemonium. No time for clear thinking. But rest assured, I told that Chinese bastard nothing. Not one word."

"I believe you." The man from the CIA took a breath and then, as if reciting a comforting prayer, said, "Charles, didn't I make it clear to you the consequences of violating our agreement?"

"What are you going to do? Read me my rights now?"

"What rights?"

One of the agents stepped forward and cuffed Merrick's hands in front of him. The second knelt and shackled his ankles. Merrick watched them do it with a mixture of fascination and disbelief. "This is completely unnecessary. I didn't tell him anything."

"And we're going to keep it that way."

"You can't do this."

"Good-bye, Charles."

Merrick turned his fury on Gibson, lunging for him. "You. You did this. You stole my money."

"I left you a penny," Gibson said. "Wasn't that enough?"

A black hood came down over Merrick's head, cinched tight around his neck. He howled as the two agents dragged him to the plane. Damon turned to Gibson and put out his hand.

"The Agency appreciates the assist."

"We're square?"

"Still don't know whose side you're on, but for now we're square."

Gibson shook his hand. "So you have something for me?"

"Jenn Charles and George Abe—"

At the top of stairs, Merrick twisted around and cried, "Gibson Vaughn! It's Peng Bolin."

Damon froze. Everything on the tarmac seemed to slow, and it was Gibson's turn to be confused. He stared up at Merrick, who kept screaming the same name over and over from under his hood: "Peng Bolin! Poisonfeather! It's Peng Bolin, you son of a bitch!"

Gibson looked at Damon for some kind of explanation. Damon looked back apologetically.

"I really wish he hadn't done that," Damon said.

"Done what?"

Damon nodded slightly to his men, who took hold of Gibson's arms.

"Wait? What are you doing?" Gibson asked, dimly aware of how much he sounded like Merrick.

"I'm sorry," Damon said as a hood came down over Gibson's face.

Gibson fought them all the way to the plane; it did him no more good than it had Merrick. On board, they cuffed him and strapped him into a seat. The needle in his arm sent a wave of cold through him. The drug worked quickly, and by the time the plane bumped forward, Gibson had forgotten why he'd been upset. Calm settled over him. A short time later, he felt his ears pop and wondered why.

"Daddy. Will you teach me to keep score?" Ellie held up a scorecard and a stub of a pencil.

Gibson felt so happy to see her that he didn't stop to wonder how she could be here with him. Nicole must have dropped her off. This was the life, wasn't it? The game was just starting; the players bounded out of the dugout and took their positions around the diamond. He smiled at his daughter; it looked to be a beautiful day at the ballpark.

Maybe Teddy Roosevelt would even win this time.

———

Big Jack Ketch parked his truck in front of his office at Dule Tree Airfield. He hadn't had his coffee yet, and his temples ached from lack of sleep. Nine a.m.—it would be a long-ass day. He'd been at the hospital until an hour ago, waiting for news about his nephew who'd been badly burned fighting the Wolstenholme Hotel fire over in Niobe. His poor sister had about lost her mind. The hotel had burned clean down to the ground, and a lot of strange stories were beginning to emerge over there. Phone lines tampered with. A gun battle that sounded like war had broken out. Dozens of dead bodies, burned beyond recognition. A bartender who worked across the street from the hotel had still been in surgery when Jack left for work. Such a mess. The state police had cordoned off the entire town, and word was that the FBI was on the way. They said so on the radio anyway.

He opened up the office and put some coffee on. While it percolated, he sorted through yesterday's mail and looked through the airfield logbook. He ought to see about Mo Davis's Cessna today. That would take a few hours. Maybe this afternoon, once he'd caught a nap.

He took his coffee and went outside to smoke. His lighter was about empty and kept blowing out in the morning breeze. He glanced out to the runway. Some jackass had parked a green Nissan at the end of the runway. *Oh, for Pete's sake.* Probably some fool kids out to get loaded and smash empties on the runway. Wouldn't be the first time, and it made him mad. Especially after the night he'd had. Or maybe a couple lovebirds doing the dirty.

Either way, they were in for a rude surprise. Jack set off across the field for the runway.

Whoa . . .

There'd been a lot more than one car out here last night; the field had been torn up by tire tracks. By the look of the fence around the hangar, someone had crashed a car into it as well. Looked like someone had hosted a NASCAR derby out here. Pissed Jack off, but on the bright side, it gave him the ammunition he needed to finally convince the owners to install the new gate he'd been lobbying for the last two years.

He felt something crunch under his heels, looked down, and saw something shiny. Brass. His first thought was car keys, but then he saw shell casings. Hundreds of them scattered like confetti after a parade. Someone had decided to use Dule Tree as an impromptu gun range to fire off some toys. In his mind, Jack began to draft a stern letter to the state police . . . until he saw where the earth had been stained red.

What the hell happened here?

He looked at the abandoned car at the foot of the runway and then back toward his office. He saw a man in a fishing vest walking toward the Sentra. The fisherman raised a hand in greeting.

Jack waved back.

He stood there in the grass, waiting for him. By the time he saw the gun, it was too late.

ACKNOWLEDGMENTS

Everything they warn about writing the second book is true.

When you write your first book no one cares. Not cruelly but in the casual way that most people don't care about other people's hobbies. In retrospect, disinterest in my writing proved a godsend. When no one cares that you're writing, then no one cares when you're finished. It'll be done when you say it's done and not before. Then if you're lucky, as I have been, a publisher says, "That's great, we'll publish your book. Now do it all again." Suddenly there are stakes, expectations, pressure. After writing your first book on your own time, writing the second on a deadline is akin to learning the steps to a familiar dance, only backward . . . and in heels. There's a great deal of graceless stumbling about accompanied by the absolute certainty that Ginger Rogers is gazing down and having none of it.

The only thing that kept me from tripping and landing square on my back while writing *Poisonfeather* was the steadying presence of family and friends. I'm grateful for all your encouragement and support; this book would be a shadow of itself without your wisdom, insight, and expertise. My love and thanks to Steve and Marcia Feldhaus, Ali FitzSimmons, Rennie O'Connor, Vanessa Brimner, Eric Schwerin, John and Betty Anne Brennan, Michelle Mutert, Giovanna Baffico, Drew Anderson, Garner Mathiasmeier, David Kongstvedt, Garth Ginsburg, Geoffrey Sparks, Miguel Barrera Prado, Kit Manougian, Daisy Weill, and a small army of Hugheses: David, Doug, Drew, Karen, Nate, Pat, and Tom.

Thank you to my agent, David Hale Smith—half man, half BBQ . . . entirely awesome; to the brilliant Ed Stackler for editing both of my books without once wringing my neck; and to Gracie Doyle, my editor at Thomas & Mercer, who stepped into a new role midway through *Poisonfeather* and made it her own with tremendous style and aplomb.

Lastly, I am indebted to the entire Field School community—you are a truly remarkable group of individuals.

ABOUT THE AUTHOR

Photo © 2015 Serena Kefayeh/Creative-Ideation.com

Matthew FitzSimmons is the author of the bestselling first novel in the Gibson Vaughn series, *The Short Drop*. Born in Illinois and raised in London, England, he now lives in Washington, DC, where he taught English literature and theater at a private high school for over a decade.